LINDSAY McKENNA

TAKING FIRE

HQN™

HQN™

ISBN-13: 978-0-373-78505-6

Taking Fire
Copyright © 2015 by Nauman Living Trust

Excerpt from Running Fire
Copyright © 2015 by Nauman Living Trust

www.HQNBooks.com

Printed in U.S.A.

To Abe Koniarsky, one of my many male readers.
He's a hero to me, having served during WWII.
Thank you for your service, Abe.
You're a wonderful role model for all of us!

Dear Reader,

Taking Fire is a military term which means the position you are protecting is taking enemy fire. In other words, you are being attacked. Sergeant Khatereh Shinwari, US Marine Corps sniper, was born in the USA. Her father was from Afghanistan. Her mother is an American. Growing up, her father infused her with his strong moral code of always being loyal to one's village, one's tribe, taking care of the young and the old. That was her duty. Khat took her duties to heart.

For five years, Khat is a fierce protector of her tribe and the villages where her relatives live. She is deep black ops, a part of the Shadow Warriors, and she thwarts the Hill tribe from murdering her people with her brave acts of courage. Riding her black mare in the dead of night or during dangerous daylight hours, she becomes the greatest thorn to the Hill tribe and the Taliban.

She lives alone in the caves of the Hindu Kush, until one evening, while setting up a sniper op on thirty Taliban below her, she spots a four-man SEAL team coming up the slope. They are unaware that the enemy is setting up an ambush to kill them. Khat intercedes, gives the SEALs a warning, taking down her enemy with her Win-Mag sniper rifle. When one SEAL is blown into a wadi by an RPG, the other three are able to retreat and escape.

Khat thinks the SEAL is dead and quickly rides down into the wadi to find his body. Her whole life changes when she finds Petty Officer Michael Tarik wounded but alive. As she rescues him, takes him to her hideout, she's powerfully drawn to the man with the gold-brown eyes.

Whether Khat admits it or not, they are destined and bound to one another. Both their hearts are under fire. Will Khat decide to stay in Afghanistan to continue to protect her family, her tribe? Or will she heed the call of the tender love that Mike offers her instead, and go back to America with him?

Visit me at my website, lindsaymckenna.com. Please sign up for my free quarterly newsletter! Chock-full of exclusive information only subscribers will get!

Lindsay McKenna

TAKING
FIRE

CHAPTER ONE

THE SEAL TEAM BELOW, where Marine Corps Sergeant Khatereh Shinwari hid in her sniper hide, was in danger. The June sun was almost setting in the Hindu Kush mountains of Afghanistan. Khat made a slow, sweeping turn to the right with her .300 Win Mag rifle along the rocky scree slope. She spotted fifteen Taliban waiting behind boulders to jump the four-man SEAL team climbing up the nine-thousand-foot slope.

Lips thinning, Khat watched the inevitable. She knew the team was looking for Sattar Khogani, the Hill tribe chieftain who was wreaking hell on earth to the Shinwari tribe. Her tribe. Her blood.

Pulling the satellite phone toward her, she punched in some numbers, waiting for her SEAL handler, Commander Jim Hutton, from J-bad, Jalalabad, to answer.

"Dover Actual."

"Archangel Actual." Khat spoke quietly, apprising Hutton of the escalating situation. She shot the GPS, giving the coordinates of where the SEALs were located and where the Taliban waited to ambush them. She asked if Apache helos were available.

No.

An A-10 Warthog slumming in the area?

No.

A C-130 ghost ship?

No.

A damned B-52 on racetrack?

No. All flight assets were tied up with a major engagement to the east, near J-bad.

"What the hell *can* you give me, Dover?"

Khat was only a Marine Corps staff sergeant, and her handler, a navy commander, but she didn't give a damn at this point. Four good men were going to die on that scree slope really soon.

"No joy," Hutton ground back.

"You're going to lose four SEALs," she snapped back in a whisper, watching through her Nightforce scope. "Do you want another Operation Redwings?"

She knew that would sting him. Four brave SEALs had walked into a Taliban trap of two hundred. They were completely outmatched and without any type of support because their radio failed, and they couldn't call for backup help.

It had been one of the major reasons she'd gotten into her black ops activity and become involved. Khat didn't want any more fine men murdered because a drone wasn't available, or a satellite, or a friggin' Apache combat helicopter.

More men had died that night when a hastily assembled QRF, Quick Reaction Force, was finally strung together out of J-bad. The MH-47 Chinook had taken an RPG, rocket-propelled grenade, into it, and it had crashed, killing all sixteen on board. More lives were wasted. She had cried for days after it happened, unable to imagine the tragedy inflicted upon the families involved. None of their husbands, brothers or fathers were coming home.

It can't happen again. She wouldn't allow it. Khat

knew without a sat phone, radio calls into this area were DOA, dead on arrival. The radio call would never be heard. She wasn't sure the leader of the patrol had one on him.

"There are no assets available."

"You said this team is out of Camp Bravo?"

"Affirmative. I'm initiating a QRF from Bagram. But it will take an hour for them to arrive on scene."

"What about a QRF from Camp Bravo?" Khat wanted to scream at this guy to get off his ass and get involved. Sometimes she wondered why they'd given her Hutton. He was a very conservative black ops handler. She wished she still had Commander Timothy Skelling, but he'd just rotated Stateside. Hutton reminded her of a slug; as if he didn't know what to do quickly, when pressed.

"I'm calling them, too. They can be on scene, providing they aren't already engaged elsewhere, in thirty minutes."

"Roger," she said, her voice hardening. "Get a call patched through to that platoon and warn them." *Like fucking yesterday.* She felt her rage rising. It always did in situations like this. She didn't want to lose Americans.

"I've sent a call over to Chief Mac McCutcheon of Delta Platoon."

"I'm waiting five minutes," Khat growled. "If I don't see that team stop and hunker down for an incoming call from Bravo, I'm engaging. The least I can do is warn off the SEALs, and they'll take appropriate action."

Shifting her scope, she saw more of Khogani's men sneaking up on the other side of the ridge. There had to be twenty of the enemy in all. Smaller boys with the Taliban group held the reins of the horses far below the slope. Sweat ran down her temples, the heat at this time of day unbearable.

"Archangel, you are *not* authorized to engage. Repeat. Do not engage. Your duty is to observe only. Over."

She cursed Hutton in her mind. "Roger, Dover Actual. Out." She hated Hutton's heavy, snarling voice. All they did was spar with one another. *To hell with him.*

Khat wasn't about to take on thirty or so Taliban with one sniper rifle. But she could fire some shots before the muzzle fire from her rifle was seen by the Taliban. They would be fourteen-hundred-yard shots, and she set up to take out at least two or three of the hidden tangos. A .300 Win Mag didn't have a muzzle suppressor. Khat knew she could become instant toast when the sharp-eyed enemy spotted her location.

In the back of her mind as she checked elevation and windage, she knew Hutton would get a QRF up and pronto, if one was available. A quick reaction force would be needed because she knew Khogani's men would attack these four SEALs. Camp Bravo, a forward operating base, sat about thirty miles from the Af-Pak border, near where she was presently operating.

She knew SEALs carried the fight to the enemy, but sometimes it was wiser to back off and wait another day. Frustration thrummed through Khat.

Settling the rifle butt deeply into her right shoulder, her cheek pressed hard against the fiberglass stock, she placed one of the Taliban in the crosshairs. They were in a rocky stronghold waiting to spring the trap on the unsuspecting SEALs. Khat wished she could contact the team directly. She didn't have their radio code because it changed daily. And that's what she'd have to have in order to call that lead SEAL and warn him of the impending ambush.

The SEAL patrol members were all carrying heavily packed rucks and wearing Kevlar vests and helmets, which meant they were going to engage in a direct-action mission. Usually, she saw some patrols with SEALs wearing black baseball caps, or field hats, their radio mics near their mouths and carrying light kits, making swift progress toward some objective in the night.

Not this patrol. These guys were armed to the teeth. The lead SEAL's H-gear, a harness that held fifteen pockets worn around the man's chest and waist, held a maximum load of mags, magazines, of M-4 rifle ammo where he could easily reach it. These guys knew they were going into a firefight. But in broad daylight? Who authorized that kind of crazy mission? SEALs worked in the dark of night to avoid being seen by the enemy. It was rare they would be out on a daylight mission. What a FUBAR. Whoever put this op together was crazy.

Taking a deep breath, prone on her belly, she was glad she had on a Kevlar vest so she wouldn't have small stones biting deeply into the front of her chest. She had a 24X magnification on her Nightforce scope and could clearly see in the late-afternoon sunlight the man she'd chosen to kill. Glancing at her watch, she had two minutes before those five minutes were up. Hutton had better damn well have gotten his SEAL ass in gear.

The sun's slant was changing. Khat patiently watched

her target. Every once in a while, she'd twist her head, glancing toward the SEALs slowly making their way up the steep slope. They blended in, but the Taliban had sharp eyes like her.

Two minutes.

Nothing from Hutton.

Nostrils flaring, Khat settled the scope on the nearest man holding an RPG casually over his shoulder. There were seven tangos in total who had RPGs. That was more than enough to kill these four SEALs. And they were a hundred feet of being in range of them. Slowing her breathing, she sighted, her finger brushing the two-pound trigger. Exhaling, she allowed her lungs to empty naturally. There was a one-second beat between inhale and exhale. The snipers referred to it as the still-point. And that is when she took the shot.

The booming sound of the .300 blasted through the silence. The jerk of the rifle rippled through her entire body. Khat instantly shot again. And a third time. She released the spent mag and slapped in another with the butt of her palm. All the Taliban targets went down. Jerking her rifle around, scope on the SEALs, she saw them instantly flatten out against the rocks. They were looking in *her* direction! *Damn it!*

She didn't have to wait long. RPGs launched, even if out of range, toward the SEALs. Khat swung the scope toward the Taliban. A number of them were angrily pointing her way. Yeah, they had her location. But she was fourteen hundred yards out of range, and those SEALs were four hundred yards from the enemy. Were they going to send tangos after her or not? Her heart started a slow beat as she scoped the enemy.

There was confusion among their ranks. They were yelling at each other.

And then her blood iced. There was Sattar Khogani, the young punk of twenty-four years who'd just taken over his father's leadership as chief of the Hill Tribe. His father, Mustafa, had recently been killed by a SEAL sniper. She'd celebrated. Sattar was in the center of his commanders, too short to take a shot at.

There were a lot of arms and hands waving, and she could see his lieutenants yelling and pointing at the SEALS and some pointing in her direction. Who to go after? She was counting on that confusion among the enemy.

Smiling grimly, Khat settled down again, muzzle and sights on the Taliban. She heard the throaty answer of the SEALS M-4 rifles as they engaged, firing off careful shots at the Taliban hidden behind the walled, rocky fort.

Not waiting, she began to fire into the crowd of Taliban officers, picking them off. Her shoulder felt bruised after firing nine rounds, the buck of the Win Mag terrific. Below her, her hearing keyed on the SEALS, they continued to return fire, spread out in a diamond formation on the scree to protect their flanks.

The Taliban suddenly surged out of the fort, waving their AK-47s, firing wildly at the SEALS. The RPGs were launched.

Khat swung her rifle, sighting on the closest man, taking him out before he could lob an RPG into the SEAL team. Damn! There were too many for her to stop! Cursing softly, she heard the RPGs explode. The pressure waves reached her, but she was spared, hunkered down a hair beneath the ridgeline.

Khat couldn't look to see how the SEALs were doing. She was taking out the enemy systematically, one at a time. There were more than thirty of the enemy and it seemed more and more arrived, and they started realizing they were caught in a deadly crossfire.

Khat pulled out two more mags of three bullets each. She released the spent mag and slapped in the full mag, settling in, swiftly looking through her sites. She saw one man shoulder the RPG. She shot before he did. Sweat was rolling down her face, burning into her eyes, making her blink, her vision blurring momentarily. With a hiss, she remained focused, continuing to pick them off.

The Taliban grudgingly retreated.

Khat waited, taking a deep breath, watching them through the scope. Lifting her head, she checked down the slope at the SEALs. They were quickly retreating in diamond formation. Smart guys. *Get the hell outta Dodge because you are way outnumbered, guys...*

Wiping her face with the back of her cammie sleeve, she quickly focused on the stone fort. More hand waving and shouting among the Taliban officers. The group had just lost half its men. More fists waved angrily in the air.

Sattar was still surrounded, and she couldn't draw a bead on him. *Damn.* She'd really like to take out the little bastard. Partial payment for what his sick monster father had done to so many innocent young boys and girls over his one-year reign as chief. He'd turned into a sex slave trader, and had so many young Afghan children kidnapped and sold across the border in Pakistan. She hated Mustafa, and she was sure his son was going to pick up where his sick sexual-predator father left off.

MIKE TARIK ORDERED his men to retreat. He'd made calls to Camp Bravo, finding out the QRF was out on another run in the opposite direction from where they were located. There were no flight assets available. Worse, no drone or satellite was available over their area to understand the field of battle.

They were essentially blind in the fog of war, and engaging a much larger force than was anticipated. And they were caught out in the open on the scree with no place to hide.

Breathing hard, he kept watch over the other three men that he had responsibility for. Their comms man, Ernie, couldn't raise shit in this dead zone. The sat phone he had in his ruck had taken a bullet earlier. They were in a bad situation. The only thing they could do with the sun setting was retreat and then melt into the landscape of darkness and wait for pickup sometime later. They *had* to get off this scree ASAP.

Tarik heard a scream. Then more screams. He was playing rear guard to his men, higher on the slope than they were. Lifting his M-4, he saw at least fifteen Taliban charging them. Fuck!

He moved backward, slipped and fell among the rocks. Rolling, he managed to hang on to his rifle that was clipped to a harness across his shoulder and chest. He stopped his slide at the edge of the ridge, a hundred-foot drop into a wadi, or ravine, below.

Sighting, he began to slow fire, choosing his targets, remaining crouched. Again, he heard the booming sound of a Win Mag far above him. Who the hell was that? He wasn't aware of any SEAL sniper assets in the area. Who, then? Whoever was firing was help-

ing his team out a helluva lot. The sniper was giving
them a chance to retreat.

Tarik heard the dreaded hollow *thunk* of an RPG
being fired. He jerked a look up and saw the damn
thing sailing lazily through the air—right at him. Cursing, he dived to the ground, the rocks biting and bruising him. He automatically put his hands behind his
head, buried his face in the rocks, opened his mouth
and waited. If he didn't open his mouth, the blast pressure waves would make Jell-O out of his lungs, the
air in his chest not equalizing with the air surrounding him.

The blast went off. The last thing he remembered
was flying through the air.

KHAT JERKED IN a breath, watching the RPG explode,
the SEAL tumbling out of the rock and dusty clouds,
flung over the side of the ridge, disappearing into
the wadi. Her heart banged in her throat, underscor-
ing the terror she felt. She whipped her attention back
to the Taliban soldiers running down the slope toward
the other three SEALs.

Khat continued to fire, taking them from the back,
their bodies flying forward five or six feet before crum-
pling into a heap. Was part of the group going after
that SEAL that had been blown off the ridge? Not if
she could help it, dropping the enemy who began to
retreat beneath her withering fire.

Finally, Khat quit firing, the escaping SEALs and
the Taliban out of her range. Leaping to her feet, she
grabbed the rifle and trotted about a tenth of a mile
down a narrow goat path. There, she'd have a better
view of the slope down into the wadi. Halting, Khat

hefted the rifle to her shoulder, and she looked through the scope, moving it from the top of the wadi, working downward.

Breathing slowly, she hoped to locate the SEAL. Doubting the man survived, it was her duty to find him, retrieve his body and then make a call to J-bad. Hutton probably couldn't even cut loose a damned Medevac, he was such stickler for regulations.

Wait.

She steadied the scope, holding the rifle still in her arms. *There!* The body of the SEAL was just at the edge of the wadi. She saw his M-4 nearby. The light was getting bad. He still had his arms and legs. Was he breathing? She didn't know. Looking up, Khat heard smatterings of fire rising from far below her between the SEALS and the Taliban. There was nothing else she could do to help the SEAL team. She'd done everything possible. But maybe she could rescue this SEAL in the wadi. No way did Khat want his body to fall into Taliban hands.

Turning, she slid down the hill where her black Arabian mare, Mina, was standing quietly below. Khat had tied her reins to a branch of a tree where she was hidden. The mare wore a Western saddle, something Khat had insisted on when she started working alone out here. She wasn't about to ride one of those torturous Afghan wooden saddles. The Arabian mare's fine small ears pricked up, her huge brown eyes watching her progress down the rocky hill.

"Good girl, Mina," Khat whispered, leaping off the slope. She quickly slipped the Win Mag into the nylon sheath beneath her left stirrup. Picking up her ruck from beneath the tree, Khat shrugged the sixty-pound pack across her shoulders. She pulled her black base-ball cap out of her lower cammie pocket and settled it on her head. Mounting, she urged the small horse into a trot, heading for a goat path that would lead them to the wadi.

By the time Khat located the SEAL, it was dusk. She had put on her NVGs, night vision goggles, and moved cautiously into the wadi, not wanting to make any noise. She knew Sattar Khogani had more men in the area. Taking no chances with the Hill tribe on patrol like a bunch of angry bees running around on the mountain, she wanted to remain the shadow she was. Her mare carefully picked her way through the trees, winding in and around them, her small hooves delicate and avoiding coming down on branches. If a branch snapped, it could alert the Taliban they were in the wadi.

Khat spotted the body of the SEAL. Half of him was still on the scree, the other half hanging down into the wadi. She dismounted, dropping the reins. Mina was trained to remain where she was.

Slipping out of the ruck, she set it quietly on the ground near the mare. Her heart picked up in beat. Was he dead? Injured? Or playing dead? If he was faking it and she came upon him, he could rip her throat out with a KA-BAR knife. SEALs were taught that they were never helpless. If a rifle or pistol wouldn't do it, a knife sure as hell would.

Approaching cautiously, soundlessly, she had her NVGs on, the grainy green showing there was blood leaking out from beneath his Kevlar helmet and down his bearded cheek. With green filters on, Khat couldn't see what color his flesh was. His mouth was open. He seemed unconscious. His one arm was hanging down into the wadi. She carefully reached out, placing two fingers on the inside of his thick wrist.

He didn't move.

She felt his pulse. It was weak and thready.

He really was unconscious. Moving quickly, Khat pulled him into the wadi so no one could see him from the slope. Rolling him over, tipping his head back so he could breathe, she held her ear to his nose. His breath was shallow, but it was there.

Grimly, she realized she'd have to get that heavy ruck off him in order to get him on the horse. Kneeling, she pulled him toward her until his tall, lean body rested mostly against her knees. Pulling the straps apart, making no sound, the ruck slid off his back.

Next, his Kevlar helmet. It had a pair of NVGs on the rail. Fingers moving quickly beneath his chin, she released the strap. His blood was on her hands now. Gently as she could, Khat lifted the helmet away from his head. Grimacing, she saw his temple was nothing more than a huge clot of blood. Grade three concussion, for sure. But how bad? Her mind was already running over medical possibilities. He was out cold. She removed the heavy H-gear harness from around his chest, another thirty pounds of weight.

Khat left him on his back, trotted down the slope and picked up Mina's reins. Leading the mare up beside the SEAL, she knew there was no way she could lift a hundred and eighty pounds of his dead weight and place him across the saddle.

"Down," she told the mare, making a signal for the Arabian to lie down.

The mare bent her front knees and then lay down, all four legs beneath her.

"Good girl," Khat whispered, patting her mare's sweaty neck.

Now for the hard part. She hooked her hands beneath the SEAL's armpits and hauled him forward. Grunting, she clenched her teeth, digging in the heels of her boots, inching him forward. Damn, he was heavy! Breathing hard, she got the SEAL close enough.

"Lie down," she told the horse, giving her another hand signal.

Mina stretched out on her side, laying her head down near Khat's feet.

Now it was easier hauling the SEAL over the saddle. Khat worried about her mare. She was on an incline, and she would be pulling herself into an upright position. Could she do it with someone this heavy?

"Sit up," she whispered, signaling the mare. Khat watched the horse heave herself back into a sitting position, her legs beneath her body once more. Relieved, Khat moved quietly around the mare, coming to her head, picking up the reins in one hand and keeping her other hand on the unconscious SEAL's body. She hoped he didn't slip off when Mina lurched to her feet.

"Up!" she whispered.

Mina grunted, flinging out her front feet first. She shifted her weight to her rear, the muscles bunching, then shoved her hooves into the dirt and rock in one smooth motion to gain purchase. Khat felt more relief, holding the man in place so he didn't accidentally slip off. The SEAL lay on his belly across the saddle. It wasn't great that his injured head was hanging down, but she didn't have the strength to haul him upright and hold him in the saddle. She hooked his ruck and harness over the horn of the saddle. Nothing could be left behind to indicate an American had been in this wadi.

Leaping up behind the saddle, Khat turned the horse around, and they started back up the goat path in the dark. Only the night winds, cold and howling from the north, were heard. Keeping her hearing keyed, Khat gripped the SEAL's cammies to keep him from sliding off.

As they rose out of the wadi via the goat path, Khat saw the stars hanging so close she felt like she could reach out and touch them. Halting at the juncture of another goat path, she waited and listened. She hadn't survived four years in the Hindu Kush by taking chances. Her hearing was extraordinary. No human voices. Chances were, the Taliban retreated back to that rock fort and were making tea and eating. Probably arguing like hell among one another for their major losses this evening. She grinned.

Once more on familiar territory, five miles down the slope, Khat guided her horse into a group of thick bushes and trees. The horse pushed through the vegetation, coming to a halt at the entrance to a large cave. Khat dismounted, walking in front of the mare, her hand on her .45 pistol. This was one of her safe caves, but she never, ever took for granted that the Taliban wouldn't find it someday. Worse, make camp in it. The mare's small feet moved through the fine silt dirt on the cave floor.

Turning to the right, Khat walked half a mile, went into another cave and through it. Her NVGs no longer worked when a cave was completely black. She halted, pulled them off her eyes, switched them off and reached into her cammie pocket. Flicking on a laser flashlight, the whole area lit up.

They were safe now, and she breathed a small sigh of relief. Making a few more turns, at least half a mile deep within the mountain, Khat finally came to the pool cave. She heard the musical sounds of the twenty-foot waterfall. *Water.* Even Mina picked up her pace. She was thirsty. So was Khat.

Once inside the last tunnel, she could see the small pool of water and the waterfall above it. Khat dropped Mina's reins. Grabbing a kerosene lamp, she picked up a box of matches and lit it. The warm yellow glow highlighted a twenty-foot radius. Moving to the other side of the tunnel, she pulled out a sleeping bag and laid it out on the floor. Grabbing two other blankets, she quickly rolled them up. One for the SEAL's neck and the other for beneath his knees. She grabbed her paramedic ruck, opening it up and placing it next to the sleeping bag. Pulling out a pair of latex gloves, she also retrieved a bottle of sterilized water.

Moving quickly to the SEAL, he was close enough that if she angled him just right, he might fall directly onto the sleeping bag.

Hooking him beneath the armpits, Khat pulled. He slid off a lot faster than she was prepared for, and she just about had him fall on her. Using her arms, Khat turned him over as his legs slid off the saddle. Breathing hard, she positioned him on the bedroll. By the time she got him on it, Khat was huffing.

For the first time, she got a good look at the SEAL. He had a square face, strong chin and a nose that looked like it had been broken at least once. She liked his mouth. Even unconscious, it was well shaped, the lower lip a little fuller than the upper one. His brows were straight across his well-spaced eyes.

Taking a battle dressing, she wet it and began to blot away the congealed blood at his temple. He had taken a terrific concussion wave from that RPG exploding so close to him.

For fifteen minutes, she cleaned the wound. There was swelling, but not massive, which was good. A cut at least two inches long was the culprit—a scalp wound, and they were notorious for heavy bleeding. In no time, Khat had the cut stitched up and closed. Rubbing antibiotic ointment on the dressing, she gently pressed it against the wound and wrapped gauze firmly around his head to keep it in place as well as clean.

Quickly, she started from his neck down to his feet, feeling, squeezing, gently moving his other joints to see if anything was broken. When she moved her hands to his lower forearm, even in unconsciousness, he jerked. Brows dipping, Khat used scissors to cut open his sleeve. Grimacing, she saw a bone pushing up. It had not come through his sun-darkened skin, but it was a bad break.

Turning to her medical bag, she pulled out a bottle of morphine and a syringe. The only thing to do was give him just enough morphine to dull the bone setting she would have to perform. With head injuries, morphine had to be used very carefully.

Cutting the sleeve to his shoulder, she pulled it open and administered the shot. Watching his face, she saw his features begin to relax as the morphine eased the pain in his arm.

Khat took a deep breath, one hand above the bone, near his elbow, the other below the break. This was going to hurt him like hell. She made two quick motions. He groaned, his brow wrinkling, the corners of his mouth pulling inward with pain.

"Sorry," she whispered, seeing the bone was set. Beads of sweat formed on his brow. His face was darkly tanned and he had longish black hair. He almost looked Middle Eastern to her.

Shaking her head, Khat was exhausted, sure that her mind was playing tricks on her. Quickly splinting his lower arm, she wrapped it and then made a sling to hold it against his chest. She tied the ends of the cotton sling around his strong, thick neck.

Khat found no other injuries during her thorough examination, except a lot of bruises, swelling and scratches. She pulled off the latex gloves and threw them near the wall. First things first. She had to give him a shot of antibiotics. After giving it to him, she quickly cleaned up and put the medical ruck away.

Getting off her knees, she walked over to Mina who stood patiently watching, her ears flicking back and forth. Taking the sat phone, Khat had to make a call to J-bad and alert Hutton she had one of the SEALs in her care. She hoped she was in time so that no wife and parents of this man would get a call from a casualty officer, telling them that he was missing in action. Pushing a strand of red hair off her brow, she punched in the numbers.

Hutton came on the other end, and Khat told him what had happened. The best news was the other three SEALs were picked up down at the bottom of the slope an hour later by a Night Stalker helicopter. And Hutton was surprised to hear about her patient. Everyone thought he was missing in action.

"That's Petty Officer First Class Michael Tarik," he told her. "He was leading the team."

"I rescued him out of a wadi. He's unconscious. I'm hoping he'll wake up pretty soon." She chewed on her lower lip, watching him beneath the glow of the lantern. Even now, he looked hard. A warrior.

"Report in tomorrow morning. I hope he makes it. There's no way we can drop a Medevac in there to pick him up. We just got a drone up, and that mountain you live on is crawling with Taliban. We've counted about a hundred so far, so keep a low profile."

Khat snorted. "Don't worry, I will. I'll contact you tomorrow. Out."

Walking back to her mare, she tucked the sat phone away in the huge leather saddle bag. "Come on, girl, your turn. I'll bet you're starving." Khat led the mare to the other side of the tunnel, about ten feet away from where Tarik lay. She stripped the mare of her saddle, the SEALs gear, brought her a bucket of water, curried her and then retrieved a flake of alfalfa hay from a nearby room. She shut the gate because Mina would wander in there and eat herself into colic. Khat didn't need one more emergency on her hands right now.

It was her turn. She grabbed her small towel, a washcloth and Afghan lye soap from a hole in the cave wall. She smelled of raw-fear sweat, and she could feel the grit of dirt chafing her flesh. Grabbing the kerosene lamp, some unscented shampoo, a comb and brush, she walked the fifty feet into the waterfall cave. She had fashioned a bench out of rocks with a piece of wooden plank across the top of it a long time ago. Laying her towel over it, she quickly stripped herself of boots and clothes. The water was going to be seventy-five degrees because that was the cave's temperature.

Stepping into the sandy bottom of the small pool, the coolness felt wonderful against her hot, sweaty body. Closing her eyes for a moment, she pulled the rubber band out of her hair and allowed it to swing free. Soon she would be clean. This was one of the few perks of living in the Hindu Kush that she looked forward to. The light spread out, eventually graying at the edges as she moved into the clear green, waist-deep water beneath the waterfall.

Every once in a while, Khat would look in the direction of the SEAL to see if he was conscious yet or not. She hoped he would awaken. With head wounds, one never knew.

Tipping her head toward the falling water, she groaned with pleasure as the wetness soaked into her long, thick hair. In moments, it would be soaped up, the grit and dirt cleaned from her strands and scalp. This luxury didn't happen often. Tonight was a special gift to her.

CHAPTER TWO

MIKE TARIK AWOKE SLOWLY, pain throbbing through his head, making him frown. His ears were ringing badly, and he fought to become conscious. What had happened? His mind felt unhinged as he struggled to fight the darkness. There was pain in his head and pain in his left arm. His mind focused on that, and he felt incredibly exhausted, unable to move.

It took him a good ten minutes before he could force open his eyes. A ceiling of what looked like a cave was above him, grayish and deeply shadowed. Licking his lips, dying of thirst, he tried moving his hands and feet to see how badly wounded he was.

The memory of an RPG sailing through the air finally grounded him into reality. Yeah, the ridge. His men? Panic settled in him for a moment. Where was his team? And where the hell was he?

Mike heard water running. The ringing in his ears would lower for a bit and then return to near normal volume. Knowing he'd been close enough to the explosion to pop both his eardrums, he wouldn't be surprised if they were blown. He felt pain in his ears when he focused his concentration there. Vision blurring, he blinked several times. Wherever he was lying, there was something soft beneath him. He slowly moved his right hand, his dirty, sweaty fingers encountering something soft. *Fabric.*

Vision blurring again, he shut his eyes, concentrating and trying to figure out where the hell he was. He'd been on a scree slope, nothing but rocks. The RPG had been fired by a Taliban.

Opening his eyes, his vision cleared. His head throbbed with unremitting agony. It hurt even to blink his eyes. Moving his right hand, Mike encountered his left arm in a sling. A sling? He was in a cave. This wasn't making sense to him. The sound of rushing water, like a small waterfall, caught his attention again. As much as it caused hellacious pain, he slowly moved his head to the left, toward the sound.

Tarik simply wasn't prepared for what he saw. He had to be having some kind of hallucination. Or the wound he'd sustained to his head was playing tricks on him. His eyes narrowed. There, maybe fifty feet away, was a tall, naked woman beneath a waterfall. She was washing herself with a cloth, her face tipped up, water splashing around her head and shoulders.

He closed his eyes. No, this was his messed-up head. One didn't find a naked, beautiful young woman under a waterfall in the Hindu Kush. *No way...*

His hearing returned briefly, and he heard the water again. Opening his eyes, he was sure the hallucination would be gone.

But it wasn't. Mike watched, mesmerized as she walked slowly out of the pool, picked up the towel and began to dry her dark, very long hair. *What the fuck is going on here?* Closing his eyes, frustrated, Mike touched his head, his fingers running into a bandage around it. Exploring further, he felt a heavy dressing where the pain was originating from along his temple. He wasn't in a Medevac. He wasn't at Bravo's dispensary, nor was he at Bagram hospital's emergency room. He'd been to all those places at one time or another. The trickling sound, the music of water falling, surrounded him. This was all his imagination. His brain was scrambled.

Opening his eyes, he saw her. Again. He watched as she sat on a bench and combed her long, damp hair. Mike could see her very clearly. Her profile looked Afghan, a broad brow, strong nose, full mouth and a stubborn-looking chin. She was probably in her late twenties, maybe.

Every motion she made was graceful. Her skin had a golden sheen to it. The rest of her body was lean, glistening with water as she sat there and allowed the air to dry her. Her breasts were small, her hips flared. It was her long, long legs that caught his attention. Beautiful thighs, curved and firm.

Groaning, Tarik shut his eyes. He had to be hallucinating! That was all there was to it. The pain in his left arm nagged at him when he tried to move it. *Not good.* Lying there, breathing raggedly, mouth dry, he tried to get a hold on where the hell he was lying.

Opening his eyes, he watched her, finally convinced that she wasn't an apparition. Or a ghost from his imagination. She was combing her hair, getting out the snarls in the long strands. When she was finished, she took the brush, taming the drying strands. Once, she turned her head away, and he saw her hair was a deep, rich red color. It glinted for just a second in the lamplight.

This was real. Friggin' real. Mike felt as if he'd stepped

into a Tim Burton movie, *Alice in Wonderland.* There
was a sense of calm, of peacefulness where he lay. And
then, his ringing ears caught another sound.

Munch, munch, munch.

Mike turned his head very slowly to the right. There,
five feet away, was a black horse with a halter, eating
alfalfa hay on the cave floor. He could smell the alfalfa,
a sweet scent filling his nostrils. One he was very familiar with. But how did alfalfa hay get into the Hindu
Kush? The more he saw, the less made sense to him.
Alfalfa did not grow in this country.

He slowly turned his head back toward the woman.
She had moved her long hair that was nearly halfway
down her long back and brought it over her naked right
shoulder. His eyes narrowed. What was he seeing on
her back as she stood up? He scowled. Her back was
heavily scarred. Dark, puckered ridges indicated she'd
been whipped with something that had metal on the
ends of the tips. He felt himself getting angry. Afghan
women were punished with whips like this when they
didn't "behave" properly toward their husband.

The woman shrugged on a muscle shirt of dark olive
green. She sat down and pulled on a pair of camouflage
cammie trousers. They weren't SEAL cammies. His
memory was barely functioning. Maybe marine? He
watched her pull on a set of olive-green wool socks and
then a pair of combat boots. She quickly laced them
up with her elegant fingers. When she was done, she
stood up, used her hands to spread that cloak of red
hair about her shoulders, fluffing it in a fully feminine
gesture. He saw glinting waves of crimson, burgundy
and gold shine beneath the kerosene lamplight.

He was torn. He could pretend he was still unconscious, or he could reveal to her he was awake. As she picked up her toiletry articles in her left hand, Mike decided to let her know he was conscious. Curiosity was burning him alive. He'd seen no weapons around. Just her and the horse, contentedly consuming hay.

As she drew near, Mike watched her gaze lock on his. She slowed her pace toward him, wariness coming to her face. She was deeply tanned, face oval and eyes that made him drag in a deep breath. She carried the kerosene lamp in her hand, and the light flashed up for a moment, revealing the most incredible green color to her large intelligent eyes.

KHAT FELT HER heart wrench in her chest as she drew close to the SEAL. He was awake, looking at her with confusion. His face was dirty, sweaty, but those gold-brown eyes of his were clear and pinned on her.

What Khat didn't want was for him to try something stupid, like leap up and grab her or try to find one of her weapons and point it at her. She halted a good ten feet away from the SEAL. "I'm Khat," she said in a low voice. "You're safe. I'm your friend."

He stared up at her like she was a ghost. Khat was used to that reaction. How many women were riding around a fifty-square-mile area of the Hindu Kush? No one else she knew of.

He had large eyes, and she could see they were a light brown color. He was intensely assessing her, and she could feel it.

The SEAL was confused, and Khat didn't blame him. What she didn't want was for him to go into defense or attack mode. Because he would. He was completely out of his element. She'd removed his pistol and his knife from him earlier.

"You're in a cave," she explained, keeping it simple. "I saw an RPG explode very close to you. Later, when I found you in the wadi, you were unconscious."

She gestured toward his head. "You've got a pretty bad concussion, and you have a broken left arm. You need to stay calm and relax."

"Are you thirsty, Michael Tarik?" she asked when he didn't say anything. She put her toiletry items back into the cave wall hole. The damp towel hung on a peg she'd pounded into the walls years earlier. Khat turned and picked up one of the plastic quart bottles from a box filled with them.

TARIK BLINKED. HER RED HAIR was drying like a cloak around her proud shoulders. Cat? Her name was Cat? Or was it a lie? She looked somewhat bemused by his confusion, that wide, beautiful mouth of hers turned up on one corner. His gaze moved to the water bottle in her slender hand. Immediately recognizing it as SEAL issue, he growled, "Who the hell are you, really? And where am I?"

The tension rose in him. She stood casually, her green eyes holding his. There was no fear in them. No sense that he was a prisoner, either. His hands were not bound. And then, Mike focused on the leather thong hanging around her neck. His gaze fell to the pendant at the end of it, and he rasped, "That's a hog's tooth." And then he lifted his chin, glaring at her. "Are you a Marine Corps sniper?" It made sense to him. She wore marine cammies. He remembered someone had fired a .300 Win Mag from the ridgeline, alerting them to the Taliban ambush. But a woman marine sniper? He'd never heard of such a thing. Mike tried to figure out just who she was. A hog's tooth was given to every marine who successfully completed one of the toughest and most vaunted sniper school courses in the world.

Khat shrugged. "I'm many things, Michael Tarik. What you need to know is that I'm on your side, and that I saved your sorry ass earlier this afternoon." She leaned down, offering him the bottle of water. "You need to stay hydrated. You were in a really bad firefight earlier."

He took the bottle, their fingertips meeting. She had a placid expression, her voice husky and smoky. Damn, he was dying of thirst. He set the bottle down and tried to push himself up into a sitting position. Grunting, he struggled, angry he was so damned weak.

KHAT SAW THE FRUSTRATION on his face with his helplessness. SEALs hated feeling that way. Beads of sweat popped out on his bleached-out flesh. "Stop. I'll help you sit as long as you don't try CQD on me."

Freezing, Tarik looked up at her, breathing hard. He was a damn rag doll, and he hated feeling weak. She was watching him, her hands relaxed at her sides. How did she know about CQD, close quarters defense? SEALs were taught how to hold or kill a person very quickly with a sharp, quick movement.

Wiping his face with his right hand, he muttered defiantly, "How do you know my name?" The bottled water looked so damned good to him, but he couldn't even twist the lid off it to drink from it.

Khat came within six feet of him, crouching down on her haunches, her elbows resting on her thighs, hands hanging relaxed loose between them. "I called someone to find out who you were. I wanted to let them know I'd rescued you, gave them your medical condition and serial number on your dog tags." Her thin brows moved downward. "I didn't want your wife or parents to be called and be told you were missing in action."

Her husky voice riffled across him, tamping down his anger. The look in her eyes was sad. For him? Mike's nostrils flared, the pain in his head increasing. "You must have contacted someone in the SEAL HQ, then," he growled. He saw neither confirmation nor rejection of his statement. She just crouched there, that incredibly beautiful red hair around her shoulders, framing her Middle Eastern face.

"What's important," Khat told him seriously, "is that the right people know I have you, and the Taliban doesn't. Your team is safe. They were picked up about three hours ago by a Night Stalker. They were flown back to Camp Bravo. None were wounded, except for you."

His eyes rounded. "And you know this how?"

"That's something I can't tell you."

"YOU'RE AN OPERATOR."

The frustration in the SEAL's voice was real. Khat understood why. He was in a crazy situation, something completely out of his league of reality. She remained patient, wanting to get him up and over his bristling defenses and earn his trust so she could give him the water.

"I told you. I'm many things." She gestured toward the bottle. "You need to drink a lot of water. I'll come over and help get you into a sitting position, but I don't want you locking my head and neck and snapping it." She allowed a hint of a smile. "I'm going to die, but I don't want to die that way."

All his anger dissolved as Mike heard the gutting sadness in her voice. Worse, he saw it in her gleaming green eyes. "I'm not going to hurt you," he muttered.

"Your word?"

His mouth quirked. "Yeah, my word. I need the water."

Khat nodded and said softly, "I know you do." She stood and knelt at his right side, sliding her arm beneath his sweaty neck. He grunted as she brought him up into a sitting position. His mouth went flat from pain.

"I'll give you some morphine as soon as I can get you settled against the wall. Can you scoot back for me?"

It took him more minutes than he cared to think about, but Mike finally had the wall at his back. She was so close. He could smell her, the lye soap she'd used, the clean scent of a woman. When she leaned down to pick up the bottle, the veil of red hair covered her profile. She screwed off the lid of the bottle and looked up at him.

His eyes were feral looking, not quite trusting her, but there was something else that Khat couldn't decipher. Tarik was ruggedly handsome, and she felt herself being pulled into his lion-gold eyes. She placed the bottle in his right hand. "Here."

Mike watched her as he drank down the quart of water. Nothing had ever tasted as good as water out in this mountainous desert region.

He watched as she stood, moving like a graceful gazelle. She walked over to the other tunnel where there was a huge stack of water bottles in cardboard cases. They were American. Was she an operator? CIA? He was sure she was Middle Eastern. Her green eyes held a slight tilt to them, giving her face an exotic look.

Khat brought two more bottles, opened them and placed them beside him. She retrieved her medical ruck and knelt at his left side. She watched as he wiped his mouth with the back of his hand. "How much pain are you in?" she asked, opening her case.

"Enough that I can't get up," he growled unhappily. Mike watched her pull on a pair of latex gloves, pick up a syringe and place the needle on the end of it. "What are you doing?"

"Giving you some pain relief," she murmured, picking up the bottle of morphine. "You'll heal faster if you're not in pain."

Mike watched Khat pull a very small dose into the syringe. "Are you sure that isn't a truth drug of some sort?"

She smiled. Taking an alcohol swab, she pulled the flap of his sleeve aside on his upper arm. "Positive."

Fascinated, he watched her give him the shot of morphine. Or at least, he hoped it was. Every move she made was graceful, and he found himself absolutely mesmerized with Khat. As she put the needle into a sharps container, he asked, "You're black ops?"

"Don't try to figure me out, Michael Tarik." She pulled off the gloves and threw them where the other pair was. Closing the ruck, she looked deep into his eyes. He was wary, and she couldn't blame him. "I need to examine you." She pulled a small flashlight from her pocket, slid her hand beneath his chin. His flesh tingled. "I'm going to shine the light in your eyes. I need to see if your pupils are equal and responsive or not. Just look straight ahead at me?"

She was so damned close to him. Her touch was firm but gentle. Her breasts beneath that muscle shirt were inches away from his chest as she slowly moved the light from one eye to the other, and then back again. She smelled of fresh air, sunshine and her own unique woman's scent. He dragged it into his lungs, feeling his entire body respond.

Khat eased away from him. She placed the light in the bag and then pulled out her stethoscope. "I'm going to listen to your lungs and heart now."

She opened his blouse, exposing his chest covered with a tan T-shirt. When she placed the stethoscope against his heart, his muscles tightened beneath it. Strands of her hair tickled his nose and cheek. Her hand lay lightly upon his left shoulder.

When Khat straightened, she picked up a small note-book and wrote down the information. He rasped, "Are you a physician?"

"No. I'm a paramedic." She placed the stethoscope into the bag. "Last but not least, your pulse." And she stood up and walked around to his right side.

Khat knelt and placed his hand against the curve of her thigh, two tapered fingers coming to rest upon the inside of his wrist. Mike felt the coolness of her fingertips. She looked at the Rolex on her right wrist, following the second hand's movement. Her touch was electric. He was so damned hot and sweaty, her fingers soothing. He stared at the scars he saw across her shoulders just barely exposed beneath her shirt. They were deep. Ridged. What the hell had happened to her?

It angered him on another level that she was beautiful, young and yet someone had either beaten or tortured her. The ridges were white, indicating there were probably four or five years old. Damn, he had a helluva lot of questions for her.

"Good," Khat murmured, pleased. Removing her fingers, she picked up his hand and placed it against his belly. "You're stabilizing."

Mike watched her. She put the medical ruck away. And then she walked down the tunnel, past the horse to where he saw a Western saddle sitting balanced on a gate of some kind. She pulled out a sat phone from the nearest saddlebag. Only operators got them. He had one himself and it had a bullet hole in it. His ruck was nowhere in sight.

Khat walked out into the other cave, and she made a call. She reported Michael Tarik's medical condition to her handler, Hutton. She knew it would be passed on to Bagram. There, someone would decide when he should be picked up.

Right now Khat said he couldn't ride ten miles down the mountain on a horse to reach a Medevac. He couldn't even sit up on his own.

Mike heard the entire conversation. She wasn't hiding it from him. He watched her return and put the sat phone away.

"Are you hungry?"

"No. Just thirsty."

Nodding, Khat knelt beside him and handed him the opened second bottle of water. It wasn't uncommon on a long SEAL patrol for a man to go through two gallons of water. When she placed the bottle into his hand, she felt small, electric sensations move through her fingers. He was watching her. But it wasn't an uncomfortable feeling. She sat down, bringing up one of her knees, her hands wrapped just below it. Khat watched him chug down the water. He was sweating freely, dirty and still pale beneath his tan.

"I'd offer you the waterfall," she said, gesturing toward it, "but you can't even stand yet. Would you like me to get a washcloth and some water in a basin? I'm sure you'd feel better if you got a little bit cleaned up."

Mike set the emptied bottle aside and stared at her. "I'm feeling pretty damned wary of you."

Khat nodded. "I understand," she said quietly. "I realize it's a strange situation."

"Who were you talking to on that sat phone just now?"

"Someone who will send your vitals to an ER doctor at Bagram hospital. That physician will decide when you should be airlifted out of here."

"Move me?" His wariness shot up. She looked so damned calm about it all. Okay, he got she had to be an operator. Khat was a marine sniper. And she had a sat phone, and whomever she'd talked to was high up on the black ops food chain.

Khat lifted her hands and pulled her dried hair off her shoulders, the mass tumbling down her back. "Yes. As soon as you're ambulatory, I'll take you to a place, providing it's not got Taliban around, and they'll fly in a Medevac for you." She smiled a little. "And then you'll be home, in familiar surroundings once more."

Mike couldn't stop staring at Khat. Her arms were lean and tightly muscled. She was feminine, but in damn good shape. There was nothing weak about this woman.

"Would you like to get cleaned up a little?" she asked. She smiled a little and stood up.

From another of the many holes in the cave wall, she pulled out a large aluminum bowl and walked to the pool, dipping it down into the water. Bringing it back, she stopped and took the washcloth she'd been using earlier, plus a dry, clean towel.

Kneeling beside him, she took his right hand and placed it in the water, gently washing all the dirt, sweat and blood off. He had large square hands, long fingers and she saw many small white scars across them as she washed each one individually.

"Tell me about yourself?" she asked, glancing at him. "Is your team out of Coronado?"

Mike felt his entire body go hot with longing. He hadn't expected her to wash his filthy hands. Her movements were gentle, careful. "I don't really want to say anything to you. For the same reasons you're not sharing anything with me. For all I know, you could be Taliban."

Her lips curved ruefully as she soaped the cloth and slid it up to his hairy wrist and lower arm. He felt his muscles leap and tense beneath her ministrations. "I understand," she answered. "In our business, it is a need to know only."

Mike wanted to talk to her. His mind plunged through ways to get information out of Khat. He looked at the water in the bowl. It was filthy. That's how the rest of him felt. He wished like hell he could stand and go over and bathe under that waterfall.

"Your horse?"

Khat nodded. "Yes. She's my best friend. She's saved

my life so many times…" Holding his clean hand, she brought the towel over and dried him off.

"That's no Afghan mountain pony," he said, hoping this line of conversation wasn't going to end in a box canyon.

"She's purebred Arabian."

"My father has an Arabian horse ranch," he said. Mike saw her chin lift, her eyes widen.

"Really?" Khat searched his shadowed golden eyes. The morphine was helping him to relax. When a partial smile pulled at his chiseled mouth, a white-hot heat moved down through her. Shocked by her body's response, Khat swallowed. "Can you tell me more?"

Hearing the sudden excitement in her husky voice, those green eyes so large, reminding him of green tourmaline, he said, "My father was born in Saudi Arabia. He became a renowned cardiac surgeon, met my mother, who is American, and came to the States. After I was born in San Diego, he decided to have a small, select herd of Egyptian Arabians at their ranch in Alpine. He was able to acquire a stallion from the House of Saud."

She released his hand. "That is wonderful. We share a love of Arabian horses. I need some clean water."

"Yeah, I'm pretty dirty," he agreed drily. Watching her rise, those thick red strands of hair tumbling across her shoulders, Mike felt hungry for her on a purely sexual level. Rubbing his jaw, he watched her walk into the other cave. There was a gentle sway to her hips, and those long damn legs of hers went on forever.

Then he stopped himself. He had no business reacting to Khat like this. She'd saved his life. She deserved better than his male reactions, and he was unhappy with himself.

When Khat returned with a clean bowl of water, she handed him the cloth so he could clean his face. There was a lot of dried blood along his temple, across his high cheekbone and matted in his black beard. She rested her hands on her thighs. "Do you still have Arabian horses?"

"My parents do," he said. God, the cool cloth felt so damn good against his gritty, filthy skin. He closed his eyes, wiping his brow, eyes and cheeks.

"Then, they are Egyptian Arabians?"

He squeezed the cloth into the water, quickly watching it become dirty. Lifting it out, it felt good to wipe his nose and lips. When he rubbed the left side of his face, it was swollen and tender. "Yes. They keep one stallion and six broodmares. It's a hobby of my father's. He likes the fire of the Egyptian Arabians."

Excitement bubbled through Khat. "Mina, my mare, is also of Egyptian lineage."

Mike smiled a little, rubbing his right temple and his beard. "I thought she might be. How old is she?"

"Nine."

"Has she been with you long?" He squeezed the cloth into the bowl. There was so much dirt in the water, he must have looked like Godzilla to her when she found him.

"Five years." Khat pointed to the left side of his face. "There's a lot of dried blood and dirt on your left temple."

"Hurts too damn much to touch it," he muttered.

Khat went and got a third bowl of water. She knelt

down near his left side. "May I try? The blood will draw flies tomorrow morning. They'll eat you alive."

That wasn't a pleasant thought. Mike nodded, holding her gaze. "You have a gentle touch." He tipped his head back against the wall and closed his eyes. God help him, but he wanted her to touch him. He didn't care where or how, he just wanted those long, cool fingers on his flesh.

Khat lowered her lashes as he gave her an intent, burning stare. It was a look a man gave a woman. A man who wanted his woman in his bed. She felt heat sweeping up her neck and into her face. His eyes were closed, and she inhaled a ragged breath, moving closer, her knee grazing his hip. Placing her right hand against the other side of his face, the soft prickle of beard making her fingers tingle, she used a very wet cloth and gently placed it against the area of dried blood. In time, the dried blood would soften.

Her heart was waffling in her chest, and Khat felt unexpected emotions leaping through her. His face was hard, weathered and tough looking. He beckoned to her, man to woman.

Trying to still her reactions, she carefully worked the blood loose, cleaned off his temple and the left side of his hard jaw. He reminded her of a snow leopard at rest but still possessing that coiled tension and power within him.

Khat closed her eyes. Fear skittered through her. She knew the power of men only too well. But for whatever miraculous reason, she was not afraid of Michael Tarik. She saw his nostrils flare, as if drinking in her scent. His mouth… Her gaze fell to that strong, chiseled mouth of his. Something unbidden, bright and clean exploded through her lower body. It took her by surprise. For whatever crazy reason, Khat felt desired by this SEAL.

Shaking her head, she released his face and quickly washed the bloody washcloth in the bowl.

"You have the touch of an angel," Mike murmured, barely opening his eyes. He saw the ruddiness in Khat's cheeks, her lashes lowered, refusing to meet his eyes. Her lips were pursed, too. As if…as if she hadn't wanted to touch him?

"You're Middle Eastern, aren't you?" he asked, keeping his voice purposely low and nonthreatening. He saw Khat's head snap up, her eyes widen for a moment, and then Mike saw terror in them. Why?

Khat rose, carrying the bowl to the pool, refusing to answer his question.

Mike rubbed his damp beard. Yeah, she was. Only question was: Which country? Was she a CIA operative? They were actively and aggressively courting Middle Eastern people into their ranks.

Something told Mike her reactions were typical for a woman from the Middle East. They were brought up chastely, surrounded by family, protected from men, virgin until they were given away in marriage. Even her English had a lilt to it. He had Saudi blood, and it was easy to pick up another Middle Eastern accent. And when he'd told her he liked her touch, she'd blushed. Was she not used to being around men? But then Mike scowled, remembering the scars on her back and shoulders. Okay, something else was falling into place. What if she was a CIA operative? Got caught by the Taliban? Tortured? Probably raped. That would explain her sudden shyness around him. She might see all men as a natural threat to her.

Mike watched Khat return. She walked as silently as a SEAL. No one heard them coming, either. The look on her face was closed, and he saw chagrin in her eyes, maybe. He didn't know Khat well enough to be sure. God knew he was starving to death to get to know her. He owed her something for saving him, didn't he?

CHAPTER THREE

WHILE KHAT MADE tea for them, something she loved doing every night before she slept, she felt the SEAL's eyes on her. She had a small copper kettle on a grate and used an old-fashioned magnesium tab to create the intense heat to make the water boil. There was the chemical equivalent in her MREs, but she preferred this way.

After setting it up, she moved out of her crouch, turned and went to find a rubber band. Her hair was thick and long. And it often got in the way, which was why she tamed it into a ponytail or a single, long braid down her back.

Out of the corner of her eye, as she did so, Khat saw a vulnerable expression fleetingly cross Mike's face. A wistful sort of look, and then it was gone, replaced by his game face once more. It made her feel things she'd never felt before. Bewildered by all these new emotions, Khat brought two chipped mugs from another hole and placed them on a nearby tray.

"Do you like sugar with your tea?" she asked, barely turning in his direction.

"SEALs can use all the sugar energy they can get," he answered wryly, half smiling. Mike liked the way shorter, softer strands had stolen out of her ponytail, caressing the sides of her face, emphasizing those breath-stealing green eyes.

"Ah," she said, nodding.

"How do you take your tea?" He watched her work on the drinks, her fine, long fingers mesmerizing him. Mike wondered if she'd ever taken dance lessons because that is what she reminded him of—a ballerina.

"Plain."

And then Khat joked, "Like me."

Scowling, he said nothing. "Why did you warn my team there was a Taliban ambush set for us?"

Pushing a tendril of hair away from her face, Khat looked up. His eyes were hooded, his face contemplative. He was trying to figure her out. "Because it's my job."

"Do you always shadow SEAL patrols?"

Shrugging, Khat said, "Luck of the draw." She loved teatime, having grown up with it. Taking some of her favorite cookies, shortbread, that her mother had sent to her, she pulled some out of a tin box from another hole in the wall.

Mike shouldn't enjoy watching her so much, but he did. "How tall are you?"

"Too tall for a woman," she answered. Bringing over a tray, she set it next to him.

"Six foot?"

"Close."

"How the hell were you able to get me out of wherever you found me?"

Khat gave him a serious look. "Very carefully. I rode my mare into the wadi and retrieved you." She watched the steam starting to rise out of the spout. Placing a tea bag in each cup, she removed the teakettle and poured the boiling-hot water into the awaiting cups. As she did, she told him how she got him from the wadi to the cave.

Mike shook his head in disbelief, turning and giving the black mare, who had eaten and was now resting, an appreciative look. Her head was drooped and one rear leg cocked, resting on the other three, eyes closed. "Unbelievable." And he gazed at Khat as she walked toward him with the two cups in her hands.

Kneeling, she set them on the rusty tray, gave him three cookies and three for herself. She nudged the open jar of sugar with a spoon in it toward his good hand. Settling down, crossing her legs, she faced Mike. He did everything with focus. Adding a teaspoon of white sugar to his cup, he stirred it and set the spoon on the tin tray.

Khat held the cup with both hands, inhaling the scent of the tea. It always made her smile. It reminded her of happier times when she was young and at home with her family, until she joined the Marine Corps. Her father strongly disapproved of her choice. Her mother remained loyal to her, however, and sent her these tasty shortbread cookies every few months. She worried constantly about her.

"Is this something you do every night?" Mike asked, picking up the cup. He saw her eyes half close, a look of satisfaction on her face as she sniffed her steaming tea.

"When I can."

"Does that mean you usually operate at night?"

"Like the SEALs?"

"The night's our friend."

"Sometimes, during the day, sometimes at night." Khat sipped the tea, the taste giving her pleasure. She regarded him through her lashes, watching him think and plot and try to get something out of her that he could use. But to what end? Khat didn't feel threatened by Mike, surprisingly. Was it his driving curiosity? Most likely.

"If I were a man in black ops, you wouldn't be asking me so many questions, would you?"

He raised his brows and grinned. "Probably not. No women I know of in black ops out here in Dodge City." He saw her lips curve just a little, her eyes gleam with amusement and secrets known only to herself.

"There are many ways to fit in and not be seen."

"Do you like doing this?" Mike gestured to the horse.

Shrugging, Khat murmured, "It is my destiny."

Mike felt that damned sadness around her again. A sort of surrendering over to the inevitable within her. She avoided looking at him, as well, paying attention to eating a cookie with her delicate fingers instead. Okay, he'd try another approach. "What touches your heart, Khat?"

His voice was deep with sincerity, and it riffled pleasantly through her. Lifting her chin, she met his thoughtful-looking gaze. Lion-gold eyes. A fierce warrior. But her instincts told her this man also possessed strong morals and values as all SEALs did.

She licked her lower lip and bent her head. "To walk out into the desert as a storm hits. To smell the perfume of the dry earth rise up and embrace me. To—" she lifted her chin, meeting his gaze "—have a baby born and slip into my hands and hear her first lusty cry." Khat sipped her tea and added, "To see my people free and unafraid, to be able to walk out of their homes and not get their leg blown off, or to lose their children to those who would abuse and kidnap them."

His heart squeezed with pain over the last whispered words. Her brows had drawn down, her gaze moving away, looking into the darkness, eyes filled with anguish. Mike heard it in her voice, too. "Those are heart-worthy passions," he agreed, powerfully moved by her words.

"Why are you a SEAL?"

His mouth twisted. "That's a long story. My father wanted me to follow in his footsteps, which most first sons do when their father is from the Middle East. I was a wild child, loved riding the Arabian horses, loved anything athletic, track, hurdles, gymnastics. You know, boy sorts of things?"

"Mmm," Khat said, sipping her tea, enjoying sharing something important with him that had nothing to do with black ops. "Did you not want to become a surgeon?"

He laughed a little, holding up his right hand. "With these hands? Look at them. They're good for fixing cars, fixing weapons, but I sure as hell wouldn't trust these hams with a scalpel, would you?"

Khat laughed softly, feeling her heart blossom at his engaging smile. She liked his humbleness. His eyes... She sighed inwardly. His eyes gleamed with gold in their depths beneath the low light within the cave. "You have a point," she agreed. "But you have hands of a man of the land who would work the soil, shape things and coax plants to grow."

He didn't want to be affected by how she saw him, but Mike was. "Farmer hands?"

"Maybe. I love looking at people's hands. They tell me so much about them."

He looked at his. "What do my hands tell you?" He saw redness come to her cheeks. "No, really. I'm not teasing you. I'm interested in how you see the world, Khat." And God help him, he was. Her face was so damned readable, it shook him. There was no coyness. Just shyness. And gentleness that she tried to hide from him, but she couldn't. Mike was having a hell of a time seeing her out there as a sniper and then drinking tea with her now. Two very different people.

"Your hands—" she shrugged "—are hands meant for molding and shaping things. Such as a loving father who would mold his children by supporting them, showing them the way, but not pushing them. You have hands that are sensitive to texture, to how something feels beneath your fingertips. I could see you being very gentle with a baby or supporting an elder who had trouble walking. You have helping hands." Khat was so taken by his hands that she wondered what his fingers would feel like across her body. It was a vivid curiosity. And at the same time, Khat knew that would never be. No man would ever want her.

Mesmerized by her low voice, the almost lyrical quality of it, Mike was shaken by her insight into him. He set the cup down and stared at his right hand. "Then I'm in the wrong business," he said, grinning. SEALs took the fight to the enemy.

"Not necessarily," Khat said, picking up the second cookie from the tray. "I know many SEALs who do charity work with the villages they are near. Some bring in clothes, others shoes, food or medical support. They care about the people of the village. To those

SEALs, they are not just a number. They are human beings with a heart. With a soul."

Mike considered her quiet, passionate response. This woman lived in her heart. Something terrible had happened to her, though; that was why she was here. "Many of our guys do help out villagers," he agreed somberly. "It isn't always about killing the bad guys. It's really about nation building, giving those who have practically nothing, something."

"I like the way you see your world," she said softly. "Your eyes tell me you see much more than you reveal to others." And he was a passionate person just like herself, Khat realized. But he hid that element of himself, too, but not from her.

"Now you're making me nervous," Mike joked. Looking into her green eyes was, he swore, like looking into a well so deep that he couldn't see the bottom. Khat had complexity and levels to herself. Maybe layers like an onion. Peel one layer off by asking the right question, and you saw another side or facet to her. She was an enigma and a mystery.

"My mother called me a seer," Khat admitted fondly, remembering her happy childhood. "She said I had the power to see through people with my eyes."

"I think your mother was right," Mike said. He saw a faraway look in Khat's eyes, her lips softly parted, not really there for the moment. "What would you say about your hands?" he asked, gesturing toward them.

She looked at one. "Oh." And then she shrugged and made a sound. "My mother said I had beautiful hands. I played the piano when I was a child." She looked at her left hand, moving her fingers. "She wanted me to play piano, but I wanted to dance."

"As in ballet?" Mike guessed.

"Yes, I dearly loved ballet. But my parents could not afford it, only piano lessons. I love music, but I loved dancing and movement even more."

"So, do you have dancer's hands?" he wondered, seeing the animation in her eyes, hearing it in her husky voice. He saw her eyes grow dim, her expression grow closed. Nothing like stepping on a land mine with her. Mike felt bad because they were beginning to build a trusting connection with one another. He didn't want to lose it.

"I have hands that—" her mouth quirked, brows drawing down "—that heal and kill."

The silence fell heavy in the cave. Mike felt a sharp, jagged energy around her, as if some unknown thing was a constant abrasion to her heart, perhaps. He was very attuned to the subtleties of energy. Maybe it was reading a person's body or their voice. Mike really didn't know. "I think your hands are beautiful, Khat. When I first saw you, I thought you might be a ballerina." He gave her a gentle look, hoping she wouldn't take his compliment the wrong way.

Sitting up, she shrugged. "I dance every day. I dance on the edge of a sword. On one side is life, the other, death." She finished her tea and abruptly stood. "One day, I will fall on death's side. It is inevitable."

Near midnight, she gave Mike pain pills to take so he could rest comfortably.

"I will be gone when you awake tomorrow," she told him. "And I won't return until dark. I'll leave you everything you need."

"My gear?" he demanded. If he was going to be alone in this cave, he wanted his own weapons in hand. He watched her expression become serious as she cleaned up the area and walked to the cave with the gate across it. She brought out his rifle and pistol, placing them near him. If Mike had any doubts about whose side she was on, it was gone now. Next came his heavy rucksack.

Khat moved to her medical ruck and opened it. "I'm leaving you enough pain pills for while I'm gone tomorrow. Take them every four hours. And if you can, get over to the waterfall and get cleaned up."

"Can you leave me your sat phone? I have one but it's got a bullet hole through it," he said, watching her walk back and forth, collecting items.

"No. I'll need it." Khat saw him frown. "When I'm done with my day, on the way back here, I'll check in and see if your people are willing to come in and pick you up. Much depends on you getting to your feet and being able to walk without falling sideways." She gestured to his head wound. "You took a hard hit when you landed. And I can't move you until you can walk and stay on your feet."

"You've got a point," Mike admitted. He saw her pull a sleeping bag from the cave that had bales of alfalfa stored in it. She gave her horse another bucket of water and then picked up her M-4 rifle and headed into the other cave. Khat silently melted into the darkness, but he could pick up faint sounds of where she was moving.

When she walked back, minutes later, she said, "I'm leaving you the kerosene lamp. I'll be sleeping in another cave, keeping guard. I have motion-sensor detectors at the opening. If you hear shots, take cover and hide. I don't think the Taliban will find us because we're so far back in this mountain, but you don't count on anything."

"Got it," Mike said. He pulled the kerosene lamp toward him. "Do you have a flashlight?"

She held a small one up in her hand. "Sleep well," she whispered, and turned and disappeared into the black gloom.

Mike waited a few minutes. He placed his rifle nearby, his pistol within easy reach. Dousing the flame in the old lantern, he set it aside and lay down on his back. He worried about Khat. He wanted to protect her, not have her protecting him. Frustration overwhelmed him as he closed his eyes. Tomorrow he was going to be on his feet and become ambulatory—or else.

Mike heard a horse approaching his area in the darkness. He stood near the cave opening to the waterfall area, M-4 in hand. The glow from the kerosene lamp revealed Khat leading her mare out of the gloom.

To his surprise, there was another horse behind her, but it was packed with supplies beneath a tarp. Khat looked tired.

When she spotted him, she lifted her hand in greeting. Khat was dressed differently than yesterday. She was in Afghan male clothes, dark brown trousers, boots, a black shirt with a brown vest over it. There was a white-and-blue-checked *shemagh* around her neck, the ends of it hanging down between the front of her breasts. He saw no weapons on her. What had she been doing? And why the change of costume?

"We're clear," she told Mike. For a SEAL, *clear* meant no enemy was present. And he needed to know that.

Khat felt her heart surge as she caught sight of him.

He stood alert, the M-4 in his right hand. She saw he'd taken the sling off his broken arm. His eyes were narrowed, and his mouth was in a hard line, as if expecting trouble. Fortunately, there was none tonight. The Taliban had moved off the mountain and were north of her location.

She brought the two horses to a stop and dropped Mina's reins. Lifting the stirrup, she put it over the horn of the saddle and quickly loosened the cinch and hauled the gear off her tired mare. "How was your day?" she asked as she passed him and walked down to the cave that held the hay.

"Better," Mike said. "Can I help you at all?"

She disappeared inside the cave and came out a moment later, pulling off the *shemagh*. "No, thank you. How is your arm doing?"

"It hurts like hell when I let it hang too long," he admitted.

Nodding, Khat saw his chagrin. "Took it off to wash up?" He looked clean. His hair was mussed, but the dirt and sweat were off his body. She was sure Mike had taken off the sling to get out of his blouse. He'd done a poor job of closing it up, however, but considering he had one hand, he'd managed to get his clothes back on.

"Yes. No choice." Mike walked over to the second horse, a black Arabian that looked identical to the one she had ridden. "What's under the tarp?"

Khat led Mina to her place, where she fed her and took the bridle off, tying the halter lead rope to a large iron ring in the wall. "Medical supplies," she said.

"I didn't know you had two horses."

"I need two," she said, patting Mina's rump as she walked up to the other mare. Leading the horse closer to the tunnel, she added, "If Mina goes down with a sprain or something, I have to have a backup." She managed a slight smile in his direction. "I'm like the SEALs—one is none, two is one."

Nodding, Mike put the rifle down against the wall where his sleeping bag was located. "She's nice looking, too. Are they sisters?"

"Yes. Her name is Zorah." Khat quickly unstrapped the canvas over the load the horse carried. In moments, she had the tarp pulled off and folded it up. "This one is eight years old. Same sire and dam as Mina."

Mike saw two huge leather panniers, one on each side of the small horse. Inside, he recognized American bottles of drugs and other medical supplies. "Can I help you carry these things somewhere?"

"Yes," she said, grateful. He looked like he was bored out of his skull. SEALs didn't sit down well doing nothing for twelve hours. His skin looked better; his eyes were clear. "Did the pain pills work okay?" she asked, removing a carton.

Mike was able to reach in with one hand and find another box and draw it out. "Yeah, fine."

"Follow me," she said, moving past the cave with the gate.

In minutes, they had the horse unpacked, the harness taken off, and Khat tied Zorah to a second iron ring a few feet away from where Mina stood. Giving them each a flake of alfalfa hay, she said, "Okay, you're next, Mike. Take a seat on your sleeping bag."

Mike sat down, back resting against the cave wall. She was a marvel of efficiency, as if she had done this all her life. Khat brought her medical ruck to her side as she knelt by him. "Why are you dressed in male Afghan clothes?"

She met his gaze. "Now, I think you know the answer to that one," she said, and she quickly cut away the dried bandages around the splints. They'd gotten wet when he'd bathed and had become wrinkled and loose. Quickly, she removed the dressing, took the splints away and gently held his forearm between her fingers. Mike's arm was black-and-blue and swollen. She moved her fingers lightly across it. His fingers looked like sausages because he didn't wear the sling. "No heat," she murmured, pleased. "Rest it against your chest." She turned and gathered the supplies she'd need and dug out a new sling.

Mike looked forward to her gentle touch. He did as she asked, watching her. The lamplight emphasized her green eyes. He saw shadows beneath them. "Tough day?" he wondered. Her lips thinned for a moment and then relaxed.

"It's always a mix," she murmured, re-splinting his arm. Leaning up, she fashioned the dark green cotton sling so it supported his broken arm once more.

The nape of his neck tingled wildly when her fingertips brushed his flesh as she tied a knot in the sling. "Thanks," he murmured, "it feels a hell of a lot better in this position." He inhaled her scent, a mix of sunshine, fresh air and her. It made him very aware he was hopelessly attracted to Khat.

Khat eased away, wildly aware of Mike's nearness, his maleness. For whatever unknown reason, he never felt threatening to her. Instead, she felt protection radiating from him, surrounding her. She saw the liquid darkness in his eyes as he followed her movements.

His look held desire, and she once more felt flummoxed by the feelings Mike automatically ignited deep within her body.

Almost breathless, Khat said, "I'll bet it does feel better. Your fingers are swollen because your arm hung down for most of the day. It's hard for the circulation to get back up into the area of the break because the tissue is swollen around it." She took his fingers, squeezing them gently, assessing the situation. Khat would never admit she liked touching this man as she gently massaged each finger, pushing some of the fluid out of them and into his arm. "The swelling will probably go down in a few hours," she murmured.

Picking up her stethoscope, she listened to his heart and lungs. With her small pen flashlight, she moved it across his eyes, watching his pupil response. Moving to his other side, she took his pulse and wrote all her observations down in her small notebook.

"Am I going to live?" Mike asked drily, absorbing her profile, the light glinting through the thick strands of her hair that she had captured in a ponytail.

"Definitely," she murmured, looking up at Mike. He was so masculine but dangerous to her in a new and unexpected way. Her throat tightened. "I figured you'd rebound today. You're in great shape, and your body is responding quickly."

"When can I be picked up by Medevac?" Part of him wanted to get back to the FOB; the larger part of him didn't. Mike found her lifestyle fascinating. And he knew Khat put herself on the line. Taliban were all over these mountains like fleas on a dog. She had to be careful where she rode so she wasn't seen or discovered.

Khat stood and put everything back into her medical pack and closed it up. "Shortly. I took a chance you'd be improved today." She hauled the ruck to the wall and then pushed some tendrils of hair off her cheek. "One is scheduled in at 0100 this morning." She glanced at her Rolex. "It's 2200 now. I've got time to change, eat and get the horses ready. It's going to take us an hour to ride down a steep goat trail to reach the valley below." She saw his face light up, and she smiled a little. "Then you can be with your own kind once again. I imagine everyone on your team is looking forward to seeing you back in the fold."

Mike sat there watching the shadows across her face. "I'm going to miss you." That wasn't a lie. He saw her cheeks grow pink as she walked to her kitchen hole and brought out the grate and a magnesium tab.

"You'll be happier back at Camp Bravo, Mike. This kind of life isn't for a SEAL." She brought out the tea-kettle and set it on the grate. Khat would miss him, too, but she bit back the comment.

Rubbing his beard, Mike growled, "I'll worry about you."

She made a sound in her throat. "I've been out here for five years, and very few people know I'm here. Don't worry about me. I'll be fine." She was touched by his gruff reply and sincere concern. She rocked back on her heels, watching the magnesium tab begin to heat the water.

Scowling, Mike said, "Don't you get lonely out here?" She was young, beautiful and he couldn't imagine this kind of isolation for a woman her age.

"No."

"If you took a packhorse with you this morning, you

must have gone somewhere to render medical aid. To a village, maybe?"

Khat grinned at him. "I'm going to miss all your observations and trying to put them together to figure out who I am." She saw his eyes narrow upon her and once more, her heart started a slow pound. Her gaze fell to his hand resting on his knee. Beautiful hands for a man. If only... And Khat gently tucked those thoughts away. She was damaged goods. Her parents had been shocked by what had happened to her. Her angry, upset father had said no man would ever consider her wifely material.

Khat brought the two mugs down and placed the Darjeeling tea bag into each.

"Have you saved other men like you saved me?"

"Yes. But not often."

"Was I the heaviest?" He grinned.

Khat laughed softly. "Yes, you were."

"Were they SEALs?"

"One was. The other was a Marine Force Recon sniper."

"And you got them out of here like you're going to get me out? By horseback?"

"Yes." Khat poured the boiling water into the cups. Placing them on the tray, she stood and brought down her box of shortbread cookies. "Different locations, but the same scenario. They were wounded, too."

"Did they make it?"

Khat placed the cookies on the tray and then closed the box, taking it back to the hole in the wall. "Yes."

Mike watched her bring the tray over. She set it on his right side and knelt down on the other side of it.

Picking up the spoon, she placed the sugar into his cup and stirred it for him.

"I don't want to lose touch with you, Khat." Mike held her startled gaze as he picked up the mug.

"That can't be."

"Why not?" He watched her expression over the rim of his mug. For a moment, Mike swore she wanted to keep their connection, but then decided against it.

"I have all the help I need." Her heart was doing funny things in her chest. He had seen her naked beneath the waterfall. That realization alone had shocked her. But Mike had treated her with nothing but respect. He didn't try to grope her or speak in sexual innuendos to her.

There was a reflective look in his gold-brown eyes now as he considered her answer. She watched his lips curve around the mug's rim, and she felt a sudden, white-hot heat stab through her lower body. Surprised, she hid her reaction. No man had ever affected her like he did. All they were doing was drinking a cup of tea together!

"Well," Mike said gruffly, "out here, you can never have enough. Bravo is roughly twenty-five miles from here."

Giving him a sad look, Khat whispered, "I know your heart is in the right place, Mike, but we don't operate the same way."

He grimaced. Yeah, he got that. The black ops food chain had a lot of levels. And she was somewhere unreachable, far above him. "Still," he said patiently, "I'd feel better if you'd take my platoon's sat phone number. If things happen, we might be the QRF you need."

"You're not going to take no for an answer, are you?"

Her lips twitched with amusement. He was endearing with his stubborn protectiveness, and it made Khat feel good. No one else ever cared that she was out here, operating on her own, an American surrounded by enemy Taliban every day.

"You're alone out here," he said in a low tone. "I've got five rotations under my belt in this area, and I know it crawls with Taliban. You might someday find yourself in a situation. And if your handler, or whoever he is, can't cut loose the air or ground assets you need, you might find us an alternative. That's all."

"There's no harm in taking your platoon's number." So much of her wanted to remain in contact with Mike. The past five years had been some of the loneliest times in her life. Khat knew he was drawn to her; he'd made no bones about that from the beginning. A man didn't ask the questions he did if he wasn't interested in a woman. She knew he'd remember everything she'd said, trying to put the pieces together on her operator status. Khat hoped she hadn't given him a direct line into her black ops mission. She could see that strong willed look in his darkening eyes that he was damn well going to turn over everything he knew about her in order to find out who she really was, what she did and who she worked for.

Khat seriously doubted, though, that Mike would ever uncover her status.

"Good," Mike said, relieved. Khat was contemplative, her eyes half-closed, those green tourmaline eyes shadowed beneath her thick red lashes. She was torn between saying nothing and divulging more to him. He could feel it. And dammit, he was going to research her when he got back to Bravo, no question.

He had some contacts in the black ops community. His good friend, Gabe Griffin, who had just left the SEALs to marry Bay Thorn, had been in this area. Maybe he knew something about Khat. Mike was sure as hell going to find out from his best friend. If he tried to go up the black ops food chain, they'd stonewall him. No, he'd have to search among the SEALs at Bagram and J-bad, nose around to find out if they'd seen her or knew anything about her. And he wasn't the type that let something go until he got the answers he was seeking.

"When we leave, I'm going to let you ride Zorah, my packhorse. I have only one saddle, and I want you to have it. I don't think your balance is all that good yet, and I don't need you to fall off."

"Good planning," he said drily. "Last time I threw a leg over a horse was just before I left to join the SEALs."

"I'll ride bareback." Khat gestured to her legs. "I've got thighs of steel from being in the saddle so much."

The words, *you have the most beautiful legs I've ever seen*, almost tore out of Mike's mouth. She'd take it the wrong way, of course, and he wanted to leave their relationship, as thin as it was, intact between them.

"That's fine," he murmured. He sipped the tea, branding Khat's clean profile, the shadows and light across her face, into his mind and heart. "What's next for you after you get rid of me?" He said it half in jest, but he wanted to try and get something out of her that would give him a lead. *Any lead.*

"Every day is different." Khat smiled a little sadly, feeling his protectiveness embrace her. "I'm like the wind. You never know which way I'll flow on a certain day."

"Were you always like this, Khat?"

Her smile dissolved. She held the mug in both hands, sipping from it. "No."

"What were you like as a little girl?" Desperation clawed at his chest. The hunger to know her was eating him alive, and no woman had ever intrigued him like Khat did.

Sighing, Khat placed the cup down beside her and clasped her hands around her one leg that was drawn up against her body. "Happy."

"Do you have brothers or sisters?"

Shaking her head, she said, "I was an only child, but a very welcomed child into my parents' lives."

"I know you have Middle East blood in you," he said, watching her expression closely. "I've wondered all day whether one of your parents came from another country and moved to the States like my parents did."

"Yes," she said, holding his sharpened look. "We share a common background in some respects."

"The way you speak English," he pressed, "it sounds like you're Afghani."

Khat gave him a wry look. Mike was part Saudi. He would be able to hear the dialect differences, the pronunciation of certain words, and most likely be able to know if a person was from one Middle Eastern country or another. "I think you missed your calling. You should have been a linguist."

He snorted. "No chance in hell. Not my game. I like doing what I do as a SEAL shooter."

"Mmm," Khat said.

"Your profile reminds me of the women in this

region of Afghanistan. Each province has different
bloodlines, different gene pools. This region saw a
Mongolian influence." Which would account for the
slight tilt of her eyes, but Mike didn't add that important point.

He was getting too close for comfort, and Khat
avoided his direct, digging gaze. "I think you had too
much time on your hands today, Mike." She forced a
smile she didn't feel. He was like a bloodhound on a
scent. Khat agreed with him that the genetics of each
tribe were unique. And there were marked differences
in hair color, eye color and skin color, as a result.

"I've seen a lot of red-haired women in our area.
Green and blue eyes. Fair skin," he continued. "And
you fit that model."

"I could be Irish," she teased, now uncomfortable
beneath his intense scrutiny.

"No way. At least," he amended lightly, "in this province we're in."

"I'm not giving you any information, Mike."

"And," he went on, ignoring her statement, "the
women and men in this area are much taller than the
other tribes in other provinces. You're about an inch
shorter than I am, and I'm five foot eleven inches tall."

Khat said nothing. He was on a mission of discov-
ery, and she could see it in the tenacious look in his
gold eyes. "I need to get something to eat before we
leave." She unwound from her position on the floor,
feeling his unrelenting inspection.

Following her with his gaze, Mike felt tension rising in Khat due to his interrogation of her. He sensed
he'd gotten close to the truth about her but he wasn't
going to gloat about it. The more he questioned her, the

more he saw fear deep in the recesses of Khat's eyes. And that delicious, full mouth of hers had thinned, as if a defensive reaction. Why? His gut told him it had to do with the scars across her long, beautiful back and shoulders.

She brought back some dried beef jerky and handed him some. "I'm sure the first thing you will do once you land at Camp Bravo is call your wife. And then your parents. They will breathe a sigh of relief and be glad to hear from you."

"I don't have a wife," he said, watching her sit down near his feet, long legs crossed. He saw surprise in her widening eyes.

"Surely, a special woman, then?" Khat couldn't conceive of this ruggedly good-looking man, who obviously was intelligent, not being in a relationship. That simply wasn't possible.

"I don't have anyone." So what did he see in Khat's eyes? Surprise? Shock? Desire? Happiness? Mike decided to turn the tables on her as he chewed the salty beef. "What about you, Khat? Do you have a husband?"

Heat swept up from her neck and into her face. "No."

"Someone here in Afghanistan that you love?" He could think of a hundred men who would stand in line to get her. She suddenly became nervous, licking her lower lip. Shy with him, unable to hold his gaze.

"No one," she answered softly. "My line of work is too dangerous." That wasn't a lie, but it wasn't the truth. No man would consider her whole. Her back and shoulders were nothing but scars, ridges and were ugly. Men did not want a scarred woman with a shameful past. Her father, who had been born in this province, once he had seen her scars for the first time, had cried.

He had told her mother that no man would ever consider her for marriage. He cried for the grandchildren he would never hold in his arms. He was shamed by her scars.

Khat had felt even more wounded by her father's patriarchal Afghan attitude, but she was at a place in her life that his words had cut even deeper than the lashes she had received during interrogation by the Taliban. And when she had survived and healed physically, she'd come back here four years ago. Her father said she was a dead woman walking. He was right.

Mike felt Khat leave, her thoughts elsewhere, her eyes growing clouded. Sensing pain or suffering around her, he said, "You're right, in our business, we can have a short life. It's hell on anyone who loves us. That's why I'm not in a serious relationship. I wouldn't want someone worried about me all the time over here."

Pensive, Khat forced herself to eat because she knew her body needed the nutrition and energy. "My parents are very unhappy about what I do. They don't understand it. Or me."

"That's too bad. You're doing important but dangerous undercover work." The hurt in her face moved Mike. He wanted to open his arm and ask her to come and lean against him. Khat needed to be held. It was so clear in her darkening eyes. Her mouth was pursed, as if holding back unknown pain and memories.

If one of her parents was Afghan, it was probably her father. He would have made the decision to move the family to the States, not the woman. And Afghan males were patriarchal as hell, superprotective of their daughters, wanting only two things from them: being a virgin upon their wedding day and giving them grandchildren to carry on their family lineage. He imagined if his thinking was accurate, Khat was seen as a misfit as a woman to her father. And it would have put a lot of pressure on her to live up to her father's expectations of her, versus what she wanted to do with her life as an individual. Which was to become a Marine Corps sniper.

Khat wanted to move away from her painful past. "Your name? Michael? That is one of the archangels of heaven. Did your parents name you that because they knew you'd be a warrior someday?"

"My father named me after my grandfather. He fought in tribal wars that helped bring the House of Saud to power a long time ago. He was a warrior." Mike gave her a wry look. "I think my father was hoping I'd become like him. Instead of picking up a scalpel, I picked up the sword."

"Just as in the Koran, Michael the archangel is the one who battles, protects and defends."

"I do my share of battling," Mike agreed. "And I am protective of those I love." His voice became gritty. "And I'm a sucker for women and children who need protection."

Her skin riffled with the darkness of his voice. "Don't look at me. I can protect myself." Khat would never let on that she'd never felt as safe or shielded as the past two days with Mike's presence in her life.

"It's my nature," he said seriously, seeing the haunted look come to her eyes. Something told him Khat rarely received any protection from anyone. She'd learned a long time ago to take care of herself and never expected help from another quarter. What the hell had happened to her to make her think like that? He shouldn't feel so damned elated to discover she wasn't married or wasn't in a relationship presently.

"Your last name, is spelled *T-A-R-I-K*?"

Now why would she want to know that? "In the old country it was spelled *T-A-R-I-Q*, but when my father came to the States, he changed it to make it easier for his patients to pronounce and spell."

"It's my understanding the name means one who uses a hammer?" She lifted her chin and stared at him.

"Guilty on all counts," Mike said, giving her a slow smile. "There's various meanings to it. One is it means a bright, shining star that leads the way."

"You are a leader. There is no question."

"I try to be," Mike said. "Another, the name of the Morning Star, Venus."

"I think you've taken two of the three definitions to heart," Khat said lightly.

"What? I'm not a star?" He chuckled. "I did love astronomy when I was a kid. My dad even bought me a small telescope so I could look at the stars."

"But that lost out to becoming a warrior? Your first name, Michael, combined with your last name pushes you toward being a man of action. Someone who can use the sword."

"You're right." He lost his smile. "If I had one wish before I left you, it is to know your full first name. I know Khat is your nickname."

Feeling her heart move beneath his humble request, Khat saw the sincerity in his narrowing eyes. "I can't. I'm sorry. Besides, my name does not have the glory and power that yours does." She managed a small smile, appreciating him for who he was: a very brave SEAL. The joke was, her Pashtun name, Khatereh, simply meant, "memory." And so it had been. There were branding memories in her mind about her scarred flesh and fractured soul she could never forget. And she was never the same after her capture. So much for *memory*.

She rose. "It's time to go."

CHAPTER FOUR

MIKE STOOD NEXT to Khat as they waited beneath the edge of a wadi that spilled out onto a plain where the Medevac would land shortly. It was a quarter moon night. He could hear the wind gusting off the mountains, sliding into the desert plain before them. The stars were bright. The horses had been hidden and tied farther up into the wadi. Nothing moved. He breathed a sigh of relief that a drone was overhead with thermal imaging capability, not picking up anything but animal body heat. There were no humans in the immediate area except them. Still, he was alert and took nothing for granted.

Damn, he didn't want to leave Khat out here alone. It ground against every protective mechanism Mike possessed. Hell, yes, she was competent. She said she'd been doing this for five years, and she was still alive. So who did he think he was? She was the one who saved their sorry asses a few days ago, not vice versa. Mike smiled a little, his eyes glittering as he swept the rocky scree slope to his right, the same slope his team had damned near been killed on. If not for Khat.

His hearing was slowly returning to normal, not as sharp as it had been, but he could hear Khat talking in a very low voice on the radio transmission to the Medevac coming their way, giving the pilot the GPS position to land the bird five hundred feet from where they were hidden. She'd already gone out earlier, like a shadow, and removed rocks or limbs that could be kicked up by the whirling blades of the Black Hawk, potentially causing them injury. She knew her job.

Mike kept hearing the call signs Archangel and Boulder. Which sign was hers? If he could pick up her black ops code name, that was a piece of vital intel he could use.

Khat signed off the sat phone, everything in place. She shoved it into a pocket on her H-gear she wore around her torso. Her M-4 was in a harness across her chest. Her mouth was dry with tension. Even though the drone's eyes were above the exfil point, she was wary. The wind rustled the tree leaves. Her hearing was cocked toward any other sound out of place. Leaning down, she placed Mike's rucksack to her right, where she could easily pick it up and sling it over her shoulder in a run to the Black Hawk. He couldn't do it; his left arm was in a sling.

She straightened, pulling the NVGs around her neck, pushing her fingers through her captured hair in a single braid down her back. Nerves always got her at moments like this. Murphy's law of "if anything could go wrong, it would," was alive and well in a combat zone. Her mind was racing over the rally point in case they were jumped by unseen and undetected Taliban. It would be their only escape route. Khat felt the heat of Mike's body close to hers and could sense his alertness. Amazed he didn't feel tense, she realized it was a different kind of training. Join the SEALs and you knew you would be facing combat continuously.

It took a special kind of person to be comfortable in such a situation. She wasn't one of them.

She felt Mike turn, his shadow looming over her. The thin wash of moonlight only made the gloom even scarier for Khat. Her gaze caught the faintest movement of a leaf, a change in it, indicating someone could be sneaking up on them. It wasn't; it was just the wind playing havoc on her senses, but her nerves were taut.

In the distance, she could hear the Black Hawk and the two Apache combat gunships, escorting it, the thumping of the rotors cutting through the darkness toward their position. They would land with no lights on. Everyone was wearing NVGs. The night hid them from attack up to a point.

Mike eased the NVGs on his helmet. Khat's face was tense, her eyes narrowed, in complete guard mode. She'd pulled off her goggles, the black baseball cap pushed up on her head. A powerful surge of protection nearly overwhelmed him. He was so damn invested in her emotionally, and he didn't want to extricate himself. Watching her scan the area, her profile clean, those soft lips accentuated, he thought the unthinkable. He wanted to kiss the hell out of her, feel her mouth beneath his. Feel her respond. A flood of heated emotions coursed through him as he stood beside her. *To hell with it.* He set the M-4 against a tree trunk, easily within reach if he needed it in a hurry. Lifting his hand, he placed it gently upon her shoulder, so as not to startle her.

Khat felt the warmth of Mike's strong hand come to rest on her shoulder. She was wearing her cammies and even through them, she could feel the male heat of his fingers. Surprised, she turned quickly, thinking he saw something and was silently warning her. Instead, as she looked up into his darkly shadowed face, her lips parted. The look in his glittering eyes was focused on her. Her breath hitched as he pulled her toward him. He was going to kiss her! Panic mingled with shock. And then, Khat felt an even more powerful emotion sweep through her, erasing the other two feelings. Her mind shorted out. Mike was going to kiss her. Nothing was further from her reality. For five years of loneliness, Khat had accepted her twisted fate.

Until now.

Her eyes widened as he bent his head, his mouth curving softly against hers. His hand was firm, guiding her as close as they could get to one another. The gear they wore prevented any real intimacy. She closed her eyes, inhaling his scent, feeling his mouth tentatively explore hers. The prickle of his beard against her cheek sent tingles racing through her. His hand slid from her shoulder, fingers curling gently around her nape, tipping her head upward, angling her just enough to deepen their kiss.

Her world exploded, and Khat moaned, her hand moving to his chest, her fingers curving against his Kevlar vest. She tasted his maleness, his power, his coaxing, asking her to participate. It had been so long since she'd kissed a man! And she wanted this. She wanted to taste Mike Tarik, feel his roughened lips rasp against her softer yielding ones.

Breath ragged, Khat sank against him, and he took her full weight, welcoming her into his partial embrace. He was giving her so much that it brought tears to her eyes. It was as if Mike somehow sensed she was fractured and terribly vulnerable to a man. He parted her lips more, inviting, asking her for greater entrance. A hunger roared up through her, and Khat responded to his scalding invitation. She felt him groan. There was no sound, just vibration. It sent elation through her as her fingers curved shyly around his thick neck, pulling him closer, wanting deeper connection with him.

Her knees felt like so much jelly as his tongue slowly traced her lower lip, explored the corner of her mouth and slid deeper, finding her tongue. Suddenly, Khat felt a bolt of white-hot heat clench in her channel, and it was almost painful in its swift contraction. A whimper escaped her.

They were out of time. Two Apaches thundered high overhead, guard dogs to protect the Medevac when it landed. They would be on the lookout for enemy. Mike regretfully eased his mouth from hers, breathing unevenly, staring hard down into her drowsy-looking eyes. Her lips were glistening, slightly swollen from the power of his kiss. He released Khat but kept his hand lightly on her shoulder. She looked bewildered as she stared up at him. There was burning arousal in her dark eyes. He'd felt her innocent response in their kiss, sweet and unsure with him. Her slender fingers tightened against his shoulder.

He framed her face with his hand, leaning close, inches between them. "Listen to me, Khat. I've got your back. You call me anytime you need help. All right?"

His guttural growl sifted through her shaking body. Khat had never been kissed like this. She felt weak, hot and needy. All from one kiss! The palm of his hand was rough against her cheek. She saw the hunter's intensity in his slitted eyes, heard the growl in his low voice. He meant it. Barely able to nod, she couldn't find her voice, so shocked by his molten kiss. So many emotions were running through her, some good, some terrifying monsters from her past, that she felt a lump form in her throat as she rested against his tall, strong body. Mike exuded an animal-like protection toward her, as if she had just been claimed as his mate. There was an overwhelming sense that she was his woman. She could feel it.

Mike was taken aback as he saw tears form in her eyes, slide silently down her cheeks. He felt their warmth slide beneath his palm, dampening his flesh. He used his thumb to push the tears away from the high slope of her cheek. The sound of the Black Hawk grew closer. A minute out, maybe. Damn! Frustrated, he could read her eyes like windows into her soul, seeing desire mingling with terror, and he couldn't translate all of what was going on within Khat. Fear of him? Impossible! She could have stepped away from him at any point. She could have refused to kiss him. But she was here, standing before him, her face a map of how she was feeling inwardly toward him. Her lower lip trembled, and she looked away, shame in her expression.

"Khat," he growled, gently forcing her to hold his gaze, "this isn't over, Angel. Not by a long shot. I'm going to find you. Do you hear me? And when I do, you aren't walking away from me again. I want to get to know you."

Khat closed her eyes, giving a bare nod of her head, his hand trapping her against him. She could hear the Black Hawk's arrival, the blades puncturing the night air. Pulling away from him, she quickly wiped her eyes, turned and put on her NVGs. Her heart was in utter

turmoil, torn, hurting and wanting Mike all at the same
time. Compressing her lips, she picked up his ruck and
walked to the edge of the bushes and trees.

The Black Hawk landed. Trying to clear her blown
senses, shake off the shock of his unexpected kiss, Khat
crouched and then started her run toward the helo. Dust
and dirt kicked up, eighty mile an hour gusts created
by the rotors. She saw the door slide open, and one
aircrew chief hopped out. Giving him the ruck, she
stepped aside.

Tarik was right behind her. He saw Khat remain
crouched, quickly moving away, fading into the dust
clouds raised by the helo. The crew chief took his M-4,
and Mike grabbed the frame of the door, hauling himself inside the cabin. He was going home, and it was
the last place he wanted to go right now. As the combat
medic guided him to a litter, he sat down, not wanting
to lie down. He traded his Kevlar helmet for another
helmet, pulling it on, in instant communications with
the four men on board.

"I'm good to go," he growled. "Thanks for picking
me up. Let's exfil…"

In seconds, the Black Hawk broke gravity with
the earth and quickly turned, heading out over the
open, empty desert plain. It picked up speed and al-
titude swiftly, the twin engines roaring, shaking the
helo with rhythmic vibrations. Mike felt suddenly sad.
And happy. It was a mix. He'd wanted to kiss Khat
ever since he'd become conscious. And she'd *liked* his
kiss. She'd responded to him. He had known there was
something special between them; invisible, but raw,
alive and heated.

His hand curled into a fist, and he focused on the

combat medic who was asking him a lot of medical questions. He'd have to go to the dispensary, get the arm x-rayed and go through the medical system. Once done, he'd be expected to see the chief of the platoon come tomorrow morning. He'd go back to his tent in the SEAL section of Camp Bravo, climb into his cot and sleep. If he could...

KHAT BLINKED BACK the hot tears that continued to fall. She quickly ran back to the wadi to where the horses were tied. The sound of the Black Hawk and guard dog Apaches would draw any enemies who were around. She would be in danger. Leaping up on Zorah, she used her calf, not the reins, to turn the mare around. She tied the rope to Mina's halter on the back of her saddle. They would slowly pick their way out of the wadi and up to another goat trail. Khat never took the same route twice.

In a village where she posed as a nurse, the Taliban had caught and tortured her. Khat savagely shoved down those memories. She had to ride through the night and remain alert for her enemy. Once on a safer trail, her mind revolved back to that capture. She'd been holding medical clinics for a year with great success; gathering intel from the villagers and giving it to her handler in J-bad. The villages along the border were grateful for her riding in on her horse, a packhorse in tow with medical supplies for the men, women and children.

Her cover was solid because her father had been born in the village of Dur Babba, and she was his daughter, part of the Shinwari Tribe.

The days of being held, questioned and tortured by

Sangar Khogani, chief of the Hill tribe, had changed her life forever. And if not for the village women who risked their own lives to save hers, she wouldn't be here today. The week they'd hid her in a nearby cave, her back a mass of bloody strips of flesh, had passed in a semiconscious, feverish daze.

It was weeks later, septic and near death, that one woman villager had walked ten miles into an American forward operating base, asking for help, that Khat was rescued. And it was when she was hospitalized at Bagram, that the terror of nearly dying, the flay that had stripped her flesh from her body, had welled up through her. Khat understood her soul was fractured by the capture and subsequent torture interrogation. She had shut down her violent emotions, stuffed them into a deep, dark hole within herself. As she lay in the hospital recuperating, she became emotionally numb to everything. A robot of sorts, her Afghan blood thirsting for revenge against the Hill tribe for what they did to her and her people.

The past four years, Khat had left a trail of blood, and she never blinked when killing a Hill tribesman. They'd murdered so many of her people over the years. They had raped Shinwari women, girls and boys. They murdered their husbands, sons and brothers. She stood between her tribe and Sangar Khogani's Hill tribe.

It hurt to feel those violent emotions once again, reliving them all, and Khat hated it. Mike's kiss, his care, ripped the lid off that dark, wounded place within her. She understood he didn't know what he'd done to her. His intent had been pure and unselfish because she could still feel his strong mouth curved against her own, giving to her, not taking anything away from her.

Rubbing her cheek, the tears continuing to flow, Khat couldn't stop them. Mike had unknowingly released all the demons from her past, but he'd also released her as a woman from a dormant state, too.

Wiping her cheeks dry as she rode, the horse moving silently down the narrow, rock-strewn goat path, the mountain's giant shadow covering them from the thin moonlight, Khat didn't want to remember that time. Mike's kiss had been completely unexpected. He'd blindsided her and yet, she felt no anger over what he'd done. After all, she'd been a willing participant. She could have said no. She could have stepped away. But she didn't. *Why? Why?*

The goat path curved. In another mile, she would be home to her pool cave. Her mind was spewing out memories of her torture at the hands of the Taliban.

The Marine Corps had sent her home to recover. Her parents had been horrified over the extent of her wounds; her back and shoulders flayed by a whip, the metal tips tearing up her tender flesh, forever marking her.

Her father, Jaleel Shinwari, was a civil engineer who had moved from Dur Babba precisely because the village was closest to the violent, aggressive Hill tribe. He had moved to San Diego, California. There, her mother, Glenna, met and married him. Khat was the result of that union, half Afghan, half American.

It was hard enough to deal with the torture for Khat, but her father nearly went insane because of what had happened to her. He was Afghan and believed in an eye for an eye. He wanted revenge, but was helpless to make it happen, so his anger had turned toward her.

Recovering at the San Diego Naval Hospital, Khat

had enough to deal with. He'd gotten into an argument with her mother at her bedside one day, saying that her life was ruined, that no man would ever look at her again. Jaleel wanted her to marry, to give him grandchildren, carry on their proud Afghan lineage to the next generation. His words were just as deeply scarring and life changing to Khat as being whipped by the Taliban.

She was damaged goods, he'd cried, pacing the room, filled with anger and helplessness. No man would want her once he saw her scarred body. She was ugly. Her mother had heatedly argued otherwise, but on that day, something fragile and beautiful to her as a woman had died.

Now, by the time she arrived back at the cave, Khat felt shattered inwardly once more. Only in a very different way. She'd gone through the motions of caring for her horses, watering and feeding them. It was nearly 0200 in the morning. Her hands trembled as she made herself some tea. Just the custom of making it calmed her somewhat.

Only this time, Mike wasn't here with her.

Drawing in a ragged breath, Khat closed her eyes, waiting for the water to boil. He was larger than life. He was a man. And somehow, he'd slipped into her closed heart. Khat didn't know how it had happened or why. But it had. The cave seemed sterile without his presence.

As she sat on the sleeping bag, her back against the cave wall, mug in her hand, Khat swallowed hard. Tears were just at the periphery of her eyes, her heart and mind in utter turmoil. Nothing could change. It didn't matter. She wasn't going to change the trajectory of her life because of his one kiss. But Mike's guttural challenge to her, that he'd find her, that he wouldn't allow her to walk away as he had this time, scared Khat. And it called to her, a whisper in the halls of her shattered heart.

His kiss had awakened her from a deep sleep of ignoring herself as a woman with a rich palette of emotions, of normal human needs and desires. His mouth had been like a key opening up the treasured awareness of her own body, igniting it into bright, burning life once more. He'd uncaged her yearnings she'd had before this had happened. Before that, she'd always known that someday, she'd meet a man who would hold her heart gently between his hands, respect her, love her. Khat had dreams and hopes. And yes, she'd wanted children by this man and to live happily ever after.

Mouth twisting, Khat stared into the gloom of the other cave in front of where she sat. She had been so young and naive, in her early twenties, so filled with idealistic dreams, hopes and desires. And it had all come to a crashing, violent end when she was twenty-four.

Lifting her gaze to the ceiling, hot tears stung her eyes. Khat was helpless to stop them this time. She'd stopped crying the day her torture began. Tonight, after Mike's kiss, she cried long and hard. When she doused the light of the lantern, Khat lay on the sleeping bag Mike had used. It gave her comfort, and she could still smell his masculine scent in the fabric. It was as if he were still here.

Closing her eyes, feeling sleep pulling at her, Khat realized that she wanted to see Mike again, too. His kiss had made her aware of just how lonely she really was. The cave was now a symbol of a different sort for her. Before, it had been safety, hiding from her pain. It served as a buffer, an isolation, so that she didn't have to live again, only exist.

Tears slipped from her eyes, warm and trailing down her face. To acknowledge all of this was too much for Khat to accept. Five years had hardened her resolve; her focus was on her people, not herself. It was a sacrifice she was willing to make. Sometimes, Khat understood, her personal needs, whatever they were, were quietly tucked away for the good of others. And it had to remain that way.

"So, who the hell is she, Mac?" Mike asked Chief John McCutcheon.

He sat in the office with the man who held the daily reins of Delta Platoon. Mike had awakened early the morning after arriving at Camp Bravo, sat with Mac, as they all called him, and told him the entire story.

The chief was forty, had been a SEAL since he was eighteen, was married and had two grown sons. His wife, Pamela, was a schoolteacher in San Diego.

Mac rubbed his black scruffy beard and scowled. He sat with all the notes that Tarik had written down. "Black ops, for sure." He pulled his laptop over and entered a password to get into the top secret network of SEALs and other agencies, like the CIA, Army Delta operators, Army Special Forces and Marine Force Recons utilized. Pulling up a map of their area, thirty miles between Bravo and the Pakistan border, he clicked on Marine Force Recons. It would show where teams or single operators, who were snipers, were presently located.

For safety reasons, all assets out in the Hindu Kush, no matter what black ops group it was, were updated out of Bagram four times a day. When identified as a friendly, it meant air assets or other black ops groups in the same area would not shoot each other by mistake, thinking they were the enemy. Mac stared at the map, zeroing in on where Tarik had been picked up.

"Come over here," he said, gesturing for him to pull up a chair and sit next to him. "Look at the area where your team was." He pointed to the enlarged map.

Mike came over, turned the chair around, sat down, his arms across the top of it. The doctor had put an old-fashioned plaster cast on his lower left arm. It was a nuisance. Looking at where Mac placed his finger, he scowled. "That's the area," he muttered. He saw no red dot that indicated a friendly operator in the area. "Why the hell wouldn't she be marked as a friendly?"

"Could be deep ops, but still, someone has to know her whereabouts."

"Can you try typing in Boulder and Archangel? See if you get a hit?"

Mac moved to another program and typed in "Boulder." Nothing came up. He typed in "Archangel." Immediately, a box with big red letters said "Access Denied." Below it was a request for a password, which Mac didn't know. "I can't get any more intel on this code name."

Staring at the box, Tarik cursed softly. "What about a work-around? Go to the Marine Force Recon network?"

Mac nodded and moved over to it. He typed in "Archangel." The same box appeared again. "Look, you have to get a ride to Bagram today because the doctor said that arm has to be given an MRI." Mac studied him. "Why don't you get over to SEAL HQ? They've got intelligence officers over there. Talk to them. See if you can find out anything on this woman."

Growling, Mike stood up. "Yeah, I'll do it. Thanks, Mac."

Tarik walked out of the small office and headed down the passageway to the big room where the SEALs gathered. A number of his team was there, drinking coffee and talking to the other men. He frowned and left the building, going to his tent to get his kit, his rifle and then head over to Ops.

The morning sky was pale, the sun barely edging the mountains surrounding the forward operating base. It was cold even in June at eight thousand feet. He broke into a trot to warm up. His mind, and if he was honest, his heart, were never far from Khat. Kissing her had been the most right thing in his world, and Mike didn't regret it.

As he kitted up, hauled the ruck onto his right shoulder, clipping his M-4 rifle onto the harness across his chest, images of Khat filled his thoughts. Mike was glad to have the time to do some serious investigation to try and find out more about her. He knew the SEALs had a staff of men and women who did nothing but intel. As soon as he got done going through the medical gauntlet, he'd get over to the SEAL HQ. It was the main go-to place for anything black-ops-wise going on in this country.

LIEUTENANT ADDISON SINCLAIRE sat listening to Mike Tarik's tale of rescue. She had a small office at SEAL HQ. Writing down the specifics, she saw the stubborn glint in the petty officer's eyes when he told her he wanted to know who this black ops woman was. Mike sat with her at her desk. She had a large PC screen, easy to see and read.

Mike liked Addison the moment he met her. She was a petite blonde with sharp-looking blue eyes. Like the rest of SEAL HQ, she was a navy intel officer and wore SEAL cammies. Sinclaire was part of an eight-thousand-person force who supported the two thousand SEALs who took the fight to the enemy. He had a cup of coffee nearby as he watched her take the information and start her hunt.

"Hmm," Addy said, "getting nothing on this gal. I'm going over to the Marine Corps net."

Mike watched her hit "Access Denied" on everything. Frustrated, he said, "What about tapping into personnel files? Try her first name? See if something pops up?"

"Good idea," the intel officer murmured, switching screens. "C-A-T?"

"Yes."

"Nothing. What about Cathy or Cathleen? It's probably a shortening of her original name."

Nodding, Mike watched her type them in. A number of Cathleens came up, but every lead showed a woman marine, her MOS or skill, her rate or rank and none of them were presently deployed to Afghanistan.

"Your gal is very secretive," Addy muttered. Her blond brows dipped as she thought about it. "Okay, let's go another direction. She wore a hog's tooth. Only snipers who actually graduate from marine sniper school are given one." She brought up the names of Marine Corps sniper graduates for the past ten years. Gaze moving slowly down the list, she said, "Hmm, here's a Shinwari, K. Listed here as having graduated seven years ago." She tapped the screen. Turning to Mike, she said, "You did say she referred to the villages of that area as 'her people,' right?"

"Right."

"Well," Addy said, thinking about it, "the Shinwari tribe is four hundred thousand strong. And Afghan names are not like English names. They would *all* use 'Shinwari' as their last name because it denotes their tribe."

Excitement thrummed through Tarik as he stared at the entry on the computer. "Maybe that's her? And her first name is a K, not a C. Her first name has to be Afghan, then, not an American name."

"Let me see if this will let me find out more. There's an asterisk by her name, and I don't know what that means." She clicked on the name.

"Damn," Mike growled. The box "Access Denied" came up. Again. Frustration ate at him like acid.

"Yeah, she's really protected." Addy twisted her lips in thought. "Okay, we think we have the correct name on this operator. We have Marine Force Recon snipers all over Afghanistan. They're small in number, like our SEAL snipers, out there operating alone for weeks or months at a time, tagging the bad guys and usually going after high value targets." She tapped her chin. "Let's see if they'll let me into the whereabouts of marine snipers along the border."

Mike saw a map pop up, the same one Mac had accessed earlier. This time, the intel officer typed in Shinwari, K. The box "Access Denied" appeared.

Mouth thinning, Mike stared at the screen.

"You said she was a medic of some sort?" Addy asked.

"Yes, she is. She said she was a paramedic. But it could be a lie to throw me off her trail, too."

"Maybe an Army 18 Delta combat corpsman," she said, "but I'm not aware they're allowing women to take that eighteen-month course." She went to the army website and to the 18 Delta area. Typing in the name, nothing came up. Dead end. "Okay, let's take another angle on this, Tarik. You said you saw scars on her back, right?"

"Yes."

"How old do you think they were?"

He shrugged. "Hell, I don't know. The scars are white, not pink. Pink would denote they happened in the past year or so."

"Okay, so let's play 'what if,' here. What if she was here in Afghanistan? A covert asset? Posing as someone else? She got caught by the bad guys? Tortured? And she survived it. But if that was so, she'd have been taken here, to Bagram hospital for treatment. Right? Or, if bad enough, sent to Landstuhl Medical Center in Germany."

Mike shrugged. "Your guess is as good as mine. She could have been whipped because the scars were long and deep across her back." He didn't tell the intel officer he'd seen Khat naked. He wanted to protect her, not expose her to the world in that way. Or maybe he was just plain damned protective of her.

"Okay, off to Bagram's database on patients." She typed in the name. Her brows lifted. "Ah, a hit!" She traced her finger across the screen.

Mike leaned forward, his eyes narrowing. There,

five years ago, was a Shinwari, K., admitted to the hospital.

"Let's pull up her medical record."

He cursed softly. The box "Access Denied" glared back at them.

"She is deeper than deep," Sinclaire muttered, frowning and studying the screen.

Mike twisted a look up at the officer. "What does that mean to you, then?"

"That she's working a special black ops. Probably straight out of the E ring of the Pentagon. She's a 'need to know basis' only. In other words, Tarik, if you didn't directly work with her, you'd never know she existed." She shrugged. "You just got lucky and intersected with her. Right time, right place. But you're like two ships passing in the night, and one doesn't overlap with the other insofar as information goes." She tapped the screen. "They're *really* protecting her."

Rubbing his chin, he muttered, "Okay, so let's take it another direction. On the second night when she rode in, she had a packhorse with medical supplies. I saw them, and they're all from the US. She was dressed in male Afghan clothes. She was wearing a blue-and-white-checked *shemagh* around her neck and shoulders. She'd gone somewhere. Where? And I know she's a medic of some sort. If she's got supplies with her, then she's got to be going into a village. Giving people medical aid, maybe?"

"Yup, good lead. That blue-and-white *shemagh* she was wearing is indicative of the Shinwari tribe. Every tribe has different colors. Maybe she's connected with an NGO? Nongovernmental organization? A charity that's working here in this country?" Addison brought up the list of NGOs and then typed the name into the database of people associated with each charity.

"Zip," Mike muttered.

"Yep. But we're not done. If she's giving medical aid to Shinwari villages, then there has to be a record of it somewhere. She's using US supplies, and those are tracked. You said she gave you morphine, right? For your broken arm?"

"Yes. Why?"

Dipping her head, Addy said, "Well, morphine is the most carefully tracked drug in our medical supply. Not just anyone can have it. Let me prowl for a second here…"

Mike watched her fingers flying over the keyboard. Different web pages whipped by. He was grateful that Sinclaire knew her business. Sooner or later, something would be revealed.

"Aha!" Addy crowed, grinning. "Got her!"

Mike looked at where she was pointing.

"This is a list of morphine distribution for this year to Afghanistan through the navy supply depot here at Bagram. There's her name, Shinwari, K., and there's what she is. A paramedic. So, she didn't lie to you. Hold on, let me see how this morphine is being distributed."

Mike's heart started to beat harder as he waited.

"Okay," Addy said, scowling at the screen, "the morphine goes from Bagram to J-bad. It's the northern SEAL HQ in the country. Smaller than us, but important. Let's see who this morphine is going to."

The name "Hutton, J., CDR" came up.

"I know Hutton," Mike said. He didn't like the man, but didn't say anything.

"Hmm. Commander Hutton handles deep black ops

over there." She said, "I can make a call and see what I can get."

Grateful, Mike said, "I'd appreciate it. This woman saved four SEAL lives. She deserves to be put up for a medal."

"Yep, I get where you're coming from." She picked up her phone and made the call.

Tarik sat back. He liked Sinclaire's can-do spirit. She was like a dog on a hunt. He listened as she spoke to Hutton. And it was clear she was getting stonewalled. She tried asking all types of different questions, giving him her intel she'd accessed on Khat already. When she hung up, she grimaced.

"Well, he was none too pleased I was snooping around," she muttered. "She's deep black ops. Off-limits to us. And he about shit when I mentioned Archangel. He wanted to know how we knew that code name. You heard the conversation."

"Yeah," Mike said glumly, sitting back in the chair, thinking. "She's got to have a very unique job assignment, then. Something more than just being a marine sniper out in the mountains shooting HVTs."

"Yes." Addy pushed some blond tendrils away from her cheek. "Maybe you need to go at this in a different direction."

"Oh?"

"Look, there's SEALs in all these villages along the border off and on. They know the elders of these villages. Maybe you should go out and talk to the operators out of Charlie platoon based here at Bagram. Ask if they've met a red-haired, green-eyed woman who is a nurse. Or a paramedic. Giving medical aid in a village. Too bad we don't have a photo of her."

"Well," Tarik muttered, "there aren't that many women rendering medical aid out in those villages because it's too damned dangerous. And all I can think is she would be aligned with an NGO. They go into a village, protected by the military, by SEALs. They protect the NGO people while they do their thing."

Addison grinned, her voice becoming excited. "Right! And so if some of the SEALs pulled for a detail like that, they might have seen her."

"She's damned easy to spot," Mike said, "she's almost six feet tall." And she was beautiful. No, a SEAL who had seen her would damn well remember her.

"Right. Look, you nose around on this angle, okay? In the meantime, I don't like being stonewalled. I love a challenge like this. I know where to reach you at Camp Bravo, and Mac is a sweetie. I can give him a call if I find anything, and he can let you know. Okay?"

Good intel officers were worth their weight in gold. Mike rose and shook her hand. "Thank you, ma'am, for all your help. This is important to me."

"I know it is. But also, don't forget, if she's deep black ops, she's writing up reports and sending them in, too. *Someone* is receiving her reports, more than likely, Commander Hutton. And then, he's probably sending them to the E ring of the Pentagon, where this operation or mission was created." She rubbed her hands together, grinning up at him. "I'll keep looking for you."

Tarik spent the rest of the day talking with the SEALs of Charlie Platoon who were assigned to Bagram. None of them could remember Khat. All of them agreed her red hair, green eyes and height was something that would stick in their minds.

As he left for the barracks across the base, Mike felt

hopeful. At least he had some info on Khat. And he was missing her. The huge army base was a beehive of 24/7 activity. It held twenty thousand military and civilian people. But the only person he cared about, his priority, was Khat.

As he took a base bus to his barracks, he had time to think. What bothered him the most was the haunted look deep in her eyes when he told her he was going to find her. She'd been admitted to Bagram hospital five years ago, so something had happened to her when she was undercover. Maybe that was the terror he'd seen in the recesses of her eyes? He recalled their conversations, her shyness toward him.

Then again, what if the name Lieutenant Sinclaire had found was not her? Was he barking up the wrong tree? Dammit, he wished he had a photo ID on her. It would then verify K. Shinwari was Khat. He hoped against hope that Sinclaire, who was passionate about her job, could uncover a photo.

His mind clicked over so many possibilities. If he went to the Bagram hospital and asked about K. Shinwari, he'd be blocked. If he wasn't family, he had no business having access to her records. If he went over to the Marine Force Recon HQ here at the base, they'd tell him to fuck off. They'd see him as a navy SEAL making inquiries. Yes, he had top secret clearance and so did the Force Recons. But that didn't mean they were going to give him anything. She was a marine sniper, and they were aggressively protective about their fellow—or sister—snipers. He would be laughed out of the office.

When he got to his barracks where he was TDY, temporary duty, he'd make a call to his best friend and fellow SEAL, Chief Gabe Griffin. Mike checked the time on his watch and made mental calculations as to the time in West Virginia, where Gabe lived with his wife, Bay. A warmth flooded his chest. Mike had gone to visit them last year, and Bay was very pregnant with twins. He had been shocked when Gabe told him they were going to name the boy after him: Michael.

Staggered by the gesture, Mike was touched beyond words. Bay was a wonderfully warm person, originally an 18 Delta corpsman. The first woman to be allowed in, and she passed the course. He scowled, remembering some of the conversation he and Gabe had had on the porch during that visit. Bay had been part of some deep black ops, too. Rubbing his brow, he tried to remember the name…Shadow Warriors? Was Khat a part of it? Cursing softly, Tarik felt like he had a hold of an octopus with thirty arms, trying to wrestle it to the ground in order to get answers.

The bus dropped him off at the huge three-story men's enlisted barracks. It was 1400, and he needed to eat. There was a chow hall nearby, and he headed for it. As a SEAL operator, he was in his normal uniform and always carried his M-4 with him, his pistol in a drop holster on his right thigh and a SOF SEAL knife in a sheath on his lower left calf. Settling the black baseball cap with the SEAL insignia on it, he watched people move aside on the sidewalk. SEALs had a special aura, and people gave him furtive looks, curious but wary. He'd grown used to this over the years. His mind and heart were centered on Khat. His hopes rose thinking about calling Gabe. Maybe he could give him a lead. Maybe…

CHAPTER FIVE

BAY GRIFFIN ANSWERED Mike's phone call, much to his surprise.

"Bay, this is Mike Tarik. How are you?"

"Mike!" she cried, "it's so good to hear from you!"

Mike waited patiently, finding out Gabe was at his woodworking store in town. He also had a part-time job as a security consultant to Special Operations Command, the heart of black ops for the US military. He heard about the fraternal twins, Michael and Dawn, and at one year old, they were healthy and walking, driving her and Gabe crazy in a good kind of way. He smiled, hearing the happiness in her voice.

"Listen, I'm glad you answered the phone," he said heavily, and he launched into a quick explanation of what had happened and what, if anything, she could provide to him in the way of information. When he got done, there was silence on the other end. Finally, Bay spoke.

"And you need this why, Mike?"

His mouth quirked. "Because she saved our lives."

Bay snorted. "What is it about you SEALs?" she demanded, laughing. "That's not an entirely honest answer, Mike, and I'll tell you why. Every time you mentioned Khat's name, your tone went softer. In my world that means you like her. Or, maybe love her? And that's why you're wanting to contact her?"

Squirming, Mike knew from meeting Bay that she had a depth and ability to look straight through a person and know what was in their heart whether they wanted to admit it or not. "Yeah, okay, it wasn't a total fabrication, Bay. Khat *did* save our lives. But—" he drew in a deep breath and released it "—I like her a lot. She's out there all alone. And I worry about her."

"That's more than *like,* then, Mike."

Pushing his fingers through his hair, he growled, "Gabe must have one hell of a time trying to hide your birthday or Christmas gift from you."

Chuckling, Bay said, "He's not the fibbing type, although," she drawled, "he sometimes hedges, and I do catch him. And I'm very good at finding out what gift he bought for me."

"Look, I can't sit and tell you I love her. I was with her only two days. That's not enough time."

"You're right. It isn't. I'm sensing a serious connection between you."

"You know what?" he said, exasperated. "You should have become a navy intelligence officer. You truly missed your calling, Bay."

She laughed heartily. "Okay, you're worried about her being out there all alone? That she needs some backup or protection?"

"Yes."

"I can make a phone call to someone in the know. I can't tell you anything more than that, Mike. You said her handler is Commander Hutton in J-bad, right?"

"Yes."

"Okay, I'm writing all of this down. Because the

person I have to contact doesn't want to know you're invested in her. What this individual will consider is her being in danger or possibly needing help or backup. I can't promise you anything, Mike. This person is in charge of this operation. All I can do is give her the info."

"You were a part of that operation, right?"

"Yes, I was."

"Shadow Warriors, by any chance?" Mike heard silence at the other end. *Bingo.* Bay had been a part of it even though she'd deny it.

"Mike, I can't go there. You know that," she said, her tone somber.

"That's all right, I got it. You were and so is Khat. Your secret's safe with me. I just want to help her…or… hell, protect her, I guess," he muttered in frustration.

"SEALs are very good at protecting the people they love," Bay agreed, her voice low with emotion. "Gabe saved me."

"I know," he rasped. Bay had been captured by Mustafa Khogani, raped and nearly choked to death by the Hill tribe leader. She'd managed to escape, and if it hadn't been for his best friend, Gabe, who was a sniper, being nearby, Bay would have been tracked down by the furious Hill leader and killed.

"Well," Bay murmured, her voice lighter, "when you use the word *protect*, I think there's a serious, deep connection between the two of you. If you don't want to call it love, that's okay. I'll make the call. I have no idea when I'll be able to call you back."

"I'm grateful you'd do it, Bay. Be sure to tell Gabe hello from me. And tell him I'll get better about emailing him more often rather than less." He grinned.

"That will make my ex-SEAL husband very happy. He might be out of the teams, but all his friends are still in, and he worries about you guys."

"HEY, MIKE," MAC CALLED as he walked past his office door three weeks later. "Got a minute?"

Tarik was glad to have any interruption. The doctors at Bagram had taken an MRI of his broken left arm. They were impressed with Khat's setting of his bones. But the break was severe, and they insisted he had to stand down eight weeks, two months, and that about killed him. He was planning on four weeks and then pleading with Mac to let him start running patrols with his team at that time. As it played out, Mike was now Mac's gopher, and he was up to his ass in mission planning. He was sitting in an office, dying for sunlight, fresh air and exercise.

"Yeah?" he said, sticking his head in the door.

"Shut the door," Mac said, gesturing for him to come in.

Mike saw the chief's wrinkled brow, a somber look on his square face. Something was up. He knew Mac well, having worked with him four out of the five rotations into Afghanistan. He sat down. It was nearly noon, time for chow.

"What's up?"

Mac raised a brow. "Remember our little talk about this woman, Khat?"

"Yeah." Mike saw a funny look in the man's blue eyes, almost amusement. Almost. Since calling Lieutenant Sinclaire three weeks ago, he'd heard nothing. He'd had such high hopes, but as the weeks wore on,

Mike realized it had been a shot in the dark. Nothing was going to happen.

"I just received an interesting call from Commander Hutton out of J-bad."

Mike's heart leaped. "Yes?" Tension swirled through him. Mac grinned a little and pushed some notes he'd taken on the phone call to one side of his hand.

"You must have stirred up a hornet's nest, Tarik. Either that or that cute blonde Naval intelligence officer at SEAL HQ did some digging and poked the bear with a stick."

"What the hell are you talking about?"

"Commander Hutton called to tell me that in a week, I was going to become the liaison for a Marine Corps Staff Sergeant Khatereh Shinwari. She's the woman who saved your ass, by the way. Hutton confirmed it."

His mind exploded with surprise. And then questions. "What do you mean *liaison*?"

"Hutton said that from now on, all supplies, including bales of alfalfa hay for her horses, were coming from Bagram to us here at Camp Bravo. We have the facility and space for her medical supplies and for the hay, no problem. And the handoff is happening next week. She's been ordered to ride in here and talk to me so we can meet, get details nailed down and get to know one another. Hutton said Bravo was much closer to where she operates, and the handoff was simply an economic decision. He'll still be her handler. But I'm to coordinate times and dates of when she can ride in and store up on supplies."

Stunned, Mike sat there, digesting it all. "Khat's going to be *here*?" His heart started to race in anticipation. He'd get to see her. At least, from time to time.

It was better than nothing. Bay must have said something to her contact that had gotten the ball rolling. Mike knew he'd never know.

Mac nodded, grinning like a Cheshire cat. "Yes. And I'm assigning you to coordinate drops of her equipment by helo from Bagram to here. You'll have to get some of the boys from the army maintenance to load up the pallet and bring it over here and put it in that spare room we have."

He was going to get to see Khat! Mike kept his expression neutral, but inside, he was jumping up and down for joy. "I can do that."

"Also, Hutton said they want her to stay here five days with us, to get used to us, to our routines, learn the layout of Bravo, all the ins and outs. I expect you to be her mentor and show her around. She needs to know where women's showers are located, the chow hall, the dispensary and stuff like that. Plus, she's to stay here." He pointed across the hall to a small bedroom that was available.

"Oh, Sarah's room?" On the door there was a plaque with that name on it. Mike had heard from the departing platoon that the room was painted and decorated for a Medevac pilot, Chief Warrant Officer Sarah Benson, who was engaged to Ethan Quinn, one of the SEALs in one of the platoons. She had been treated like a little sister by the men and with Master Chief Hunter's direction, cleaned up the small room and made it habitable. It was painted a light pink by the SEALs.

Mike had been in the room as a matter of curiosity, checking it out shortly after their platoon had arrived. No one used it. So it was a perfect place for Khat to get some seriously good sleep in a very safe place. Or, as safe as any forward operating base could be.

"Yeah." Mac scratched his bearded jaw. "They're also going to be doing their yearly physical and psych evaluation on her. From what Hutton told me, the people in this Pentagon op, which he did not name, go through a yearly protocol. Just routine maintenance, I guess." He shrugged. "And that's going to take three days. So, you'll be her guide and mentor. You got a broken arm, and I'm sure you'd rather be with her than doing mission planning all day with me," he added drily, grinning.

Mike felt as if the heavens had suddenly opened up and piled more bounty on him than he could ever have imagined. "You got that one," he said, smiling a little.

"Well, you're a known quantity to Sergeant Shinwari, and Hutton agreed to allow me to pawn her off on you."

"I'll make sure she's welcomed and comfortable with us."

Mac raised his brows. "Be careful. Hutton warned me she's a loner and is not very socialized." He shrugged. "It would take that kind of personality to do what she does. He said she's not diplomatic and has a hair-trigger temper."

Mike chuckled. "She's got red hair. What the hell else should we expect?"

Mac grunted. "He called her 'wild.' I wasn't sure how to take that. Hutton meets with her once a year. They fly her into J-bad, and she goes through this five-day protocol. He said she's brutal on those she works with, and she flouts authority."

"She doesn't suffer fools," Tarik agreed quietly,

thinking about how Hutton was describing her. That's not the woman he met in the cave. It wasn't the one who saved his life. So what was going on?

"Between you, me and the fence post," Mac said, "I don't think Hutton likes her one bit, but he's stuck with her. He may be the one who is moving her over to Bravo just to get her off his back. He was saying no one looked forward to her coming into J-bad for those five days. She pissed everyone off, including him. She's angry about something, that's for sure, so be forewarned."

"I never saw any of that with her," Mike argued strongly. "She was wary of me because she is black ops. She never spoke about anything she did, but she was never disrespectful or angry toward me." He never forgot her scarred back. Maybe she had something to be angry about.

Shrugging, Mac said, "Maybe you're the right guy to tame her, then."

Or, maybe they had a deep connection that he wanted to explore more than anything else. Mike didn't say anything. "Does she need new cammies? Other gear replacement?"

"I don't know, but apparently when she's in-house, whatever she needs, she gets, no questions asked. I'm to send the bills to Hutton. If she needs new cammies, then you'll have to fly with her to Bagram and get over to Navy Supply. We don't have anything like that around here."

"I always like going to Bagram."

"Yeah, who doesn't? A little piece of the US on base," Mac growled.

"Do you have a personnel file on her?"

"Hutton's sending it by pdf email later today to me. The officers, me and you will be the only ones privy to it. Don't need to tell you, she's classified up to her ass and back, so say nothing to anyone."

Mike was anxious to read her personnel record. It would tell him so damn much and rip away the mystery surrounding Khat. "Roger that," he agreed.

"I don't want to have to 'handle' this woman, Tarik. If she's upset or bitching, you're handling it instead. I've got my hands too full as it is."

"I'll take care of her and anything she needs," he promised.

"So, get Sarah's room ready for her. Make sure that air conditioner is working. Get someone over from electrical to fix it, if it isn't. We need to make her feel welcome."

"She's got two horses, Mac. I want to look at that room. We need to make some kind of small corral for them."

"Good idea. I'll contact the Seabees lieutenant that's here at Bravo and get him to build something. I'll let you handle the details."

Tarik knew those two horses meant everything to Khat. She'd relax more if she knew they were going to be well cared for while she was here. "Mac, did Hutton give you her call sign?"

"Yeah, it is Archangel." He smiled. "You have a good set of ears on you."

"You think there's anything in her personnel record about what she's doing?"

"Hutton said it would be redacted. Not for our eyes or knowledge. We're like a supply depot for her, that's all. The less we know, the better. Hutton was getting his knickers in a twist when I asked more questions than I should have."

"Okay," Mike murmured, thinking ahead. There was a key to Khat; one that he wanted to open and understand. Maybe after reading her record, he could go back to Lt. Addison Sinclaire, the Navy intel officer at Bagram, and she might be able to find out more. Naval intelligence worked closely with all black ops. An intel officer often knew more than anyone else. He'd give it a try because his gut told him Khat's life changed five years ago, and he wanted to know what had happened. She wasn't going to tell him, that was for damn sure.

"Get back to work. I need that mission PowerPoint by this evening," Mac said.

Getting up, Mike picked up his laptop. "I'm on it." Planning a mission took weeks, even a month, sometimes. Especially a complex one where a team would be out for days or a week.

He hurried out into the big room, sat down at the desk and plugged in his Toughbook laptop. Joy cascaded through him. Mike knew he couldn't show any of it. If anyone, even Mac, suspected that he was emotionally connected with Khat, he'd have been removed as her mentor. As he sat there waiting for his Toughbook to power up, he wondered how Khat was taking the news from Hutton.

"You can't be serious!" Khat growled into the sat phone. She was sitting on Mina, hidden in a grove of trees just above a goat trail, coming back from a sniper op. The sun had set, and it was getting dark.

"The paperwork is already complete, Archangel."

"Who did this to me?" she demanded, anger rising in her along with fear.

"Look, I take orders just like you do. This came from the Pentagon. That's all I can tell you."

Fear snapped at her. She was reassigned to Camp Bravo for her five-day evaluation? Not J-bad? "When am I expected to arrive there?"

"Three days from now. A Petty Officer First Class Mike Tarik will be waiting for you at Bravo's secure gate at 0200. You won't be allowed in without security confirmation no matter who you are, and he's your mentor while you're there."

Shock made her gasp. Mike Tarik! Confused, her heart sank. Biting on her lower lip, Khat continued to look around, the place unsafe. She kept her voice very low. "But you're still my handler?"

"That's affirmative. You contact me once you're back in position in your op area. It will take you two days to travel by horseback one way from where you're at to Camp Bravo. Just be careful."

"Roger that," she muttered, signing off. Well, hell! Stuffing the sat phone in a pocket on her H-gear, Khat shifted in the saddle. She'd been out on a sniper op since 0400. Three Taliban leaders riding with Khogani were now dead. And like a disturbed nest of wasps, the other twenty riders had spread out, aggressively searching for her.

Patting Mina's sweaty neck, she could feel her mare's flanks heaving in and out from the long gallop and trot for the past ten miles. She'd varied her movement, taking rat line trails used to carry fertilizer to the bomb makers in her country, to goat trails that were thousands of years old. That way, their trackers would become confused or at least be slowed down, allowing her to escape.

Khat couldn't afford to be distracted, but the news from Hutton was an unexpected bombshell. Almost akin to Mike's kiss. Mouth pulling in at the corners, she squeezed her calves to her mare, asking her to move out. *Mike...*

The sky was turgid above them, summer bringing violent thunderstorms. She could smell the rain in the air, a cell about five miles away from her position. Nudging Mina into a slow trot, knowing her mare was tired, Khat wanted to try and get to her pool cave before it started raining. Floods, rock avalanches and inches of water would pour off the slopes. It made for bad riding, and it was dangerous to her horse and herself.

The rain began just as she got to her cave complex. Dismounting in the outer cave, Khat patted her mare's wet neck and pulled the reins over her head. After making sure there were no surprise visitors, Khat made her way back to the internal safety of the cave structure.

As she unsaddled Mina and brushed her down, her mind was free to range over the sudden turn of events. Frowning, Khat felt a new fear. Fear of Mike Tarik. His one kiss had opened up a Pandora's box of emotions she'd hidden from for five years. And they were loose and howling inside her, with no way to stuff them back from where they had come.

Mike scared her. She scared herself. Putting the saddle over the gate, Khat pulled out a flake of hay for her mare. Her heart seethed with ecstasy and then crashed with anxiety. Mike's kiss had reminded her too vividly of her physical needs. And dammit, it had all remained under wraps until his mouth curved hotly against hers. And she'd become lost in him, warmed by him, protected by him. Shaking her head, Khat wrestled with herself. Five years of celibacy. Five years of not feeling alone, but on an important mission of revenge. And his kiss had exploded her carefully choreographed reality. In one moment Mike had initiated a warmth and healing into her wounds she'd been unable to repair by herself.

She couldn't forget his mouth on hers. Ever since then, she'd begun to have torrid, colorful dreams. They replaced her nightmares for the most part, and Khat felt she should be grateful for that. Giving her mare two buckets of water, she settled down to take care of herself. Tea first.

Just the familiarity of her nightly routine helped calm some of her nerves. She was going to see Mike. For five days. Would he try and kiss her again? God, she couldn't let it happen. Khat had seen his kiss turn her world upside down. And his promise to find her again had come true. The look in his eyes that night as they waited for the Medevac to land, told her he meant what he said. It had been no idle threat.

As she poured hot water into the mug, the sweet smell of the Darjeeling tea wafted to her sensitive nostrils. Inhaling it, Khat closed her eyes, head hanging down, feeling her way through the lightning-bolt changes of her life and how it might affect her mission. She hungrily absorbed Mike's roughened hand on her cheek, his strength monitored, his protectiveness embracing her. His voice did something sensual to her, unstringing her, opening her up to her own vibrant, pulsing appetite. His kiss...well, the man knew how to kiss a woman, no doubt. Khat was sure he had a lot of practice. From what she'd seen, SEALs drew females like bees to honey, and they never wanted for women.

There was a powerful charisma to Mike Tarik, and Khat couldn't explain it any more today than the first time she had met him. Maybe it was because he was of Middle Eastern blood like her. Blood was thicker than water. And he had the magnetism that reminded her of a powerful sheik she'd met years ago. A natural leader. A man whose confidence oozed from his pores. "Damn," she muttered, sipping the tea and burning her tongue.

Counting the days ahead, Khat knew she had to get squared away within herself. His kiss had dissolved her hardened barriers against all men. He'd melted them away with one soft brush of his mouth against hers. Mike wasn't anything like the men who had kissed her before when she was much younger. He wasn't sloppy or in a hurry. Instead, he had tasted her lightly, as if barely sipping a fine wine to discover all its layers and complexities. He'd asked her to participate and didn't assume she wanted to kiss him at all.

Rubbing her eyes with her hand, she muttered, "Dammit!" What it really came down to was that she was afraid of herself. Afraid of her newly released feelings, hormones or whatever the hell it was, that appeared when she'd decided to return Mike's warm, coaxing kiss. Khat had no one to blame but herself. She could have pushed away. Told him no. But she hadn't. Because in that single moment, she *wanted* to kiss this man. His mouth fascinated her, called to her, and she felt nearly helpless when he had been so damned close, so incredibly masculine and confident. Those all turned her on, not off.

Worse, she thought as she finished her tea and stood up to go bathe in the waterfall, he was not presently in a relationship. Just like she wasn't. What were the odds? Trudging wearily down the tunnel after grabbing her towel and toiletries, Khat was scared. How to tell Mike no? Every time she was in the general vicinity of him, Khat could feel her lower body clenching, wanting…

Later, as she turned out the kerosene lamp and settled down on her sleeping bag, Khat was too tired to think anymore. Her world of five years had just been deconstructed. Feeling lost, lonely and scared, she knew it meant big changes. Khat wasn't sure she was strong enough internally to deal with all of these new and overwhelming challenges. If she hadn't been nearly beaten to death, if she hadn't lost part of herself, if her soul hadn't been fractured by the torture, she could have dealt with Mike, with her growing feelings for him. Where she was at right now, Khat simply didn't feel she had the strength to remain immune to the man, and that scared her more than the flaying she'd endured.

CHAPTER SIX

MIKE WAITED IMPATIENTLY near the guard gate entrance to Camp Bravo. It was a last quarter moon, the darkness diluted. The two Marine sentries knew Khat was to arrive at 0200. The wind was sharp and cold, even in the middle of summer. He'd worn his heavy cammie jacket. Pushing his baseball cap up off his brow, he tried to tame his anxiety. Was Khat angry over the changes? Accepting? How would she react to him? Mike was sure she knew he was going to be her mentor while she was here. Hutton would have told her.

Pulling his NVGs up, he could see moving shadows. Two horses. He saw Khat, and she was wearing male Afghan clothes, her head swathed in a black turban, the material across her face, only her eyes covered with a pair of NVGs visible. His heart picked up in beat. Damn, he'd missed her so much. He'd enjoyed their sparring, their verbal dances around one another. They were two operators playing a mental chess game with one another. What he felt in his heart for Khat wasn't a game, however.

In fifteen minutes, Khat arrived at the gate. She pulled the material from her face and pulled the goggles down around her neck so she could be recognized. Mike walked up to her, patting Mina's damp neck.

He gave her a warm smile. "Welcome to Bravo," he told her.

Khat was exhausted by the long ride. "Thanks." His smile was like warm honey being poured through her stiff, tired body. How handsome he was.

"Any problems getting here?"

"No," she answered, leaning over and rubbing her mare's neck. "The usual. Avoiding Taliban in an area." Khat saw he was all business. The two Marine guards were alert. She saw Mike give them a nod of approval. The gate lifted. Mina trudged forward, her head hanging a bit.

Mike walked ahead of Khat, taking her through rows of tents and then angling off to the right. Finally, he stopped.

Khat stiffly dismounted. Forty miles a day was hard on horse and rider. Pulling the reins over Mina's head, she kept her distance from Tarik. There was enough moonlight, and he pulled his NVGs away from his eyes. Instantly, her heart started beating harder. She was wary of him, unsure of how he was going to treat her. "Do you have a stable for my horses?"

Mike smiled a little, seeing the weariness in her deeply shadowed eyes. "Our Seabees built you a small corral and barn. It's right around here." He led the way.

Pleasantly surprised, Khat saw the twenty-by-twenty corral made of sturdy posts and rails. Mike opened the door to a small barn, stepping aside. Once Khat was inside with her horses, he closed the door and turned on a low light, giving Khat a good look at the facility.

"Don't worry," he said, "the light can't be seen from outside."

"Good," she said with a grimace. "I draw enough Taliban to me without light leaking out of a building."

"Want some help?"

Khat was moving slowly. Mike wanted to show her to Sarah's room, but knew she wouldn't leave her horses until she was satisfied they were properly taken care of first. The light clearly showed her skin was tight across her high cheekbones.

"Could you unpack Zorah?" And then she looked at his arm. "How is it doing?"

He smiled a little and held it up. "The docs were very impressed with how well you set the bones. I just graduated to a removable splint. Bad part is they said eight weeks before I could get out on patrols again. I'm not happy about that." For the first time, he met and held her gaze. He was already sensing Khat was wary, tired and something else that he couldn't define. Maybe tense. On guard. He wondered if she was remembering their kiss. He sure as hell was. How many times a day did he rerun that moment? Mike had lost count. Her eyes were cloudy, not the clear green tourmaline color he'd seen before. "You must be tired." He quickly released the straps and pulled the tarp off the horse.

A warmth spread through Khat. She didn't want to respond to his slight smile, his caring gaze, but she felt it right down through the center of her, and straight into her lower body. The man literally oozed sexuality. As exhausted as she was, Mike had the ability to electrify her senses with just a slight smile. And those lion-gold eyes of his seemed able to gaze into her wildly beating heart and know she was secretly drawn to him. "It's been pretty active in my sector," was all she'd say.

She stripped Mina of her saddle and placed it on a

metal saddle rack. There were two box stalls filled with thick, fresh straw for the horses to bed down upon. The place was so new that even the timbers smelled good. "This is a wonderful barn," she whispered, leading Mina into the first stall. Khat realized the water trough was already filled. There was a feed box for the oats she fed them. A flake of alfalfa hay lay on the floor. Mike had done this. She would have bet anything. Only another horseman would know what was needed.

Mina plunged her small muzzle into the large container, drinking deeply. Khat left her halter on and closed the door. She turned to see Mike taking Zorah into the other stall. Wiping her face, she felt dirty, sweaty and gritty. The floor was concrete, and on the wooden walls there were plenty of hooks for bridles, halters and lead ropes.

"Did you help the Seabees lay this place out?" she wondered. Mike was dressed in his cammies and wearing a Kevlar vest. He wore only a pistol on his right thigh. Beneath the light, his face was strong and angular, that tension always radiating from him. He was the snow leopard in repose, but not asleep.

Locking the gate, he said, "Yeah, the Seabees officer wasn't up on barns, so I drew him a few pictures, and he got it right." He lifted his head and smiled. Wanting to stare at her but knowing it would make her nervous, he said, "Come through this side door." He opened it for her.

Khat stepped into the other room. There was a pallet of supplies in the center of it, plus fifty bales of alfalfa hay stacked in one corner. She inhaled the sweet scent, loving it. "Wonderful. I won't be outside."

Mike rested his hands on his hips, a few feet separating them. "Right, no Taliban sniper to take shots at you. What would you like to do first? Food? Shower? Or bed?"

All her tension and anxiety fled beneath his dark, inquiring gaze. He was making no move to crowd her or try to kiss her. Instead, he kept his distance, and Khat was grateful. "I would die for a hot shower."

"Not necessary to die," Mike teased with a slight grin. "The showers are located in the center of Bravo. I think we have enough light to see okay without our goggles. Let me show you your room first. I've got towels, washcloths and soap on the dresser waiting for you."

Khat was glad for the warm wool Afghan clothes. It was cold as they walked out the other end of the supply room. She could hear Apache helicopters spooling up at Operations and the airfield area of the FOB. Everywhere she looked as she followed Mike, it was dark.

Mike opened the door leading into SEAL HQ. She waited just inside the hall, not sure where to go.

"In here," he murmured, opening another door. "This is Sarah's room, and now it's yours."

Khat was amazed at the amenities. A twin bed, not a cot. A real dresser, a desk, a small lamp, a television set and a large rectangular mirror above the dresser. Best of all, it was air-conditioned for the summer heat. That was a true luxury. She spotted the toiletries on it and walked over, picking up a thick white towel, a pair of flip-flops, a washcloth and the soap. There was a thick blue terry-cloth robe hanging on a hook, and she took it. "This is wonderful," she said, looking around. And then she lifted the pink soap, inhaling it deeply. "I love the smell of roses..."

"Like it?"

"Very much." And then she added with a weary smile, "SEALs rock."

It made Mike feel good. He and his team had worked hard for a week to get the barn and corral built, helping the Seabees. He'd scoured the FOB to find the specially scented soap for Khat. Mike had noticed on the tin of her Darjeeling tea that there were red roses painted on it. He thought she might like roses. On a hunch, he'd walked over to the Black Jaguar Squadron and gotten one of the women Apache pilots to donate a bar of her rose-scented soap for Khat. He led her to the concrete block set of showers. Taking her to the women's side of the facility, he said, "I'll wait out here for you."

It was cold. She frowned. "I won't be long, Mike."

"Don't hurry on my account, all right? Enjoy that hot water."

Mike leaned against the building, arms across his chest. The thick jacket kept him plenty warm. He heard a shower turn on, and he smiled a little. Maybe all these amenities would convince Khat to spend more time at Bravo. He could wish. Concerned, he realized Khat seemed to have lost weight since he last saw her. His mind went over her personnel file that he'd pretty much committed to memory. Deciding to let Khat tell him about herself, it gave him a leg up on some of her mysterious responses to him.

In the file it stated she had been a POW for thirty days. All the rest of the information had been redacted. It had happened five years ago.

Khat emerged later wrapped in the blue robe, the white towel twisted up on her head, her Afghan clothes in a bundle. He smiled and eased the clothes and her boots out of her arms. "You look like a blue teddy bear."

She grinned tiredly. "A blue teddy bear?" She looked down at the huge robe that must have belonged to a guy weighing three hundred pounds. She could have wrapped it around her twice. "That hot water was divine. That's something I miss so much. A hot bath."

"No bathtubs here at Bravo," Mike said, "but they do have them at Bagram." Mike checked his stride to walk with her, leading her back to the HQ. He opened the door for Khat, and she flip-flopped into the hall. When she opened the door to her room, he halted at the opening. "You can sleep in tomorrow," he said. "And down the hall on the right is the head. The guys know you're coming in, so no worries. It becomes a unisex head for a week."

"Hope I don't scare the bejesus out of some guy by walking in on him tomorrow morning." She smiled and turned around and released the towel around her damp, thick red hair.

Mike grinned. "They're animals, but they'll get over it." Mike felt his body go hard as she stood there. Khat's long hair was like a red cloak about her shoulders. The robe was voluminous. She looked lost in it. Or maybe, she was lost. The haunted look deep in her green eyes had returned.

"Where can I find you after I wake up? I don't know where I am."

"Just come down the passageway," he told her, "I'm doing mission planning, and you'll find me in the big room at the desk in the corner."

"Okay," she murmured, drying her hair with the

towel. "I need clothes. I forgot to get a set of clean cammies out of that one pannier container."

"I'll get them for you."

Khat gave him a bewildered look. "I'm just not thinking," she said apologetically. "I need my small red bag, too. It has my comb and brush."

"Anything else?"

"Just sleep," she muttered, eyeing the bed.

"Be back in a minute."

The door quietly shut. Khat felt so many emotions, she couldn't process all of them. Mike looked healthy. And happy. And fit. And so damned masculine and sexy that it was blatant. It wasn't anything he was doing. It was just *him*. She'd missed that playful glint that was in his eyes. And his mouth. Oh, she was in such trouble, it wasn't even funny because she felt sexual hunger gnawing at her, and she wanted to kiss him again. The way Mike looked at her, the care burning in his eyes, melted all her defenses. Khat knew she was tired. Her mind just wouldn't work.

There was a light knock at the door.

"Come in," she called.

Mike brought in her clean cammies and her red toiletry bag. She was sitting on the bed, the low lamplight gleaming off her crimson hair. Did Khat know how classic her features were? How clean the bones of her face? How damned tempting her soft mouth was? He kept a tight leash on himself. Khat wasn't a woman who rushed into anything. He was going to have to build trust with her first. "Okay?"

"Yes, thank you." She tilted her head a little and gave him a grateful look. "I'll see you whenever I wake up."

He lifted his hand and said, "Good night. Sleep the sleep of angels, Khat."

The silence took his place. He was like strong, warm sunlight to her dark soul. Khat got up and pulled the blankets and sheet back on the bed. *A real bed.* She turned off the lamp, placed the towel on the pillow and lay down, even though her hair was still damp and uncombed. Exhaustion tunneled through her, and she told herself tomorrow she would comb and brush her hair.

The last thought Khat had was of Mike, smiling. Her body was still restless and needy, that smile of his touching her, awakening her in ways she never knew possible.

AT 0800 THE NEXT MORNING, Mike was at his desk in the big room, working on a mission plan. He noticed that a number of the SEALs were hanging around a lot more than normal. At this time of day, the big room was usually empty and silent. He smiled to himself. They all wanted to see Khat, their curiosity getting the better of them. All week, they'd talked about her arrival. The noise level was constant, some of the men sitting on the bleachers talking about patrols, others getting coffee from the machine in the other corner.

And then the room felt silent. Mike could have literally heard a pin drop. He lifted his head and saw every man in the room staring at Khat. She stood resolutely at the end of the passageway where it opened up into the big room. Dressed in her cammies, her red hair in a thick braid between her shoulder blades, Mike saw Khat's eyes were clear and beautiful. And damn, she looked like a tall, proud Afghan warrior. She radiated strength and confidence. Mike got up and met her narrowed eyes. She surveyed the SEALs coolly, her black baseball cap gripped in her left hand.

"Good morning," he murmured, coming over to her. Her cheeks turned a dull red, and he felt the tension in her body as she stared back at the ten SEALs in the room. Mike deliberately placed himself slightly in front of her and to one side, a protective reaction.

"Okay, you animals, stand down," he called with a grin. "Meet Marine Corps Staff Sergeant Shinwari. She's going to be with us for five days, so make her feel welcome."

Most of the men gave sheepish grins, nods and smiles. Each of them came over and introduced themselves to Khat, politely shaking her hand. Mike stood aside, watching the men's faces. Half were married, and the other half were not. They were all smitten by her, and he wondered if Khat realized her effect on men. It wasn't often they'd gotten to meet a nearly six-foot-tall woman warrior. And to give Khat credit, she was the model of decorum, shaking each man's hand and meeting his eyes. Hutton's assessment of her not being socialized was a lie as far as Mike was concerned. She was attentive, respectful and sincere with each SEAL.

"Okay," he said turning to her, "now that we got their curiosity out of the way, are you ready to eat?"

Khat settled the baseball cap on her head. "I need to feed my horses first."

"I got up at 0500 and went out and rubbed them down and fed them. I gave them each a quart of oats, too. That all right? They've done some serious traveling."

Her heart tumbled because Mike was kind enough

to take care of her horses. He was a horseman himself, and he understood animals came first before a person ate a meal. "Yes, a quart each is fine." Her voice grew husky with feelings. "Thank you…" Every time Khat tried to distance herself from him, to stop from feeling so drawn to him, Mike did something utterly kind or thoughtful, and it blew all her defenses apart. *Again*.

Tarik threw his black baseball cap with the SEAL emblem embroidered in gold on the front of it on his head. "You'd do the same for me." He gave her a boyish smile. "Let's go, I'm starving. You have to be hungry, too."

Khat got her first good look at Camp Bravo. Mike told her it was strictly a black ops forward operating base with a thousand people. They had an Apache squadron flown only by women, a Medevac squadron, drones, the CIA and all the other major black ops groups from the various military branches. As they walked, she saw row upon row of tents. Mike pointed out the SEAL section.

"And I have a room with a real bed in it?" she asked.

"Yep. We treat our women right." He smiled over at her. Mike saw the look of awe she gave him at his comment. "Did you sleep well last night?"

"I did," she muttered. "Real sleep. Not having to sleep light, waiting for the enemy to sneak up on me."

Mike watched the men turn and stare at Khat. Maybe because she was too tall to miss, or maybe because she commanded their attention simply because she was a beautiful woman. She frowned, and he watched her mouth draw in at the corners. Groups of men made her tense up and become guarded.

"Not used to a lot of men staring at you?" he asked, catching her downcast eyes.

"I *hate* it."

"You can't hide yourself, Khat," he teased, trying to get her to relax. "A beautiful woman always turns the heads of men. You can't blame the poor bastards."

She shrugged, putting on her wraparound sunglasses. It was a defense, but it helped her. "I'm hardly beautiful."

Mike wasn't going to argue with her. They reached the chow hall, and he led her into it. Most of the lines were short, breakfast for many long past. He found them a table in a corner with no one else nearby and sat down. She wanted to sit with her back to the wall so she could see who was coming in the doors. Mike acquiesced, understanding her survival reactions. More than anything, he wanted her to relax.

As they ate, he noticed she was tucking it away. That was good. Looking down at his tray, which was piled with protein and carbs, he was going to eat heavy, too. In their business, one never knew when they'd be able to eat the next time.

"What's my schedule, do you know?" she asked him, sipping her mug of black tea.

"Dr. Johnson, a navy woman doctor, is going to give you your physical at 1000. You've got plenty of time to eat and relax before that."

"I'm glad it's a woman," she said, enjoying the eggs, grits and toast. "I hate being examined by a male doctor."

She said it with passion. And with distaste. He held her gaze, which had grown upset. "Tell me if I'm being too nosy," he said quietly, "but men seem to threaten you. Am I wrong about my observation?"

Khat compressed her lips. His voice was caring. She could feel that protectiveness emanating off him toward her. Setting her hands on either side of her tray she looked at him. "I wasn't always like this," she managed in a strangled voice.

His heart tore a little, her voice suddenly emotional. Mike knew she had to be referring to the POW period in her life. He felt frustrated. The chow hall wasn't a good place to have a raw conversation like this. He saw shame in her eyes. Plus, he had to back off from stirring upsetting things like this in her life. She had a physical today and psych eval tomorrow.

"Life has its way with us," he agreed gently, holding her shaken gaze. "The good news is that life usually puts a person or people to help support you at times like that, too." He wondered if she had support after being released as a POW. "Like you," he said, giving her a slight smile. "You were our guardian angel that afternoon we were on that scree slope, and the Taliban ambushed us."

"I like your philosophy," she said simply, picking at her food, no longer hungry. Khat felt her stomach begging for food, but lately, her emotions got in the way. And when she was upset, she did not eat.

"Listen, I've been meaning to ask you if you need replacement gear. I understand this is the time you get it."

Nodding, she said, "I need to go to Bagram, to Navy Supply. I've worn out five sets of cammies. The trousers, that is. All the hard riding. They don't make cammies for riders." She gave him an amused look. Her emotions were soothed beneath the warmth Khat found in his eyes. He cared deeply about her. She could feel it.

"Yeah," Mike said, smiling, "no double-sewn fabric and seams like you'd find in a pair of equestrian breeches. Okay, I'll get a helo flight set up for us. You're free on day three, four and five." And then he had an idea.

"I could use some downtime," Khat admitted. She pushed the fork around in the potatoes. "Sleep. Honest to God, deep sleep."

"I have an idea," he murmured.

"Oh?"

"My father donates to an Afghan charity run by Khalid and Emma Shaheen. They live outside Kabul. He's an Apache pilot in the US Army and is stationed out of Bagram. His wife, Emma, is American and was in the US Army as an Apache pilot. Unfortunately, she got kidnapped by the Taliban and suffered some nerve damage to her left hand before she was rescued by Khalid. She had to leave the Army, but she flies her husband's Chinook helicopter, and she takes educational and medical supplies to all the villages along the border."

"Really?" Khat sat up. "Why haven't I heard about this before now?"

Shrugging, he said, "Hey, the border area is large. They're the only charity flying in to help because all the other NGOs have pulled out to protect their people from attack. With Khogani on the loose attacking all those Shinwari villages, they had to leave."

"Those murdering bastards," she breathed.

Her anger was startling. Mike saw her tense up, her face becoming hard. "Khalid and Emma have a villa outside of Kabul. They're always asking me to come visit when I fly into Bagram. I could call them and ask if they have two suites available at their villa for us. We could have dinner with them. I think you'd really enjoy Emma." And then he grinned. "She has red hair and green eyes like you."

Khat became excited. "Yes, I would like to meet them. I want to know all about their charity and how they are helping my people."

"I thought you might," he said, looking at the hope suddenly flare in her flawless green eyes. "Let me make a call to Khalid while you're getting checked over with Dr. Johnson, okay?"

"Yes," she said, feeling her appetite come back. "I would love to meet them."

CHAPTER SEVEN

KHAT DAWDLED OVER the Darjeeling tea, her fourth cup. Riding for long periods of time, she didn't always stay hydrated. The chow hall was pretty much emptied out. Looking at her watch, she saw she had forty-five minutes before having to go for her physical. Mike had eaten a ton of food. Considering how tight and lean he was, she wondered where it had all gone and smiled a little. SEALs burned through thousands of calories on a mission. Right now, his guard was down, and she enjoyed his company.

"You're so different from when I rescued you," she murmured, meeting his eyes.

"I was a little uptight at the time," he agreed, finishing off the last of his six pancakes.

"Does Camp Bravo get hit often?"

"No, not much. A mortar every now and again to keep everyone on their toes, but that's pretty rare."

"You look relaxed," she noted.

He felt her curiosity. "I have my SEAL brothers. When you've got forty of them surrounding you, you feel pretty safe." He grinned.

Brows dipping, she asked in a low tone, "My handler, Commander Hutton, said my personnel file was being sent over to your chief."

Taking a breath, Mike nodded. "Yes, it was sent over."

"Have you seen it?" She was concerned about how much he knew about her.

"I had to read it, Khat. I'm the one responsible for you while you're at our FOB. A lot of your record is redacted, marked out in black, because you're deep black ops."

Tense, she didn't know what had been revealed about her. "What did you see?"

He was uncomfortable with the direction their conversation was going, and he did not want to lie to her. "Just general info, Khat. The usual stuff like your birthdate, family contact info, your height, weight, color of eyes and hair." Well, that wasn't a lie. "We need to get you over to security because you'll be given a photo ID for when you're coming and going from Bravo."

Chewing on her lower lip, she felt a little of her anxiety dissolve. "Nothing else about my present status?"

"No, only that you have a top secret clearance." God, Mike hoped she did not ask too many more questions. The worry was in her eyes, however. "They also showed the ribbons and medals you've earned. The schools you've attended. Typical jacket stuff." He tried to sound noncommittal. Would she buy his explanation?

Sipping her tea, Khat felt her stomach unknot. She knew her record showed POW status. It was the last thing she wanted anyone to know about. "That's good," she murmured.

Mike wanted to detour this conversation. "I'm curious about why you have to have a psychological evaluation every year. I've never heard of something like that."

Wrinkling her nose, Khat said, "It's part of the operation I've volunteered for."

He decided to try and ease into her black ops world. "Look," he said, keeping his voice low, his gaze on her, "I know about Operation Shadow Warriors." Thanks to Lt. Sinclaire's snooping around; she had called him two days ago with the intel. And judging by Khat's rounded-eyes reaction, he'd struck pay dirt. Mike knew operations hatched in the Pentagon were as dark and deep as the belly of the military whale. But his need was driving him to understand where Khat fit into the larger picture.

"How did you find out?" Khat demanded, wary. She saw no triumph or pleasure in Mike's expression.

"Let's just say that a good friend of mine was once a part of that operation. She's out now, but she let it slip to her husband, who was my best friend when he was in the SEALs." He added, "Don't worry. Your secret is safe with me. Even the chief doesn't know about it. I'm not telling anyone, Khat. I just wanted to understand more about you, that's all." She was worried and somehow, Mike wanted her to trust him with that knowledge.

Dipping her head, Khat stared at the cup of tea between her long hands, her mind racing. Mike was the only man in five years that she trusted. And it had been instantaneous, from the moment he'd become conscious. She knew he'd seen her naked beneath the waterfall. Khat was sure Mike had seen her scars on her back; it would have been impossible not to. He'd never brought it up, respecting her privacy, respecting her. At every turn, he'd proven he was trustworthy.

Something broke inside her. It was something ugly that had been created out of her torture. He was a man. Men had hurt her and nearly killed her. The corners of her mouth drew in as she contemplated their tenuous relationship. Maybe Mike was a new chapter in her life? A positive male figure? She'd never been distrustful about him, and she should have been. Maybe some of her emotional wounds had healed sufficiently to allow him into her life. Khat didn't know all the answers because she always felt good in his presence. Every time she saw Mike, she felt lighter, more free, and she yearned for his company.

"I trust you with this information," she said huskily, holding his golden-brown gaze. She saw instant relief come to his face.

"You're always safe with me, Khat." Mike saw her expression change, soften, and the wariness in her eyes dissolved. For a split second, he thought he saw moisture in her eyes, but then it was gone. "I swear, I want to earn your trust." That came from his heart. "I have your back. I told you that the night before I was picked up by the Medevac. I meant it then, and I mean it now."

She set the cup down and rubbed her wrinkled brow, so many rainbow emotions shattering the blackness that always dwelled within her since the torture. Just from the warmth radiating off him, she felt as if he'd held and kissed her again, but he hadn't. That was how powerful an effect he had on her and God help her, she was so damned lonely, so at odds with where her life was going, she trusted him more than anyone. Whether

Mike knew it or not, he held her heart between his large calloused hands.

"I'm scared," she murmured.

He gave her a slight smile. "So am I." Mike thought he understood. She was trusting him fully. And he was damned frightened of somehow blowing it with Khat, failing her in some way. The burning look in her green eyes seared his soul and squeezed his heart.

She shook her head, looking down at her hands. "In a way," she whispered, "it's nice to finally have someone I can talk to."

"I've seen where you're operating, Khat. I understand the pressures and demands on you." And she was in danger all the time. He wondered if Khat ever got leave or a chance to feel safe or unthreatened.

"In some ways, you do." And then she lifted her eyes to his. "I don't know why you care, though."

His mouth flattened. "Because in my eyes and heart, Khat, you're an extraordinary woman. I don't know of too many men who could do what you've accomplished out there for five years. And you're still alive. That's a remarkable achievement under any circumstance."

Khat felt her heart open, spilling out yearning and need for Mike. His voice was low, cultured and filled with veiled emotion. He was opening up to her, and it felt good. Healing. "Thanks," she murmured. "From the moment you opened your eyes, I felt a connection with you. I guess—" she shrugged her shoulders "—I didn't want to admit it…"

"I understand," Mike said. He saw the tension dissolve in her face, and she looked more at peace. Knowing he had an influence over her, he had to be damned careful how he used it. "Listen, I asked Dr. Johnson how long your physical would take, and she said about an hour." He looked at his watch. "I'll come back and pick you up at the dispensary and introduce you to our canteen for lunch. I'll buy." He grinned a little. "I don't know about you, but an American hamburger and French fries sounds damn good."

Khat felt a sheet of heat flow through her. "Yes, I'd like that. Do they have cold beer? I love beer, and I so rarely get it."

"Oh, yeah, cold beer," Mike said, nodding. "Nothing like coming off a hot, long patrol and hitting the canteen and knocking back a few."

She stood and picked up her tray. "I'm really glad Hutton sent me here," she said. In more ways than one.

MIKE MET HER at the dispensary at noon. Because Khat had yet to get security identification, he had to sign off on her physical for Dr. Johnson. Khat appeared with what he called her game face on when he'd come to the nursing desk to deal with the paperwork. There was something deep in her eyes, but damned if he knew what it was about.

Outside, the sun high and hot for mid-July, he asked, "How'd it go?"

"Dr. Johnson said I needed to eat more." Actually, she'd made a fuss over her scars and that unsettled Khat. It was the *last* thing on earth she wanted to talk about. So what if her skin was leathery and wasn't as flexible as it could be? Did it bother her when wearing a heavy ruck? When she was riding for miles with sixty pounds on her shoulders? Did it affect her ability to use or swing her arm if she was holding a weapon? A

sniper rifle? Khat could recite the questions every physician who examined her extensive scarring asked her.

Mike swung down another lane used by Humvees
and trucks. "Well, we'll fix that. The canteen has half-
pound hamburgers." He noticed men stopping and staring at her. Some gawked. She wore her sunglasses and
ignored their attention.

"Half pound?"

"Yeah, sometimes when my team comes off a mission, we'll come over here and order three a piece."
He chuckled.

"I think I'll start with one." She gave him an imp-
ish look.

The canteen was centrally located to the rest of the
busy base. The place was bustling; mostly men, although she saw two Apache women pilots sitting together and eating at a table. There was a huge U-shaped
wooden bar, and she saw a lot of army black ops types
at it, swigging down beer. The noise was high, and
there was a lot of laughter. It seemed like a happy place.

Mike briefly touched her arm. "This way," he told
her. There was a round table in a corner. The patrons
were just getting up to leave. He got there before a
couple of other guys could claim it. He told Khat to sit
down and teasingly asked her to defend their position.
Picking up the dirty plates and emptied beer bottles,
Mike brought them to the bar where another man took
them off his hands. Mike ordered their meals and got
two icy beers.

As he walked back through the crowded tables, he
saw most of the men giving Khat long, studied looks.
She was relaxed, her hands clasped on the table, her
baseball cap pushed up on her head. She looked like

an operator, and that probably stopped these guys in their tracks. In the larger military world, there were no women operators.

He handed her the cold beer and sat down at her right elbow. Holding his beer up, he said, "Welcome home, Sergeant Shinwari." He clinked her bottle. She flushed and then took a drink.

Home. Did Mike realize she felt homeless? The beer's bubbles delighted her mouth and tongue. It had been a year since she'd had her last beer, and it tasted damn good.

Mike sat back, tipping his chair on the two rear legs, balancing it, his hand around the beer sitting on the table. Khat had closed her eyes, savoring the beer she'd sipped. He understood her reaction. Noticing a number of guys shooting him a jealous look, he didn't respond to the mano a mano challenge. SEALs ruled this place, and everyone knew it whether they liked it or not.

Khat gasped at the size of the platter of food the waiter brought to their table later on. On Mike's were two hamburgers. She had one. There were enough French fries to feed an army! The food smelled good, and she was starving. Soon, her fingers were gooey from the mustard and ketchup leaking out of the over-size burger. She shifted hands and licked her fingers and continued to hungrily consume the burger.

Mike saw a couple of guys watching her lick the ketchup and mustard off her fingers. He could tell by their faces they were thinking below the belt with her innocent actions. Khat seemed unaware of it all, focused on that thick, juicy burger. When they were finished, both platters were clean.

"No prisoners taken," he murmured, running his hand over his belly.

She grinned, drinking her second beer. "No kidding. It was delicious." She patted her belly. "I feel like I've eaten a ton of food."

"You needed it," Mike said, serious, holding her gaze. The red tendrils at her temples emphasized her incredible green eyes. She seemed a bit giddy, a little looser, and maybe it was from drinking two beers. Whatever it was, Khat was the most relaxed he'd seen her. He watched her move her thick braid with her slender fingers, pulling it across her left shoulder. It was a purely feminine gesture, and it tightened his lower body. She wasn't mannish even though the clothes hid her body. She was always graceful and a feast for his eyes.

"I'd like to go check on my horses."

He roused himself. "Sure. Let's go." He knew the noise and crowds were probably playing hell on her nerves. Pulling back her chair, he watched her gracefully stand. She took her wraparound sunglasses from the top of her baseball cap and slid them on.

Way too many men were now watching her, and Mike could feel the fine tension in her. He stepped out in front of her, making it clear body-language-wise that no one was to hit on her. That she was his. They left a trail of broken hearts behind when they left the canteen.

Walking through the avenues of tents, Khat said, "This is a nice base. Not too big, not too small."

"Didn't you like J-bad?"

"It was different. And Hutton, who's been my handler, is a pain in the ass."

"Why?"

Khat lifted her hat off her head and pushed a number of loosening strands away from her cheek, tucking them behind her ear. "He's too conservative. He thinks I'm a bitch who is disrespectful of him." Her mouth stretched into a wry smile. "After all, I'm *just* an enlisted person, and he's an officer."

Mike turned down the last street that would lead them to the SEAL compound. "Why did you join the Marine Corps?"

Lifting her face to the sun, appreciating the breeze, Khat said, "Long story."

"Hey, I've got an idea. Let's give Mina and Zorah a good rubdown, and you can tell me your long story. How about it?"

What would it hurt? Khat nodded. "Okay, but it's really boring, Tarik."

He shook his head. "You don't get it, Khat. There's *nothing* boring about you."

"Then you're a sucker for punishment," she chuckled. They swung around the building to the rear. Khat saw her two mares out in the paddock, standing and resting. They had rolled earlier, dust coating them. Mina nickered softly when Khat opened the gate as she and Mike strolled through it.

The Arabian mare's ears pricked forward, and she turned around, coming up to her mistress. Khat had saved the lettuce from her hamburger and gave her mare half of it. Zorah nickered and came over, curious.

Mike leaned against the corral fence, watching the interaction between Khat and her mares. They loved her like children. She had taken off her sunglasses, and he could see the softness in her eyes. With them, there was utter trust and love. How he longed to see

that look in Khat's eyes for him. The more he was
around her, the more he was sure about her becoming
a part of his life.

Bay Griffin's statement about being in love with her
needled his conscience. Was he like all the rest of those
men who salivated after Khat? Seeing her as nothing
more than a night of sexual gratification? A challenge,
maybe? Mike scowled as he dug deeper into himself.
Hell, being attracted was a mix of sex and…

He heard Khat laugh, the lilting, husky sound sending riffles of pleasure through him. Lifting his head,
Mike watched the two mares nosing around her emptied hands and then nudging the pockets of her cammies, searching for more lettuce. Khat's mouth was
pulled into a tender smile. Mike knew that he wanted
this woman in his life for more than just sex. And sex
would be good with her. He sensed it as only a man
could. But he also saw the hurdles he'd have to leap to
get her into his arms, too. Mike wanted Khat to vol-
untarily come to him. He'd made the first move that
night out in the Hindu Kush mountains. This time, she
had to come to him of her own free will and accord.
Or it wouldn't work.

"I know where there are some apples. Our chief
always likes a bowl of them on his desk," Mike suggested.

Khat felt happiness blossom in her heart as she
glanced over and met his hooded look. She was aware
of the intense, burning expression in Mike's eyes. He
wanted her. So much of her wanted him, too. Her heart
was pleading with her to give in to him, to show him
with a kiss once again, that she liked him. Her memories,
however, waived her off. She'd struggled for so many

years trying to tell her mind and body that not all men were hurtful. She knew that from her younger years. The scars on her back were also inside her soul, and that was what stopped her from reaching out to Mike. What would he do when he saw her scars? Felt them? They were disgusting to Khat. "Apples? Out here?"

"Yeah, can your girls have one a day?" he teased, easing away from the fence. He walked over, sliding his hand across Mina's dusty back. She was in top shape, not an ounce of fat on her short, compact body.

"Of course you can. I know they would love to have an apple a day. Do you have a hose and water around here?" Khat wondered, looking around the area.

"I can rig up something," Mike said. "Why? You want to wash them first and then give them an apple?" He saw a sparkle in Khat's eyes.

"Are you reading my mind?"

Shrugging, he murmured, "I learned a long time ago not to try and figure out what's on a woman's mind."

"We're that complicated to you men?" she teased.

He grinned. "Complex but worth it." He ran his fingers across Mina's black coat. "They've rolled and now they're dirt bags. I imagine they'd enjoy having their own kind of shower and feeling clean for once. Get rid of all the salt accumulating on their skin?"

"I'd love to do that," she said. "I've got some jeans and a tank top in the other pannier. I'm going to change into civvies, and I'll meet you back here. We can wash both of them."

Mike nodded. "Sure. It'll bring back fond memories of me working in my father's barn, washing all our horses once a week." He patted Mina's rump and walked toward HQ.

KHAT HAD NEVER enjoyed herself so much as she had putting Mina in the cross ties within the barn and washing her from stem to stern. It felt good to be in a pair of comfortable jeans and a pink tank top. She'd unbraided her hair and used rubber bands to make two pigtails. With a bucket of water, a mild soap and rubber curry comb that would loosen the deep dirt and sweat that had accumulated on her mare, she went to work. Mike worked one side of Mina, dressed in a set of jeans and a tan T-shirt that showed off his powerful upper body.

Mina's eyes were half-closed, her hind leg cocked, telling Khat she felt comfortable and absolutely loved all this attention. "I think Mina has gone to horsey day spa." She laughed, looking over her gleaming back at Mike. His T-shirt was damp with splotches of water, some suds caught in his dark hair. She liked to watch those lean, powerful arms and hands of his at work. He had a protective waterproof removable cast on his lower left arm.

Chuckling, he said, "I like that. Horsey day spa."

"She's more than earned this downtime," Khat murmured, crouching down and rubbing her legs with a soft brush instead of the currycomb.

"Speaking of downtime," Mike said, crouching opposite her, getting Mina's other leg with soap and water, "what kind of leave do you get with this op?"

"I'm supposed to get six month rotations on and off from combat. When I go Stateside, they like me to take more training in my area of expertise. In my case, upgrading my paramedic skills."

Mike took the hose and stood, allowing the water to flow from the Arab's wither down across her leg and

hoof. "Six on and six off? That's a pretty brutal schedule. SEALs get six-month deployments, but then we
go Stateside for eighteen months." Damn, six months
off from combat and then getting thrown back into the
mix seemed like a crazy plan to him.

"The operation is in its third year of seven-year
trial," she said. "I didn't want to leave my op area. I
could see the difference I was making, and the Shinwari villages were beginning to feel a sense of protection because I was in their vicinity all the time."

Mike handed her the hose around Mina's chest.
Their fingers touched briefly, and he ached to kiss
her. The ends of her long pigtails were wet and curled
against her upper chest. Her tank top was soaked,
outlining her breasts. Worse, her nipples were clearly
straining against the fabric. He was in a special hell.
He'd never seen Khat happier, discovering a dappling
of gold in the depths of her eyes. To Mike, she looked
like a young teenage horse-crazy girl. And his heart
expanded with a grinding hunger and a driving desire
to see her happy like this with him.

"What does that mean, 'all the time'? You mean
six months out of every year?" He straightened and
began to wash Mina's long thick black mane. It had a
lot of snarls in it, and he used a shampoo conditioner
to unknot most of them. They came out quickly as he
gently combed down through the strands.

Khat stood up, brushed some damp tendrils away
from her flushed cheek. She saw concern in his eyes.
"The first year I was with the operation, I took a week
to visit my parents." She shrugged. "That didn't go
well, so I went after my upgrade training instead.

When I finished the schooling, I deployed back to Afghanistan."

"You didn't take that six months off?" Mike probed carefully.

Khat gave him a grimace and began to wash Mina's neck from her ears down to where it intersected her sloped shoulder. "No, I came back here."

Damn. Mike couldn't believe what she was doing to herself. He'd seen the train wrecks with the marines and army personnel who would spend a year in combat, go home for four to six months and then get slammed with another year of deployment back into combat. Mike had seen men commit suicide after two or three such brutal tours. The amount of PTSD they accumulated was stunning, and their symptoms grew worse with each deployment. What the hell was her handler thinking? Hutton should realize Khat needed downtime to recharge and get back to a somewhat normal life Stateside.

He continued to comb out the snarls in Mina's mane, opposite where Khat stood. "Tell me something. Didn't your handler care that you came back too soon into combat?"

Khat heard the grate in his voice. It was veiled, but it was there. The look in his eyes was narrowed and filled with concern. She felt Mike was upset although he appeared relaxed. "No. The Shinwari villages were being regularly plundered by Sangar Khogani of the Hill tribe. With me being boots on the ground, I was making it hell for him to keep attacking my villages and not lose five or ten men at a time."

Mike scowled. "So the handler decided that?"

"No, I did. He wasn't happy about it, but he saw the

value of me being in the breach and making the difference. I was able to slow Khogani down. I was also providing actionable intelligence in an area where it was desperately needed."

Anger rolled through him, but he kept it to himself. "So do you go Stateside every year, then?"

"No."

"How long has this been going on?"

"Past three years," she muttered, seeing Mike was clearly concerned. She took a soft cloth, wet it and cleaned out Mina's ears and then gently washed off her face and tiny muzzle.

"Because?"

"Because I wanted to protect my father's tribe," she answered, defensive. "You don't understand, Mike. My father, Jaleel, was born and raised in Dur Babba. He was second of two sons and three daughters. He wanted more than a dirt poor farmer's life. Since he wasn't the firstborn son, he was able to leave the village. My father went to Pakistan when he was twelve years old. He got a job at a concrete plant outside of the capital and saved money. When he was eighteen, he went to the university and worked for five years to gain a degree in civil engineering. Then he went home and told his parents he was going to immigrate to the US, to find a good-paying job."

"And he'd send money home to his family after that?" Mike guessed, washing out the conditioner from Mina's mane.

"Exactly."

"How did he meet your mother?" He saw some of the defensiveness leave her face.

"My father was taking English classes at San Diego

State University. My mother is an English teacher. They fell in love and got married a year later. My father got a good-paying job at a construction company, and my mom kept teaching until she became pregnant with me." Khat smiled softly, cleaning Mina's large, delicate nostrils, wiping the fine dirt out of them. "I was born two years after they were married."

"That's a nice story," Mike murmured, meaning it. "You said you didn't like going back after coming home from Afghanistan?"

"That's another long story," Khat whispered, standing back and looking at how Mina's black coat now shined.

"I've got all day," Mike teased, wringing out a cloth into the bucket. He glanced over and saw pain lingering in her eyes.

"My father hated that I joined the Marine Corps," she admitted, overcome with sudden grief. She took a towel and began rubbing Mina's neck dry. "He said a woman's place was at home, having children and all that. He couldn't understand why I joined the Marine Corps."

"I'm sure it raised hell with his customs. Was he a strict Muslim?"

"No, he was actually pretty worldly considering where he was born. It's just that he's a neanderthal about what women can or can't do. He hated that I went into the military. And then, when the Corps asked me to join USMC Counterintelligence group, because I spoke flawless Pashto, was half Afghan and had ties in the country, that's when he lost it."

"You wanted to go over and help your family?" Mike saw the tears in her eyes for a moment, and then she swallowed them back, continuing to dry Mina's neck with the towel.

"You know, Mike, I grew up in the States. I was like any other girl. The freedom I enjoy there wasn't here in this country. It was like stepping back into the Stone Age for me. Like being caught in a time warp. Girls are chattels in Afghanistan. They were imprisoned. But at the time, I didn't know all that until I got training in counterintelligence."

"I imagine it was a helluva jolt coming over here after being born and raised in America."

She snorted. "It was a stunning revelation, believe me. My parents made decent money. I grew up with my father's stories about Afghanistan, about his huge, extended family. In my heart, I felt this driving need to get back to the place of his birth. He was very proud that he was Afghani. I grew up on his knee, listening to fabulous, wonderful stories of Afghan heroes and warlords, fighting for their tribe, keeping them safe and out of harm's way." She smiled a little, resting her hands on Mina's back. "I guess I wanted to give back to the other side of my family, to meet them, know them and love them."

"And you did get to meet them eventually?"

Wiping the sweat from her brow, she nodded, tears in her eyes. Her voice wobbled a little. "I got to meet my father's brothers and sisters. When I drove into Dur Babba with a SEAL unit a long time ago, it was one of the most amazing and happiest days of my life." She gave Mike a self-conscious look, wiping the tears from the corners of her eyes. "I finally felt like my soul had come home. Father had always told me Afghan blood ran deep and wild in a person, and he was right. I've committed whatever's left of my life to my people. It is in my blood. And nothing and no one is ever going to tear me away from this part of the world. I'll die over here, and my body will someday be thrown to the vultures, my bones bleached white by the sun. But my spirit will be happy."

Something broke inside him as she whispered those last words. It scared the hell out of him. "Hey," Mike said, walking around the horse. He turned her around, placing his hands on her shoulders. "I want you around, Khat." She felt so damned fragile in that moment that it triggered every protective mechanism he owned.

Mike was so close that it made Khat dizzy. She felt his hands on her shoulders, monitoring the amount of strength he held her with. The intimacy he automatically established with her. His face blurred for a moment and without thinking, she leaned upward and placed her mouth upon his. For a second, he tensed, surprised by her action. And then he swept her into his arms, his mouth taking hers with a fierceness that flooded her entire being. Desire plunged through her, electrifying every nerve ending, triggering a wild hunger that howled through her awakening body.

THE WORLD CEASED to exist for Khat as his mouth plundered hers, giving and taking, wanting her. As she strained to get even closer to Mike, the length of her body plastered against his, she felt as if she'd come home in a different way. A good way.

His hand cupped her cheek, deepening his exploration of her, the hunger flaring bright within her. Khat couldn't get close enough to him, her breasts pressed urgently against his chest, her heart a staccato against his. And as Mike eased his palm across her nape, his calloused fingers incited flares of building heat down through the core of her body. His mouth skimmed her, tasting her, giving her lower lip a small nip.

Khat moaned, her arms curling tightly around his shoulders, absorbing his strength, his masculinity. Her breasts tightened, and her nipples hardened, and she wanted him to touch her so badly. The fear of him discovering the thick scars on her back was erased as his hand drifted from her nape and he enclosed her hip, bringing her hard against him. A softened cry tore from her, his thick erection against her belly, bright, white heat flooding her core, dampening her thighs as his mouth pleasured her.

Khat's senses were blown by his sweet assault upon her. She inhaled Mike's masculine scent, dragging it deep into her lungs. His beard sent prickles across her cheek and jaw, his hands exploring her, awakening her until she trembled in his embrace. And without realizing it, he'd moved his hand lightly across the damp fabric stretched across her scarred back. The one thing she'd lived in fear of had not made him recoil, had not stopped him from continuing to kiss her. Her fear dissolved as his tongue moved slowly against hers, suggestive, hot and sending more ripples of heat exploding through her lower body.

Mike didn't want to stop kissing Khat. But they were out in the open and someone could walk around the building and find them practically making love to one another. Easing from her mouth, he dragged his eyes open, staring into her drowsy green and gold gaze. Yes, that dappled gold sunlight was there, her black pupils huge, a green crescent around them. He kissed her nose, her cheek and then her brow. "We're a little exposed here," he said gruffly, regret in his tone.

Dazed, Khat released him, but not wanting to. She felt so damn needy that she could barely think coherently. Her lips throbbed with the power of his kiss, and her heart was fluttering in her chest. "Y-yes," she whispered. Her knees felt unsteady.

Mike needed her softness, her woman's strength as he framed her face. Khat's cheeks were flushed, her breathing uneven, her nostrils flared, drinking in his scent. "It's damn nice to kiss you again," he rasped against her ear, nuzzling her temple, the red tendrils tickling his nose and cheek. "Do you know how many times I replayed our first kiss?" He pulled away, smiling into her softened eyes. There were no more tears, just arousal and a keen hunger for him in them. More than anything, Khat had come to him. His heart nearly burst with joy. It told Mike that what he felt for her was mutual, not one-sided. He saw Khat give him a tremulous smile.

"I've wanted to kiss you, Mike, from the first minute I saw you again…"

Her voice was husky with sensuality, and it flowed through him, making him ache even more than before. "I like what we have, Khat," Mike grated, still trapped in the blistering heat coursing through him.

He tamed several strands of her hair and tucked them behind her ear. "I want to build upon what we have, Angel. And I hope you do, too."

Khat's voice throbbed with emotion. "I'm afraid, Mike." Afraid that if she undressed and he saw the extent of her scars, that it would disgust him. He would think her ugly. She was damaged goods. Her father had said so. She saw his lion-gold eyes grow hooded. That mouth of his, strong and chiseled, called to her again then moved into a very confident, male smile.

"We can both be afraid as long as we run toward one another, Khat, not away from one another." Mike's voice lowered. "I'm serious about you. This is no one-night stand. I need you to know that." Mike saw her eyes grow moist.

"How do you know?" she demanded, her voice breaking.

"From the minute I became conscious and saw you, I knew." The indecision in her eyes was from her self-consciousness about her scars, Mike sensed. Yet, he'd purposefully run his hand across her back, seeing if she was going to shy away or freeze because he'd grazed that injured area of her body. Khat had done neither. Mike felt it was a sign of trust on her part toward him. "You're so damned breathtakingly beautiful to me, Khat. I can't think two thoughts in a row without thinking of you."

Her heart swelled. She saw he meant every word he'd said, his gold eyes darkening, intense and desiring her. "Every time I'm around you," she admitted softly, her hands on his upper arms, "I feel myself flying apart inside." Khat drowned in his primal look. "Maybe I'm afraid of myself, more than you." She gave him a bewildered look.

"Khat, you're in the driver's seat here. It's your call. I want you to come to me on your own terms and time. Otherwise," he said wryly, "I'd be like every one of these men on this base who want you."

His words helped dissolve her feeling anxious. "It's been a long time, Mike, since I had a relationship with a man." She forced herself to hold his gaze. "Things have happened. Things I haven't told you yet."

The worry was back in her eyes, and Mike knew what it was about: her scars. "We'll take this as slow or fast as you want, Khat." Well, that was a damned lie, but Mike wasn't about to destroy the trust they'd just built based upon his sexual needs. Her expression calmed. She licked her lower lip nervously, and stepped away from him, her arms falling to her sides.

He reached out, grazing her cheek, the skin soft velvet beneath his fingertips. "Come on, let's finish up here." She nodded and picked up the towel she'd laid across Mina's back. Mike walked to the other side of the horse.

There was a new sense of building yearning escalating and throbbing between them now. He swore he could feel it, and it wasn't a bad thing. It was something alive, something triggered by their kiss. A waiting. A promise. And it was galvanizing. He was going to have a hell of time keeping his hands off her.

CHAPTER EIGHT

SOMETHING WAS WRONG, and Mike could feel it. What was it? After washing the horses, Khat wanted to go lie down for a while and rest. He went back to work on his mission-planning duties. Finally, toward 1600, he got up and ambled into the chief's office.

"Come on in," Mac said, "I'm ready for a break." He leaned back in his chair.

Mike shut the door and sat down. "I need to talk to you about Sergeant Shinwari," he said, scowling. He filled in Mac on what he'd found out.

Mac scratched his brown beard, looking up at the ceiling, considering his thoughts. "Bottom line is she needs her ass hauled off that op."

Mike nodded. "That's what I think, but I wanted to run it by you."

"This is a FUBAR," Mac muttered, turning around in his chair and putting his hands on the desk, pushing a few papers around. "You know, some of these handlers just let their people run loose, not enough oversight."

"Do you know Commander Hutton?" Mike asked, well aware any master chief in the SEALs knew everyone, their reputation and background. Mac's blue eyes grew hard.

"Hutton, unfortunately, got deep-sixed into that job because his shit is not tight."

Which meant to Mike, Hutton wasn't living up to the SEAL ethos, and so the officer was put someplace where he could do the least amount of damage to the personnel around him. Just great. Now Khat was suffering the consequences under his authority. "Okay, but I'm worried about her. She's on a razor's edge, Mac. She's got PTSD, and she's been tortured. And I know she hasn't taken the shore leave to get help or even begin to assimilate those experiences."

"And her family is a no-go?"

Mike grimaced. "Her father is Afghani. He was against her decision to go into the Marine Corps. And she hasn't brought it up, but I'm sure after she was captured, her family knew she was MIA. And then, thirty days later, were told their daughter was rescued after having been tortured. That bends minds, Mac. No parent wants their child in this kind of place."

"But it's especially tough on an Afghan father who has grown up believing his daughter would be married young, have a passel of children and he'd be a grandfather. Yeah," Mac mumbled, "I got the picture."

"What can we do?" Mike knew he was too low on the SEAL food chain to influence much of anything. But Mac, as a chief of a SEAL platoon, had incredible power. He watched him, holding his breath. If Mac wouldn't take up Khat's cause, he was stonewalled.

"What I need to do," Mac said, thinking out loud, "is get to the head of that black op she's working with."

"It's called Operation Shadow Warriors."

Brows raising, Mac cut him a glance. "And you know this how?"

Giving him a sheepish look, Mike told him about Lt. Addison Sinclaire, the intel officer at SEAL HQ at Bagram.

"You're pretty good at work-arounds, Tarik," he said, grinning. "Does Lt. Sinclaire have the head honcho's name?"

"Yeah, a US Army General Maya Stevenson. She's in the E ring of the Pentagon."

Rubbing his beard, Mac considered the information. "Okay, here's what we need to do. I can't go upstairs to the admiral with this because I have to have proof." He drummed his fingers. "I need to get those psych evals they've been doing on her. That should show us something."

"What about getting her leave history for those years she's been in Operation Shadow Warriors?" Mike suggested. "I consider psych evals useless. I don't have much faith in shrinks, sorry."

Snorting, Mac said, "Yeah, I hear you. But maybe there will be a pattern I can pick up or see in those evals. Something… Anything to show she's been out there too long and needs to be reeled in for her own good."

His heart rate went up with hope. "Then you'll follow this up?"

"Sure. Someone has to have her back." Mac smiled a little. "She saved four of our SEALs. We owe her."

"She's going in for that psych eval tomorrow morning," Mac continued. "Some shrink's flying in from Bagram to sit and ask her questions," he said, frowning. "You know her better than I do. Is she smart enough to trick a shrink?"

"I don't know. I think she is. Which is why I suggested, instead, that you get her leave and schooling background for the years she's been with this operation."

"Good point," Mac grunted. "Okay, so noted. Go back to work. I'll let you know what I can find out after nosing round a little. I'll probably contact Lt. Sinclaire. She seems to be a dog that'll hunt. Intel officers can be worth their weight in gold." He grinned.

"You LOOKING FORWARD to this psych eval?" Mike asked Khat as he walked her over to the headquarters for Camp Bravo the next morning. She had her game face on. Dressed in her Marine Corps cammies, she was back in the harness of being an operator.

Khat shrugged. "It's a pain in the ass," she muttered. The air was beginning to heat up, the sun having crested the Hindu Kush to the east of the camp. The smell of aviation fuel kerosene filled the air. A number of helicopters were warming up, getting ready for the day's missions at Operations, which was near where they were going.

"Why do they put you through it?" Mike wondered.

"They're evaluating women in combat. I agreed to this when I volunteered to be a part of the experiment. I hate doing it because I always get some idiot who has never been in combat asking me stupid questions."

"I wouldn't like it, either," Mike admitted sourly. He felt the tension in Khat as they walked down a long row of tents on either side of them. "Is there such a thing as failing a psych eval, then?"

"I don't know. I try to stay in touch with some of the women friends I made when we went through the one-year training before being turned loose in combat over here. They all consider it a pain in the ass, too. I've never heard of any of the volunteers being yanked out of combat because of their psych eval."

"I see," Mike murmured. "So it sounds like the general is accruing long-term information that, after the seven-year op is over, will show a larger picture of women's mental and emotional fitness for combat?"

Khat smiled a little. "Nothing gets past you, does it, Tarik?"

He gave her a bemused look. "Not much." He gestured to the left and said, "That's the building. Just go in, show them your brand-new security identification, and they'll get you to this shrink." He looked at his watch. "Meet you here at noon? We'll go over to the chow hall and grab some lunch."

Halting in front of the cinder-block building that was two stories high, Khat said, "Yes, I'd like that."

"See you then." And then he smiled. "Good luck with the eval. Better you than me," he teased. He saw the tension in her eyes. Khat was not looking forward to this three-hour session at all. She managed a slight smile.

"See you then."

Climbing the stairs, Khat dragged in a deep breath and then pushed through the door. She hated this testing. And she was scared because she knew a bad psych eval or a failure as the shrink saw it, could potentially haul her off the operation. Her hands were damp with anxiety, and she pushed them down the sides of her trousers.

In no time, she was escorted into a small office. When she opened the door, she saw a Marine Corps officer with wire-rimmed glasses. He was short and lean, his eyes a watery blue color. She came to attention and gave him her name and rank.

"At ease, Sergeant Shinwari," he said. "Have a seat. I'm Captain Robert Carter."

Khat's nostrils flared as she sat down in front of the desk. He wore cammies like her own, and he carried a side arm. She wondered if this officer had any combat experience. Most likely not. She nervously watched him open her thick personnel file. Everything about her was in there. It wasn't a redacted copy like the one Chief McCutcheon had gotten from Commander Hutton.

Forcing herself to relax, she knew Carter would be watching her like a proverbial hawk. That's what they did: observe. The problem was, their observation was skewed because they were human, too, and they had their own set of problems and projections. So how was this man going to honestly see her?

MIKE WAS WAITING for Khat at the bottom of the stairs at noon. She was about fifteen minutes late. He sensed her coming before he heard her. Turning, he looked up and saw her. Her game face was in place; he really couldn't interpret how she really felt.

"Ready for lunch?" he asked, walking with her toward the chow hall.

"Yeah," she snapped.

Ouch. Mike watched her face change. Her full mouth was thinned, and she was upset. "How'd it go in there?"

"The usual. The little twerp doesn't have a clue as to what combat is. He sits back in his air-conditioned office at Bagram playing head games." She pushed her black baseball cap off her head and ran her fingers distractedly through her hair caught up in a ponytail.

"What's the upshot? Or do you know?"

Khat didn't want to go there. Why the hell Carter homed in on her lack of leave, of staying in the war zone without taking the six months back to the States, really wore on her nerves. "Let me come down, Mike. I'm pretty upset."

While they ate lunch, finding a table in a corner that was occupied by many others, Mike felt anger radiating off her. It was nothing overt, except she was stabbing at the steamed broccoli on her tray like she was sticking a KA-BAR into Carter, most likely.

"I got a hold of Emma Shaheen earlier," he told her. "They'd like us to fly in this afternoon. She's really looking forward to meeting you."

"Who will take care of my horses?"

"I asked one of our SEALs from our platoon. He's from West Texas, and his name is Travis Cooper. He grew up on a cattle ranch, and he knows horses. Said he'd enjoy feeding and watering them." Mike saw the worry leave her eyes. "You okay with that?"

"Yes, that's very nice of him to do it for me."

"The guy likes animals," Mike said, finishing off his meal and pushing the tray aside. "Travis found a starving puppy at a village, and the little guy started following him around. Travis asked the villagers if it belonged to anyone, and they said no." Mike grinned. "So he brought him back to the platoon. Named him Cheese because the puppy loves cheese." He chuckled. "Your horses will be in good hands with Travis."

"Sounds like it," Khat said, pushing her tray aside.

She hadn't eaten much. Her stomach was in knots over the intense three-hour session with the shrink.

She picked up her cup of hot Darjeeling tea, wrapping her fingers around it. Mike's presence automatically soothed her. "Are you getting tired of being my babysitter?" she asked, a partial smile tugging at her mouth.

"No," he said, sipping his coffee. "You're a feast for my senses. Why would I trade being your mentor for sitting on my ass doing mission planning all day long?"

She nodded and smiled, feeling his compliment flow through her. "I like your company, too," she admitted softly, not holding his gaze. Moving the mug in her hands, she sighed. "That shrink was on a mission," she muttered, brows drawing downward.

Mike watched her wrestling with a lot of emotions, her lips pursed, her brow wrinkled. "Want to talk about it?"

Rolling her shoulders as if to get rid of unwanted tension, Khat lifted her head. "The bastard homed in on the fact I wasn't taking my yearly allotment of leave. And that when I did rotate back to the States, I'd do my paramedic upgrades then immediately deploy right back to Afghanistan." She blew out a breath of air. "He didn't get it. He doesn't understand."

"That your Afghan blood calls you back here?" he asked quietly. Khat's eyes were dark and filled with frustration. She kept moving the tea mug around between her hands.

"Yes. I tried to explain it to him, but honest to God, I felt like I was talking to an alien from another planet."

Treading carefully, Mike said, "Have you considered taking your leave? The kind of work you're doing is damned intense, Khat. Not to mention dangerous. Everyone needs a break from combat."

She glared at him. "Now you sound just like him."

Holding up his hands, he said, "Whoa. I'm asking as a concerned friend, Khat. I don't have any axes to grind with you."

She sipped her tea, eyeing him. "I don't see any problems. I *like* what I do. It's a calling. A passion, Mike. That man did not get it. I doubt he understands passion at all," she growled. "He was a robot."

Mike wondered if Mac could get ahold of this shrink's evaluation. It would certainly support what he was seeing in Khat. "Well, let it go," he suggested. "Would you like to get a hop to Bagram this afternoon? Emma will have their driver meet us at Ops, and he'll drive us to their villa. It would be a nice change of pace." Never had he wanted anything more than to get Khat disconnected from her military obligations as she saw them.

Shrugging, Khat said, "Sure." And she didn't add anywhere was better than being near that damned psychiatrist. Worried, she wondered if General Stevenson read every psych eval on every woman in the program. If he put anything in there about her being in too much combat and not rotating back under the rules of the operation, she could be screwed. The last place Khat wanted to be told to go was Stateside. Her people, the blood of her tribe that ran through her veins, was her life, her focus. She didn't want to leave her area of operation because it would leave those villages open to attack by Khogani. He'd kill men, women and children.

Sickened, Khat felt miserable and filled with angst over the eval. That bastard could hurt her objectives.

Hutton didn't care what she did. Out of sight, out of mind, was his philosophy. But someone else above him, back in the Pentagon, might care, and that had her deeply concerned.

MIKE STEPPED INTO Mac's office later, making sure he got permission to leave for Bagram with Khat. The chief motioned for him to shut the door and sit down. When he sat, Mac gave him a triumphant look.

"Seems Commander Hutton is authorizing background reports on Khat to us."

Surprised, Mike said, "That's unexpected."

"Yeah, I made a personal call to him, feeling him out. He's more than happy to offload anything having to do with her to me. I didn't tell him why I wanted the info."

Shaking his head, Mike snarled, "He's sandbagging her. He doesn't give a rat's ass if she's burned out or not." And then he quickly filled Mac in on their lunch conversation.

"Well," Mac said after hearing the info, "if this shrink puts that in the report, it's a nail in her coffin insofar as being allowed to operate without proper oversight. Hutton's not monitoring her at all. He doesn't care, or they're getting such good actionable intel from Sergeant Shinwari that they don't want to lose her contacts if she left." Drumming his fingers, he said, "Hutton's sending over the pdf documents on her psych evals to me later this afternoon. When you get back from Bagram, we'll talk."

"Good enough," Mike said. "Give me my TAD orders so we can get going?"

Mac nodded. "Yeah, drop by in thirty minutes."

Mike found his good friend, Travis Cooper, out back with the horses. The lanky West Texan was leaning against the rails, idly observing the two black mares resting. Travis was nearly six feet tall and relaxed. Anyone who knew Travis well, knew that casual look around him wasn't for real. He struck like a rattler when necessary, out on patrols. He was twenty-six years old, laid back and easygoing.

Mike had always liked Travis. He was one of their snipers and the best of all of them. He was a country boy raised in Rush City, Texas, a small West Texas town. There, he'd been a local football hero. His team had taken the championship, no small feat for such a little town.

"Hey," Mike called, joining him, "doing some wishful thinking about throwing a leg over one of them?"

Travis gave him a welcoming nod. "Now, there you go again, Tarik, mind reading me."

Mike liked his slow Texan drawl. "Those horses are worked pretty hard," he said, gesturing toward them.

"Yeah," Travis murmured, "that one mare has a puffy front right leg. That comes from overwork. Mare must be doing a lot of fast, quick, tight turns to cause the condition. Thought I'd do some massaging of her legs while you're gone. You think that Marine Corps sergeant who owns them would mind?"

"No, I think she'd be grateful."

Travis pushed the baseball cap back on his longish black hair. "She's a fine-lookin' woman, Tarik. How'd you fall into that pot of honey?" He grinned.

"It's no pot of honey," Mike warned him, resting his arms on the rail.

"Never realized there were women in black ops," he drawled.

"It's coming," Mike said, not wanting to give away any info on Operation Shadow Warriors.

"Your lady can do the job," he said, watching the horses. "You see the look of an eagle in her eyes. Back home, on my dad's ranch, we had a pair of golden eagles that made their nest in a one-hundred-year-old cottonwood tree out by the bunkhouse. I used to watch those two eagles, and I saw them up front and close a few times." He shook his head. "Your woman has that same look, Tarik. Doesn't miss much of anything."

"She's not my woman, Travis."

"Hmm," he said, giving him an appraising look. "Coulda fooled me, bro. When she looks at you I see her face go soft. She looks at anyone else, that hard alertness is there instead. Women are like a campfire. You have to tend them regularly."

"Well," Tarik muttered, uncomfortable, "she did save my sorry ass, and I did spend two nights with her up in that cave of hers. You know she's a sniper?" He turned to see Travis's reaction.

"No." And then he shrugged. "Figures, though. She's got that look."

"You have it, too, and you're a sniper."

Travis nodded. "She's not very laid-back, pardner. Most snipers are pretty easygoing and patient," he observed. "She kinda reminds me of a person who lets in too much reality, so there's no room left to dream."

Mike couldn't disagree with him, but Travis didn't know her background like he did. "Well, she's a helluva shot. She was taking Taliban out at fourteen hundred yards. That's nothing to sneeze at."

"No, that's damn fine shooting. She carry a .300 Win Mag?"

"Yeah."

"Where you takin' her this afternoon?"

"To Bagram. Gotta replace gear for her," he said.

"You're going to be gone three days," he said, giving him a raised eyebrow look.

Mike knew just as Travis did, that it didn't take long to get gear replacement. It was a half-day turnaround trip from Bagram back to Bravo. "Chief wants to get her some downtime," he explained.

"She's lookin' mighty thin," Travis agreed. "Maybe workin' too hard out there?"

"I think so," Mike said. Travis missed nothing. No sniper ever did. "I'm hoping the rest will help her recoup."

"Well, like us Texans say, a good huntin' dog is hard to keep on the porch. If she's good at what she does, then her handler is probably abusing the privilege of her. What she needs is a partner. Someone who can take over for her when she needs to rest and catch some downtime. Hell, I'm fine sniping alone, but when we're out on a weeklong op, I like having one of the other snipers with me. That way, we can trade off, sleep while the other keeps watch through the scope."

"Well—" he sighed "—she isn't ours to handle or direct. She's overseen by people far above us over at J-bad."

Travis snorted and kicked some dirt clods with the toe of his combat boot. "Pity, because that gal of yours is lookin' like she's on the edge and you know? Being a sniper is hard work, but it's like quicksand. You don't know how deep you're in until it's too late. Hope whoever has responsibility for her reels her in a bit for her own good."

Mike said nothing. Leave it to Travis to observe Khat and evaluate the dilemma in a split second, just as he had. Mike wasn't a sniper, but he'd had two nights alone with her to observe her in her environment. They had both come to the same conclusion. He slapped Travis on the shoulder. "I'm going to get my TAD orders from the chief and head out. Thanks for taking care of her horses. Can I bring you anything from Bagram?"

Travis grinned. "Man, if you could find a coupla cases of Lone Star beer, I would be beholden. It's a crime for a Texan to drink anything else but Lone Star," he chortled. "Have fun at Bagram. You're one lucky son of a bitch."

Mike laughed. "I'll see what I can do. Later, bro."

"READY?" MIKE ASKED as Khat sauntered into the big room. She had a small duffel bag over her shoulder.

"Yes." Khat saw the room was empty save for Mike doing his patrol planning. Her heart opened as he unwound from his chair and gave her a warm smile. She'd been chewing on the eval interview, and he automatically lifted her spirits with that slow, heated smile of his for her alone.

"We'll head over to my tent first. I'll collect my gear, and we'll be off." He patted the TAD orders for both of them in his shirt pocket. "Chief gave me our orders, so we're good to go."

"I just met Travis Cooper out at the corral with my horses. He's a nice guy."

"Yeah, he's our Texas boy. He's one of our snipers. Did you know that?"

Nodding, Khat said, "Yes, we started talking about horses. He was in the corral working the puffiness out of Mina's front legs. He knows their anatomy, too."

Mike opened the door for her. "He's a good person. Someone you can count on. He'll take care of your girls while we're gone," he promised.

Khat didn't know where Mike's tent was, but it was located on an avenue near SEAL HQ. It looked like all the rest, a desert camouflage color. The tent was set upon a thick plyboard floor, keeping it off the ground. She peeked inside as he got his M-4, pulled on his Kevlar vest and other gear he had to wear. Any helicopter flights over Afghanistan meant full combat gear and weapons in case it crashed and they survived it. The country was never safe.

Mike pulled his floppy bucket hat onto his head, slid on his sunglasses and hauled his duffel bag over his left shoulder. He saw Khat's expression held some excitement. Her eyes looked more clear, less worried than before. He stepped out of his tent and said, "Let's rock it out."

"We can get your gear replacement first," he told her as they walked toward Ops. "We can stow it at the SEAL HQ at Bagram in a locker and then pick it up on the way back to Bravo."

"Good," Khat said. And then she smiled a little. "I'm really looking forward to meeting Emma and Khalid Shaheen."

Nodding, Mike said, "I think you're going to enjoy staying at their villa." And then Khat could get some desperately needed sleep. Would it be enough to bring

her back from that edge she walked on? Mike didn't
know. Desperate to help her, he felt like he was walking on another kind of edge—balancing gaining her
trust and trying to rein in his personal need for her as
a woman. Nothing in life was ever easy.

CHAPTER NINE

KHAT SAT WITH Mike opposite Emma and Khalid Shaheen at their dinner table that evening. She could hardly contain her excitement with the couple who ran a charity organization for the border villages.

Khalid was intense, lanky and had dark blue eyes and military-short black hair. Like his wife, Emma, they wore jeans and T-shirts, so she didn't feel underdressed for dinner.

"When you were at Princeton, Khalid, did you miss Afghanistan?" Khat asked.

Khalid cut into the succulent lamb on his plate. "I always missed Afghanistan." He shared a warm look with his wife. "It's the blood. Even though I'm only fifty percent Afghan through my father, and my mother is Irish, my soul is here."

"How do you cope?" she wondered.

"It's not easy," he murmured. "We live in a war-torn country. I worry about Emma. We've agreed not to have children while living here. I want my wife and my children safe, in America."

"I was born and grew up in America," Khat said, "but when I was sixteen, I began feeling like I was lost. I didn't feel a part of America as I should, I guess."

Emma said, "Maybe it was your Afghan blood calling you home?"

Khat truly liked red-haired, green-eyed Emma. She was tall, lean like her husband and had that look of alertness in her eyes. "Yes, it was. I didn't understand it until I took my feelings to my father, Jaleel. He laughed at me, thought it was funny. He told me my soul was pining away for Afghanistan." She saw Khalid dip his head in understanding. She cut into the spicy lamb and said, "My father said that yearning would always be there in my heart. He said it never left his heart, but he wasn't going to come back here."

"Because he wanted something better for you," Khalid said, "and for his wife. I'm sure he made that choice because it's much safer to live in America."

Emma took a bowl and added more couscous to her plate. "Khat, are you intending to stay here when your military service is up?"

"I am."

Mike said nothing, learning by listening. Khat was intrigued and animated by the couple. She was trying, perhaps, to understand herself through the experiences of Khalid, who was like her: half-Afghani.

"Do you have plans?" Khalid asked.

"No. I thought I might hook up with an NGO, but most of them have left because of the danger to their volunteers."

"What about your parents?" Emma asked gently. "Do they know of your wish?"

"I haven't told them yet." Khat shrugged, frowning. "My father is not at all happy with my career choice. Nor does he want me doing what I've been doing for the past five years."

"You're his child," Khalid remarked in a kindly manner. "You live a very dangerous life, Khat."

"I'm used to it," she said. "I enjoy what I do."

Emma said, "If you feel like it, tomorrow afternoon I'm taking some clothing donations to two women's charities in Kabul. Want to come along? See what we do?"

"I'd love to," Khat said. "I was so excited when Mike told me about your charity. It's inspiring. You're helping so many."

Mike heard the emotion in Khat's voice. He reached over and squeezed her hand. "Maybe Afghan blood is fierce, but it's also generous."

Khat squeezed his fingers, his touch unexpected, but welcome. "I'm still finding out who I am."

Kahlid smiled sympathetically. "I was a lost wanderer in my early years, too," he said. "I was a half and half. I felt like I had a mission in life, but I honestly didn't start finding it until I was allowed to join the army and flew Apache helicopters."

"Just as I became a Marine Corps sniper."

"Sometimes," Emma said softly, "to understand peace, you have to experience war."

Mike saw the expression on Khat's face. The words sank deep into her, and she was digesting them. "Some of our greatest peacemakers were in the military first," he added.

"Well," Khalid said, "it gives you a unique look at what war does to everyone. No one is left untouched or unchanged by it. When you see that, I think many turn to peace as the only real answer."

"I guess I haven't reached that point," Khat admitted, finishing off the food from her plate. "All I see is Khogani murdering my people, and I want vengeance."

"An eye for an eye," Khalid said. "And sometimes,

you have to wage a war against someone like him. They're never going to come to the peace table and talk."

"Aren't you lonely out there by yourself?" Emma inquired, handing her plate to her Afghan housekeeper.

Khat rolled her eyes. "Well, before Mike came along, I wasn't lonely." She gave him a warm look. "Now...well, he's reminded me of many things I stuffed down inside me in order to do my job."

"Mmm," Emma said, grinning as she got up, "none of us go through life alone."

Mike watched Khat color prettily. She had allowed her long, red hair to hang loose, a gleaming crimson cape about her proud shoulders. The jeans she wore made her long legs look even more tempting to him than before. She'd worn a dark green T-shirt with a light green long sleeved blouse over it. Khat was also wearing a pair of what looked to be very old, antique Afghan earrings that hung nearly halfway to her shoulders. She looked exotic, tempting, and he wanted to kiss her until they melted together.

The housekeeper brought over a special dessert, strawberries that were grown in the large garden within the villa walls. They were piled high on shortcake and smothered with whipped cream. Emma helped the housekeeper clear the dishes from the table. When Khat started to get up, she waved her down, saying, "You need to just rest."

Khat looked at Mike with question in her expression. Had he told them about her?

He gave her an amused look. "I didn't say anything to them."

Emma came back and set a bowl with the dessert

before Khat. "You're too thin, Khat. You need to put on twenty pounds, at least. That mission is wearing you out. Literally."

"I might be thin, but I'm strong," she said.

Khalid said, "Emma wasn't being unkind, Khat. She's a big, nurturing mother to everyone who comes here." His blue eyes sparkled. "And believe me, she'll pile the food on your plate if you don't tell her to stop."

Emma laughed and brought the desserts to the men. She sat down and placed the linen napkin across the lap of her jeans. "Well, Khat, he's right. That's why I love this charity so much. We can reach out to the children and improve their lives. I love children, and I suspect you do, too."

Khat felt her heart swell with happiness. "The children are our future. And like you, I'm a mama bear of sorts myself."

Mike heard the passion in her husky voice, saw the fierce look come to her green eyes. "Come on," he teased, "eat this strawberry shortcake or I'm going to swipe it from you."

Khat's pulse bounded with the intimate look Mike gave her. Having him at her side made meeting two strangers easy for her. She picked up the strawberry and tasted it. She made a purring sound in her throat and said, "This is wonderful, Emma."

"I love strawberries, so I nagged Khalid into getting me some seeds from America. Our plants are three years old and what we can't eat, we freeze. Some things about America I miss, and this is one of them."

"After coffee or tea," Khalid said with a smile toward Khat, "would you like me to show you more about our charity and what we do?"

"I'd love it, Khalid, thank you."

Emma gave Mike a grin. "You want to play a round of chess? I know you're good, and Khalid hates the game." She held up her hand. "I have to keep sharp, and you'll give me a run for my money, Mike."

"You're on," Mike said. "But I've played you before, and you're a lot better than you think."

Khat smiled. "Chess player? I didn't know that about you."

"You didn't have a chess set in your cave," he said drolly, chuckling. "Or I'd have challenged you to a game."

Khat laughed.

EMMA WAS SITTING with Mike at the cleared dining room table with the chessboard. Night had fallen, and she had put on some classical music in the background. They had been sitting for about half an hour when Emma said, "Khat is in terrible shape, Mike. What's going on with her?"

He looked up and made his move on the chessboard, telling her what he could about Khat not taking leave or going Stateside when she should have. He finished up by saying, "Khat doesn't see it. She's got tunnel vision."

"Damned Afghan blood."

Mike looked up, surprised at her statement.

Emma sighed. "Khalid's the same way. His Afghan blood runs him. He doesn't see it, either."

There was frustration in Emma's tone, her green eyes dark. Mike waited for her to study the chessboard. "You've been married three years. The charity seems to be growing, and you're doing good work here."

"That's all true," she admitted, making a move.

He rubbed his chin. "Why are you upset, Emma?" She had always been the quiet, stable one in the marriage, a rudder. Or maybe an anchor.

Pushing her red hair off her shoulders she sat up and said in a quiet voice, "Because those two feel guilty. Guilty that they had it better, that they made it out of this pit. I see it in Khat's face. I see it in Khalid's. It wasn't their fault who they were born to, but their damned Afghan blood makes them want to do something…anything, to atone for who they are and what they have."

Mike scowled, her words hitting him hard. "Why don't they orient to their Irish or American mother, instead?"

"Because America is the land of plenty. I watch Khalid go back to Ft. Rucker, Alabama, to take upgrade training on the Apache helo, and he always comes back depressed. He sees that people in America having so much, and the people here having nothing."

"I worry for Khat," Mike admitted, picking up a chess piece, deciding where to put it. "She's passionate."

Snorting, Emma said, "Those two are fanatics. Only they didn't turn into terrorists, they turned into saviors for the weak, the downtrodden and the women of this country."

"There's plenty of fanatics in the world," Mike murmured. "Look at the SEALs. We're fanatics." He grinned a little. Emma looked distressed. "So why are you worried? What's going on?"

"Khalid promised me that by our third wedding anniversary, we would be moving back to the States. His military contract is up in three months, and I just wonder if he's going to re-up for another six years." She gave Mike a brooding look. "I want children, Mike. I'm thirty-two years old now. I can't wait much longer."

"Khalid's caught between two worlds?"

"Precisely. Some days I wonder if he had to make a choice, who would he choose? Afghanistan or me?"

Mike reached over and touched her hand. "He loves you so damn much. That's obvious."

"He may love Afghanistan more. I'm racking my brain, trying to come up with a workaround plan. We can hire an ex-military pilot to fly the Chinook. Hell, we could hire anyone to do what we're doing right now. He's a multimillionaire so many times over, money is not an issue." Rubbing her brow, Emma muttered, "I miss my family. I miss the US. I don't mind doing my part over here, but I'm lonely for my sisters and my parents."

"Want me to help you with your workaround? I'm pretty good at mission planning." He gave her a warm look. Emma was like an older sister to him. "Maybe with two sets of eyes on this issue, we'll come up with different ideas."

She smiled a little. "Yes, I can use some help. I think once Khalid is presented with a solid alternative, he will go back to the States, and we'll live there."

"The work you do here is always dangerous."

"We both know that, believe me. Sometimes, when I fly the Chinook and he's taking off for his duty at the Apache squadron, I wonder if I'll ever see Khalid again." Her eyes grew moist. "I love him so damn much it hurts, Mike. I love him even more now than when we met, if that makes any sense."

Nodding, Mike murmured, "It does." He set the chess piece down.

"What about you?" Emma asked. "I can tell Khat is head over heels with you."

"It's been rocky from the start, literally and figuratively speaking. She found me on a rock pile, unconscious." He smiled a little.

"She's got PTSD really bad, Mike. I think you know that."

"Yeah. I'm trying to get her off the front lines, Emma. But dammit, she's flouted military authority and has pretty much gone rogue and done her thing. Her handler is a jerk and lets her do what she wants. There's no oversight on her like there should be. My platoon chief is working with me, and he's in the breach on this one. He's got the power to get her off that op."

"Does Khat want to stop?"

"No." The word came out flat. Hopeless sounding. He pushed his fingers through his hair. "If Khat knew what Mac and I are doing right now, I think she'd take those two horses of hers and fly the coop. Go disappear back into the Hindu Kush."

"Because she's driven by the passion of her Afghan blood."

He lifted his gaze to Emma's dour-looking face. "That's what I'm discovering." And then Mike said to hell with it and quickly told Emma the rest of Khat's story, her capture, becoming a POW and then being tortured. As he did, Emma's eyes rounded with horror and with sympathy.

"My God," she whispered. "I was kidnapped for two days and got kicked around a lot by them, but nothing like what happened to Khat."

Mike rubbed his palms on his trousers. "Most of the time I feel like a fish out of water with her, Emma. Khat likes me and when we met, I kissed her just before I got airlifted out of the mountains. It did something to her. Threw her into some kind of crisis." He shrugged. "Because now she's really unsure of herself and what she wants out of her life. I see her being torn about it all the time."

"That's because she's falling in love with you," Emma said gently. "She may not even be aware of it, Mike. But by you stepping into her life, it's given her a chance to reevaluate those years in the mountains as a hermit. She may be realizing it's not been all that it's cracked up to be." Emma gave him an understanding look.

"Your explanation sounds better than anything I have," Mike muttered, shaking his head.

"You love her, don't you?"

Squirming, Mike finally said, "I've never been in love, Emma. I don't know what it feels like. Do I like Khat? Yes. Do I want to make love to her? Better believe it. Am I worried for her? Hell, yes."

"Do you want to protect her?"

He gave Emma a flat stare. "More than you can ever know."

"Then you love her." She smiled a little. "You guys are always the last to know."

A lot of emotions stirred within him as he gazed at Emma's gentle expression. "Well," he breathed, "all I know is she needs holding. She needs to feel safe, because ever since her capture and torture, she's not had a safe haven. It's classic PTSD symptoms."

"By you suddenly falling into her world," Emma

mused, "you short-circuited her life. Khat is sort of like a gerbil running inside a wheel. The gerbil is moving but going nowhere. If she never received proper help after her torture, somebody really screwed up. She should have been taken Stateside, gotten long-term therapy, emotional support and continual, ongoing help. The military should never have allowed her back over here. You and I both know that."

"It didn't happen," Mike growled. The tension in his chest increased, and he unconsciously rubbed the area of his heart where it felt so damned heavy.

"If she loves you, and I feel she does, then you've given her an alternative, Mike. She might be ready to live again. And if that's true, then living alone in the mountains isn't going to be very appealing to Khat. You're making her reassess what she's been doing. That's what you're feeling around her. I would put money on it."

"You should have been a shrink," he said, giving Emma a grateful look. "Since you're so wise, what the hell should I do next?"

Emma sat up and took a drink from her coffee cup. "Continue being her anchor, Mike. You know what you want to do—hold Khat, give her a safe place to ramp down, protect and love her. That's what she clearly sees in you right now, but I honestly think the layers of PTSD combined with her captivity is like a dirty lens she's looking through. I don't think she's at all in touch with why she's so drawn to you."

"Well," he said, scratching his head, "I'm about in the same boat as her. I've just been following my heart and gut with her, Emma."

"That's good enough. The heart never lies to us,"

she said, giving him a sweet smile. Emma's green eyes grew merry. "You've *never* been in love, Mike? I can't believe that! You're eye candy. You can't tell me women don't drape themselves all over you?"

He had the good grace to flush. "No serious relationships, okay?" he defended. "You know how women are when they find out you're a SEAL."

Emma's brows moved up, and she laughed. "Yeah, you studs don't want for women, that's for sure!"

Mike patiently tolerated her humor. It felt good to hear Emma laugh and look happier. She was one brave woman, and he admired her so much. She came from the Trayhern military family and dynasty, and being a warrior was in her blood. Just as being Afghan was in Khat's blood. "Okay, okay, it's probably true."

She tilted her head, grinning broadly. "Seriously, Mike? Never found love?"

He shook his head. "Honest to God, Emma, I haven't."

"But what you feel for Khat is different than the feelings you had for all the other women in your life?"

"Yes," he muttered, again on the defensive. "What I feel for her, I've never felt before."

Emma rubbed her hands together, giving him a gleeful look. "Finally, you met a woman who is your equal."

"Don't go raving about it," he muttered, giving her an amused look. Emma was beautiful, her auburn hair soft around her shoulders. She had the most amazing emerald eyes he'd ever seen. Khat's eyes were a shade darker, but just as spectacular to him.

"You know I love you, Mike. And I want only the best for you. You and your father, Bedir, have done so much for our charity. If I can be of help with Khat, let me know."

His voice grew low with gratefulness, "You already have. How did you get so smart?"

Blowing air between her lips, she said, "Life 101. I'll be there for you and Khat. Just know you can call and talk to me anytime. I really like Khat. She reminds me so much of Khalid. It's like looking at fraternal twins who were split apart and sent to different families after birth."

Mike heard the door that led into their garage off the kitchen. "They're back." He picked up his piece and said, "Check."

Emma laughed, holding up her hands. "I surrender."

Mike stood up, hearing Khalid and Khat speaking in Pashto. He smiled a little. Khat had a big brother now. Again, he was grateful to Emma and Khalid. They were very busy people with stress-filled lives, and yet they were giving him and Khat the gift of three days at their villa.

As he walked around the table, Mike felt his heart lift when Khat entered the kitchen, all smiles. Khalid was following her, grinning. It made him happy to see her smiling; something she rarely did. What would tonight bring? Did she want to kiss him again? Was she ready to be loved by him?

Everything was tenuous, but Mike promised himself he'd go with whatever Khat wanted from him. Emma's words rang in his head about falling in love with her. His chest warmed with deep feelings that had never surfaced before in his life.

Maybe it was love.

CHAPTER TEN

AT 2:00 A.M., Khat couldn't sleep. She sat out in the quiet living room, drinking hot Darjeeling tea, curled up on the couch. Her heart was in turmoil. Mike's suite was right across the hall. He was a few steps from her room. Her mind whirled with excitement over all that Khalid had shown her earlier about their charity to help Afghan people.

"Want some company?"

She lifted her chin and saw Mike standing at the end of the couch. He was dressed in a T-shirt and a set of dark blue pajama bottoms. His hair was mussed, drowsiness in his eyes.

"Did I wake you up? I had a nightmare, and I woke up screaming. I was worried I'd disturb you." Her heart started to pound. Mike called to her heart, her body. She saw him push his fingers through his hair and give her a concerned look.

"These walls are pretty thick," he said, exhaustion torn from him. Khat sat with her hair down, flowing across her shoulder, her eyes shadowed, her skin stretched tight across her sloping cheekbones. She wore a sleeveless pink T-shirt and a set of pink capri cotton pajama bottoms. Her feet were tucked beneath her. He felt his body instantly react, and it was the last thing he wanted to happen right now. She looked fragile again.

Before going to bed, Khat had been high with excitement on all that Khalid had taken the time to show her about their charity. But it was short-lived from where Mike stood.

Giving him a look of relief, she uttered, "Good…I was afraid I'd wake you up."

"You didn't," he said, coming over and sitting on the couch. He sat near enough but not so close that Khat would feel crowded by him. He saw her eyes half close and she pursed her lips. "Hell of a way to lose badly needed sleep."

She set the mug of tea on the coffee table and felt a desperate need for his company. "I know," she whispered. Hitching up one shoulder, she said, "I wish I could control them, but I can't."

Mike felt her turmoil, saw it in the darkness of her eyes. He decided to take a step that could shatter the trust he had built with Khat. But as long as no one challenged her, got her to see herself or where she'd entrapped herself, nothing would change for her. He leaned his elbows on his knees, hands clasped between his thighs as he studied her in the silence. "Do those nightmares have to do with the scars I saw on your back?"

Khat froze beneath his quietly posed question. Her eyes widened. There was no judgment in his expression. His voice had been gentle. And his eyes told her he had put it together. Gulping, she felt a lump forming in her throat. "It does," she managed in a strangled voice.

Mike saw the fear leap into her eyes. He straightened up and said, "Why don't you come over here and I'll just hold you, Khat?" It was a helluva bold step for him to take, but his heart was screaming at him to hold her. He held out his hand toward her. "Sometimes," he rasped, "having a safe place to go to helps."

Khat stared at Mike, her heart wrenching and starting to pulse strongly. The look in his eyes was tender with care for her. Moistening her lips, she nodded. Moving beside Mike, she felt his arm go around her waist and pull her up against him. Closing her eyes, Khat rested her head on his broad shoulder. It was such a change for her. She had been alone for so long and now, suddenly, to be in the arms of this man...

"That's better," Mike rumbled, pressing a kiss to her hair. Leaning back against the couch, he couldn't believe Khat had come to him. Emma's observation that humans weren't made to live alone struck him. She was curved against the right side of his body, and he could feel her breasts pressing against his chest. Her palm lay over his thudding heart, and Mike felt good. Felt whole. As if Khat fit him like a long lost puzzle piece he'd been looking for, but never found until just now. He smoothed some of her thick hair across her shoulder, revealing her face and slender neck to his gaze. She smelled of roses and he inhaled it and her woman's scent. Mike felt her slowly relax and inwardly, he breathed a sigh of relief. The trust was still between them.

"Do you ever get nightmares, Mike?"

He heard her faraway tone. "Sure. You can't be in combat for as long as I have and not get them every once in a while." He smoothed her hair from her temple, wanting to touch her, soothe and love her. Mike wasn't sure where tonight would lead. "Do you have nightmares often?"

Khat nodded, nuzzling against his neck and jaw. This felt so right. And she was was so hungry for his tenderness. His fingers grazed against her temple, sifting through her hair, her scalp tingling with pleasure over his touch. Her mind gnawed on what his reaction would be to her if he saw her scars. Would he be so disgusted by her disfigurement that he wouldn't want to be around her? Wouldn't want to hold her? Yet he'd already seen them in the cave. Khat had just thought it when he skimmed the length of her back. A light touch, a warming one. Without thinking, she tensed as his large hand came and rested in the center of her back.

"Does that bother you?" he asked, kissing her temple. He placed his mouth against her jaw, kissing her again. She began to melt into his arms, her tension dissolving.

"No," she whispered unsteadily, moving her hand across the material spanning his chest. He had powerful upper body strength, and she could feel the muscles beneath his flesh leaping, responding to her exploration. She dragged in a deep breath and released it. "I— I'm afraid, Mike..."

"I know you are, Angel. Your scars don't define you to me. Did you know that?" He deliberately moved his fingers in a grazing motion across her back again, wanting her to get used to his touch. Understanding that he wasn't disgusted by her scars, that he wanted her anyway, despite them. Even beneath the thin cotton fabric, he could feel the thick ridges, the tension in her scarred flesh. It made Mike angry. He wanted to find those bastards who had done this to her.

Shoving all those feelings deep into a box within himself, he focused on Khat. On what he knew they both wanted. It was just a matter of getting her to trust him and release her worry about what he thought about her scars.

"You don't care, then?" Tears burned in Khat's tightly closed eyes. His fingers continued to gently skim her back from her shoulders to her hips. His touch brought out her shame, and Khat couldn't believe it didn't matter to Mike. Her father's words rang in her head, warning her no man would ever want her. Mike did. With each stroke of his hand across her back, Khat began to lose the worry and tension that had held her prisoner for so long.

Mike smiled a little, kissing her wrinkled brow. "Remember? When I became conscious in the cave? I saw you naked beneath that waterfall. I saw your back then, Khat. I figured something really bad had happened to you. I thought you might have been tortured…" His voice deepened, and he held her a little tighter. "The woman I saw in that moment stole my heart. I didn't see your scars, Angel, I saw *you*. All of you. Your beauty. My God, you are incredibly beautiful to me," he breathed, placing his finger beneath her chin, guiding her lips toward his and curving his mouth gently against hers. Mike tasted the salt of her silent tears, and it tore through him that she'd borne the pain for so long by herself. If he had anything to say about it, from now on, he was going to show Khat just how precious she was to him.

He heard her moan as he skimmed her wet lips and absorbed her salty tears, moving his tongue lightly across her lower lip. Khat's breath hitched and then grew uneven. Her fingers gripped the fabric across his chest, and she automatically strained against him, telling Mike she wanted him. Lifting his mouth from hers, he saw her eyes slowly open. He smiled down at her. "Let me show you just how much you mean to me," he growled, holding her softened gaze. He saw no more worry, no anxiety in her eyes.

"Yes," she choked, holding his burning gaze.

Mike nodded and released her. Standing, he held out his hand toward Khat. A fierce love tunneled through him as he watched her slowly unwind and stand. "You're mine," he growled, slipping his arms around her and picking her up.

Gasping, Khat placed her arms around his shoulders, not expecting him to lift her into his arms.

"Relax," Mike whispered, holding her, kissing her brow. "I've got you."

"But your arm…"

"The doctors don't know what they're talking about," he muttered, carrying her easily from the living room and down the hall toward the suites. "My arm was fine at six weeks. That's why I don't wear that removable cast anymore."

Content to be held, trusting him utterly, Khat rested her head on his shoulders and closed her eyes. Mike was so male, so confident, and she felt protection emanating from around him. A fierce kind of feeling that wrapped her in a blanket of security she'd never felt before. She was his. Hadn't she always been from the moment their eyes had met?

Mike carried her into his room and shut the door with his foot. He brought her over to the king-size bed, where a 1930s art-deco lamp in the form of a pink lily shed just enough light into the room from where it sat on the black walnut antique dresser.

He laid Khat down, her red hair a blazing halo about her head and shoulders. He was hard, and he ached, but he knew tonight, more than any other, had to be for Khat. He came second this time, not first.

He sat down, their hips touching one another, and he leaned down, caressing her lips. "Tell me what you want, Khat." Mike wasn't about to blunder into this. He had no idea during her time in captivity if she'd also been raped. There was no way to know. He sifted his fingers through her silky strong hair. He eased from her mouth, holding her shining green gaze.

"I haven't had sex in six years, Mike." She grimaced. "More like a virgin who is not a virgin," she joked, feeling nervous.

He moved his fingers across her flushed cheek, feeling the velvet quality of her warm skin. "That's okay, we can handle that. Anything else?"

"I wasn't raped when I was in captivity," she said, choking on emotions, "if that's what you're asking."

Mike nodded. "I needed to know. Are you protected, Khat? Or do I need to use a condom?"

Her mouth pulled. "Mike, I so rarely have a period… I'm not on anything, but I don't get a period for months at a time…"

Nodding, he murmured, "It's the stress. You know your body better than I do. Want me to use a condom? Just to be safe?"

"I think so." Khat didn't want to end up pregnant.

"Okay," he said, opening the bed stand drawer and pulling out a packet.

Khat closed her eyes and felt his fingertips eliciting tiny fires across her cheek and down her neck, as if he were memorizing her. Opening her eyes, she stared up at him. "I trust you…"

Her whispered words about broke Mike. He felt his heart tear as he saw the unshed tears glistening in her eyes, her face open for him to read. "If," he rasped, "at any time, something doesn't feel good or you don't want me to do it, Khat, tell me." He frowned, wanting her to realize she was in control. A person couldn't go through captivity and not feel imprisoned in many ways, even if it were only in their mind. "This is important," Mike urged, cupping her cheek with his palm. The moment he'd said the words, he'd seen a change in Khat's expression. It wasn't obvious, more a feeling than an actual facial movement.

"Yes," she said huskily, "I will tell you." She lifted her hand, sliding it up across his jaw, feeling the soft bristly quality of his beard. "I know you won't knowingly hurt me, Mike. I've known that about you from the beginning."

He gave her a wry look, catching her hand, kissing her palm. "But I'm human, Khat. I'm not a mind reader. When I love you, it's two people here, not just me. Not just what I want." He curved his fingers around her hand and pressed it to his heart. "Tonight, I want to please you. I want to give back to you."

She'd had so much of her soul stripped from her, but Mike couldn't say that. Her lips parted, and he saw turmoil and desire in her green eyes. Maybe she wasn't used to a man giving back to her, pleasuring her, bringing her along with him. Mike didn't know. All he could do was show her how much he loved her, wanted her and needed her.

"At least for tonight," she told him.

He gave her a slight smile. "Yes, we have two more nights here besides this one. We'll make every one of them count, Angel…" He began to wage a sweet, hot campaign upon her, wanting to melt her mind, engage that magnificent, courageous heart of hers and entwine it within this own. Leaning down, Mike placed a series of slow kisses against her slender neck. He would take a slight nip of her tender flesh, move his tongue across it and then gently kiss the area. Instantly, she closed her eyes, gripping his arms, a soft sound in her throat, telling him she enjoyed it.

Mike moved slowly, inhaling her, tasting her, feeling her response as he outlined each of her collarbones. Her breasts were so close, covered by the soft material, the nipples hardening, pushing against it. Curving his hand around her right breast, she gasped, turning and filling his hand. Her breathing became uneven, her face flushed and he leaned down, capturing that tight nipple hiding beneath the fabric.

Khat gave a soft cry, arching against him, her hand restless, pulling at his T-shirt, gripping his shoulder.

"Like that?" he whispered, moving next to her delicate ear. Her hair tickled his nose, his cheek, as he caught her lobe, nipping it just enough, but not causing her pain. Mike heard her call his name, pleading, her voice hoarse with need. Her hips were restless, straining against his. He wanted her naked against him.

Standing, it was easy for Mike to pull the T-shirt over his head. He dropped it on the floor and pushed out of his pajama bottoms. As he straightened, Khat's eyes were half-open, drowsy looking with arousal, staring at him, drinking in his entire body. There was no question he wanted her. Mike moved to her side and eased the camisole over her head, revealing her small perfect breasts. He saw the scars that had come across her shoulders, and he leaned down, kissing each of them, trailing those kisses down to each breast, licking near her nipple, her flesh tightening in anticipation.

As his mouth settled on the first flushed peak, Khat mewled. He suckled her, and she thrashed her head against the pillow, rasping cries spilling from her throat. She was so damned sensitive, so hot. He moved her to the center of the bed and lay down at her left side. She turned against him, her hips pressed against him. Gritting his teeth, he felt her lust, her hunger. He took her mouth powerfully. At the same time, Mike slid his calloused hand downward across her soft belly, sliding his fingers beneath the elastic band. More than anything, he wanted her ready for him, wanted her aching for him as much as he ached for her.

Khat gave a whimper as he moved down the cleft of her mound, searching, discovering how wet she'd become. He'd barely touched her, barely begun, and still, her inner thighs were damp. Slowly removing his hand from beneath her pajamas, Mike pulled away from her mouth. Her eyes were wild-looking with a hunger so deep that it made him smile down at her. Khat was restless, moving against him, silently pleading for him to take her. To complete her.

Mike sat up and helped her off with her pajamas. He tossed them over the side of the bed, marveling at her long legs, so tightly and firmly muscled. He skimmed his hand from her slender ankle, up across her calf, knee and splayed out his fingers, appreciating the curved firmness of her thigh. "You are so beautiful," he rasped, turning and holding her glittering gaze.

Her lips were parted, and she was swiftly unraveling beneath his exploration.

Slipping his arm beneath Khat's neck, Mike drew her upward just enough to capture the nipple lightly between his teeth. At the same moment, he slid his hand over the inner curve of her thigh, opening her. Khat's fingers dug powerfully into his shoulders, her hips pressed tightly against his exploring fingers. Oh, no question, she wanted him. It humbled Mike as he slid his fingers along the outer rim of her entrance, the fluid so thick and hot that he wondered if she had already orgasmed. He suckled her strongly, while slowly easing his finger through her opening, testing her, wanting to make sure she wouldn't freeze or become fearful of being penetrated.

Just the opposite happened. The moment he moved his finger within her, she groaned, arching into him, her hand gripping his shoulder, fingers digging spasmodically into his flesh. She was wild beneath him, twisting, trying to pull him deeper into her. Sobs tore out of her, begging him to enter her.

Mike eased out of her, lifting his head and allowing Khat to lie down on the bed. Reaching across her, he found the condom and rolled it on.

"Please," Khat begged, her breath coming in ragged gasps, "enter me. Don't keep teasing me, please…"

Mike smiled and settled over her, keeping most of his weight off her, elbows near her shoulders. "Don't worry, Angel, we're going to fly. Hang on…" He nudged her thigh more open with his knee. She was trembling with need, her flesh damp, her breasts rising and falling quickly against his chest. She twisted and pushed up against him, wanting him to enter her.

Dragging in a swift breath, his blood blistering through his lower body, Mike absorbed her wildness. And God help him, she was exactly that. No fear. Wanting what was hers. He pressed up against her opening, and she whimpered, her hands gripping his hips, tugging him strongly, wanting him.

Mike held on…barely. He wanted to come so damn badly, his body shuddering, holding back for her sake. His mind started to melt, and he knew he couldn't plunge into her. No sex for six years and she was going to be tight. No, he had to enter Khat slowly, allow her body time to adjust. But his red-haired hellion was making it clear she didn't agree with his plan.

Her hips bucked violently against his, and at the same time she pulled him forward. Mike entered her. Just barely. He jammed his eyes shut, feeling her surround him like the tightest damn glove he'd ever experienced. Khat was moaning his name, twisting her hips, wanting more of him in her. The fluid was sweet and thick around him, and he gripped the bedcovers in his fists, sweat popping out on his brow. Damn, she was strong! In every way. He'd forgotten Khat was in top shape, just like him. And when those long, strong legs of hers tangled in his, she arched her hips and she pulled him halfway into her.

A serrating cry of pleasure ripped out of her, and she arched as he filled her. Mike felt his control disintegrating against her onslaught. What had he expected? Some sweet, tame woman? Hell, she was a warrior, knew what she wanted and knew how to get it. His heart opened fiercely to Khat as he met and held her green-and-gold eyes. Oh, yeah, she was one hot, fiery babe, no question. Easing deeper, Mike felt her tremble violently beneath him. He felt as if a hand were squeezing the hell out of him; almost painful except for the heat and fluids surrounding him.

He allowed some of his control to slip and began to slowly thrust into her and then pull back. It was slow, and he monitored her expression, heard her cries of pleasure, her fingers wreaking the hell out of his shoulders. This was a woman who wanted him, and it sent a fiery surge through Mike. She wasn't as fragile as he'd assumed. Shame on him. Well, he'd learn. He slipped his hand beneath her hips and plunged deeply into her, giving her exactly what she wanted.

She came loose in his arms beneath his body as he established a hard, driving rhythm for them. Mike could feel the building explosion within her hungry body, heard it in her mounting, keening cries, her hips matching, meeting his thrusts with primal animal energy. He angled her a little bit more, engaging that silky knot just inside her entrance, driving as deep as he could, feeling her suddenly freeze. Her back arched, and she gave a jagged scream, head tipped back deeply into the pillow, her fingers gripping his upper arms.

Nothing made a man feel better than to have his woman orgasm around him. He continued to draw the sweet juices from her ravenous body, feeling the rippling, gripping effect of her muscles contracting around his thick erection. It was almost too much for Mike to bear as he continued to thrust, continuing her pleasure.

Her cries suddenly became strident once more, and Mike felt her violently orgasm again. He watched a rose flush sweep across Khat's upper body, and Mike had never felt more powerful as a man as right then.

Finally, when Khat sank weakly against him, her

eyes closed, Mike knew she was satiated. At least for
this moment. Now he allowed himself off that steel
leash, driving into her sweet, hot body. He felt her
move, tip her hips upward, aiding him, pleasuring him
on his journey. Khat's hands settled on his hips, and
he ground his teeth, feeling the coming, scalding explosion as it ripped through him. He strained, groaned
and locked himself against her damp, strong hips, his
world nothing but fire tunneling out of him. The release shattered him in every way, his body shuddering
violently as the fire engulfed him, threw him into an
orbit of nothing but edgy pleasure and fulfilled lust.

Mike collapsed against Khat, his brow against hers.
They were both breathing like animals locked in a sav-
age battle with one another. His mind refused to work,
but he kissed her closed eyes, her flushed, damp cheeks
and grazed her parted lips that were pulled upward in
a soft smile of fulfillment. He groaned. "You are one
helluva lover," he rasped, kissing her lips more surely,
feeling her smile bloom beneath his mouth.

"You feel so good in me," she quavered, barely
opening her eyes, meeting his narrowed, fiery gaze.

Mike felt perspiration leaking down his temples.
Hell, his whole body was in a sweat. So was hers. He
liked what he saw in Khat's eyes; a kind of fearlessness, a woman knowing she'd pleased her man, and
he'd pleased her. "Angel, I think I'd like to die just
this way. Inside of you." He shared a heated look with
her. When she laughed, it was throaty, and he felt it
through every cell of his body. He eased out of her, got
rid of the condom and rejoined her. This time, he slid
into her welcoming confines, the sensations creating
pleasure tearing through him once again.

"Come here," Mike said thickly, remaining fused together with her. He wrapped Khat in his arms, wrapped her body around his and lay down on the pillow. He felt the warmth, the dampness, the tightness of her around him. And he knew she was going to be sore. His plan didn't exactly go as he'd expected. He'd taken her more roughly than he'd wanted, and he knew she'd be feeling the effects of it later. For now, let him remain within her, stretching her and allowing her body to accommodate him. Later, he'd take her to the hot tub down at the end of the hall.

Moving damp strands of her hair away from her face, Mike kissed her gently, nuzzling her ear, kissing it and feeling her moan, her hand gliding up against his hairy chest. "Are you okay?" he asked.

"Very," she whispered, smiling weakly.

"You're a wild woman. Do you know that?"

"I should have warned you. My Afghan blood."

Laughter rumbled out of his chest. "I like discovering who you are as we go along." And then Mike gave her a wicked look. "Sort of like hunting for treasure. Beautiful, breath-stealing treasure of your body, your heart and soul."

His words flowed like a warm, secure blanket across Khat. "You're a poet, Mike."

"No," he groused, "I'm not. But you inspire me, Khat." And she had touched his heart, held his soul in those scorching moments that they'd gifted one another. He saw her give him a lazy smile, her lashes nearly closed, satiation in her expression. There was no more tension in her face, none in her eyes. He felt relief. Leaning upward, Mike grabbed the sheet and pulled it up to her shoulders.

"I've never felt so good," Khat murmured. "And I've never felt more tired, Mike."

He caressed her thick, silky hair and eased his arm around her back, keeping her close to him. "Go to sleep, baby. There won't be any more nightmares tonight."

Because he was going to protect her with his body, his heart and give her the sanctuary she so richly deserved for so long. Hearing Khat's softened sigh, feeling the weight of her body sag against him, he knew she was drifting off to sleep. In his arms. Where she belonged.

Closing his eyes, his head against the top of hers, Mike had never felt happier in his life.

CHAPTER ELEVEN

KHAT AWOKE SLOWLY. Mike was no longer beside her. She frowned, missing him. Automatically, she slid her hand across where he had been lying, the sheet cool to her touch. She heard the door open. Turning, she saw Mike quietly enter the room, wearing a white terry-cloth bathrobe.

"You're awake," he said, leaning over, capturing her mouth, drinking in her softness. Lifting his head, he said, "Come on."

"Where?"

He took her hand, removed the sheet off her naked body and helped her sit up. "To the hot tub." He picked up the other robe from a nearby chair and helped her put it on. "The heat will take away your soreness."

Her heart spilled open with his concern, and she allowed herself to be pulled to her feet. "I'll be okay," she said, her voice husky with sleep, tying the robe. She saw Mike raise his eyebrow at her.

"Angel, the way we went at it last night, you've got to be sore. And I want you comfortable. Okay?"

Khat had never been treated this way. "Thank you..." She stopped at her suite and retrieved two large tortoiseshell combs and wrapped her hair haphazardly on top of her head. Mike led her down the hall. It was barely dawn, the house quiet. It felt good to be cared for, Mike's arm around her waist. "I slept so deeply." She sighed, laying her head on his shoulder for a moment.

Mike opened the door. "So did I." He smiled a little. "Good sex always makes you sleep well. Come on in. This is their little piece of heaven, as Emma calls it."

Eyes widening, the spa room was covered in light-blue-and-gold tiles. Soft, unobtrusive lighting made it feel as if dawn was on its way toward the horizon. There were thick dark blue rugs near the round-shaped spa that could easily hold ten people. The warmth within the room was humid and moist, but not overwhelming to Khat. There was a silver tray holding two glasses of water. And, to her surprise, a cup of hot Darjeeling tea and a carafe beside it on another tray. She drowsily realized Mike had gone to a lot of trouble for her.

Khat turned around, slid her hands over his shoulders and kissed him deeply. Her body hotly responded as his hands curved possessively around her hips, holding her captive against him, letting her know he wanted her all over again. She smiled against his strong, cherishing mouth. "Thank you," she breathed, her voice trembling. "For everything…" Khat released him and stepped back to take off her robe.

"You need some attention and care," he told her, slipping out of his robe. He took hers and placed each of them on a wall hook. Turning, Mike watched her move gracefully into the inviting, bubbling warm water. He saw the scars clearly on her back. Instantly clamping down on his rage, Mike wanted Khat to enjoy the goodness in life, not be reminded of the bad.

Khat groaned, trailing her hands across the surface as she walked to the other side of the hot tub and sat down on the blue-tiled bench. "This feels wonderful, Mike."

He climbed in. "It does a body good," he agreed. "Cold water or Darjeeling tea?"

She gave him a grateful look. "Tea, I think." She held out her hand and took the large mug. "Come sit beside me."

Mike took a glass of ice water and sat near enough and at an angle, so he could see her. There was soft instrumental music in the background. A small waterfall in the corner, complete with green living plants completed this intimate spa. He looked at the tendrils of her hair, curling in the humidity against her relaxed face. As Khat sipped her tea, Mike remembered those long, tapered fingers of hers around his hips.

The hot water felt good on her scarred back, some of the tightness melting magically away. Leaning against the wall, Khat closed her eyes and uttered, "Am I in a dream?" Her mouth stretched into a soft smile. She tipped her head back, leaning against the tiles.

"If you are, I'm in it, too," Mike murmured, drinking the glass of water. He set the emptied glass on the wooden teak deck, far enough away so it wouldn't accidentally fall into the tub.

"I didn't realize how hungry I was for you," she said, opening her eyes and catching his gaze.

"Six years is a long time. Besides, I'm not complaining." Mike reached over and brushed her flushed, damp cheek. "We were good together last night."

Khat became serious. "My father told me after seeing my scars, that no man would want me. I believed him."

Angered, Mike kept his expression neutral. "They sent you home after you were rescued?"

"Yes. They did as much as they could for me at the naval hospital in San Diego. The counselor said I should go home for thirty days, that I needed a place where I felt safe…"

He heard the sadness in her voice…saw it linger in her eyes. "What happened?"

"My father lost it," she muttered. "He got angry and blamed me for it. If I hadn't joined the Marine Corps, this wouldn't have happened and a whole bunch of other stuff. I was a POW for thirty days. I was still in shock from the captivity and torture when I arrived home. His anger totaled me. I felt so broken anyway, and when he laid into me, I just felt that much more fractured. I couldn't protect myself from his anger. I felt like a piece of raw meat." Khat's heart grew heavy thinking about those confrontations, and she finished her tea, setting the mug on the teak deck nearby.

Mike's mouth tightened. "Did he ever give one thought to the realization you were tortured? That you needed to be helped? Not yelled at or blamed for what happened to you?" His hand curled into a fist, and he put a choke chain on his growing rage toward her father.

"No. My mom did, though. She had her hands full with my father's anger toward me. He went ballistic. I had to get out of there. I couldn't handle it. There was no way I was staying with them for a month and dealing with my father's blaming me every day."

"What did you do, then?" Mike asked, his heart breaking for Khat. She'd just been tortured and had come home, thinking it was a place of safety. Only

Khat stepped into another kind of war that was being waged against her shattered soul by her own blinded father. *Dammit, anyway.*

Shrugging, Khat moved her arms slowly through the warm water, luxuriating in it flowing across her limbs. "I went back to my op. A year later, I was contacted by General Maya Stevenson. She asked if I would consider volunteering for Operation Shadow Warriors. I liked what I heard about the plan, and I said yes. The rest is history."

Mike reached out for her elbow, levering her up and floating her across to where he sat. She laughed like a child, eyes alight with joy as he settled her across his lap.

"What was that for?" she asked, breathless, sliding her arm around his shoulders.

"Because," he growled, lowering her into the water just enough so that he could bring her lips to his. "You're an incredibly brave woman, and I want to kiss you…"

Closing her eyes, Khat absorbed the power of his mouth wreaking fire through her. Instantly, as her breasts glided against his chest, her nipples hardened, and she moaned. His hand swept from her curved back, cupping her hips, bringing her fully against him. She felt his erection and went hot and hungry all over again. His mouth was commanding, and she surrendered to his arms, happiness and hunger threading through her.

Mike eased his mouth from hers. Khat's head was tipped against the edge of the spa near his, her eyes warm and shining. With love? For him? He wanted to hope so. Her mouth was plundered and slightly swollen. When she kissed, it was with that fierce Afghan passion that drove her. He cradled her in his arms, lifting his one leg and resting his heel on the tile bench below the water. That effectively trapped her long legs and hips against him.

"You're such a water baby." She laughed, lifting her hand and running her fingers through his damp hair. His eyes grew stormy-looking, narrowing on her like a hunter would his prey. His hand glided across her curved thigh, down her lower leg, caressing her, letting her know how much he cared for her.

"Did you expect anything else?" he teased. "I'm a frogman by training."

Nodding, she touched his broad, lined brow, her fingertips sliding down his temple. There were fine lines at the corners of his eyes, and they grew more obvious when he smiled. "I like water."

"Yes, you do." Mike caught her fingers and kissed each one of them. "I'll never forget seeing you beneath that waterfall. That just blew my mind."

Laughing, Khat said wryly, "You probably thought you'd died and gone to heaven, right?" When he kissed her palm, licks of fire radiated from the center, making her so aware of the ache centering in her core once more.

Raising his brows, Mike murmured, "Yeah, I'd seriously thought I was dead, and I was in heaven." And then he gave her a wicked look. "I thought, man, this is great. I'm in heaven, and I have this beautiful, naked babe in a waterfall waiting for me."

They both laughed.

Mike became serious, enjoying her in his arms. "Feeling better?"

Nodding, Khat kissed his cheek. "You were right. I was sore."

"That's why I'm not going to take you here and now," he told her, catching her green gaze that was dappled with gold flecks.

She pouted. "But I'm ready."

"So am I, but you can't abuse your body, Khat. You need some downtime. We have tonight." Mike held her sultry look. Khat had shown an extreme tendency to take her body for granted. She didn't seem to understand that she was human and needed rest, not always pushing herself to the edge with exhaustion.

"Okay," she murmured, gently outlining his mouth with her fingertip, "you're probably right."

"I've got a better idea," he growled, catching her finger and kissing it. "I want to put some seriously good lotion on your back."

Stunned, she frowned. "But—why?"

"Dr. Johnson called me over to the dispensary after you'd had your physical. She said you forgot the bottle of special lotion she gave you when you left the building. I picked it up. She told me it should go on your back morning and night."

"I didn't forget to pick it up."

"No? Why?"

"Because I can't reach the worst parts of the scarring in the center of my back."

"She said it would help you a lot, take out the stiffness that the scars have caused. Don't you want to try it?"

The truth was, she didn't want Mike to see how bad her scars were. Would he be repelled? It was one thing

to run his hand over them. It was another for him to really look at them and then rub lotion on them.

"What are you thinking?" Mike coaxed, seeing hesi-
tation in her eyes. He had felt her withdraw from him.
"Your scars don't scare me, Khat. I don't mind putting
the lotion on them. Do you?"

Some of her trepidation melted beneath his roughened voice, the tenderness burning in his eyes. "I—
well, it's just that no one has ever touched them. Except
for the doctor I have to see once a year. I don't care
what they think." She forced herself to look him in the
eyes. "I do care what you think."

"That I'd get up, walk out of your life because I saw
the extent of your scars? Touched them and become
disgusted? Is that what you're thinking?"

"Well," Khat whispered, "when you put it that way,
it sounds kind of dumb of me, doesn't it?"

"Angel, I love every inch of you," he rasped, bringing her mouth to his. "And read my lips. You're mine."
Mike kissed her gently, feeling all the tension dissolve
within her. Cupping her cheek, holding Khat's gaze, he
added, "I told you that the night we were on the mountain. Nothing's changed since then. I don't blow hot
and cold. I know what I want. And that's you, Khat. I
accept you just the way you are. Your scars are a part
of your life, but like I told you before, I wasn't going
to be defined by scars, nor should you."

The passion in his gruff tone affected her deeply.
Khat felt one more door that she'd hidden behind crack
and fall away. The fierce look in his burning gaze told
her he meant every word of it. Mike had never lied to
her, always done what he said he'd do. "Okay," she

whispered, resting her brow against his head and closing her eyes. "Let's go do it, then."

"Good," he praised. "Then I'll make you breakfast. Did you know I'm pretty good in the kitchen?"

Khat smiled, feeling his strength feeding her, holding her, and she opened her eyes and murmured, "This I've got to see…"

Mike carried her in her bathrobe back to his room. He disrobed Khat and urged her to lie on her stomach. Khat hid her face in the pillow, and he understood why. He opened the floor-to-ceiling drapes, allowed the dawn light to spill into the large room. Sitting down at her side, their hips meeting, he squeezed the thick, unscented ointment on his fingers.

"This might feel cold," he warned. He saw her nod, her face hidden. For the first time, Mike got a look at her back. Unprepared for it emotionally, he gently began at the top of her shoulder, lightly applying the cream. He felt the fine tension running through her body, as if holding herself against what he might see or think. His stomach turned as he saw the skin had been ravaged, never sewn up, but laid open and healed back together in ragged, thick keloid ridges. It was as if she'd been whipped three or four times, days apart from what he could tell with the way the skin had healed, one on top of the other.

The welts were real, and he choked back rage as he continued to apply it to her moist, heated skin. The damaged flesh had turned darker over time, nothing but layering of scar tissue. He saw how the thickened scars were pulling the unbroken flesh of her back. Some lashes had been deeper than others, and he could almost feel those metal tips digging deep into Khat's long, beautiful back, slicing through her skin, ripping into her muscles beneath.

"Feel okay so far?" he murmured, keeping the horror, the rage, out of his tone. He knew how to stuff his emotions. Khat had been through enough. She didn't need to see his violent reaction to her torture. Her father had done enough damage to her already.

"Mmm-hmm."

Mike smiled faintly. "I think this cream will help over time. Dr. Johnson said it had a lot of vitamins in it to help soften up those scars. It will stop them from pulling on the surrounding skin."

"Mmm-hmm."

Okay, he understood. Khat was mortified. He got that. By the time he was finished, her back gleamed beneath the low light. As he sat there, Mike watched her skin absorb it, thirsty for more. So he put on another layer. Every once in a while, he'd glance down at Khat. Her hand had fallen away from her face, and she had fallen asleep. His heart opened with powerful emotions as he sat there ministering to her. She'd trusted him in the end, and was still so damned exhausted by the unending years of combat that she'd fallen asleep.

A slight smile curved Mike's mouth as he continued to feed those thirsty scars across her back. Maybe it was his touch. Maybe it was because she finally believed him that he loved her, and he didn't give a damn about what kind of scars she carried. The more he worked the ointment in, the more pliable her flesh became. In the end, he gently massaged her back, feeling the tautness of her muscles from the grueling work she did every day. Her skin was flushed, and after the massage, appeared rejuvenated. He even saw a lightening of the darkness that had once been in the scar tissue, some normal color returning because of improved circulation into those areas.

Getting up, Mike covered Khat with a sheet and light blanket. He quietly padded into the bathroom to take a shower. If Khat was still asleep when he was finished, he wouldn't wake her. More than anything, she needed deep, uninterrupted sleep.

Turning at the door to the bathroom, he saw the dawn light caress her soft, relaxed features. Her hand was slightly curled near her flushed cheek. Her hair was tousled and still somewhat tamed within those two tortoiseshell combs she'd used. Thick crimson tendrils curled softly at her temples, and Mike ached to walk over, gather Khat into his arms and hold her safe.

KHAT YAWNED SLEEPILY, staggering down the hall, dressed in the dark blue terry-cloth robe. She'd taken off her watch and didn't know what time it was. All she knew was sunlight was cascading brightly through the open curtains of Mike's room. Rubbing her eyes, she walked out of the hall that spilled out into the kitchen and living room area.

"Feel better?" Mike asked from the sink. He was washing his hands after making two beef sandwiches for lunch. Khat looked like a lost child in that voluminous robe, her hair loosened, her eyes half-open, a drowsy look in them.

"I think so," she muttered, heading to the kitchen where he was. "What time is it?"

"Noon."

"What?" Her eyes rounded. "You're kidding me!"

"No." He wiped his hands on the towel. "Emma

just left for Kabul, and she said for you to take it easy
today. She thinks you're tired."

Wrinkling her nose, Khat walked across the cool
tiles of the kitchen in her bare feet, rubbing her eyes.
"You should have woken me up, Mike."

"Oh," he teased, "so this is *my* fault?"

She made a noise in her throat and looked around.
"Is there tea?"

"I'll make you some," he said, picking up the kettle
and putting it on the gas stove.

"Thanks," she said, yawning again. And then she
rubbed her face as she leaned her hips against the gran-
ite counter. "I feel drugged," she muttered.

"You slept a long time," he said, opening a cabinet
door and bringing down a plate. "How's your back
feeling?"

She lifted her hands from her face. "A lot better.
It's not pulling and stiff like it usually is. I feel like
my back has turned to hard leather, but it doesn't feel
like that now."

"We'll keep putting the lotion on it."

She gave him a tender look. "Sometimes," Khat
admitted huskily, "I think I've made you up. I'm so
desperate, so lonely, and my imagination has created
you..."

Mike walked over, taking her into his arms. "I think
you know how physical I am from last night." He kissed
her brow.

"Really," she mumbled, laying her head beneath his
jaw. Content to be held, she leaned fully against him.
"I liked it, liked you. A lot. And I want to do it again."

Pursing his lips, Mike whispered against her temple,
"You're not leaving my bed while we're here."

The teakettle began to sing, and he reluctantly released her. "Want to have your tea in the living room?"

"I'd better get out of this robe," she said, gesturing to it.

"Emma and Khalid are gone until this evening. It's the housekeeper's day off. We're alone here at the villa. So why not kick back?"

"Wonderful," she murmured, moseying toward the couch.

When Mike brought in her cup of tea, he sat down on one corner of the couch. Khat snuggled into his arms, wanting to be held, starving for his nearness. Unable to explain her neediness, she felt her entire life slowly revolving in a new direction. It left her feeling uncomfortable in some ways. And in others, she was running toward it with open arms, joyous and anticipatory as never before.

"My life hasn't been the same since I met you," Khat said, sipping her tea.

"Well, my life hasn't been the same, either," he chuckled. Khat lay against his left side, his arm over her shoulders, her legs tucked beneath her. The robe had opened, revealing most of her curved, firm thigh.

She blew some air across the surface of the steaming tea she held between her hands. "You're like a lightning bolt that crashed into my life, Mike."

He moved his fingers across her shoulder. "Are you sorry?"

"No." Khat leaned her head back on his arm and looked up at him. "You just worked me up and over my worst fear of a man who liked me until he saw my scars." Mike made a face and shook his head. She laughed softly. "You're such a little boy sometimes."

Moving his fingers along her temple, pulling some of the strands away from her eye, he growled, "I wish you could see yourself through my eyes, Angel. You wouldn't worry about that at all."

Content, she raised the cup to her lips, feeling a happiness she'd never felt before. "Well," she whispered, "I like what we have."

"Makes two of us."

"What are we going to do, Mike? When I have to leave?"

"Let's cross that bridge when we get to it." He knew Mac was getting information together to try and take her off that op. Inwardly, Mike felt panic because he knew it was Khat's entire life and reason for being. They would literally be taking her life, her passion, away from her. She'd be made to stand down and probably rotate Stateside for a minimum of six months. He drew in a deep breath, worried for her, worried for their blossoming relationship. He'd just found Khat, and he sure as hell didn't want to lose her. If she ever found out he was a part of trying to get her off the op, he knew she'd hate him. Hate him enough to walk away from him forever.

"My life feels like it's in transition," she said, worried. "You're the only stable part to it right now."

"Then let me be your anchor. We'll take this one day at a time." Mike drowned in her gaze and saw her mouth pull into a sweet smile that set his body on fire once again. Hell, he was already hard. Just being with Khat aroused him. Having her in his arms sent him into a constant ache. He knew she had no idea of her effect on him. But tonight, Mike was going to love her, bind her to him so that when the storm came into her life, she would stay with him, not run away from him.

CHAPTER TWELVE

"THIS IS OUR last night together," Khat whispered, moving her naked body against Mike. She felt as if these past three days were some kind of magical respite never to happen again. His arm curved around her waist, and Mike pulled her solidly against him. "I don't want it to end, Mike. I feel like a pouty little child having a temper tantrum about it." Khat closed her eyes, nuzzling against his shoulder, her fingers tangling through the soft, dark hair across his chest.

"I don't, either," Mike said, kissing her hair. She had just washed and made love with him in the shower. The thick, dark red strands of her hair were not easily dried. Mike had spent time with her afterward, helping with the hair dryer. The deep scarring on her back prevented her full range of motion upward, so he held the dryer while she did the combing and brushing. They were a good team. He felt her tension and trailed his fingers down her upper arm, her skin warm and velvet.

"We'll be able to come back again. There's always an open door for us here at Khalid and Emma's home," Mike added. He felt Khat take a deep breath. "Do you want to come back when we can?"

"Yes," Khat murmured, feeling his solid heartbeat beneath her palm. "You keep my life interesting in the nicest of ways." Mike was so masculine, so confident of himself, he lured her, intoxicated her senses and made her want him twenty-four hours a day. After two nights of sex with him, she found him to be a consummate lover, always wanting to please her first, gratify her and share their love with one another. Khat had never met a man like him. It made the reality coming tomorrow morning much more excruciating for her.

Mike had awakened her body from dormancy. He'd introduced her to pleasures that could be shared between a man and woman, some of which she'd never known before he'd dropped into her life.

"Like making love in the shower?" Mike teased and pulled away just enough to see her shadowed face in the near darkness of his bedroom. The glint in her eyes told him everything. He wanted to keep Khat's mind off tomorrow and frankly, he didn't want it to arrive, either, for different reasons. He felt her laugh, her breasts pressed suggestively against his chest. Khat could arouse a man from the grave with that sinuous body of hers.

"I've never made love in a shower before. It must be a SEAL thing. Water, maybe? Being a frogman?"

A laugh rumbled through his chest. "No, sex in the shower isn't a US Navy thing, Angel. Lots of people do it, and they aren't in the military." He shook his head and grinned. In some ways, Khat was so damned American, but having left at age eighteen and spending the rest of her life in the military, most of it in Afghanistan, shortened her personal life experience. It had protected her from growing up in the States and learning from different life situations everyone took for granted. In a sense, she'd been socially and personally marooned. By age twenty-nine, she had been fully shaped by the military world. As a teen, she was a young American girl on the verge of womanhood. Walking into the military at eighteen had honed her life as a woman in different ways.

Mike prayed that he'd get a chance to teach Khat about the many ways a man could love his woman. It sure as hell wasn't confined to a bed, but for now, Mike was okay with it. After six years of celibacy, about all Khat could handle was something tamer and within her limited and accepted experience.

However, the episode in the shower was new. And it made for a lot of laughs along the way because she simply didn't know how to participate. That was all right, he got to show her, and he had fulfilled her. At least for a while, and he smiled. Khat would never make it as a nun. She'd been celibate because of the choices she'd made.

He'd met his match, that was for sure. She was strong, assertive and certainly as far away from meek as a woman could get.

His body warmed once more because he liked her fire, her fearlessness beneath his hands and body. Mike got to thinking that many men would have been threatened by the power of her fierce womanhood, but he wasn't.

"I want you," Khat whispered, nibbling at his ear, moving her hips suggestively against him.

Mike turned his head, meeting her gaze. Oh, there was no question there was arousal in her shadowed eyes. "I get the feeling I'm being stalked."

She laughed softly, rising up on her elbow, kissing his chest, moving her hand lower until he tensed and groaned as she wrapped her fingers around his erection. "You are," she said softly against his ear, watching his eyes close, pleasure coming to his face. There was a power swirling within her, understanding herself as a woman and how she could tease and influence Mike as an equal. She'd never experienced it before him, but Khat found it empowering, and it spurred her sexual appetite to even brighter life within her.

"Now, be careful," he rasped.

"Why?" Khat licked his lower lip, feeling him tense. Moving her fingers teasingly up and down his erection, she saw him clench his teeth. There was something magical being able to have a man become malleable within her exploring hand. "I am stalking you, Michael Tarik." She met his mouth with passion, moving her tongue against his lower lip, going on the offense. He groaned and gripped her shoulders, pulling her away. Surprised at his strength as he lifted her over him, and Khat found herself straddled across Mike. Her thighs settled against his narrow hips. What was even more wonderful was her damp core gliding against his thick, warm erection. That sent earthquakes of fire tremoring through her, wiping out her mind, and her objectives melted away. He was experienced; she was not. And somehow, her youthful attempts to stalk him, please him, had turned out differently.

As she opened her eyes, her palms resting on his shoulders, she gave him a feral smile. "You don't play fair."

Mike gave her a slow, heated smile. "Never." He relished the arousal gleaming in her eyes. Sliding his hands down across her hip, he rasped, "Angel, we're both winners. I can feel you, and you're so wet."

His words made her clench her thighs, and Khat

pressed downward upon him, a sheet of skittering fire lacing up through her, making his belly spasm with need. She was going to say something, but his roughened hands caressed her breasts, his thumbs moving teasingly across her hardened nipples. A small cry echoed in her throat, and she moved forward, wanting more of the wild, shocky sensation that flowed hotly through her core. He thrust deep inside her.

Her lips parted, head tipping back as he filled her, triggering every sensitive spot within Khat. A choking sound of pleasure tore from her lips. She was paralyzed with the excruciating, scalding sensations he was creating by holding her captive against him. Another sound of raw satisfaction tore from her as he leaned up, suckling deeply upon each of her nipples. Her world started flying apart. She felt his deep thrust, felt her channel become heated, the fluids within her saturating him, building toward orgasm.

Mike released her nipple and wrapped his large hands around her hips, grinding her firmly down upon him. Her fingers spread in sudden ecstasy across his chest as he moved his hips, angling them, moving so deep she couldn't breathe. He maintained the hungry rhythm, triggering her core. The wild pace made her cry out, white-hot pressure built and consumed her. It was as if she were riding a beautiful stallion, her body glowing hotly, being held in the perfect position, giving her continued, indescribable, electric sensations.

The cauldron of pressure exploded within her, and Khat felt faint as the orgasm rolled throughout her like a tsunami. Lost in the heat of the powerful orgasm, his strength carrying her, he milked her willing body of every last vestige of hunger. Khat eventually collapsed against him; her breath came in pants as she heard Mike rasp her name and then surge into her, taking her, claiming her once and for all.

Khat could do nothing, so weak and spent. She closed her eyes as he filled her with his power, his thrusts deep, an animal growl rolling out of his chest as he spilled into her and made her feel claimed as never before. Mike could be a tender lover, but tonight…well, tonight was like the Fourth of July. Only, Khat thought, lost in the lust haze of sexual fulfillment, their bodies had created the delicious fireworks between them.

Mike smiled, gratified, as Khat lay limply against him. Finally, she was no longer hungry, and neither was he. He ran his hand lightly across her damp back, the scars much softer and more pliable now beneath his exploring fingertips. Her head lay on his shoulder, her breath moist and uneven. He absorbed the way Khat draped across his body, feeling a sense of possession of her in every way. Moving his hands down her damp flanks, he took the greatest chance of all. He whispered, "I love you, Khatereh. You're mine. We've always belonged together, my sweet desert woman." Mike had never told another woman he loved her, and he wasn't sure what her reaction would be to his admission.

As he moved his hand over her silky, dry hair, a fierce sense of wanting to protect her overwhelmed him. He had no idea if Khat loved him, but she was going to know how he felt toward her and let the chips fall where they may.

Khat moved her lips, feeling incredibly exhausted. Mike had spoken to her in Pashto, her language. *His desert woman.* Her body glowed in the aftereffects of orgasms that he'd triggered deep within her. Mike loved her. The words moved sweetly through her, building a new pathway into her frantically beating heart, twining around her, filling her in a new and radiant way. Khat moved her cheek against the damp hair on his chest, unable to think or speak. All she could do was feel and then feel some more.

Mike waited patiently, knowing she'd heard his admission. Finally, she eased off him and moved beside him, sliding her arm across his chest.

"I've never been in love before," Khat whispered, pressing her cheek against his shoulder.

"Neither have I," Mike admitted, her husky voice riffling through him. He took his fingers, taming her thick, crimson hair across her shoulder. "I never expected to fall in love." And then his mouth thinned. "Especially in a combat zone." And not with a woman who was in the military.

Lifting her lashes, Khat propped herself up on her elbow and studied his shadowed face. She saw concern in his expression as he turned to hold her gaze. "I don't know how this works, Mike."

He shrugged. "Our time isn't our own. We're military."

Pushing her hair away from her face, she saw his love for her mirrored in his narrowed eyes. This was as real as it got, Khat realized. "I like what we have. I want to go forward with it, Mike, but God, it looks daunting from where I stand."

Wasn't that the truth? Mike nodded. He slid his hand across her arm that lay on his chest. "Nothing worthwhile is ever easy, Angel." He could almost feel Khat thinking, weighing and juggling her life, her old world against this new one they'd created together. Which was more important to her? The call of her Afghan blood to protect her father's Shinwari villages? Or their new, fragile, softly unfolding love? She couldn't have both, and Mike knew it. The stress, the choice, weighed heavily in her gaze. Could his love for her make up the difference?

Mike had never wanted anything more than her. Khat deserved a chance to live, not merely survive. And where she was at right now, Mike knew he could lose her if she was allowed to return to the routine she'd known for so long. People who had PTSD, when pushed beyond a certain line within themselves, became distracted. They didn't know it, but an outsider looking in could easily spot it. And he knew distraction would get Khat killed sooner or later. It wasn't if, it was *when* it would happen.

"We live day to day," Mike told her, holding her warm gaze, feeling her love for him. "It's not going to be easy, Khat. But we have maturity under our belt. We're adults, and we'll handle it."

"I feel so torn, Mike. I've just found you. I love what we have." She pursed her lips, looking off into the darkness, thinking out loud. "My life isn't my own."

"Your life *is* your own," Mike said. "You control what your priorities are, Khat." He wasn't going to let her slide on this one. For too long, she'd followed her fervent Afghan blood, allowed it to run her, not the other way around. He saw her frown and consider his words. "What you feel is most important is where you'll make your choices," he added more gently.

Hanging her head, her hair a curtain around her,

Khat whispered, "I understand it more than you real-ize, Mike."

Feeling an icy hand move around his heart, he heard the strain in her voice. "Maybe," he said, rolling onto his side and sliding his arm beneath her neck as he eased her onto her back. "You need to make some per-sonal decisions. Maybe our meeting and falling in love is a new chapter in our lives, Khat. Maybe the way you've been living needs to be reassessed? That you deserve some good things coming into your life." He felt the tension rise in her as she considered the two choices. And they were choices.

"I feel," she said, searching his somber-looking eyes, "that I'm being selfish, Mike."

"What? Falling in love with me is a selfish thing?"

"My priority has been what I do. If I'm not out there…then those villages are at risk. People will die…"

"Falling in love is not a selfish thing to do, Angel." Mike leaned over, pressing a kiss to her wrinkled brow. "It's one of the beautiful things about life." He felt ter-ror taking deep root in his heart. How anyone could see loving another person as selfish had never occurred to him. But Khat was single-minded. She'd blocked out the rest of the world of possibilities for herself.

Until just now, with him.

As he looked deeply into her confused gaze, Mike saw the battle she was wrestling with. Loving him or loving the crusade that she'd undertaken to protect the people of her father's tribe. Which did she love more? It was a hell of a choice, and he wasn't at all sure which one Khat would choose in the end.

Closing her eyes, Khat muttered, "I just never ex-pected to ever fall in love, that's all."

Mike heard her pain and confusion. He knew Khat
was recalling her torture and the words her angry father had filled her head with—that no man would ever
love her after her disfigurement.

Mike held back his anger, understanding the context
of her words. He kissed her lips softly, feeling her immediate response. "Well," he said, his voice low with
feeling, "hold on to what we have, Khat. Love doesn't
happen often, and it needs to be tended by both people's
hands and hearts. We can surmount any challenge as
long as we lean upon one another, Khat. We can use
our love as a support and not choose something that
will tear us apart instead."

KHAT WAS MET by Travis Cooper as she walked into
the SEAL HQ with her duffel bag. Mike was right behind her.

"Hi, Travis," she greeted. "How are my mares?"

He opened the door for her. "Well, we've got a problem with your one mare, Mina." He nodded hello to
Mike.

Khat opened the door to her room and placed her
duffel bag on the bed and came out where Travis and
Mike stood in the hall waiting for her. All the happiness she'd felt in the past three days dissolved. "What's
wrong with Mina?"

"Well, ma'am, why don't we mosey on out to the
corral, and I'll show you the issue?" He settled the
black baseball cap on his head and opened the door
for her.

Mike saw Khat's immediate reaction. Worry. What
the hell was up? He was going to see Mac, but that
could wait. Travis knew horses, and he wondered what

had happened to Mina. She was Khat's main mount. Zorah was her backup replacement.

Khat saw her mares in the corral. When they saw her, both nickered and came over to the fence to greet her. Travis opened the gate and gestured for them to come in. She moved into the corral, petting her horses. They looked sleek, well-groomed and happy.

"What did you find?" Mike asked as Travis crouched on the left side of Mina, his long, spare hand around her upper front leg. Khat walked around, leaning over Travis's shoulder.

"Ma'am," he said, twisting a look up at Khat, "are you familiar with a horse popping a splint?"

She shook her head. "No. Tell me."

Travis moved his hand down below Mina's left knee. "At my father's ranch, we have quarter horses. Some are cutting horses, and their job is to cut a cow from the herd. It requires a lot of athletic ability, and it puts plenty of stress on the horse's cannon bone. That's this bone." He ran his hand down Mina's lower front leg. "There's a smaller bone beside it called a splint bone. It lays up against the cannon bone. When a horse is doing some serious, hard turns, fast stops and starts, really using their front legs to move, twist and turn, then it can tear the splint bone away from the cannon bone. What you get as a result is puffiness in the affected leg. And lameness if you don't catch it and do something about it in time."

Khat crouched down next to Travis. "And this has happened to Mina?"

"Yes, ma'am, it has." He moved his fingers lightly and showed her where the splint had torn away from the tissue that held it against the cannon bone. There was a small, hard knot where the splint had appeared. "Right here. Run your fingers downward. And then feel Mina's right cannon bone and make a comparison. That splint is still attached. You'll feel the difference. One is smooth to the touch, and the other has a hard bump on it." Travis unwound from his crouched position and moved aside so that Khat could feel the injury for herself.

Mike frowned. Travis stood beside him, hands on his hips, waiting for Khat to discover the difference. The look on her face turned worried.

"I feel it," she said, looking up at Travis.

"Yes, ma'am, it's a pretty bad splint. That's why her leg was always puffy below her knee. I discovered it right after you left for Bagram. I've been putting an oatmeal poultice on it daily, and it's reducing the inflammation real well."

"What does this mean?" Khat asked, standing, her hand across Mina's back.

Travis pushed the cap back on his head. "When my father's best cutting horse popped a splint, it meant giving him a long rest. Maybe two weeks to a month. What happens is when the splint is torn away from her cannon bone, her body is gonna produce calcium to fill the space between the cannon bone and the splint bone. It takes a number of weeks or a month for that to happen."

Her heart sank. "Rest? Complete rest?"

"Yes, ma'am, I'm afraid so." He gestured to Mina's affected leg. "If you don't give her that downtime, all you'll do is make her permanently lame in the long run. A splint can usually be handled by enforced rest. The other problem is you're riding her hard. Sharp turns, stops, starts, will always make a splint that's healed more likely to pop again." He shrugged. "Maybe you can ride her less? Or not for as long or hard as you usually do? What about riding Zorah instead? Her legs are fine."

Grimly, Khat said, "That isn't possible. Zorah isn't trained up like Mina is. She's my packhorse."

Travis looked over at Mike. "Did you get the Absorbine I asked for?"

"Yeah, I managed to find some. I've got it in my duffel bag. I'll bring it over here in a little bit." His concern was for Khat. She looked shattered by the bad news.

"What's Absorbine?" she asked Travis.

"It's a liniment, ma'am. It brings more blood flow into an injured area, helps it heal a little faster."

"And you rub this on her leg?" Khat felt her stomach clench tightly. She'd had Mina for years, and she couldn't do her job without her brave, stalwart mare.

"Yes, ma'am," he drawled. "What I've been doin' since I discovered her injury is rubbing her leg and then wrapping it with warm towels three times a day. Got a can of rolled oats from a navy chief over at the chow hall, and I've been makin' a mash out of it, placing it on her leg and keepin' it wrapped for the nighttime hours." He smiled a little. "I know you're upset about this, but your mare is responding well to the treatment. With the Absorbine, I'll just mix it with the oat mash, and that will help her heal up even quicker."

Khat gave him a grateful look. "Thanks, Travis. I didn't know she had a problem."

"I know, ma'am, but if it went undetected and you worked her hard like you're used to doing, she'd have come up lame soon enough. And then she'd be hobbling around, unable to bear much weight on that leg at all. You'd be screwed, to put it politely."

Shaking her head, Khat moved to Mina's head and gently scratched her ears, which the mare loved. "I don't want to make this worse than it already is."

"Your other mare," he said, gesturing to her, "is fine."

"Even though I do use Zorah more as a packhorse," Khat said, "I do ride her. I try to give Mina a day off when I can and use her instead." The problem was, Zorah wasn't trained for the kind of dangerous, hard riding that Mina was. And it would mean she had to train Zorah, which would put her at much greater risk and in more danger.

Travis nodded. "I can show you how to care for her. I'm happy to keep doin' it for you if you want."

She gave the SEAL a grateful look. "I need to figure a lot of things out, Travis. I have to talk to the chief about this, first. I was supposed to leave and go back on my op tomorrow night."

"I'll take care of your gal here in the meantime, ma'am. You go do what you need to do."

Khat looked over at Mike. "Can we talk?"

"Sure. Come on, we need to go to the chow hall and get lunch anyway." Mike turned to Travis. "On the way back, I'll bring that bottle of Absorbine with me."

"Sure nuff," Travis said. "Hey, by any chance, did you find a box of Lone Star beer?"

Grinning, Mike said, "Yeah, two boxes, bro. They're on a pallet that's coming off that Chinook right now. You might want to wander over there and guard it."

Snorting, Travis grinned widely and lowered the bill on his cap across his eyes. "No joke it needs to be guarded. If someone spots the name on the box, they'll steal it. I'm on my way."

Mike saw Khat go over to Zorah and pet her and give

her some attention. She looked stricken about the news. Privately, he was elated. It kept her here at Bravo, not back out on that op that should have been pulled years earlier. Keeping it all to himself, Mike walked over and gave her a hug.

"I'm sorry," he said.

Khat blew out a breath of air, wanting his contact. "This is a shock. It changes everything." Worried, she looked over at Mike, a serious expression on her face. "If I don't have Mina…I can't do what I do. And if I'm gone for two weeks or a month while she rests up, that gives Khogani an opening big enough to drive a truck through. He'll start attacking the villages again…"

Mike moved his hands along her tense shoulder. "But he doesn't know you aren't there."

Grimacing, Khat muttered, "That's true."

"Come on, let's go eat. We'll talk and figure something out." His heart broke because he saw the devastation in Khat's darkening green eyes. He could feel her reacting as if gutted, her whole world suddenly ripped away from her. Well, now he got to see how she was going to react once orders came down the food chain for her to stop her op in the mountains. This was just a taste of what was going to happen.

He squeezed her shoulders and then released her as they walked out of the paddock. Back at Bravo, they couldn't touch one another or kiss. It was a special hell to be living in, Mike decided.

"DO YOU THINK the chief would let me stay here with you at SEAL HQ while Mina rested up?" Khat asked, pushing her food around on her tray.

"I'm sure he would," Mike told her. "You already

have a room, and there's nothing he has to do for you
except let you hang out with us."

Mouth flattening, she muttered, "I need to talk to
him right away."

Nodding, Mike ate heavy because today was the
day he was officially off the injured list. From now
on, he would be included on up-and-coming patrols,
no longer tied down to lesson planning and being left
behind. "You should. Maybe Travis has already alerted
him about your horse being lame."

"This is a shock," Khat whispered, running her hand
across her cheek, pushing tendrils away. "I don't want
to be gone too long. I know Khogani will find out eventually." She chewed on her lower lip, looking away.

"Take it a step at a time, Khat." Mike wondered what
Mac would say. This was potentially a bombshell for
him, too. And he desperately wanted some time with
the chief to find out what he was doing to get Khat
permanently removed from the op.

"COME IN AND close the door," Mac told Mike.

Mike shut the door, and as he took his seat in front
of the master chief's desk, he asked, "You saw Khat
already? You heard that her mare's injured?"

"Yeah." Mac shrugged. "Good timing if you ask me,
but I played along and listened to her concerns. I told
her she was welcome to stay, that it wasn't a problem."

"And what have you found out about her op?" He
waited, holding his breath.

Mac leaned back in his chair. "I got the proof she's
been out far too long and needs to be reeled back in. I
sent it to Admiral Fraser. It's in his hands."

"What do you think he'll do?"

"The evidence is there in black-and-white. He knows as well as we do, you put someone out in combat too long without downtime, they're a dead man walking. I think he'll make a call to General Stevenson and pass the info on to her. In the end, it's up to that general, because it's her op."

Running his fingers through his hair, Mike growled, "If she cares about the women in her op, she'll do something."

"I think she will," Mac said. "The question is what? The good news is Khat is grounded for up to a month. Not by us. But by her horse."

"She's uptight as hell about not getting back to her op area," Mike muttered.

"I've got to run this by our officers, but I've been thinking of bringing her along on a patrol with us. She's a paramedic, and we can always use medical help when we're out in the field. There's a load of charity clothing and medical supplies coming into a village later this week. It's a Shinwari village, and we promised the head man of it some nation-building support. Maybe get Khat involved in that way. It's a helluva lot safer than what she's been doing out there alone. At least this will keep her occupied."

Mike felt relief. "That would be good."

Mac nodded. "I'll know more after talking to the officers. They have to wave their magic wand over my idea and approve it. In the meantime, you're back on patrols."

Grinning, Mike said, "It's about time."

"I want you to head up that four-man team going to that village where Emma Shaheen is going to be flying in the charity stuff for those people. It's five days from now, so get acquainted with the details."

Mike rose and nodded. "Music to my ears." As he opened the door and left the office, he crossed his fingers Khat would be allowed on his patrol. It was a perfect mission for her. And for him.

KHAT SPENT HER TIME with her horses, feeling torn up inside. She used a brush to groom Mina, who stood quietly in the cross ties within the barn. The midafternoon sun was hot. She'd opened the door to allow the mountain breeze to chase away the worst of it.

As she smoothed the soft dandy brush along her mare's short, strong back, she wanted to cry. Feeling as if she was at some kind of invisible crossroads, guilt warred with her love for Mike. Khat worried about Khogani killing more innocent Shinwari people. They had no way to defend themselves, simple farmers who lived off the land.

She loved Mike. He'd given her hope she'd lost so long ago. And belief that she wasn't some kind of freak destined to live out the rest of her life in loneliness. He'd shown her she was worthy of being loved. And she was worthy of living her life, not hiding from it.

Khat rubbed the sweat off her brow with the back of her hand, brushing Mina's rump. For the first time, she realized just how dependent she'd become on her horses. She'd never be able to accomplish what she'd done without them. They were her transportation, her escape from the Taliban, her survival. On foot, she was in far more jeopardy than if she were on horseback. She could be a sniper, take her shots and ride off at a hard gallop before the Taliban could ever find her.

Without Mina, she was on foot and far more exposed. The chance of her being found was too high for her to take such a risk. What was she going to do?

At the same time, Mike held her heart, and Khat knew it. She didn't want to lose him, either. Hating the fact she'd have to make a decision one way or the other, sooner or later, left her feeling raw and vulnerable. She loved him. But where did responsibility begin and end? Those villagers knew her and were family to her. She had a fierce, protective feeling toward all of them. Her father's people. *Her* people. Their blood ran in her veins. How could she turn her back on them and walk away? Choose love for herself over them?

Making an unhappy noise in the back of her throat, Khat felt frustrated. And yet, every time she pictured Mike in her mind, she felt her heart swell with a fierce love equal to the love she had for her people.

Travis ambled in with the bottle of Absorbine in his hand. "Howdy, ma'am." He held up the bottle. "Mike just gave me this."

She nodded. Travis was easygoing, his voice a soft, Texas drawl. He made her feel less wretched with his quiet presence. "Thanks, Travis. I really appreciate all you've done."

Travis set the bottle up on a shelf next to the metal container that had the rolled oats in it. He gave her a loose smile and said, "Happy to do it, ma'am."

"Travis? Do me a favor? Call me Khat. I'm not a ma'am. Okay?"

He shrugged, "Just my manners, ma— I mean, Khat." He took off his cap and pushed his fingers through his longish hair. "I imagine you're pretty upset about your mare's injury?"

Rolling her eyes, Khat walked around the other side of Mina, beginning to brush her long, ebony neck. "Just a little."

"She's a fine-lookin' animal," Travis said, leaning against the wall, his arms loose around his chest. "Good legs on her. And a nice disposition."

"She's saved my life so many times, I've lost count."

"All the more reason to lay her up for a while," he said. "How long you been doin' this op with her?"

"Five years."

He whistled softly. "A lesser horse's legs would have caved in long before this. Those mountains are nothing but brutal on legs, man or beast."

"It's rough work for both of us," she agreed quietly, brushing Mina's chest and sloped shoulder. Just currying her horse was helping to ease her tension.

"I hope you don't take this the wrong way," Travis began, hesitating, "but you and your mare both need a long-term rest."

She smiled a little at the Texan. "I don't have any leg splints, Travis."

He grinned sheepishly, "No, ma'am.... I mean, Khat, I know that. You take mighty good care of those horses of yours. But I wonder if you do the same for yourself?" He gave her a curious look.

"Not you, too," Khat growled. "God, I thought Mike was bad enough, griping I'd lost too much weight and needed to put some pounds back on."

Travis scratched his well-trimmed beard. "Well, we have a sayin' in Texas. 'Never miss a chance to rest your horse.'"

"It's a good saying," Khat agreed.

"I'm applyin' it to you," Travis corrected. "You

should never miss a chance to rest yourself. It appears you've not done that. Your care extends to your horses, not yourself." He shrugged. "Just my two cents' worth. I'll drop by your room tonight around dusk. I'll show you how to make that poultice for your mare and apply it to her leg."

Travis might be laid back, his voice quiet and thoughtful, but he had an eye on him, Khat thought. "After chow?" she asked.

"Yes, ma'am…"

Well, hell! Khat leaned down, brushing Mina's hind quarter and lower leg. She smarted beneath the SEAL's observation. Mike didn't mince words about it, either.

Mouth tightening, Khat was beginning to feel like she needed to take stock of herself. Maybe she had been out alone for too long. Maybe she needed to seriously look at herself. She knew she was run-down. She wasn't getting much sleep, maybe three or four hours a night. And she could never relax knowing the Taliban were always around her. Khat felt it was just one more load on her shoulders right now.

Mike was her only safe haven; someone she could relax and talk honestly with. He never judged her. He just listened, and she appreciated that quality in him so much. Wiping her sweaty brow again, Khat wondered what the next few weeks would bring.

CHAPTER THIRTEEN

"HEY," TRAVIS CALLED urgently to Mike, trotting down the avenue of tents where the SEALs had their area.

Mike had just left his tent, getting ready for his patrol. Travis was one of his men, and he looked upset. The morning was crisp, the sun not even on the horizon yet. "What's up?" he called, moving his ruck around on his shoulders.

Skidding to a halt, Travis was out of breath. "Your lady's gone!"

"What?"

Travis hitched a finger over his shoulder. "I went out just now to check on the mares before we left. Zorah is gone, and Mina's still in the corral."

Mike's heart plunged. "Is it possible Zorah got loose? Got out of the corral?"

"No way. The gate's locked. Listen, Khat's Western saddle is gone. Everything's gone. She left the packhorse equipment behind."

"Let's go see the chief. He might know something." They both took off at a fast trot.

The first thing Mike did once he got to HQ was stop at Khat's door and knock on it. She might be sleeping, he hoped. He knocked again. No answer.

"Khat?" he called. "Are you in there?"

Travis shook his head, looking grim.

Mike opened the door. His gaze immediately flew to the made bed. There were two letters sitting on the bedspread. Cursing softly, he picked them up. One was addressed to him. The other to the master chief. He handed it to Travis and asked him to take it to Mac. Breathing hard from the run, Mike tore the envelope open with trembling fingers.

Mike,

    I'm sorry to do this to you. I am taking off for my op. I've taken Zorah and left Mina behind. I hope Travis will continue to take care of her. Please don't be angry with me. I know you felt I needed rest, but I can't ignore my people. I can't allow them to be left open to being killed by Khogani. Please forgive me. I'm already missing you.

Love, Khat

"Son of a bitch!" he snarled, whirling around, barging out the door, past Travis and heading for Mac's office.

Mac was standing and reading the letter Khat had left behind for him when he entered.

"She's gone," Mike growled.

Mac shook his head. "Dammit." He handed Mike the letter.

As Mike read the letter, which was a short thank-you note to Mac for allowing her to stay with them, he heard the chief talking to security. Lifting his head, he dropped the letter on his desk.

"Well, hell, this woman knows how to create chaos," Mac muttered, sitting down. "She signed out at the security gate at 2200 last night. She's got a seven-hour head start on us and by now, she's in the mountains."

Mike tried to think through the haze of shock and pain. "Is there anything we can do to get her back here?" he demanded.

"No, because I haven't heard anything from General Stevenson. Until or if there's a change of orders that comes down the pipeline to us, she's within her legal military rights to come and go as she pleases. She hasn't broken any regs."

Mike stood there, feeling as if the floor had fallen out from beneath him. "I said good-night to her at 2100 last night," he said. Closing his eyes, he replayed that moment. Khat had looked sad last night. He'd kissed her in the barn, and she had cried. Now he knew why. She knew she was leaving. Saying goodbye to him. *Why didn't I see this coming?*

Desperate, Mike said, "I need to go after her. Find her."

Mac gave him a hard look. "And do what? Haul her off a legitimate op? Come on, you know better than that! That would earn *you* a court martial."

Wiping his mouth, Mike knew the chief was right. "She's going to get killed out there, Mac. You know that."

Holding up his hand, he muttered, "She's an accident waiting to happen. That's why all of us were busting our asses as fast as we could to protect her against herself. But she must have sensed it. She's cagey, Tarik. She hasn't survived out there that long without developing a lot of peripheral senses."

"I didn't give her any reason to bolt," Mike argued,

feeling tears in the backs of his eyes. He gulped several times, forcing them away.

Travis rounded the corner. "I think I did," he admitted, giving them an apologetic look.

"What the hell are you talking about?" Mike demanded.

"Khat and I had a talk yesterday afternoon at the corral. I told her she should take better care of herself." Travis rolled his eyes. "I told her she should take a rest like her mare needs, that in Texas, the one thing we do is give our horse a rest anytime we can. I told her she needed to rest herself." Giving both men a sheepish look, he added, "I shoulda kept my damn mouth shut. I'm sorry, Mike." He reached out, resting his hand on Mike's shoulder for a moment. "I seriously screwed up, pardner."

"Bullshit," Mac snapped. "She'd heard the same thing from Tarik and me."

"Well," Travis drawled, "maybe I was the straw that broke the camel's back?"

Mike shook his head in turmoil. "It's not your fault, Travis. Don't go there. When we were at the Shaheen villa for three days, Emma made a big deal about how Khat was underweight, that she needed time off."

"That lady is as stubborn as a mule."

Right now Mike was ready to agree with him. "She's like a horse with blinders on—seeing only what's right in front of her, not the bigger picture."

"Okay, you boys need to put this in your box. You got an op in thirty minutes. Get your shit together," Mac ordered.

Rousing himself, Mike nodded. "We're ready," he

said, and he nodded to Travis, who turned and left the office.

As they moved into the big room, meeting the other members of the team, Mike got down to business. They'd be taking a Night Stalker helicopter to the Shinwari village where they'd make sure no Taliban were around. That way, Emma could land her helo, the charity items on the pallet safely off-loaded. She'd take off immediately because helos were the chosen prey of Taliban carrying RPGs.

When he got back from the op this evening, he'd see if Mac had heard from Khat. Probably not, because her handler was Commander Hutton out of J-bad. Dammit! If they'd had more time with one another, Mike was sure that he could have convinced Khat to stay. Somehow, she'd sensed something was coming and ran.

MAC WAS DRINKING coffee when Mike brought in his report on the patrol from earlier today. He took the papers.

"Have you heard anything yet?" Mike asked, standing at the doorway.

"A little. Come in and sit down."

Stomach tight, Mike didn't like the look on the chief's face.

"I called Commander Hutton just a little while ago. He said Khat had checked in with him at 1700, and that it was business as usual. I told him what had happened, our concerns for her."

"And?"

"He could care less. He completely ignored me."

"Dammit," Mike snarled, his hands closing into fists. "She's got her supply line through us. That means the pallet of food, ammo and alfalfa hay that just came in needs to be airlifted out to her at some point."

"Khat hasn't checked in by radio with me yet," Mac said. "She's going to want those supplies sooner, not later. My hunch is she'll get settled back into her op area and then make a call to us as to where we drop those supplies."

"I wonder if she'll use the same cave I was in?"

"Probably," Mac said.

"This is a cluster fuck," Mike snarled, feeling his heart tearing, the pain radiating through his chest.

"All we can do is hope like hell General Stevenson, who's in charge of this Operation Shadow Warriors, gives Admiral Fraser a call and she makes some changes in Sergeant Shinwari's operating orders. Until then, there's nothing we can do, Tarik. Not a fucking thing."

Opening the door, Mike left the office, staggered by the series of events. He was sure the chief knew he and Khat had a connection to one another.

He made it back to his tent in the early evening hours, the heat of the day broken. Stowing his gear, he was hungry and headed to the chow hall. Dammit, he had to think! He loved Khat. And she was putting herself in the line of fire again. As always.

He felt desperate and clawing at any possibility to get her back to the safety of Bravo. As he walked over to the chow hall, deep in thought, Mike realized Khat had a choice here. He couldn't haul her back against her will. That wouldn't serve anyone, and he'd lose her for sure with any strong-armed methods.

More than anything, Mike didn't want to lose the love he had for Khat. Their tie with one another was too fresh, too young, and couldn't compete fully with her years of being the human shield protecting her people. He didn't doubt Khat loved him; he knew damn well she did. Mike realized she thought she'd made the best decision she could. Never mind that it was a flawed decision.

Her heart, however, was a different matter. He hoped in the coming weeks, something would come from General Stevenson. She was their last hope. The SEALs and Mac in particular, could do nothing else. Their hands were tied.

KHAT WAS HOME. But the waterfall cave no longer felt like home to her. Heart heavy, Khat was exhausted from the two-day ride.

It was evening, the cool mountain air making her shiver. She'd already taken care of Zorah, fed her and gotten her bedded down for the night. The musical sound of the waterfall made her feel minimally better. Everything she did as she prepared herself an MRE for dinner, reminded her of Mike. His voice. What he'd said to her. His charismatic smile that always went straight to her heart.

Kneeling by the metal grate, Khat heated up the MRE with the chemical pouch. Tears came to her eyes as she waited for the meal to heat up. Mike… She felt as if her heart had been flayed. What must he think of her? Would he understand why she had to leave him? It wasn't because of him. He would probably think she was running away from him, but she wasn't. Would he realize she was running toward her responsibility for her people? Would he forgive her? She wiped her eyes, trying to stop a sob that wanted to tear out of her.

There was still a lifeline between them. Of sorts. She knew his platoon would be there only for another four months, and then rotate back to the States. She would probably get handed off from Mac to the next chief of the new platoon coming in to replace them at Bravo.

Rubbing her cheeks, the tears fell whether Khat wanted them to or not. She had one reason to ride back to Camp Bravo. Mina was still there, and she knew Mike and Travis would take care of her. Maybe she'd call Mike on the sat phone in a month and find out if her leg was healed. Khat would ride back to Bravo to pick her up. Then she could see Mike one last time before he left. Her heart felt shredded, and she pressed her hand against it, the pain almost unbearable.

Every time she thought of Mike leaving, Khat felt intense anguish. She felt as if she were bleeding out, the heaviness in her chest nearly too much for her to bear. She felt gutted by her decision to leave Bravo. She didn't want to leave him. Mike had been a perfect match for her. He loved her. He didn't care if her body was permanently scarred. He accepted her fully and with open arms and an open heart.

Glumly, Khat removed the MRE to the tray. Peeling back the covering, she wasn't even hungry. Too many people had told her she was underweight, so she'd try to remedy that.

After forcing herself to finish the meal, Khat took a welcome shower beneath the coolness of the waterfall. Getting the sweat, grime and dirt scrubbed off her skin felt so good. She wished Mike were here to enjoy it with her. Soon Khat climbed into her well-used sleeping bag and fell into an exhausted sleep. Tomor-

row she would make plans to hunt down Khogani and
his men anywhere she could find them.

KHAT AWOKE FEELING drugged the next morning. She'd
overslept, glancing at her watch. It was 0800. Normally,
she was up before dawn. After feeding Zorah and giving her water, she sat down to eat a breakfast MRE.
Her mind was on strategy. Tactics. Without Mina, she
had no packhorse, no way to carry her necessary medi-
cines and equipment to the villages.

Chewing on the rubbery egg omelet, she forced all
the uninspiring food down. Khat remembered Mike
making her breakfast on the second morning, working
with him in Emma's kitchen. He made them an awe-
some omelet of eggs, bacon, black olives and accom-
panied with savory Middle Eastern spices. She had
made the toast, a simple enough job. Just working beside him, their flowing conversation between one another, lulled her and made her ache.

Mike was the voice of reason in comparison to her
powerful emotional passion that lived on the surface
of her skin.

As she drank her Darjeeling tea from the chipped
mug, Khat closed her eyes and pictured Mike naked in
bed with her. He had so many scars on his body, too.
Not from torture, but from being a SEAL. She never
truly realized how much these men suffered and were
in pain. Mike had taken a bullet to his left calf, and she
knew sometimes it hurt him. But he never complained.
He just bore up under it and got on with whatever he
felt was important. It didn't slow him down. He had so
many cuts, short and long across his legs, from sliding
down scree, or being blown off his feet, landing upon

rocks. Khat had seen deep bruising on his back, the purplish color never going away.

There were other areas of his magnificent body where she had felt swelling. Again, from the hard training SEALs underwent eighteen months out of every two-year cycle. Once, he'd lost his grip on a fast rope out of the helicopter and fallen ten feet onto the deck of a carrier. That place he hit on his hip was still swollen to this day, the tissue permanently damaged. And that had occurred when he was twenty-two years old.

They were both hurt in various ways, Khat realized, sipping her tea. Hurt, but never letting any of it stop them from their objective or goal. Hurting wasn't a reason to give up or quit. They were so alike that it shook Khat on a deeper level of herself. She found Mike to be courageous. Yet why didn't she see herself in that way?

Closing her eyes, she took in a deep breath and then released it. The answer was: it was about duty. Her father had drilled into her from a very young age that the young owed duty to their elders, the helpless, the widows and the village as a whole. And she'd taken his fiercely spoken words into her passionate, driven heart.

Opening her eyes, Khat stared around her cave. The munching sounds of Zorah eating calmed her, as did the music of the waterfall. What took away her constant anxiety was thinking about Mike. Just his presence made it dissolve. He had a powerful effect upon her. His voice quieted her anxiety, allowed her to relax. His touch…oh, God…his touch electrified her, awakening her as a woman, making her aware of how beautiful she was in his eyes, and how responsive she was beneath his skillful hands.

Khat finished her tea and then saddled Zorah. She'd

been gone a week, and she knew the Taliban were constantly shifting the trails they rode upon. Needing to
test out her mare, Khat was going to ease back into
her op.

MIKE HAD JUST stepped into Mac's office with a question when the sat phone on his desk beeped. Mac held
up his hand and indicated to him to sit down.

"Chief, this is Sergeant Shinwari."

Mac's brows rose. "It's good to hear from you, Sergeant."

"I'm calling about my horse, Mina. Is her leg healed
up yet?"

Mike sat up as Mac gestured to the phone. His pulse
took off. It was Khat! Three damn long weeks had gone
by. Three of the longest weeks of his life. Mike's hands
became damp, wiping them on his trousers.

"Your horse is fine according to Travis. Are you
coming in to pick her up?"

"Yes, if it's all right with you, I'll see you in two
days. I'll come in under cover of darkness, say 0200?"

"That's fine," Mac said. "I'll alert the front gate.
You've got clearance anyway, but it won't hurt to let
the marines know a rider is coming in."

"Thank you. Second, I'd like that pallet of goods
dropped when I return with my second horse. When I
come into Bravo, I'd like to talk to you about the drop
details."

"Yes, we'll work on a plan. Stay safe coming in, Sergeant." He clicked off the sat phone and looked across
the desk at Tarik. "You heard?"

"Yes."

"Meet her at 0200 two days from now at the security gate."

"No problem." Hell, he was ecstatic! Showing it wouldn't be a good idea in front of the master chief, however.

Rubbing his beard in thought, Mac leaned back in his chair, staring up at the ceiling.

"You have a horse background, right, Tarik?"

"Yes. Why?"

Mac drummed his fingers on the desk, brow wrinkled. Finally, after several minutes he said, "We haven't heard anything from General Stevenson yet. It's been three weeks. I want you to start setting up a mission for me. I want you to ride back out with Sergeant Shinwari to her op area when she leaves with her other horse. I've been thinking of ways to get her off that fifty square-mile area that she patrols. I want you to go along with her and look at objectives, places we can put snipers. Get the lay of the land. If we can coordinate with the SEALs out of J-bad, each of us sending a rotating sniper team into that area, it could replace what she's doing."

"I'll get right on it."

"Once I approve the mission, I'll be dovetailing it with Senior Master Chief Wilson in J-bad."

Mike's brows raised. "You've already discussed this idea with him?" Senior Master Chiefs were considered the most powerful of the navy enlisted personnel. They certainly ruled the SEAL universe, Mike knew.

"Steve Wilson was my mentor," Mac said with a little smile. His eyes sparkled. "Maybe we can do a workaround on this problem and get Sergeant Shinwari a sidekick."

He grinned. "Shades of the Lone Ranger and Tonto in reverse?"

Shrugging, Mac said, "That has a nice ring to it, Tarik. Get on this. I want this mission workup like yesterday."

A DAY LATER, Mike was in the master chief's office with a preliminary workup on the mission. He had it on his Toughbook computer, and Mac was leaning over the laptop, studying his mission prep.

"You need a horse," he murmured, looking up at Mike.

"Sgt. Shinwari uses her two horses. I won't be able to use either one. I figure I can go to the nearest village and buy an Afghan pony and make do."

"Okay," he murmured, studying it further. "You're estimating three weeks with her? To see everything that's under her op?"

"Yes, but that can change. Taliban crawl all over the area where she operates. I'm estimating it due to unforeseen circumstances."

"I see you're recommending a drone overhead to cover you two?"

"I can use my laptop and satellite connection. I'm interested in getting the lay of the land, not stumbling into firefights with the Taliban."

Nodding, Mac said, "Good thought…" And then he sat up. "You know, according to Senior Chief, Sergeant Shinwari's greatest strength is her actionable intel she gives to J-bad SEAL HQ. She's constantly in and out of those border villages, picking up information on the Taliban coming over the Af-Pak border, talking to the women who know just as much, or more, than their husbands do. I think this is one reason why Hutton and her handler before him have allowed her to stay as long as she has. She has good connections and relations with the people. He was saying that her intel is always trustworthy, and you know how hard it is to get good intel out in the badlands."

Mike knew. He'd been on any number of patrols because of perishable intel given by a local farmer. And it turned out to be a dead end. Or wrong. Sometimes his team had been set up for an ambush with that kind of intel. "That doesn't give them the right to take advantage of her, Mac. I don't care what anyone says. She's spread too thin and done it too long."

"I don't disagree. Someone like her, though, is a gold mine. If I were her handler, she'd be taking six months off during the winter and rotate back to the States and decompress. Then she could return in the early spring when the snow starts to melt around here, and go back to work."

Mike kept his mouth shut. He was emotionally involved with Khat, and anything he said would prove it. So he just nodded while the chief continued to appraise his workup on the mission.

"Good, you'll go in hajii."

"I already look Afghan," Mike said. "Wearing Pashtun clothes will prove it." Going hajii meant going undercover, dressed in the clothes a Shinwari tribesman would wear.

Mac grinned. He tapped the laptop screen. "I like this. You'll be introduced as her long lost cousin from America. Good touch. People won't see you as an outsider, then."

"Might be able to talk to the boys and men. Intel comes from everywhere," he said.

"I like this idea. When people see Sergeant Shin-wari show up in the village and they want to know why you're tagging along, you're there to guard her."

"Right. I'll just tell the elders that the Taliban is actively hunting for her."

"Well," Mac said dourly, "you do know that they recently put a bounty on her head? A million US dollars."

His eyes widened. "No. I didn't know that."

"Yeah, CIA picked up radio and cell phone chatter between the Taliban on the border talking to the war lords sitting in Pakistan who fund them earlier today. They don't have a photo of her. What they do have is that she has red hair. They specifically said a long, red braid down her back."

"Shit," Mike muttered, pinching the root of his nose with his index finger and thumb. This wasn't a good thing for Khat. At all. Mike wondered if she was aware of the price on her head. Would her village start getting death letters nailed on their doors by the Taliban? Anyone home getting one, the occupants were considered dead and would be, very soon.

"I don't think any Shinwari villages are going to give her up," Mac said, "but that red braid of hers... She's going to have to hide it or cut most of her hair off."

Grimacing, Mike nodded. Khat had such beautiful, thick hair. "She won't like this."

"No, but what's the alternative? She wears that red braid where everyone can see it, and she might as well be wearing a sign that says Shoot Me."

"I assume you're going to talk to her about all this?" Mike did not want Khat to know of his involvement.

"Yeah, it's mine to handle, no problem."

"Good luck on getting her to cut off her hair." He grinned a little. Mike imagined she'd dig her heels in and refuse. He couldn't blame her. Her long hair was her only nod to her femininity while she worked in a man's world of black ops.

"I'm not a betting man," Mac mumbled, finishing reading the patrol. "This looks good. Well thought out. Get to that local, nearby village before she arrives here at Bravo."

"Mind if I take Travis with me? He's got an eye for horseflesh, too."

Mac snorted. "You couldn't stop him from coming along with you."

Chuckling, Mike stood and picked up his computer. "I want a rifle and eyes watching my back while I try to find a horse."

Grinning, Mac said, "Send your workup to the printer. I'll add a few notes and pass it up to the officers to sign off on."

As Mike walked back to the desk in the big room, he could barely hold in his excitement over seeing Khat again. He was grateful to the chief, who, as a SEAL, made it his mission in life to think outside the box. He certainly had on this one. Best of all, he'd be with Khat, protecting her. That made Mike feel better. She needed a partner. And after she arrived at Bravo and he got Khat alone, he was going to kiss the hell out of her.

CHAPTER FOURTEEN

KHAT COULD BARELY keep her expression neutral as she approached the security gate that led to Camp Bravo at 0200. On the other side of the fence, laced with concertina wire on top of it, she could see Mike waiting for her. Her heart was in chaos. The moon was full, and she didn't need her NVG goggles to see his deeply shadowed face twenty feet away.

The marine guard came forward, and she handed him her identification. Once the marine nodded, she dismounted from weary Zorah.

The gate rolled open and she pulled the reins over her Arabian's hanging head and trudged forward up the slightly angled slope. Mike's glittering gaze never left hers. He was dressed in his SEAL gear, only a pistol at his side. There couldn't be any sign of affection between them and as she walked up to him, she didn't avoid his gaze. She tried to prepare herself for his anger, but she saw none in his expression.

"Let me take your horse," Mike coaxed softly, taking the reins from her gloved fingers.

Nodding, Khat felt the brush of his calloused fingers against her own. Heat tunneled through her. Her pulse skyrocketed. Mike fell in step with her. They didn't talk for fear of being overheard and instead, moved in the direction of the SEAL compound and the barn with the paddock behind it. Was he angry with her? He didn't look it, but he had his game face on, which meant she couldn't know what was going on emotionally with Mike.

Once they left the security area, she looked over at him. He felt somber to her, but her normal ability to sense things was partially gone because of the exhausting two-day ride. "How are you?" she asked in a low tone. When they turned down an avenue without tents on either side, she reached out and briefly touched his lower arm. She saw him react. His mouth softened.

"I'm okay," Mike answered, glancing to his left, studying her. "How about you?"

"Usual," Khat said quietly. "The Taliban is grouping near Bravo. I had to dodge a lot of patrols. I need to tell Chief McCutcheon tomorrow morning. I know you have drones, and he might already know about it, but if he doesn't, someone should be made aware. It smells like a buildup to me, Mike." She rubbed her gritty brow. "It doesn't feel good to me."

"Mac knows about it. He wants to see you tomorrow morning after you wake up, though," he told her. He led the horse around the single-story cinder-block building and halted in front of the small barn. "I'll open the door for you."

Taking the reins, Khat waited. It felt good to be on the ground and not riding. She was stiff and sore from the journey. Her heart squeezed with trepidation as she watched Mike open the barn door for her and the horse. Feeling scared that he was angry with her, although he didn't look that way nor had his voice indicated it, Khat led her horse into the barn. She automatically took off the bridle and attached the cross ties to the mare's halter. The door quietly closed, and the low lights snapped on.

Mike turned, getting his first good look at Khat in three weeks. She had pulled off her black hood, and it fell around her shoulders, revealing her mussed red hair bound in a single, long braid down her back. He took the bridle from her hand and placed it on a hook on the wall.

"Come here," he growled, sliding his arm around her waist. If she was going to push him away, it would happen now.

A soft gasp of surprise tore from Khat, his movement swift and sure. Mike hauled her into his arms, his eyes narrowed and gleaming. As his hand cupped the back of her head, the other low on her back, he tipped Khat's head, leaving her mouth available to him.

Breath catching, her heart leaped with joy as he leaned down, his mouth moving powerfully against her lips. A moan tore out of her, and she threw her arms around his shoulders, meeting and matching the fervor of his welcoming kiss. Lashes sweeping downward, Khat strained to be as close as she could against his hard, masculine body. An ache grew in her heart as she matched his hunger for her. His breath was moist, punctuated against her cheek. Her chest tightened with unshed tears, with unraveling emotions she'd stuffed deep within her since leaving Mike. He held her gently in his arms, but his mouth let her know he hadn't stopped loving her for one second. Guilt flooded her, and tears came.

Khat tasted the salt of them as their lips melded against one another. Her heart was wild with need of his touch, his smell, his beard rasping against her sensitive skin. The heat of her tears continued, and she couldn't stop them.

Mike eased from her mouth, brought Khat upright, holding her in his arms. Their breathing was chaotic. Her lips were parted, wet with her tears. Her eyes...oh, God, her eyes were distressed, and he saw the anguish in them. He framed her face, using his thumbs across her cheeks to remove the tears. "Why are you crying, Angel?" he asked huskily, holding her gaze.

Khat felt her whole world cracking and falling into shambles around her feet as she stood against him. "I'm sorry," she managed, moving her hands across his shoulders. "I didn't mean to hurt you, Mike. I—I didn't think you'd forgive me for leaving you like I did." She closed her eyes, feeling as if her heart were being crushed in her chest. "I thought you would try to stop me from leaving. I didn't want to do it that way, but I had no choice."

When Khat lifted her lashes, Mike growled and leaned down, taking her trembling mouth, tasting the salt of her tears. "Angel, if you love someone," he whispered against her mouth, "it doesn't get destroyed that easily. I would not have stopped you from leaving. Okay? All you had to do was find me, sit me down and we'd discuss it like adults. Next time? Give me a chance."

Sniffing, Khat pulled out of his grasp, wiping her cheeks with the backs of her hands. He shifted his hands to her shoulders and she saw the warmth burning in his eyes. "You're right. I handled it very badly. I—I didn't trust you, and I should have." Khat gave him a look of abject apology.

He smiled a little; his voice was low with emotion.

"I'm just glad to see you again. Relationships are built a day at a time, Angel. We just have to keep talking to one another. We'll work up and over these hurdles together. All right?" Mike saw instant relief in her expression, her cheeks damp, her eyes showing her raw vulnerability. He could feel how stressed Khat was, and he had no intention of making her feel guilty about her decision. "Come on," he rasped, "let's get your mare put away for the night. Why don't you go over and say hello to Mina while I get Zorah unsaddled?"

She nodded, a lump in her throat. Everything seemed so natural between them, as if she hadn't walked out of his life three weeks ago. Khat opened Mina's box stall, calling softly to her mare.

Mina nickered and walked up to her, nuzzling into her opened hands. She heard Mike speaking softly to Zorah as he unsaddled her. Everything seemed so right. An ache built in her heart as she turned and watched him quickly brush her horse down, the care he took and his gentleness toward the mare. He was that way with her, too.

Feeling adrift, guilt savaging her for walking out of his life without any kind of an explanation except for a letter, Khat leaned her head against Mina's sleek neck. What was she doing? Torn between wanting Mike, wanting the life he offered her and her duty to her people, she trembled inwardly, miserable. Patting her mare, she rubbed Mina's small, delicate ears, the mare's eyes closing with pleasure.

"Come on," Mike called from the entrance to Mina's stall. "Want a shower?"

She hugged Mina, kissed her on the neck and then turned. "I'd love a hot shower. All I was thinking about

the past twenty miles tonight was seeing you again."
Khat stepped out of the stall, and Mike slid the door
closed. Holding out her hands, they were dirty and felt
gritty. The sand was so fine in Afghanistan, it got into
every crevice and crack of a person's body.

Mike nodded. "As soon as Mac told me you were
coming in, I couldn't sleep. Let's go," he murmured,
shutting off the light and opening the door.

Outside, Khat waited for him. "You don't have to
walk me over to the showers. I know where they are."

"I want to escort you over there. Let's go to your
room first. I got everything you need in there to take
over to the shower," he said, his hand against her back,
guiding her around the building.

Mike wasn't angry with her, and he wasn't going to
leave her. A little more of Khat's fear melted. Just his
voice calmed her. It always had.

He reached the door to the HQ first and opened it
for her. "I'll wait for you out here. The door to your
room is open," he told her quietly.

Tiredness combined with emotional distress weighed
on Khat's shoulders as she stepped into the quiet, dark
HQ. The moonlight was enough for her to see the door
to her room, and she quickly gathered up all the items,
including the blue terry-cloth bathrobe that was three
sizes too big for her. Khat smiled, grateful for Mike's
thoughtfulness.

She met him outside, and they walked to the showers
without speaking. Khat slipped inside while he waited.
The sense of protection was strong around him tonight,
and she could see it in his dark eyes, feel it radiating
powerfully around him and invisibly embracing her.

Mike waited patiently outside, leaning against the wall near the shower entrance, always alert and watching.

It was quiet at this time of morning. Cold, the wind blowing off and on, near freezing, and the black velvet sky above held glittering, diamond-like stars so close it was breathtaking. Whether it was because Bravo sat at eight thousand feet in the Hindu Kush mountains or the lack of air pollution, Mike always found the stars amazingly beautiful.

His thoughts swung back to Khat. She looked absolutely wary upon seeing him. But her kiss told him she loved him, wanted him. There was nothing shy about her passion for him. That she was anticipating he would be angry and upset with her bothered him. Was it her father who had taught her to be wary of a man if she made a mistake? That she would be punished with anger? Disinherited? She'd acted that way with him just now.

Rubbing his beard, Mike didn't know. But he was going to find out sooner or later. They had a lot of talk, exploring and discovering of one another to do yet.

As he stood there in the silence, his heart seethed with love and concern for Khat. She was vulnerable tonight, more so than usual. What had gone on with her those three weeks when she left Bravo and was alone once more in her mountains? He saw the fierce love for him burning in her eyes. Relief of another kind trickled through him. Their love was intact, despite the setback. Mike felt a keen gratefulness for Khat being able to transcend her duty and continue to reach out to him. It gave him hope. And God, he needed that sign from Khat.

He wiped his hand across his face, his gut in knots.

He felt as if he were walking on the blade of a sword with Khat. One wrong move...

He wished he could make love to her, but it would be impossible. There was no place to go, so he'd have to be content to kiss her at moments when he could steal the opportunity. He'd seen the fire in Khat's eyes after their first kiss, the arousal.

Mike dragged in a deep breath, releasing it, white vapor created by the freezing temperature. Tomorrow was going to be a bitch of a day, and he knew it. What would Khat do? How would she react to Mac's mission plan? Would she willingly go along with him being her partner when going back to her operation area? How would Khat react? Damn, life got fucking complicated sometimes, and Mike tiredly rubbed his smarting eyes, feeling like a marathon runner in the twenty-eighth mile of a twenty-nine-mile race.

Khat appeared at the entrance, her feet in the shower clogs, bundled up in the blue terry-cloth robe, her hair twisted up in a white towel on top of her head. Mike eased away from the building, took her clothes and toiletry items from her arms. She walked closely at his side.

"What time do I have to see the chief?" she asked.

"Sleep in," he told her gruffly. "He's okay with whatever time you can meet with him. I'm going to be out in the big room all morning working on a mission plan. Why don't you come and get me after you wake up and then we'll get breakfast at the chow hall? I'll feed and water your horses tomorrow morning, so don't worry about that. Then you can go see Mac."

Licking her lower lip, Khat hugged the thick robe around her body, the wind sharp at times. "Thank you,

Mike…" She glanced over at his darkened profile. His brow was creased, and his mouth was set. She felt a fine tension in him but was unable to interpret it.

Mike opened the door to the HQ for her. There was no way he was going to kiss her good-night. Not here. If Mac ever saw it or heard about it, all hell would break loose. Mike knew the chief understood there was a relationship between them. But it remained unsaid that he was to conduct himself accordingly. And HQ was off-limits. This was the chief's house.

Khat took the dirty clothes from his arms. "I'll see you tomorrow morning, then?" How desperately she wanted to kiss Mike, but she saw him step back. And he wanted to kiss her. Wrong time and place.

"Yes," he rasped. "Tomorrow morning."

"HOW IS SERGEANT SHINWARI?" Mac asked Mike the next morning when he walked into his office with a bunch of papers beneath his arm.

Mike shut the door and stood, coffee cup in hand. "She's tired, which is understandable," he said. "And she noted that there's a buildup of Taliban in our area. She had to dodge more patrols than usual. I know you briefed us the other day on that buildup."

"I got word from the CIA a little while ago. Looks like more Taliban movements than normal around our base. They're watching it. I'm going to have an Apache helicopter roll out and make a circuit around the base using thermal imaging and then have the video sent back to us. They're probably massing for another attack on the base. That would be everyone's guess."

"Not a good sign," Mike agreed, scowling as he sipped his coffee. Bravo took sporadic RPG and mortar fire two to three times a year. It looked like it was going to be one of those times shortly.

"So, how is Sergeant Shinwari otherwise?"

"It looks like she's gained some weight back," Mike said. "Her cheeks don't look so hollow."

"That's a good sign," Mac growled. "Maybe with enough people bitching about how thin she was, she got it."

Mike smiled a little. "She's hardheaded," he agreed.

"Otherwise?"

"She looks more tired than the last time she was here." He could see the fine veins beneath Khat's eyes, the purplish shadows telling him she wasn't sleeping well. "Maybe because she was under a lot of stress dodging those Taliban patrols."

Mac shrugged. "I'm just trying to get her pulse. After you bring her back from morning chow, I'm going to have to lay out this mission we've created. It would be nice if I knew beforehand where she is."

"Yeah," Mike muttered, "whether she's going to be all for it or see us taking over her territory and feeling threatened, is up in the air." Either could happen.

"Take her pulse at chow," Mac said. "Let me know what you think, and then I'll call her in later." Frowning, he said, "It's vital she doesn't know you had anything to do with this plan, Tarik. I don't care if you have to lie to her, you do it. And I did tell her she now has a price on her head."

Mike nodded, not liking the idea of lying to Khat. He never had before. "Maybe she won't put two and two together and ask me about it."

Snorting, the chief gave him a wry look. "In your

dreams. She's not stupid. We made that mistake last time, and I've learned from it. I hope you have, too."

MIKE WATCHED KHAT eat as if starved. At least she had an appetite, and that made him feel good. She had awakened at 0900 and by the time they'd walked over to the chow hall, it was fairly empty. He was glad it wasn't noisy, and he could hear himself think. He sat with his back to the wall opposite her, finishing up six pancakes and a half a pound of bacon.

"You look like you've gained back some weight."

Khat finished off her six eggs, sopping up the yolk with her toast. "Well," she said, smiling a little, "after everyone was telling me I looked like a scarecrow, I decided to try and eat more." She drowned in his lion-gold eyes that were warm with love for her. "I think I've put on ten pounds in the past three weeks." She patted her tummy. "I hate MREs, but I'm eating more."

"You look better," he murmured. Khat had combed her hair and tamed it into a long ponytail down her back. Soft tendrils around her flushed cheeks empha-sized her clear green eyes this morning. "So you slept well?"

"I died," she muttered, slathering blueberry jam across her toast.

"No nightmares?"

"No." And then she added more softly, "I missed you beside me, though." She saw Mike's eyes grow in-tense, his mouth that she ached to kiss right now pull-ing into a slight smile.

"I wanted to be there, believe me." Mike looked around the empty chow hall, and his gaze drifted back to hers. "Military regs."

"I know." Khat sighed, understanding. She finished off all the food she'd piled on her tray. Mike stimulated her appetite. Khat realized she wanted to eat, wanted to live, when she was around him.

Putting the tray to one side, Khat picked up her mug of hot tea. Her heart rate increased as she saw Mike do the same thing. Meeting his gaze, she whispered unsteadily, "I'm so sorry I was a coward, Mike. I should have told you I was going to leave."

"Why didn't you?" He sipped his coffee, his eyes above the rim, watching her. Khat looked excruciatingly vulnerable, confusion in her gaze. He felt her being torn or undecided.

Khat placed the mug on the table, her hands around it. "Because I was afraid you'd get angry. I know you wanted me to stay here longer."

"I understood, Khat." Mike tipped his head, his voice lowering. "I love you. Nothing changes that. All right?"

She nervously turned the mug around between her long fingers. "But you'll be gone in four months," she whispered, feeling tears in her eyes. "You'll be returning Stateside."

Nodding, he said, "I know." And his heart ached because he saw Khat torn between her duty and her love for him, for what they had, which was so damned good. As much as he wanted to argue with her why she should give up what she'd done for all those years, Mike knew it would fall on deaf ears. He had to be patient and pray that eventually, Khat would get it on her own. If she could do that, Mike knew their growing love stood a chance.

"You know," he said quietly, "there wouldn't be any

harm in you returning to the States when winter comes. All the attacks stop. The snow is too deep to pass or move people or equipment. Would you consider coming back to the States then?"

She heard the longing in his voice. Yearning to be with him, not apart. Khat felt unsettled. "I usually spend my winter in my father's village of Dur Babba. I give medical help to the people during that time. Sometimes, when there's breaks in the weather, I'll ride to the surrounding villages and give medical aid. I usually stay one to three weeks in each village, but a lot of that is determined by the weather."

"I see," he murmured. "Maybe this year can be different?" Mike looked into her anguished gaze. "I'll have sixty days of leave when my platoon flies back to Coronado. It would be a nice way to spend it. With you." Mike wasn't going to lie down and let their love become a victim in this fight for Khat's heart and soul. "What do you think?"

"Where do you live?"

"I lease a thousand-square-foot condo from my best friend, Gabe Griffin. He was a SEAL until recently. The building sits about a hundred feet off San Diego Bay, and you get the smell of the ocean and the beauty of the sunsets, among other things."

"It sounds wonderful," she said. "Calming."

"Peaceful," he agreed. "I always like getting back there. It helps me ramp down from combat and kick back to a degree."

"Are there lots of seabirds?"

He smiled. "Birds, seals, dolphins, whales. You name it, San Diego Bay has it. There's a harbor seal I call Sam. He's been around forever. I started buying him some fresh fish from the fish market every Friday. He'll be waiting for me like he knows what day it is." Khat's eyes grew thoughtful, and he could feel her digesting his descriptions.

"You have a seal?"

Mike gave her a sheepish look. "Not *my* seal. Sam is a local phenomenon. Everybody feeds him. Gabe is the one who turned me on to the fact Sam didn't have any fish for Friday, so I volunteered to feed him on Fridays when I was home." He grinned.

Khat was touched by his kindness toward animals. Hell, kindness toward her. He had wonderful hands. Healing hands. She responded to his touch. Her Arabian mares loved him, too. Wistful, she said, "I've always loved the water. Especially the ocean. When I was training at Camp Pendleton for that year, I'd go out to San Onofre beach every chance I could. I learned to body surf there and loved it."

"You're a SEAL by proxy, then," he teased. "Maybe a frogwoman?"

Khat laughed. "Oh, I don't know about that!"

"If you decide to come and see me, I'll teach you how to scuba dive."

"You are *such* a temptation, Tarik."

He opened his hands and gave her a very serious look. "I love you, Khat. I want to show you another side of life with me that isn't the SEAL."

She lowered her lashes, staring at her cup of tea. "I know," she said softly, frowning. "I've had three weeks to think about a lot of things."

His heart leaped with hope. As much as he wanted to push her, Mike knew he couldn't. So he sat patiently, watching her wrestle within herself, her lips pursed, eyes down.

"So have I."

Lifting her gaze, Khat saw the tender look burning in his eyes. Her body automatically responded and so did her heart. His hands, so scarred and yet able to give her such pleasure. The heated memory flowed strongly through her. "What we have," she began hesitantly, "is good, Mike. For you, it's an easy choice. For me, it's not."

"My father always taught me to follow my heart," Mike mused, holding her unsure gaze. "He can follow his lineage back to the sheiks of the desert. I grew up listening to his stories of riding the Arabian horse during the day and then the horses were allowed into the bedouin tent at night, a part of the family. He said that stories passed down through time were stories about the heart." His lips quirked. "Maybe that's why he became a world-renowned cardiac surgeon. I can remember as a little boy when I'd be out with him and his herd of Arabian horses, he'd always tell me horses could see a person's heart. And to work with them from my heart. I grew up breaking many of the horses, but I never had to shock or traumatize them with bucking or throwing a saddle over them. All I had to do was befriend them, gain their trust and one day, I'd just quietly slip up on their back. They accepted me without any problem. They knew my heart, and I knew theirs."

"You were so lucky," Khat whispered, touched deeply by his story. "What did your father think when you wanted to be a SEAL and not follow the family tradition of becoming a surgeon?"

"He was upset at first, but he knew I was a kid who

liked adventure. I was restless, wanted to see the world, was fascinated with weapons of all kind. My father made the remark one time before I joined the navy that I'd traded in the family scalpel for a different kind of one—a military KA-BAR knife."

He saw Khat was fascinated with the story and decided to share more with her. "After I managed to graduate from BUD/S, and they came to our graduation, my father was very proud of me. At that point, he told me that I had the genes from the other side of his family—the bedouin warriors. He told me about a caliph who waged war against an invader and won. That his swordsmanship was considered the best in Saudi Arabia. I told my father at that point I'd traded in scalpels for a big modern-day sword—an M-4 rifle." He laughed in memory of that day.

"But your father, who is Saudi, did not disown you?"

Frowning, Mike said, "No, of course not." And then he blinked once, getting it. "Did your father disown you?" His heart dropped over the possibility.

Humiliation flowed through Khat. Closing her eyes, she pressed her hand against her brow. "I feel so much shame about it," she admitted in a strained tone, her voice uneven with tears. "After I came home from being captured and they met me at the San Diego Naval Hospital where I was taken, my father, Jaleel, lost it."

Mouth tightening, Mike wanted to reach across the table and grip her hand, but he didn't dare. "I'm sorry, Khat. Maybe, with time, he'll come around."

Sniffing, she lifted her head, blinking away the tears. "That's why I never go home. I go to the US to fulfill my obligations and training as a paramedic, but then I leave and come back over here."

Mike took a drink of coffee, barely containing his rage over what her father had done to her. In the Middle East, to be disowned was the most traumatic event that could happen in a child's life. It was one step down from dying. And indeed, he'd heard stories from his father about when a rebellious son would be cast out of a family. That son could never go home again. They were dead as far as the family was concerned. Son of a bitch! Now the picture was a little clearer on why Khat was over in Afghanistan so much.

"Do your father's relatives know this?"

Wiping her eyes, she shook her head. "No."

"Has he written them and told them?"

"Most of them are uneducated and cannot read or write. I usually stay in Dur Babba during the winter with my uncles and aunts." Her voice softened. "They are such wonderful people, Mike. I love them, and they love me. I'm welcomed with opened arms, and I truly feel at home there."

Mike wanted to curse so damn bad it stuck like a knife in his throat. He kept the rage out of his eyes for her sake. Jaleel Shinwari had disowned his only daughter. The bastard! Did he realize what he'd done to Khat? Hell, everyone needed to be loved. To have family who loved them. And Khat was running toward the only family she knew who wasn't judging her, but simply loving her because she was of their blood and tribe.

Beneath the table, his hand curled into a fist. Now Mike understood what their love for one another was up against. And it was daunting to him. Khat had already said once she fulfilled her military obligation, she was remaining in Afghanistan. The reason was clear to him now.

Khat was intelligent and wouldn't be bullied one way or another about their relationship. All Mike could do was appeal to her heart, which he held in his hands. She was an adult and so was he. She was fully capable of making changes in her life based upon her needs. The problem was, duty and being disowned had suppressed healthy, normal drives and desires within her. She'd taken up the mission of duty to her family, the village of her father's birth, to prove that even if Jaleel had disowned her, she was still worthy of the rest of his family's love, respect and care. He felt like he was battling a dragon without any way to defend himself against the situation.

"I think we need to get back and you speak to the chief." Mike knew putting too much pressure on Khat would distract her. And distraction was a killer in their business.

CHAPTER FIFTEEN

"WELL," CHIEF MCCUTCHEON SAID, "we normally bring in the men who are going to be on this mission. That way, Sergeant Shinwari, you and Tarik can discuss it, bring out better or different ideas."

Khat stared across the desk at Mac. In thirty minutes he'd just laid out a plan that had spun her into shock. Her notebook and the pen in her hand were frozen on her lap. "And you said that Commander Hutton was on board with this mission?" Her voice was low, strained.

"Yes," Mac said firmly. "I've been working directly with Senior Master Chief Wilson at J-bad. I'm sure you know who he is?"

"Yes," she rasped, "I do." Her heart was fluttering with dread.

"I need to get Tarik in here," Mac said, rising. "He's as much a part of this as you are."

Swallowing hard, Khat took out her bottle of water from her cammie trouser pocket. Her mouth was dry. She'd never expected this. Why was Hutton changing things up on her? Hadn't she performed well? Why fix something if it wasn't broken? Anger warred with fear within her. Khat drank deeply from the bottle. She heard the chief calling for Mike. Did he know about this and had not told her? Wiping her wet lips with the back of her hand, Khat frowned and screwed the top on the water bottle, pushing it back into the deep pocket on her lower leg.

Mike followed the chief into the office. He glanced over at Khat. She looked dazed. Her face had gone pale. Things hadn't gone well, he figured as he sat down.

Mac gave him the details of the plan for the next twenty minutes. It was an effort to trick Khat into thinking he knew nothing about it, when in reality, he was the one who had created it under Mac's direction. What Mac didn't want was distrust on Khat's part toward Mike. Finally, the chief finished giving him the bones of the op.

"Okay, I got the two of you up to speed. Do you have questions about this op?" His gaze moved to Khat and then Mike.

"Yes," Khat said strongly, sitting up, her hands curled on her thighs. "I thought I was doing good work out there for Commander Hutton."

"You are," Mac said. "Your intel is valued highly by all of us."

"Then why is he giving me a partner when I don't need one?"

Mike sat back, hands in his lap, quiet. This was the chief's battle to fight, not his.

"Because according to Senior Master Chief Wilson, he's seeing the Taliban shifting their tactics again. This time, Khogani is utilizing your area fifty percent more than he did two months ago."

"But I'm handling that intrusion fine!" Khat feared for her job. Were they going to pull her out?

"Stand down," Mac ordered firmly.

Breathing hard, Khat sat back, trying to relax. Her hands had curled into fists on her thighs.

"You know better than most the Taliban are always changing their patterns. While Khogani is favoring your op area, we want more oversight. Frankly, Sergeant, you should be relieved it's someone you know. I fought for Tarik to be your partner. They wanted someone else, and I said no."

Miserably, Khat looked over at Mike. "Are you happy about this?"

Mike kept his game face on. "I think we'll make a good team," he told her, holding her shaken gaze. "We know one another, we're both horse people. I know a little about your caves and your operating system." He opened his hands. "I think it's a good idea to take GPS on all the trails and rat lines. You're the only one who knows where all of them are. That intel could help us position a drone over a given area. It can spot Taliban coming across, and air assets can blow them to hell." He held her gaze, his voice calm and reasonable. "It doesn't hurt anyone to know this intel. It can only help everyone. Don't you agree?"

Well, how the hell could she argue that? Her lips twitched, her eyes growing hard. To argue it would be pointless and stupid. "It's a reasonable objective," she agreed huskily.

"I need to buy a horse," Mike told the chief. He'd tried at one village days ago, and it hadn't gone well because there were no horses available to be sold to him.

"Yes. I'm asking Reza, who is a Shinwari tribesman and one of our terps, interpreters, to take you down to another village. He knows the horse traders there, and he knows his horses. Buy one and make sure it's not a broken-down nag, all right?"

Mike nodded. "I think I can handle that, no problem." He glanced over at Khat. "Want to come along?"

She felt like shrieking in rage, but swallowed it. Feeling as if she were being set up for some unknown reason, Khat muttered, "Of course."

"It's going to take you a couple of days to prepare," Mac warned her. "You two work out the kinks of the op. If you can't, come and see me."

"And who am I reporting to?" Khat demanded.

"Me," Mac said, "not Commander Hutton."

Her brows flew upward. "What is happening here, Chief? First, Camp Bravo becomes my supply line. Now you're handling this op instead of my handler in J-bad."

"Commander Hutton authorized it," Mac said, holding her belligerent stare.

She snorted and sat back in the chair, crossing her legs and glaring at the chief.

"Something you want to get off your chest, Sergeant?"

Biting on her lower lip, Khat held the chief's calm stare. She was the one sweating, not him. "I feel like someone's making a back door move on me. I just can't figure out who yet," she said angrily. "I've been a good operator out there for years. I don't need to start being passed around. That's a distraction for me, dammit. And distractions get you killed out there."

Mac nodded, absorbing her anger. "I'd like you to give me and us a chance, Sergeant. I think you'll find us professional and a lot more concerned about your welfare than you are presently being cared for by that J-bad crew."

"Just what does that mean?" Khat demanded heatedly. She was fine with Hutton ignoring her. It gave her the latitude to do what she felt worked best for her and her mission. Was McCutcheon warning her not so subtly that he was a hands-on handler? Going to screw with her decision making? Worse, make decisions for her when she was the one in the field and he was here, riding a damned desk?

Mac sat back in his chair, studying her. "I think Mike can tell you what it means, Sergeant. We take care of our own. We have your back, and you have ours. SEALs operate quite differently from other black ops. We don't generally put one man out in the field alone. We know we're stronger when there's two or more of us. And I think you know that."

Her nostrils flared, and she began breathing unevenly. "I know what I'm doing out there, Chief. Do *not* screw with me. I have five years of actionable intel proof that I'm the best at what I do. I have disrupted Khogani's complete network, and all the border villages are safer because I'm out there." She sat up in the chair, jamming her index finger down on his desk, holding his stare. "You let me run on a very loose leash. You can *not* tell me what to do or when to do it. I know the rhythm of my enemy. And very often, it's my experience linked with my intuition that gets the job done." Her voice lowered to almost a snarl. "I will not be on a damn sat phone to you asking permission from my handler if I can initiate an attack or not."

Mike felt the tension amp up in the room. Khat's face was flushed, her eyes slits, her voice angry and emotional. Moving his gaze to Mac, who looked calm and unperturbed, he knew this SEAL could land hard on someone under his command. He'd seen it done before. How was he going to handle Khat?

"Fair enough," Mac said. "But I'm going to let you know why I'm going to let you have your head, Sergeant. You saved four of my men. Whether your intuition told you to be there at that spot on that given evening, you made the difference."

Some of her anger dissipated beneath his quiet, sincere tone. Khat sat back in the chair, feeling defeated. "You have to *trust* me, Chief. Commander Hutton does."

Mac nodded and thinned his lips. "This is not a question about trust, Sergeant. I think I've made that clear."

Khat nodded, swallowing hard. "Yes, you're concerned about my welfare, that I eat properly, get rest…"

"Exactly," Mac said, giving her a brief, tight smile. "Now, get out of here. See me if you need input or to fix a problem." He handed each of them a copy of the mission.

Mike rose and opened the door. Now he knew why Hutton left Khat alone. She was a damned spitting, snarling snow leopard when anyone tried to take control over her op. He ambled out into the big room and gestured for her to meet him at the planning table. Khat was drinking the rest of the water from a bottle she gripped in her hand. Her face was flushed. Anger radiated off her. *Damn.* He rubbed the back of his neck ruefully, pulling out two chairs.

Khat came over and whispered so only he could hear, "I need to get out of here and take a walk."

"Want company?"

She nodded, feeling as if she were going to explode.

Mike walked out of HQ with her. "Let's head to the horse barn," he suggested. He could feel the rage radiating from around Khat. She could blow it off, yell, scream or whatever over there, and no one would hear her but him. He'd never seen her like this and was getting a taste of her stubborn, passionate Afghan blood in action.

Khat whirled around on Mike once they were near the opening to the barn. "I'm so damned angry I could scream," she rattled, facing him.

"Why?" he asked calmly. He purposely kept his arms at his side, holding her gaze. Mike wasn't going to argue the mission with her. What he did want was to find out what was triggering this unexpected explosion within Khat. He thought he knew, but as circumstances had just shown him, he didn't know a whole helluva lot about Khat's inner world. She needed to spell it out for him. Then maybe he could be of support or guidance. Maybe not. He was feeling caught between a rock and a hard place with her right now. He loved her. That was the simplest and clearest emotion between them. But could their love survive this? He didn't know, and he felt clawing pain in his chest.

Throwing up her arms, Khat started pacing back and forth in front of him. "I want control over my op, dammit! What the hell is Hutton up to? He's always ignored me. He could care less what I did out in the field so long as it meant he didn't need to support me." Her nostrils flared, her voice harsh. "I think Hutton's trying to get rid of me."

Mike nodded, watching her. "Okay, so what?" He saw her halt and jerk around, glaring at him.

"I *liked* it the way it was! I had the freedom to do what I felt was right. And dammit, I do!"

"Chief McCutcheon said he wouldn't interfere with your judgment. What's so different, then, Khat?"

Breathing unevenly, her hands curled into fists at her sides, she stared at him like he had two heads. His expression was open, and she saw the sincerity in his eyes. "You're always the voice of reason," she accused hotly.

"One of us needs to be, Angel."

Tears pricked her eyes. Swallowing convulsively, Khat felt imprisoned by his steady, calm gaze. Her chest rose and fell sharply with anger and fear. Mike wasn't angry. He was just standing there like an anchor while she bounced around like a wild horse trying to escape an invisible cage she felt closing around her.

Trembling outwardly, she put her hands to her face, trying to stop the tears from coming. It didn't work, and she muttered a curse, wiping the moisture angrily off her cheeks. "I just feel like a trap is about to snap on me, Mike. I *feel* it!" She struck her heart with her fist. "I operate on my gut sense of things. Maybe that's why I left three weeks ago. I could feel something coming, and it scared the living hell out of me."

"So you ran from it?"

She gritted her teeth, staring at him. "I don't run from anything!"

"Could you define what you felt three weeks ago, Khat?"

"No, dammit, I can't!"

"Did you feel danger? Threat?"

Some of her anger faded beneath his quietly spoken questions. Rubbing her hands down the sides of her trousers, she muttered, "No."

"Sometimes," Mike said as he walked toward her, "we all get feelings that are uncomfortable, Khat. But that doesn't mean it's bad for us." He halted and tipped her chin up so he could look into her tear-filled eyes. "Sometimes what we feel is change. But it doesn't necessarily mean that change is bad."

His low, emotion-filled voice overwhelmed the anger raging within her. His eyes were half-closed, intense upon her. His mouth was compressed. She could feel his love for her. Tears slid down her cheeks, and she couldn't stop a sob from jerking out of her. Pulling away from his finger beneath her chin, she choked out, "I'm just scared, Mike. All right?"

He slid his arms around her, drawing her against him. It always tore him up to see a woman cry. Hell, he could handle anything but that. "I love you, Khat. We'll get through this together. All right?" Mike held her, kissing her hair as she leaned wearily against him. To his utter relief, she slid her arms around his waist.

"I'm scared," she whispered brokenly, closing her eyes, absorbing his quiet strength.

"I know you are, Angel. But it's going to be all right. Things will work out," he rasped against her ear, moving his hand gently up and down her strong back.

"I felt as if my whole world had been jerked out from beneath me when the chief told me about the mission," she choked, taking her fingers and wiping the tears from her cheek.

"I can see that now."

Lifting her head, Khat stared into his somber face,

his eyes hooded, burning with love for her. "I—I just want to belong somewhere," she admitted, her voice cracking.

"I know you do," Mike soothed, moving damp tendrils of hair sticking to her cheek and tucking them behind her ear. "You belong to me. That's a fact you can always hold on to, Khat." He shared a tender smile with her, seeing the storm of anguish in her tearful eyes. His heart winced in pain for her. She'd endured enough of it. "Look, Mac isn't a bean counter. I head up patrols all the time for him, and he leaves the execution of it to me. I'm in charge. If I need something, I call in by sat phone, and he's there to *assist* me, Khat. Not tell me what to do. He'll treat you the same way. He respects your experience and decision-making ability."

"God," she mumbled, wiping her eyes, "I really flew loose on him in his office, didn't I?"

Mike grinned a little. "Yeah, you're a force of nature, Khat, but he's been around the block, too. I think he understood where you were coming from." He caught her hand and kissed it, holding it against his chest. "Don't worry, he's not going to take your job away from you. He doesn't work that way. If he thought you'd overstepped your bounds in there, he'd have been in your face in a heartbeat."

Mouth pulling, Khat rested her head against Mike's shoulder. Closing her eyes, she felt comforted by him. "I love you so much, it hurts," she whispered, choking on another sob.

The words tore out of her, and Mike stood very still, not expecting Khat to say anything about what they shared. "That's what will get us through this," he assured her. "You're passionate, Khat. You're a fierce woman warrior. I love all those things about you, too. And I want to be here for you when you feel like the world's closing in on you, baby. I don't want to be anywhere else." He leaned down and pressed a kiss to her wrinkled brow.

She pulled away and slid her hand from beneath his on his chest. Drowning in his lion-gold eyes, Khat leaned up and kissed him. Her lips were bathed with her warm, salty tears as she skimmed the tight line of his mouth.

Instantly, Mike groaned and pulled her hard against him, his mouth curving hotly against her own. His lips deepened their kiss, parting her lips, drinking from her, giving and sharing with her. Breath uneven, the rasp of his beard against her cheek, she strained to get as close as she could to him, their hearts pounding frantically against one another. Dampness instantly collected between her thighs, and Khat felt her entire lower body radiate with keening hunger that only he could liberate and satisfy.

Mike's hand framed her face, his mouth taking hers with masculine power. Khat felt as if he were infusing her with his strength, his love and tenderness all at once. She was needy and absorbed his mouth sliding against hers, giving and taking. Her whole world melted as he licked her lower lip. A moan caught in her throat as he moved against her tongue, every nerve in her body awakening beneath his onslaught.

She wanted him. In every possible way. She wanted to feel his hands caressing her tight breasts, his mouth claiming one of her hardened nipples, his knowing hand sliding down beneath the waist of her uniform, going lower.

Her knees felt like they were going to buckle, and she felt such a powerful spasm within her lower body, she wanted to cry out. Khat had missed him terribly in those three lonely weeks. In that one moment, she felt her love for Mike deepen so much that it warred on equal ground with her commitment to her people. That realization caught her off guard. Khat surrendered completely to his sweet assault upon her, his kisses healing her, loving her.

Finally, Mike eased away from her well-kissed mouth. He opened his eyes, breathing irregularly, his erection so damned hard that he could barely stand up straight, the ache for Khat intense. Watching her lashes that were beaded with tears lift, his heart expanded powerfully with love for her alone. Her green eyes were moist, and he saw dappled gold in their depths. She wanted him just as badly as he wanted her. He could feel her trembling against him, her knees pressed against his, barely able to stand. He tightened his grip around her waist, keeping her solidly against him.

Something had changed, and Mike felt the subtle shift between them. He couldn't say what it was; only that something had happened as they'd ravenously kissed one another like starving male and female alpha wolves reclaiming each other after an enforced absence. Marking one another. Reminding one another of the power and beauty of what they shared when they met one another as equals on the playing field of life.

"Wish we were somewhere else other than here," he teased, his voice low and aroused.

Rolling her eyes, Khat whispered, "Anywhere but here…"

"One good thing about this mission..." he said, giving her a wicked look. "We'll be together."

Nodding, Khat rested her head on his shoulder once more, moving her fingers across his chest. "I thought of that."

"So it's not all bad," he murmured, no longer hearing anger in her voice, just weariness, as if she'd fought a major battle within herself. Moving his fingers across her mussed hair, he added, "We'll take advantage of what we have, when we can."

Nodding, Khat muttered defiantly, "It's the only good thing about it, Mike."

"Let's look on the positive side, Angel. I was picked for this mission. It could have been worse. You could get someone you didn't know at all."

Khat sighed. "Yes..." She shook her head. "Why the hell did I fly off the handle in the chief's office?" Pulling out of his arms, Khat stepped back, touching her brow. "All the chief wanted is GPS on all the goat trails and rat lines. Why did I overreact?"

Mike stood and watched her closely. He was seeing her waffle emotionally again, sure that PTSD had something to do with her anger and feeling unsafe. "You felt threatened," he said.

Khat dragged in a deep breath and gave him an abject look. Being around Mike was stabilizing to her in every way. "Sometimes I fly off the handle. Not often, but it happens."

"Your passionate Afghan blood?" he teased, his mouth creased at the corners. Mike saw her rally, trying to understand the extremes within herself. He knew how hard it was to see one's self. Maybe, if Khat had been given therapy and she'd stayed Stateside after her release from captivity, she would have reacted differently, more positively, to this mission.

"I guess," Khat muttered. She leaned against the corral fence, the two mares coming and standing nearby.

"Well," he murmured, kissing her brow, "I, for one, am looking forward to this mission. It means I get quality time with you. And no one to see us make love." Mike gave her a warm look. She smiled a little. Her cheeks were flushed and still damp from crying. He wanted so damn badly to ease her inner pain, but Mike knew he couldn't. He caressed her cheek. "We'll find times and ways to love one another. Guaranteed."

"YOU TWO TAKE CARE," Travis told them at the security gate. It was 0100, the sky threatening another storm and rain. Lightning danced off to the west of Camp Bravo.

Mike shook his hand. "We will. Thanks for all your help, bro."

Grinning, Travis said, "Anytime."

The marine guards at the gate opened it and stepped aside as they walked their horses through into the Taliban territory that surrounded the forward operating base. Once outside the wire, they mounted their horses, trotting down the slope toward the hilly region below.

Mike rode beside Khat. Both were in male Afghan clothing. To someone looking through a spotter scope or binos, binoculars, they appeared to be two men with a packhorse in tow. Khat had pushed her red braid down inside her cloak so that it did not remain visible to prying eyes. They each carried an AK-47 on their backs, the weapon of choice for the Taliban. Their M-4 rifles were in nylon sheaths beneath the left leg, beneath the stirrup. If they needed them, they'd be easy to reach and fire.

The rumble of thunder caromed over the area, the night air vibrating with the rolling sound. The cold wind was sharp, and he pulled the thick brown wool cloak tighter around his body. Beneath his hajii outfit, he, like Khat, wore SEAL cammies. They had to take it slow because NVGs wouldn't work in a lightning storm, their view easily destroyed by the sudden bolts flashing across the moody sky. They were taking the straightest route to the mountains that were six miles ahead of them. In the mountains, they could once more fade into the environment, less easily spotted than out in the open where they were presently.

Mike adjusted the mic close to his lips. "Test?" he asked her.

"Roger that. Loud and clear."

"Good," he murmured. Communication was essential. If they got attacked or split up, the radio was good for a one-mile radius. Mike carried a sat com phone, and so did Khat. Without them, they'd never be able to call for help from Camp Bravo.

Lightning flashed overhead. Mike ducked, it was so damned close. The horses paid no attention to it. In seconds, a torrential downpour started. Mike knew it was going to be a miserable ride. By the time they reached the halfway point, they'd be soaked, freezing, shivering and their teeth chattering nonstop. He reminded himself that Khat was active no matter what the weather, constantly patrolling her area, watching for an opportunity to kill Khogani's men. Hunkering down, he mentally prepared himself for a long, miserable night. The only time they would stop was at dawn, when they could potentially be spotted by Taliban.

His mind moved between remaining alert for a nearby enemy and Khat having lived out here for five years alone. A fierce love for her swept through him. She damn well deserved a better life than this; one that could be equally fulfilling to her. His heart ached for Khat. She'd been through so damn much, and the one thing a person always counted on in bad times was their family. And when she needed her father the most, he'd turned on her, frozen in old Afghan customs instead of allowing his daughter to spread her wings and fly. Mike counted himself lucky in comparison, silently promising Khat if she'd stick with him, he'd open up her life to happiness. Not this marginal life-and-death dance she performed fearlessly twenty-four hours a day.

CHAPTER SIXTEEN

THE CAVE KHAT led them to at dawn was intriguing to Mike. Thousands of caves littered the Hindu Kush. This one was twenty-five miles from Camp Bravo. It was hidden by a lot of trees and brush near a stream. Unless someone knew about it, it wouldn't be spotted. There were no goat trails nearby, either, which would have made it easy to find.

The rain had been off and on all night. Mike's outer Afghan cloak and clothes were soaked. His cammies had protected him up to a point and kept him warm.

Khat rode into the narrow opening of the cave. The entrance was seven feet tall and about seven feet wide; just enough for a horse and rider to enter. Mike halted his bay gelding, looking around, noting exit points of escape if they had to run. Turning, the horse quickened its pace to catch up with the other horses. The cave twisted and turned, a series of maze-like tunnels. At some points, Zorah's pannier scraped loudly against the wall. The only light was the one Khat had focused in front of Mina to show her the way. Mike felt completely lost by the time they entered what appeared to be a large dry cavern. He heard water. So did the thirsty horses, their ears pricking up.

To his surprise, he saw dawn light weakly filtering down from above. Walking across the fine silt sand on the floor, he saw it was a natural, jagged opening in the ceiling. There was just enough light to see.

"Follow me," Khat said, leading her two horses toward the rear of the cavern.

Mike could smell the dry, musty odor of the cave. Even bats didn't live back here. It would be one hell of a flight in and out every day with the twisting, winding tunnels they'd taken to get back here. He saw a small pool of water in a grotto. Khat had already taken off Mina's bridle and held the rope to her halter so her mare could eagerly drink her fill.

He walked up near where Khat stood and untied the rope from Zorah to the loop on the cantle of Khat's Western saddle. There was a lot of work to do before they could settle in.

The cave was much warmer than the outside air temperature that hovered near freezing. Mike took off his hajii gear and laid it across his saddle. His cammies were damp but serviceable. Khat went back to the cave entrance to sweep away all evidence of the horse prints in the dirt. She had motion sensors and put new batteries in them so it would alert her electronic box she kept turned on, in case someone wandered accidentally, or on purpose, into their cave complex.

Khat beckoned him to bring Zorah up next for a drink. She led Mina over to another enclosure, a rock wall about six feet tall that extended into the cave like a wing. There, she had planted a small tree trunk years earlier and tied Mina's halter lead rope around it. Turning, she removed the tarp on the load Zorah carried.

In half an hour, with Mike's help, Khat was ready to take care of the animals. The cave had a lot of alcoves to it, and she led him to one across from where the horses rested. Around a rocky corner was a crescent-shaped area, the roof of the cavern sloping downward, making it look like a room. They worked together without speaking, getting the metal grate out, two MREs, bottles of water and prepared to eat. The smell of the food made Mike's stomach growl. Damn, he was starving to death.

Khat took off the radio and headband, laying it aside. She'd shed her hajii gear, down to cammie basics. Her hair was mussed, and she moved her fingers to tame the worst of the strands away from her face.

Mike took care of the cooking while she prepared tea for them.

"Is it safe to talk in here?"

Khat nodded. "That opening at the top of the cave is down below a hundred-foot cliff. No one can get to that opening on foot or by horseback. Only way would be by rappelling down, and the Taliban aren't into that." She grinned sourly over at him. "Your butt sore?"

Snorting, Mike growled, "What do you think?"

"Those wooden saddles are a bitch."

"I'm seriously eyeing your Western saddle," he said, pulling the MREs off the grate and onto the tray.

"Dream on, Tarik. That's mine." She chuckled softly, handing him a mug of steaming hot tea. "Besides, you'll probably get a purple heart for all the nail puncture wounds you're gonna collect from that saddle."

He laughed softly and they sat down cross-legged from one another as he opened his MRE. "Are you all right?"

"Yes, just tired."

"I get to sleep with you," Mike said, meeting and holding her warm gaze.

"I just wonder how much sleep we're going to get."

"If I have anything to do with it, not much."

Khat enjoyed the gravel warning in his voice and the heated look he gave her. His hair was mussed and he looked tired, the skin across his cheekbones tight. They'd ridden a long way, and he wasn't used to that kind of time in a saddle. Her heart swelled with love for him as she watched him stab a piece of omelet with the Buck knife he carried on him.

"More like glue than eggs," she noted.

"Typical MRE. Makes me appreciate the chow hall at Bravo."

Khat looked around, the dripping of water from far above them, higher on the mountain, was eventually finding its way into the small pool at one end of the cave. "Our voices will not carry to the outer cave," she told him. "When I first arrived in this area, I did a lot of testing of noise carrying, finding adequate water for me and my horse as well as finding caves that were complex. Taliban tend to sit out in the front of a cave. They don't wander back in to see what else is there."

"Well, if that's their mind-set," Mike murmured, finishing off his food, "that's good news for us. Tactically, that's a pretty stupid action on their part."

"I've made it a point to study their weaknesses," Khat said. She put her empty MRE aside and stood up. "Why don't you get our bedding spread out in here? I'm going to wash up in that pool."

"Go for it," Mike urged, easing to his feet. The bedrolls were in one pannier. "I'm next." Even though it rained off and on all night, the fine sand had worked its way into his damp skin, rubbing a number of places raw.

KHAT BEGAN TO unbraid her hair. Mike had thoughtfully left her brush and comb on their bed. She was naked, the cave a constant seventy-five degrees, and she loved the coolness of her recently washed skin drying off. She had smiled as she'd strolled into their room, naked. Mike gave her an intense, burning look. She'd felt her body leap to life beneath his gaze. The man positively oozed sexuality. He made her feel sensual. Desired. For too long, she'd ignored her own body.

Mike rounded the corner, wiping his wet hair and beard. He knelt down on one knee behind Khat. Tossing the towel aside, he said, "Let me do that." He eased her long, thick braid out of her fingers. Because of the scarring on her back, she didn't have full mobility to reach back like this. He leaned over and kissed the nape of her neck, her flesh cool and damp beneath his lips. He heard a rush of pleasure from her lips as she tipped her head, allowing him more access. She smelled clean and sweet. Nipping her flesh lightly and then kissing each spot on her neck, Mike made it to her earlobe. "Now," he growled, "I want you to just sit there and let me take care of you. All right?" He saw a smile pull at her full lips, her lashes dropping closed.

"I'm in your hands," she whispered.

Grunting, he said, "Good to know. Still tired?"

"No. You?"

"Not even." Mike began to unbraid her thick, silky hair. Once it was released, it was a heavy cloud of red hair between his opened hands. "Beautiful, strong hair," he murmured, leaning forward, nibbling on the other side of her neck. "Like you." Her breasts had tightened, and the nipples were hard. He saw a flush coming to her cheeks, knowing that was a sign of her enjoying him.

He sat down, legs crossed and murmured, "Lean back. I'll guide your head to my thigh. I'm going to brush your hair."

Khat trusted him completely. Mike placed his hands on her shoulders, guiding her backward. Her head rested on his long, powerful thigh. As he pulled the brush slowly through her hair, her scalp tingled wildly, tiny flames of pleasure coursing down to her breasts and then to her lower body. Already, Khat could feel dampness collecting between her thighs, and Mike had barely touched her.

His long fingers moved through her strands of hair, skimming her scalp, making her utter a moan of enjoyment. He took his time, taking one long strand and brushing it until he could run his fingers through it. Mike knew the quality of foreplay was everything. Anyone could have sex. And it was more than sex driving him. He needed, in his own way, to show Khat what a man could do for his woman. The many ways he could love her, without having sex. Judging from the tension melting away from her face, her lips softening, she was cocooned within the aura of the care he was surrounding her with.

"I've never had a man brush my hair," Khat murmured, so incredibly relaxed, she felt as if she were melting a little more beneath each stroke he took with the brush.

"When you love someone," Mike told her, leaning over to catch her barely opened eyes, "there's a hundred thousand ways to show your woman she's not only loved, but worshipped."

"Mmm, I like being worshipped."

Mike saw, even in the low light, the slight waves in her crimson hair gleam. The strands were clean, barely damp between his fingers. Did she realize that touching her was making him so damned hard, he could barely control himself? Did it matter? Not right now. Khat was obviously aware of his erection, so close to her shoulder where she lay. He placed his hand beneath her neck and knees, easing her up across his lap and into his arms. Her hair fell like a warm cloak around both of them.

Khat gave him a drowsy smile, her eyes half-open. She was hotly aware her thigh was pressing into his erection as she slid her arms around his damp, cool shoulders. "You love me so well," she murmured softly, laying her head on his shoulder.

"I haven't even begun," Mike rasped, pulling her against him. He felt the hard pebbles of her nipples tangling in the hair across his chest, felt her arch into his arms, wanting to get closer. She caressed the column of his neck, and her warm, moist breath sent fire streaking through him.

Khat inhaled softly as her nipples were teased, the feelings like tiny charges bolting through her body. She slid her hand against his bearded cheek, guiding Mike's mouth to hers, kissing him hungrily, her lips seeking.

She felt him smile and then gently nip her lower lip. There was a fine line between pleasure and pain, and he always landed on the side of pleasure. Still, as she moved her tongue boldly against his, he groaned like a snow leopard who was cornered, waiting to spring. She felt him pull away from her mouth, his lips finding her nipple.

A small cry vibrated in her throat as Mike held her captive, suckling her as he laid her out against him. Feeling his calloused fingers easing around her breast, her skin charged and electrified by his touch, she moaned, pressing her belly against him, wanting more. Her breath was irregular, her pulse wild as he sought and found the other peak, lavishing it with his tongue. As he placed his teeth around it, she quivered, eyes tightly shut, feeling the flash of fire rip down through her. Fingers frantically digging into his heavy shoulder, Khat arched upward and toward him.

"You are so damned responsive," he rumbled against her breast, licking the flesh around the outer edge of her nipple, feeling her twist frantically in his arms.

His dark voice only triggered more yearning for his touch, for his body. "Touch me," she pleaded huskily. "Please... Touch me, Mike." She moved her hips in a twisting motion against his erection. Instantly, Mike froze, growled and then she felt his fingers moving lightly across her damp thigh, easing her open. Her breath caught in anticipation, her pulse skyrocketing. He pressed her face against the crook of his neck, wanting, waiting... And then she felt his fingers move against her heat and dampness. Moaning his name, she thrust her hips toward him, wanting much more. Khat heard him give a gruff laugh.

"You are always in such a hurry, sweet desert woman of mine."

As he spoke to her in a roughened tone in her own language, her entire lower body spasmed, sending a cry from deep within her.

"You are so wet," he rasped against her ear, kissing it, kissing her temple. "So ready..."

Khat wasn't helpless, and he must have felt or read her mind because he eased his fingers within her. It tore away all her thoughts. He was exploring her slowly, thoroughly, and all she could do was tremble and whimper as her body contracted around him.

As his mouth captured her peak, she was caught off guard, the fire erupting within her core. Unable to catch her breath, moving her hips, trying to take him more deeply into her, she felt so close to orgasm, the explosion racing toward her.

He must have felt her walls begin to contract because just as she was going to beg him to go deeper, he did. And in that instant as Mike touched the deep recesses of her as a woman, that sweet spot that released so much pleasure, so vivid and scalding, she violently orgasmed. A scream lodged in her throat, and she tensed, frozen as the white-hot flow tore through her.

Khat's fingers sank deep into his flesh as he continued to prolong her orgasm. Panting, her body burning, sweat trickling off her temples, he placed his teeth gently around one of her nipples. A bolt of lightning dove from her taut breast down to her throbbing core. He'd stimulated her once more, another orgasm, to gift her, once again. Mindless, her body straining and writhing, Khat felt the thick, sweet honey of her body flowing strongly, releasing a backlog of pent-up need.

Mike heard her sobbing, her beautiful body a satin sheen in the low light as he eased his fingers from within her. Cheeks flushed, eyes closed and her lips parted, he smiled. Now Khat understood what slow loving could bring to her.

He lifted her off his lap and onto the blankets, her hair spread like living red flame around her shoulders.

Easing between her thighs, he pulled her hips up toward him until his erection was pressed against her wet, warm entrance. Her eyes barely opened, her chest heaving from the orgasms that had ignited within her. She was hot, and she was still hungry. He rolled on a condom, protecting her. And as he'd pressed against her, she had moaned, her back arching, wanting to draw him into her.

Khat whimpered as Mike slid slowly within her, filling her, understanding how tight she was. He waited, allowing her body to accommodate him, skimming his hands up toward her breasts, cupping them in his calloused palms, thumbs brushing teasingly against her straining nipples.

"Now," Mike whispered, leaning down, holding her exactly where he wanted her, "I want you to let me pleasure you…"

His words were dark with arousal and instantly, her body responded. Mike remained barely within her, teasing her entrance, that swollen pearl filled with nerve endings, sending scorching heat up through her.

Groaning, Khat gripped his arms, trying to bring him deeper, but he had her on a slant and held her a prisoner, she belatedly realized. Opening her eyes, Khat drowned in the burning, narrowed look he gave her as he leaned over to sample one of her nipples. Her mouth opened, a hoarse cry tearing out of her throat. He was going to tease her to death! His hands were like firm steel clamps on her hips knowing she'd try to buck up against him. This time, she felt helpless beneath this slow, scalding onslaught. How much could she take? Her channel was tight and hot, and she whimpered again as his teeth teased the peak, sending more shocks through her tense, needy body.

A fevered explosion burst loose from within her, and she sobbed out his name, her fingers gripping his hard, muscled biceps, frozen, back curving upward. A sound, like a hoarse cry of pleasure, tore out of her.

And then, Mike moved more deeply into her, prolonging her orgasm, beginning to touch that sweet spot so deep within her, the guardian of all her orgasms to come. He angled her hips, thrust swiftly and he heard her mewling cries grow more intense, her fingers digging frantically into the blankets. He held her, thrust as deep as he could go, and she literally dissolved like hot honey between his hands. Her flesh flushed, her back so taut he thought she'd snap in two as the next orgasm shook her to her foundation.

Only then did Mike take his own pleasure, releasing her, allowing her to slide damply from his thighs back onto the blanket. Covering her with his body, he smiled into her eyes that were dazed with more gold than green in them. "You're mine," he grated, his hands framing her face. "Never...ever forget that, Angel." Mike leaned down, curving his mouth against hers, absorbing her panting breath deep into him, giving back to her, simultaneously thrusting powerfully into her. He took her hard, not rough. Releasing control over himself, Mike felt fire explode within him, making him shudder and tense. He gripped the blankets on either side of her head, a growl tearing out between his clenched teeth, nostrils flared.

Khat lay limp, feeling the warmth and weight of Mike upon her. Nothing had matched the emotions stirring within her as he slid his arm beneath her shoul-

ders, holding her in the aftermath, his breath coming
in gasps against her neck and shoulder. Weakly, she
slid her arm over his back, slick with sweat. A smile
played at the corners of her mouth as Khat absorbed
their union. Nothing on earth had ever felt so good.
Mike held her heart. He nourished her soul.

"LET ME PUT the lotion on your back," Mike told her
later after they'd recovered. Khat lay on her belly, arms
beneath her cheek.

"I didn't do it for three weeks," she admitted.

He sat down beside her, their hips meeting as he
gently applied the lotion, starting at her shoulders.
"You don't have three arms." Her body shook from
silent laughter. He grinned, gently moving his fingers
across her scarred skin. "I'm good to have around, if
for no other reason than applying lotion to your back
two times a day," he teased. Khat barely opened her
eyes, her smile disappearing.

"You do so much more than that for me, Mike."

"Because I love you, Khat. That's what people who
love one another do. They take care of each other. They
find ways to please them, make them smile. Make them
happy." He watched her eyes close, a sense of peace
in her expression.

"That feels so good. I can already feel my skin relax-
ing." She opened her eyes and looked over at him. The
day was dawning, and she could see his hard face, the
angles, the set of his mouth. Khat knew Mike's tender
side, not the warrior side. Every touch sent tiny prickles of pleasure through her skin. Her flesh had been so
toughened over time, it had turned numb and leathery
until he'd insisted on giving her back lotion twice a day

at the villa. The change had been amazing. Whatever Mike touched was better off for it.

"Do you feel like telling me how you got these?" he asked, meeting and holding her gaze. "If you don't want to now, then some other time?" Because Mike knew he couldn't force Khat to trust him. And it was only trust that would allow her to tell him of her captivity and torture.

Khat felt mellow, none of her usual defense systems online. Mike was able to walk silently through those walls and touch the real her. That part of herself that was left after the torture. She shrugged. "It's something you should know," she agreed in a whisper. Closing her eyes because she did not want to see Mike's expression, she said, "I was trapped in a box canyon by Khogani's men. They captured me and took me back to one of their caves. Sattar Khogani, who is the son of Mustafa, is a twenty-four-year-old street punk." Her lips twitched. "He was shrieking and threatening me because I wouldn't talk. But his captain, Ramin, who actually runs the Hill tribe while Sattar learns to be a leader, had me stripped down to the waist. They tied my hands on a limb overhead, my feet inches off the floor. He asked me in perfect English who I really was. I wouldn't talk. After five questions, I had five lashes with a metal-tipped whip. I fainted. They'd throw water on me to make me regain consciousness. I took eight lashes that first day. Ramin had me held down on my stomach and they poured salt into my wounds. I screamed until I fainted from the pain."

Mike stopped applying the lotion, his hand resting protectively across her back. She spoke of it as if it were nothing. Closing his eyes, he wanted to find Ramin and personally kill the bastard. "Then what happened?" he managed, his voice strained.

Drawing a deep breath, Khat said, "Ramin let me sit in a cell with water only, starving me, for a week. Then he brought me out and strung me up again. The same thing happened again. Five questions. No answers. Eight lashes." Khat felt Mike's hand tense upon her back. "I think I've told you enough."

"No," he rasped, "I want to know everything." If he didn't, he couldn't understand what she'd suffered through or how deeply it had affected her.

"I got hauled out a third time, a week after that. By that time, I had blood poisoning because no one would tend my back. The salt created so much pain for me, and I didn't have enough water to rinse it off my back. By the time I was strung up a third time, I had a fever and was so starved, I couldn't walk. He asked me the same questions, and I didn't answer him. When they cut me down, he jerked me by my hair, screaming into my face he was going to rape me next time."

"Who rescued you?"

"The women from the nearby Shinwari village carried me to one of their homes. Another woman walked to the SEAL team in a nearby FOB and got me rescued. It was an eight-man team out of J-bad. They came in a CH-47 helicopter, and the women carried me out to them. I was out of my mind with fever, hallucinating, and I still don't remember it all to this day. You know the rest."

Gently moving his hand across her back, Mike choked out, "I'm sorry, Khat." His stomach rolled, nausea burning in his tightened throat.

"It's over, Mike. That's the good news," Khat murmured sleepily.

"Come on," he coaxed, putting the lotion away. "I want to lie down, pull you into my arms, and we'll sleep."

Khat rolled to her side and gave him a drowsy smile as he gathered her into his arms, pulling her against him. He drew up the other sleeping bag around them. His shoulder became her pillow. As she closed her eyes, she knew no nightmares would stalk her because Mike was holding her. Very quickly, Khat faded into sleep.

Mike lay awake for a long time, holding Khat. He could feel her shallow breath, her body limp against him. Rage tunneled through him. He wanted those bastards. Both of them. Stunned that she'd survived such torture, it told him just how strong Khat really was. Her body had been broken, but her spirit was intact, even though she was fractured from the trauma. Mike wasn't sure he'd have borne up half as well as she had under that kind of torture. Khat left a lot out of her explanation, but he didn't blame her. If she had blood poisoning, sepsis, she could have died from it. Mike knew plenty about medical issues as a SEAL, and blood poisoning was one of the major concerns for anyone. It could kill a person in as few as three days.

She'd probably been caught just in time and helped by the village women. Those brave Afghan women had risked their lives saving hers, and Mike knew it. The Taliban could have come back and scourged the village where they had kept Khat, killing them, their children and their husbands. *Damn.* His mouth thinned, and he was unable to wrap his mind around how much it had affected Khat on every level of herself. It increased his desire to protect her at all costs.

CHAPTER SEVENTEEN

"WE'VE GOT HALF the trails mapped in a week." Mike congratulated Khat as she made them dinner.

They were in the pool cave. He was working on his Toughbook laptop, sitting against the wall of the cave, the kerosene lantern shedding light. He lifted his chin, watching her make them tea. "Pretty good work. We're a good team, Angel."

"Half to go," Khat said wryly, pouring the hot water into the mugs.

Outside, thunderstorms loomed over the Hindu Kush. They'd just gotten in at dawn, the lightning lacing the west. It was best to traverse and do the mapping in the dark. So long as they had some moonlight, they could do it. That and using NVGs to open up the night so their horses wouldn't trip or fall on one of the rugged goat trails.

Mike took the mug. "Thanks," he murmured, shutting down the laptop and placing it beside him on the sleeping bag laid out. He watched Khat come and sit near his knee, crossing her legs. Her clean hair lay damply across her shoulders. She'd already gone to the waterfall in the other room and cleaned up. The dark green T-shirt she wore with her cammie trousers emphasized her breasts. It sent desire streaking through Mike.

Khat looked at peace. As he sipped the hot Darjee-ling tea, Mike wondered if it was because they were making love nearly every night. Or that he was working with her. He wasn't sure. One thing he did look forward to were their dawn conversations with one another. They worked through the night hours, would ride back to the waterfall cave at dawn, take care of their tired horses, get cleaned up and cook a meal. The activities helped them come down off the intense danger that always stalked them in the dark, rugged mountains.

"In another week, if all goes well," she murmured, looking over her mug at him, "we'll be done."

Mike heard the sadness in her voice. "Are you find-ing working with a partner isn't that bad?" he teased, smiling a little. Khat's green eyes were dark and thoughtful-looking. Every time he made love with her, Mike felt her moving closer to him, and a little further away from her work in the mountains. It wasn't any-thing obvious; just a feeling. He felt like he had two weeks to persuade her on other levels, that she was worthy of being loved, and that she was allowed to have a life other than this one.

"It certainly has fringe benefits," Khat drawled, grinning. Her body instantly warmed as he gave her that intense, hungry look. She had never felt so happy as with Mike being a part of her world. In his arms as she slept deeply, her dreams were turning hopeful, no longer nightmares about her torture. And then her smile faded. "Tell me what you're going to do when your platoon is rotated Stateside? What do you do with those sixty days?"

Mike pulled up his knee, resting his arm on top of it, holding her softened gaze. "Well, the first week, I stay by myself and don't do much of anything. I catch up on sleep and start to unwind from the tension combat puts you in. I'm usually pretty grumpy. I don't like crowds, a lot of noise or the normal human things that are always going on." He pushed his fingers through his damp hair, having washed the grit and sweat off his body beneath the waterfall earlier.

"Are you anxious?"

"Sometimes," he admitted. "If a car backfires, I've hit the deck a number of times," he admitted ruefully. "Sounds really get me going."

"When I had to go back to the States to upgrade my paramedic skills, I would always fly in, and I would see my mother at a nearby motel. I couldn't go back to the house since I was disowned." Khat wrinkled her nose. "My mother never stopped loving me, so I always made plans to see her for a couple of days before I left for Afghanistan. I found myself feeling too vulnerable, like you. I was happy just to hide in the room and go out to eat only when I had to."

"I'm glad you can see your mother," he murmured. Khat's expression was filled with deep sadness. He wanted to strangle that father of hers. "So you stay in touch with her?"

"Yes."

"She didn't disown you?"

"No. After it happened, my mother was very angry with my father. She cried. So did I. She said he was upset over my torture." Her mouth quirked. "So was I. But he took it out on me, not the men who did it to me."

"Old customs die hard," Mike said grimly.

"It doesn't matter anymore," Khat said, sipping the tea. "My mother and I connect by emails when I can do it." She looked around the cave. "Out here, it's impossible. I can hook up with her when I'm at Bravo, which is nice."

He didn't want to say much more, his rage pinpointed on Jaleel Shinwari. Did he know what the hell his decision to disown his only daughter had done to her? Driven her more deeply into a life that was dangerous to her on a daily basis? He shut down his feelings toward her father. "You asked what I did with my sixty days off?"

Brightening, Khat said, "Yes. So, week one you hide and acclimate?"

Grinning, Mike murmured, "That's a nice way of putting it. The second week I grab my scuba gear and head out on a boat that a friend of mine owns, and go scuba diving in the kelp beds off La Jolla. I like hunting for abalone and spear fishing for sea bass. I bring back my haul and put it in my freezer. I eat a lot of abalone steaks and fish for that week."

"You're back in the water again," she said wistfully. "A sort of healing for you, maybe?"

Mike felt his heart expand fiercely at her insight into him. Her green gaze held him in tender regard. "Exactly. SEALs are taught Mom Ocean is our safety. I found out that was true for me. Being in the water is like being held by her. It's a soothing feeling to me. I always feel better after a scuba dive."

"That sounds wonderful," Khat whispered.

"I told you if you decide to rotate back this winter, and you come for a visit, I'd teach you to scuba dive." Mike held his breath, seeing a number of emotions cross her expression. Sadness as well as hope.

"I'd like that," Khat said, her voice strained.

"Have you thought any more about rotating out?"

"I'm torn in two, Mike." She bit her lower lip and avoided his narrowing eyes. "I feel guilt if I leave. And I want so much more of what we have with one another."

"These villages are stuck in snowdrifts up to six to ten feet of snow during the winter," he said gently. "You know that better than anyone."

Nodding, Khat closed her eyes, feeling pain in her heart. She loved Mike with a desperation she'd never felt in her life. Was she throwing their growing relationship away by staying here? What would it hurt if she left the snowbound village and stayed with him instead? Her conscience warred within itself. Every day with Mike was like an unexpected blessing in her isolated life. Just his presence brought her peace and calm. Even though they were in constant, nonstop danger, his presence shifted her whole world for the better.

Khat opened her eyes and drew a circle on the sleeping bag with her index finger. "I'm seriously thinking about it, Mike."

"You'd want to stay here because of your family?" he guessed.

"Yes. I love them all. They love me. I feel welcomed. Wanted." Khat met his dark gaze. "But you are making me feel loved and welcomed in another way. It's so… beautiful…" A lump formed in her throat as she felt tears coming. Mike was showing her a bright, hopeful world. In a way, he was like a big bad guardian angel, guarding her heart, seeding it with hope and love she thought she'd never have except for her Afghan family.

Mike sipped his tea, saying nothing. It would do no good to push or argue. Slowly, he was seeing Khat realizing she had choices whereas before, she saw none. He finished off the tea and stood up. "My turn to cook dinner tonight." He touched her cheek as he aimed himself at the grate on the cave floor. He had one more week to try and convince her to come back with him. Was there enough time to do it? They weren't living in a vacuum here in the Hindu Kush. It was dangerous to them every time they stepped out of their hiding place.

KHAT AWOKE SLOWLY in Mike's arms. He was still asleep. She could feel the slow rise and fall of his chest beneath her arm. From where she lay at his side, she could see that dusk was upon them, the light coming down through the crack in the cave ceiling. She heard the soft snort of the horses nearby and closed her eyes, absorbing his lean, strong body. His heart lay beneath her palm. A powerful wave of love washed through her.

The conversation they'd had at dusk last night flowed through her drowsy mind. Would her father's family understand her not staying with them throughout the long, hard winter? Would they accuse her of being selfish? Self-serving? Her Aunt Leeda, her father's older sister, was always wise. The whole family was run by this strong-minded woman. Leeda held her dear, and she always stayed with her family during the winter time. What would Aunt Leeda say? Khat wished she had elders around her who could give her an answer to her dilemma.

She felt Mike awaken, his hand sliding down her arm in a caressing gesture. Nuzzling against his shoulder, she closed her eyes, absorbing him, his love and support. Maybe, as they swung north, they could sneak in under cover of night to the village, and Aunt Leeda could meet Mike. Khat relied heavily upon her wise aunt. She didn't know to this day whether her relatives knew of her father disowning her. If they did, it didn't show. She was always welcome and surrounded by the women of the family, spoiled with attention and lavished with their love.

Mike groaned as Khat pressed her body seductively against his, feeling her lips linger on his cheek. "I want to wake up every day like this," he muttered, wiping the sleep out of his eyes. He felt her mouth glide across his as she leaned over him. Turning, he lifted his hand, his fingers curving around the nape of her neck, drawing her against him. He felt the hardening of her nipples as her breasts brushed languidly across his chest. Her lips were soft, yielding, and he moved to his side, placing Khat on her back. There was nothing shy or retiring about her, and he smiled beneath her mouth.

"Did you just wake up?" he asked, kissing each corner of her mouth.

"Mmm," she answered, sliding her fingers through his longish hair, arching against him, feeling his erection press into her belly. Opening her eyes, she drowned in his lion-gold ones that burned with hunger for her. Mike cupped her breast, and the air escaped her lungs. Her body was incredibly sensitive to his every touch.

"Like that?" he asked gruffly, holding her breast, moving his thumb closer to her hardened nipple, watching her eyes widen with anticipation. He took her mouth gently, engaging her softness, moving his thumb teasingly across her nipple. Her reaction was always the same; a tremor moving through her, a moan of need that he absorbed into his mouth, her warm, strong body arching demandingly against him.

Mike knew by the light in the cave they were late in waking up. He wanted to take his time, love Khat and lie here with her for an hour or more. But that wasn't going to happen. There was no way he wasn't going to love her, however.

He left her wet lips and leaned down, capturing the peak, drawing it into his mouth. She twisted and moaned, her fingers digging into his back. She was his female snow leopard, so sinuous and powerful, and she was his.

Sliding his hand down across her belly, he felt her shiver as he parted her damp thighs. She was ready for him. Cursing the timing, Mike wasn't going to leave both of them sexually frustrated. His fingers lingered just outside her entrance, her fluids abundant and warm. Her hips flexed upward, wanting him within her. He took her other nipple, sucking strongly, feeling her gasp, writhing in his arms. As he did, Mike slid his fingers into her, feeling her walls spasm and contract around him. She was so damned hot and responsive. Hearing her breath going uneven, her fingers opening and closing frantically against his shoulder, he teased the taut peak with his teeth. Her cry of pleasure combined with him moving deeply within her, made her pant.

Mike felt the sheen of dampness from her body as he sought and found that remarkable spot within her, stroking the bundle of nerves that would always trigger an orgasm in a woman. It did in her. She cried out, her hips bucking against his hand, burying her face against his chest, sobbing for breath. He felt her body contract violently, felt the explosion of thick, heated fluids surround his fingers, and Mike smiled, holding her tight, giving her all the pleasure she wanted. Time wasn't on their side.

Feeling Khat sink against him, her cries softening, her body going limp, he smiled and leaned down, kissing her parted lips. Easing his fingers from within her, he brought Khat against him, feeling the fine tremors still moving through her body as the orgasm rippled outward within her.

He kissed her damp brow, her flushed cheek, loving her so damn much his heart hurt. Wanting this wild, natural, passionate woman in his bed, at his side, for the rest of his life, Mike knew nothing was set in stone. Even getting to hold her was a gift to him. Finally, he rasped against her soft lips, "Come on, we've got to get up and moving, baby, whether we want to or not…"

KHAT LAY ON her belly with the sniper rifle just below a ridgeline. Mike lay next to her with a spotter scope. It was midnight and colder than hell, the icy winds gusting and shrieking over the ridge where they lay. Below, they were watching fifteen Bactrian camels being led by Taliban soldiers. The camels were carrying heavy loads of what looked to be bags of fertilizer. She heard Mike calling in the GPS to J-bad, and requesting an air asset to destroy the group. Those bags of fertilizer, once they got through the mountains, would then be distributed by Taliban soldiers to the IED bomb makers throughout Afghanistan. The bags carried by the camels would kill many, many American and UN soldiers over the coming months.

Her heart was pulsing strongly. They were half a mile higher than the rat line trail the group was on below them. She listened to his quiet voice as he talked with J-bad. Usually, they rolled out a jet from their compound, and bombs would be dropped. The only problem was their being dangerously close to the drop. Khat knew that meant that if the pickled bombs weren't right on target, they could die and be listed as "friendly fire" casualties. It wasn't a situation she wanted to find herself in.

Listening to the communications through her ear device, she kept watch on the slow-moving group through her Nightforce scope.

Their horses were tied down below the slope, well hidden in a grove of trees. Khat listened as Mike was told to contact Camp Bravo for Apache interdiction, that none were available out of J-bad. She watched as he switched channels and made the call. In moments, it reached the Black Jaguar Squadron based at Bravo. Yes, they had two Apaches on the runway as a QRF, quick reaction force, to respond to the situation. Mike gave them the GPS coordinates of the group and signed off.

He glanced over at her and made a hand signal for them to slowly extricate themselves from their position and get the hell out of there. The Apaches would arrive in thirty minutes. With their heads-up display, their television camera and infrared capability, they'd quickly locate this group and dispense with them.

Khat slowly moved down from the ridgeline, the rocks biting into her lower legs. The Kevlar vest protected her upper body from the sharpened stones. Mike worked his way down the scree, never leaving her side. His M-4 rifle was strapped across his back, handy in case he needed it in a hurry.

The night was black except for a quarter moon in

the sky. They were exposed and knew it, hoping the desert camouflage uniforms they wore blended them into the surrounding rocks.

Finally, Khat turned and stood up, far enough below the ridgeline so she couldn't be seen. The horses focused their attention on them. They had to hurry. Khat didn't want to be anywhere near the air assault. Slipping and sliding, Mike gripped her elbow to prevent her from falling. Once down the slope, Khat quickly sheathed her Win Mag rifle and closed up the boot to protect it.

"Where to now?" Mike asked, mounting his horse.

"North," she said quietly, mounting Mina. She pointed to a lesser-used goat trail that led down off the mountain. "This way." She urged her mare into a trot.

As a pale, pink dawn crawled upon the rugged peaks of the Hindu Kush, they were once again within their cave complex. Mike had taken care of the horses while Khat got the hay and measured the oats out for their hardworking mounts.

They'd established a working routine. With two people, it went twice as fast. While Khat stripped out of her gear and washed herself in the waterfall pool, Mike was laying out their bedding and getting things set up for their MRE meals. When she came back, dressed only in a clean green T-shirt, the ends hanging halfway down her curved thighs, Mike took notice. No matter what Khat wore, she was sexy as hell. He was next and shed his gear, eager to wash off a night's worth of grit and sweat.

Over their MRE meal, Khat sat cross-legged, facing him. "I want to take a couple of days off," she told him, eating the warmed spaghetti.

"And do what?" Mike asked, leaning against the cave wall. He absorbed her drying hair, a red mantle across her shoulders. Too bad she had to put on clean trousers; he liked seeing her with just a T-shirt on.

"I want to spend a few days doing medical clinics in Dur Babba."

Mike moved the potatoes around on his MRE tray. "That's your family's village, right?" He saw her nod, her look uncertain.

"Are you okay with it?" Khat watched his expression. It was thoughtful, not concerned. She needed to see her aunt Leeda, and this would be the only way she could get to talk with her.

Mike felt Khat was in turmoil, and he was not sure how to read her request. What was the real reason for her wanting to go there? This was a specific op for mapping the mountains. Not diverting to a village to render medical aid. He ate the pears and thought some more. Khat seemed anxious. Worried. Finally, he said, "You need to see your family?"

"The truth is I need to see my aunt Leeda." Khat explained to him her standing in her father's family. "She's a woman, but even the men listen to her."

Mike nodded, watching as Khat pushed the food disinterestedly around on her MRE pouch. "She's someone you can really talk to?"

"Yes."

What did Khat want to talk to her relative about now? He sensed Khat's anxiety, but he also saw it in her eyes. She was being honest with him, but was hold-

ing back something, too. "Do they know your father
has disowned you?"

"I don't honestly know," she said with a shrug, forcing herself to eat when she didn't feel hungry. "I've not
told them. I'm too ashamed to admit it, if you want
the truth."

Mike finished off his food. He set the tray aside
and studied Khat. "Come here." He held his hand out
toward her.

Khat set her half-eaten MRE aside and moved between his spread legs, her back against his body, her
head coming to rest on his left shoulder. His arms came
around her waist, and he held her. All the anxiety dissolved beneath his embrace. "I love you," she whispered, nuzzling her face against his bearded jaw.

"I don't ever want life without you, Angel," he
rasped, turning his head, pressing a kiss to her temple. "Whatever is challenging you, we can handle." He
gently sifted his fingers through her drying strands,
knowing she enjoyed it so much.

Placing her hands over his, Khat whispered, "How
did you know?"

"What? That something's bothering you?" He slipped
his fingers beneath her hair, grazing her neck. "You
can't hide anything from me, Khat, because I love you.
We have a connection. You can feel when I'm out of
sorts, just as much as I can feel when something's wor-
rying you."

She felt the warm strength of Mike's body around
her. In his arms, she felt safe, desired and loved. "I want
to see my aunt Leeda to see if she would be upset if I
don't stay with her this winter. I want her to meet you,
Mike. I want her to understand that I love you." Khat

compressed her lips, tipped her head up so she could look up into his dark gold eyes. "She'll be honest with me because she loves me. I trust her."

"You want her blessing, then?" Mike saw the concern over what her aunt would say deep in Khat's green eyes. Mike tried to keep his elation under wraps. He wanted to scream for joy that she'd finally made a choice. And it was to be with him! Now he had to worry about this Aunt Leeda, whom Khat placed a great deal of trust in.

Nodding, she whispered, "Yes. I know if I don't stay in the village, some of my relatives will get angry. I always bring food and other supplies that I distribute among the family. That wouldn't happen if I wasn't there."

"You're saying Aunt Leeda isn't bribable, right?" Mike smiled a little, moving his thumb against the warm velvet of her cheek.

"She comes from the heart like I do." Khat sighed and added, "Aunt Leeda was the first to take me in, Mike. She was fierce about taking care of me like a mother. She isn't rich. She's a dirt-poor farmer like everyone else, but she loves me. And I love her."

Mike wrapped his arms gently around her, holding her tightly. Resting his jaw against the top of her head, he said, "Then we'll go see Aunt Leeda." As soon as he'd spoken the words, Khat released a long sigh of relief.

As he held her in his arms, he wondered if Aunt Leeda really had Khat's best interests at heart or not. If she didn't, then Mike knew he could lose Khat. *Damn.* It was another hurdle to jump in order to win her hand. Mike was very well aware of marriage customs among the Pashtun tribes. He'd have to ask Leeda's husband for Khat's hand. They didn't understand American customs of living together before marriage. In the end, the real decision would rest on Leeda's shoulders. Whether he liked it or not, he was going to have to make a good impression with Khat's relatives or else…

LEEDA GAVE A cry of delight as she opened the door at dawn and found her niece smiling a welcome at her. The woman threw her arms around Khat's shoulders, fiercely hugging her. It was barely dawn, gray light hinting at the mountains that surrounded Dur Babba. Khat smiled at her red-haired aunt, who was dressed in a long brown wool robe, her hair braided about her head.

"Aunt," she said in Pashtun, "I want you to meet my good friend, Mike Tarik. He's come with me." She turned to gesture for him to come forward.

Leeda, who had a lot of gray in her red hair, squinted her green eyes, studying the tall stranger dressed in Afghan clothes. "Ah, you've brought a friend, eh?" Her long hand snaked out of her robe, and she gripped Mike's arm. "Then you are welcome. Both of you, come in. Come in…"

There was a taper lit in the corner of the large room as Mike entered after Khat. This was a larger mud house with two or three rooms. Leeda had a small fire in the other corner, a kettle on a blackened iron grate above the small flame. He saw two other rooms. Sleeping rooms, the curtains drawn across the openings.

"What a surprise," Leeda said, patting Khat's cheek. "You look good. Have you gained weight?"

Khat sat down near the fire to warm herself. The

all-night ride in freezing temperatures was miserable. "Yes." She gestured for Mike to sit next to her as her aunt busied herself making tea for them. "Is everyone else asleep?"

Tittering, Leeda murmured, "Oh, they'll wake up now that they hear your voice, niece." Her green eyes sparkled. "They know you always bring candy and gifts."

Laughing softly, Khat pulled the hood off her head, the black scarf lying about her shoulders. She saw her aunt eye Mike warily. "Auntie," she said softly, "Mike is someone very special to me. You don't have to be afraid of him. We work together up in the mountains."

Her aunt was fifty-five, lean and tall. She had Khat's red hair and green eyes. Her father had the same color of hair and eyes, too. Leeda had told her many stories of the red hair through their family. A great warrior had come from the west and married into the family. Khat finally figured out that it might have been a Siberian Russian, as red hair ran in that group.

Leeda poured the tea, put the small ceramic cups on a tray and brought it over, serving Mike first then Khat. She set the tray aside and pulled over a very old, worn pillow and sat on it, facing them.

Leeda watched Mike for a long moment, her cup between her long, worn hands. "You are not Pashtun."

Mike said, "No, ma'am. My father is Saudi, and my mother is American." He saw the woman's deeply lined face grow thoughtful.

"Ah," Leeda said, giving Khat a curious look. "He's half Middle Eastern as you are? How did you meet?"

Mike let the women do the talking. Except for the taper and small fire in the corner, the place was dark.

Smoke rose lazily upward through a hole in the roof. He could hear the snoring of men in one room. Khat explained how they'd met. The smell of earth, the wood smoke trailing out a hole in the roof, and goats entered his nostrils. Leeda was animated, and he liked her warmth, frequently reaching out to touch Khat's hand. Now he could see why Khat loved her. She was nurturing and maternal; something Khat desperately needed.

"So?" Leeda murmured, shifting her attention to Mike, "you are a SEAL?"

"Yes, ma'am."

"We have benefitted greatly from your kind, and we are grateful." Leeda gestured toward the door. "The border area is less dangerous because of your bravery to face the Taliban."

"We're glad to be of help when we can," Mike told her seriously, finishing his cup of tea.

Leeda got up and poured him more.

Thanking her, Mike knew there could be ten or twenty cups of tea on this chat. All talk was diplomatic and roundabout. The point of the conversation was never addressed at first. Usually, hours later and many cups of tea later, the point of the meeting was finally spoken about. Leeda was wily. He felt it. And she reminded him of Khat. Leeda was very strong, her spine straight, her slender shoulders pulled back with deep pride and confidence. Khat certainly took after Jaleel's female side of the line.

"My niece has been our protector for a long time," Leeda said to him, frowning.

"Yes, she has," Mike said.

"You are aware of what she does since you work with her?"

"I am."

"My niece is getting on in years and—" she smiled kindly toward Khat "—I have wished that she would meet a good man who values her and gives her many children."

Mike kept his face carefully arranged. He heard Khat choke on her tea, coughing for several moments. Leeda's steel gaze didn't waver one iota. Neither did his. "I love your niece with every breath I take," he told her quietly, sincerely. "I want to ask her to be my wife, but Khat felt she wanted to speak with you first. You and your husband."

Nodding, Leeda said less formally, "My husband died ten years ago when he stepped on an IED. I am the head of my family now."

Okay, Mike thought, the ball is in her court. It meant Leeda had full authority to either bless their union or tear it apart. She was the oldest sister. Normally, the husband of the oldest daughter would take over, but Mike knew many women became widows in these villages because of Taliban activity. If the men didn't die from stepping on an IED, the Taliban would kidnap them to recruit them, and they were never seen by their family again. More and more Afghan village responsibility for ancient male customs was falling on the shoulders of the oldest woman or the matriarch in the family.

Two young girls came out of the other room, sleepily wiping their eyes. One was ten and the other was probably six from what Mike could judge. The moment they saw Khat, they shrieked her name and flew across the dirt floor, throwing themselves into her arms.

Leeda smiled a little at Mike. "We'll talk later, eh?"

Mike nodded, holding her curious stare. Pashtuns didn't like outsiders. They almost always married within their tribal area. Sometimes a man from another village would court a woman from elsewhere, but both were Pashtuns, the tribes friendly with one another. He was a distinct outsider. He wasn't Pashtun. His tribe was Saudi.

Unsure of what Leeda was thinking, Mike turned and smiled, watching the two young girls snuggle like wriggling, happy puppies, into Khat's lap. The expression on her face melted his heart. It was obvious she loved children. He wondered what their children would look like. Would her family's strong red-haired gene be passed on to them?

Swallowing hard, Mike felt his love for Khat so deeply that he struggled to breathe for a moment. Her profile was clean, her lips drawn into a warm smile, her eyes soft and maternal. They would have beautiful, strong, intelligent children, he knew. If only… He glanced to see Leeda beginning to make breakfast for the awakening family. Soon the men would come out, eat and then go to work in the fields all day. The women would care for the younger children and cook, the hub of Afghan village life.

Later, after Mike had met all of the Shinwari family, he and Khat walked through the village to the stable where their horses were kept. The sun was just rising, the sky a light blue with puffy white clouds. He walked at her side, noticing how relaxed she had become. There were eight boys and girls, plus seven adults in that small house. All of them shy about meeting him, but adoring and worshipful of Khat.

"You're a rock star here," he teased, looking to see her response.

Khat snorted. "I am not."

"You are loved by everyone."

"I am," she murmured, smiling over at him. "I think Aunt Leeda likes you. She thinks you're here to ask her permission to marry me."

"I am," he said bluntly. He saw Khat's eyes grow huge. They halted near the mud hut that doubled as a barn for their mounts. "Your aunt forced my hand," he said wryly, resting his hands on her shoulders. He saw her smile a little, moisture in her eyes. "I love you, Khat," Mike said, his voice roughened. "I want a life with you. Not just here in this country, either. Did you think I would walk away from you someday?"

Her heart melted beneath his dark, intense stare. "I…well…it's not been that long and I thought…" She shrugged helplessly.

"I play for keeps, Angel. I told you that night when I was waiting for that Medevac I was going to find you again. Remember?"

"I've never forgotten it," she whispered unsteadily.

"Then let me make this formal," Mike growled, holding her shaken gaze. "Will you marry me? Spend the rest of your life with me? Have my children, if that's what you want? Have a life where I can hear your laughter, feel your heart against my ear when I lay my head on your breast? Sit on the beach and watch the sunset with me?"

Tears gathered in Khat's eyes. His voice was gruff with feeling, his eyes alive with love for her, his fingers firm on her shoulders. "Or feed Sam the harbor seal fish on Fridays?" she quavered.

"Anything you want, Khat. I want to give you the world." Mike leaned down, not caring who the hell saw him kissing her. She was his woman, and he couldn't care less what anyone thought. When she came into his arms, her mouth so warm and strong against his, Mike groaned.

Khat slid her arms around his shoulders, and she strained to get as close to him as possible. Tasting the warmth of her tears as their lips melded against one another, Mike hoped they were tears of happiness, not of separation. He'd been shocked by Leeda's pointed questions and observations. She hadn't been diplomatic at all. And she'd gone straight to the heart of why Khat had come to see her. Only Khat had wanted to ask her aunt a different question. But wily Leeda saw the underlying reason. As matriarch of her family, she wasn't about to hand Khat off to just any man who courted her. She wanted to make damn sure he was a worthy husband for her.

Khat lifted her lips away from his mouth, breathing irregularly, drowning in his stormy golden eyes. "Aunt Leeda thinks I brought you here as potential husband material."

"Yeah, I got that real fast," he said, brushing her cheek, amused.

"I'm sorry, Mike. I didn't mean for this to happen like this."

"I'm not sorry at all. Because—" he tipped her chin up so he could hold her gaze "—that was my plan all along, Khat. From the moment I saw you in that waterfall, I knew you were mine. I just didn't know how I was going to do it, but my heart knew you were the woman for me. It was a done deal." And it was. For him. Mike saw the gold in the depths of her green eyes, saw the softness at the corners of her luscious mouth.

Her heart filled with quiet joy, seeing the wry look he gave her. "I'm finding my way with my heart, Mike. I need time…but I know you will give me the time I need to keep sorting through everything." Khat searched his hooded look.

"You have all the time you want," he promised thickly. "I wasn't going to mention the dream I had for us, Angel, but your aunt brought it up." He smiled.

"Aunt Leeda isn't known for her diplomacy. But I think you got that part pretty quickly."

"No kidding," Mike muttered, releasing her and giving her a wicked grin. "Kind of reminds me a lot of you."

"Now," Khat said, giving him a playful look, "you know where it comes from." She tried to steady herself with the idea that Mike was serious about wanting to marry her. All her life, she had prepared herself to be alone because of her scars and shameful past. There was so much going on that Khat couldn't adjust fast enough.

Mike led her into the barn. Together they removed the tarp over the packhorse's panniers. They unloaded the goods from each one. Khat wanted to spend the rest of her day giving a medical clinic to those who would come to Aunt Leeda's home. They would stand in line for hours to receive help. Mike would be her bodyguard, always watchful, always alert. No village, especially along the border, was ever safe.

LEEDA INVITED MIKE to tea after Khat had wrapped up her medical clinic. She was having tea with more of her relatives, who were begging her to visit them at another home in the village. He went one way, she went the other.

Mike had removed his hajii gear and put it in the barn with the horses. Wearing his SEAL uniform and all his gear, he knocked on the door of Leeda's home.

"Come in," she invited.

Mike took off his black baseball cap and entered. The house smelled of spices, of lamb cooking. The woman was now dressed in a dark burgundy robe, a pink scarf over her red hair. Mike could see that when Leeda was younger, she had probably been quite beautiful. This time, she led him into another room, the window open to draw in fresh air. A small red Persian rug was spread out, a silver tray darkened with ages of tea use, delicate white cups with small honey cakes on a dish in the center of it. He knew from experience this was a formal sit-down. Leeda was going to unmercifully grill him.

He leaned his rifle against the nearby wall, close enough to grab if he needed it. Mike sat so he faced the entrance to the room. Leeda handed him the dish with the honey cakes. He thanked her, taking only one and giving it back to her.

"You have caused a great deal of excitement by coming to our village," she murmured, pouring him tea and setting the cup in front of him. She poured tea for herself, sitting on several cushions at the other end of the rug.

"I was hoping we could come and go quietly," Mike said with a slight smile, tasting the honey cake. It was hand-milled grain with sweet, wild honey mixed with raisins, and it tasted good. Leeda had probably made them specially for this interrogation.

"My niece, as you can tell, is highly regarded here among all families." Leeda sipped her tea, her gaze never leaving his face.

"She is greatly loved," Mike agreed, wiping his fingers on his trousers after finishing off the honey cake.

"You are not of our tribe."

He felt the invisible arrow go straight to his heart. "No, I'm not. But love doesn't see tribes, color of a person's skin or even countries," he countered, watching her frown.

"I was hoping she would find favor with a young man here over time," she said, breaking a honey cake open and eating a piece of it.

"She's been here five years," Mike pointed out mildly. He saw the woman's deeply tanned face wrinkle in thought.

"And she favors you."

He nodded once, waiting to see where she was going with it.

"Do you love her, Mike Tarik?"

The fervency of her question caught him completely off guard. Leeda's eyes were narrowed and intense upon him. "I do, with all of my heart," he answered quietly, placing his hand against his chest. Now he was beginning to see where Khat got that passionate snow leopard fierceness. It was clearly genetic.

"Then," Leeda said more formally, "you know there is a dowry involved? You cannot just walk in here, claiming my niece's hand without offering a dowry."

Mike realized that Leeda has accepted him as husband material. His heart soared wildly with joy, but he didn't let it show. Already, they'd moved on to the horse haggling over the dowry. Shocked and scrambling, he was elated with the aunt's blessing, but drawing a blank on dowry. God, he hadn't even thought that far ahead!

"What would you like?" Mike asked, on the defense.

Leeda touched her heart with her hand. "That you love my niece as much as we love her. Love is not something that can be bought or sold."

Again, Mike was thrown off guard. Normally, money, horses, goats and cows were the demand for a dowry. Leeda's passionate-looking green eyes were moist, and he heard a wobble in her husky, strong voice. It was then he realized why Khat had considered this her home. Her family. Fierce Leeda was a mother snow leopard guarding her family without apology. "You're right," he whispered, giving her a kind look. "I love your niece with my life. I would give my life for her." He set the tea down and opened his hands. "She saved my life. I would never do less than that for her. I can't prove to you how much I love her, but with every breath I take, I'm grateful Khat is a part of my life."

"And do you intend to take her away from us? Will we never see her again?"

Mike frowned. "I would make every effort to bring her over here to see you and the family whenever she wanted. I have no intention of tearing Khat away from you."

"But you will live in America," Leeda said bitterly. "And then we are forgotten."

Mike shook his head. "Leeda, my blood is Saudi. I understand about family and tribe. My father makes a journey home every year to visit his relatives and friends. When I wasn't in the navy, I would always accompany him and so would my American-born mother. I think I understand your concerns better than most, don't you?"

She pursed her lips, staring at him as if he were her enemy for a long time before speaking. "You cannot know how my heart feels about this. I've worried for my niece every night for the past five years." She dabbed the tears from her eyes with a white linen handkerchief that she drew from her pocket. "Khatereh has been tortured. I'm sure you know that?"

"I do," he said, grim.

"I know her father has disowned her. But Khatereh does not know that. She thinks I'm illiterate, but I am not. I got my stupid brother's letter." She threw up her hands and groused, "What is wrong with that brother of mine, I do not know! He makes me angry! If he were here, I'd whip him so he could understand what his daughter suffered through because of his idiot decision!"

Mike believed it. This was a woman warrior sitting with him, not some cowed Afghan wife. "His words have harmed her a great deal. It's another wound to her heart," Mike grated.

"So you see what I see? That is good." She picked up her cup of tea and drained it.

"Does your whole family know she's been disowned?"

Shaking her head, Leeda snarled, "When I received Jaleel's letter, I wept for Khatereh and hated him for doing it to her. I ripped up the letter and burned it! A few of our family can read, but not many." She raised a fist into the air. "I read but I cannot write. If I could, I would have sent him back a letter that would explode into flames the moment he opened it up to read it."

Mike nodded, hiding his smile, seeing the rage in the woman's eyes, her bitterness toward her brother, Khat's father. "I would like you to help me, Leeda," he said in a low tone. "Khat is torn between staying here for the winter or coming back to the States with me. She's underweight, she doesn't sleep well and she's in danger all the time up in the mountains. I would like you to talk to her, tell her it's all right to come home with me."

Mouth turning in, Leeda whispered, "You and I are on the same side. We both want Khatereh to heal. She's never healed from the torture and her father disowning her. I believe you do love her. I see it in your eyes. I hear it in your voice. I will miss her, of course, but it's more important she go with you. At least your love will help her to heal over time."

CHAPTER EIGHTEEN

"WHAT DO YOU THINK?" Khat asked her aunt Leeda one morning after everyone had left for the fields for the day. She sat with her aunt in the room with the red Persian rug across the floor.

"I think it will be good for your heart and soul to go with Mike Tarik," she said somberly. Sipping the tea, she gave Khat a kindly look. "You've not taken care of yourself, child. You have given your blood and nearly lost your life so many times for your family and village. At some point you must withdraw and heal."

Frowning, Khat digested Leeda's gentle words. "I am tired," she admitted, pushing a strand of hair from her cheek.

"But you are happy, eh? I see the way this man who holds your heart looks at you. My beloved husband looked at me the same way, and I thank Allah I had twenty-five good years with him. It isn't often a woman is blessed to meet a man who loves and respects her."

"I love Mike," Khat whispered, sipping her tea. "Lately, he's been my anchor. I've been flying apart at the seams."

"You need rest," Leeda flatly stated, frowning. "We have all benefitted from your presence, but now, it's time for you to walk another path."

Tears gathered in Khat's eyes as she looked around

the humble abode. "I—I'll miss all of you so much, Aunt Leeda. You gave me love, and you welcomed me when I felt so alone." *Abandoned.* "I'll miss having tea with you in the early morning and talking about life, about your wonderful stories…" She wiped her cheek, seeing her aunt's face droop with sadness. Khat felt her heart grieving, and she hadn't even left yet.

"Mike will help you make a new home." Leeda gave a flourish of her hand. "Sit down and agree to have tea together. Talk. It is a good thing for a husband and wife to talk daily with one another. You are going home where you were born, Khatereh. Your spirit belongs in America, not here."

"But my blood has called me here, Aunt."

"Yes, I understand that call. It's there to remind us of our homeland, of our spirit. Our true roots for generations. And you know you'll always be welcome here. Always."

Nodding, Khat wiped more tears away. "Lately, I've become such a sop. I cry so much."

"You didn't cry for four years after your torture," Leeda reminded her. "This man has opened your heart. He's allowing you to grieve and weep for what was taken from you. When you are emptied out, he will replace that emptiness with his love for you." She wagged a worn finger at her. "Love heals all. Never forget that, Niece."

As MIKE RODE with Khat under cover of darkness two nights later, leaving Dur Babba, it was misting rain. The September weather was moody, and rain could quickly turn to snow. The horses plodded across the plain toward the fourteen-thousand-foot mountain that could be seen through their NVGs, a grainy green color.

Mike rode at her side, their legs touching occasionally as the horses plodded along. She had cried, holding on to her aunt as if she were being ripped from a mooring that had been keeping her alive. Mike reached out, gripping her hand and squeezing it gently and then releasing it. He wondered if she was still crying silently. He was unable to tell.

While Khat was saying goodbye to all her relatives, he'd gotten a radio call from Mac back at Bravo. The weather was setting in, and he told them to be careful. When weather lowered in the mountains, only Apaches had thermal imaging capability and even then, it was iffy. Fog, rain and snow were in the weather picture for the next three days. They'd have to lie low and wait it out in the cave. And then, they had another five to seven days of mapping and then they could return to Bravo.

It bothered him that no orders had come down from General Stevenson. Khat's orders should be changed. She should be given light duty or better, sent home to the States to recuperate. He'd miss her, but she'd be safe. And in a few more months, his platoon would rotate home.

The mist hid them, and that was good. Not many Taliban would be out on a miserably cold night like this. Soon enough, they'd be climbing a steep slope, heading up a goat path for another of Khat's homes. Mike looked forward to holding her in his arms at night. While at the village, men slept with men and women slept with women. He'd missed the hell out of her.

"THE SUN IS OUT, finally," Khat muttered, lifting her head from his shoulder. In the waterfall cave, sunlight streaked through the opening, a radiant shaft illuminating the cave and their area. It had taken them three days to get back, due to mist, rain, fog and snow. It was early September, and the mountain weather was fickle. It had taken them ten more days to map the rest of the area because of the inclement weather hanging around. The sun coming out meant they could begin their journey back to Bravo and make it in two days, not three or four.

Mike grunted and said, "I'm going to be glad to get some decent food." He'd lost weight.

Khat laughed and stood up, naked. She stretched fitfully and walked over and picked up a clean olive-green T-shirt, pulling it over her head.

"The view is beautiful from here," he told her, hands behind his head. As she pulled the T-shirt over her loose hair, she made a funny face.

"Do you ever *not* think of sex?" she muttered, grinning.

"Not with you around, I don't." He was hard already. And they had a lot of packing to do to get out by nightfall. She had the longest, most beautiful legs he'd ever seen on a woman. Her thighs were perfection, molded and taut from so much riding for so many years. When she pulled on her panties and then her trousers, he decided it was time to get his clothes on.

"I wish," Khat muttered, sitting down and pulling on a pair of thick green wool socks and then her boots, "that I could stay here. Why does the master chief want me to come in?"

Mike shrugged as he got dressed. "I don't know." He

gave her a patient look. "Wouldn't you usually leave the mountains about this time and go down to Dur Babba to sit out the winter?"

Shrugging, she said, "I try to stay up here as late as I can. The Taliban use the trails until there's six feet of snow stopping them. That's when I leave." She tied her laces and stood up, going over to take care of the nickering horses.

Mike said nothing. He wasn't going to stir up an argument with her on this. Khat said she'd come in. There were a lot of things to work out with General Stevenson. He knew she would be at Bravo for at least a little while. According to Mac, her original orders were to fly Stateside on October 1 of every year and not return to her op until April 1 of the next year. Curious if the chief had heard from General Stevenson, he prepared their breakfast, another MRE.

He watched Khat as she brushed each horse as they ate. Their coats were getting shaggy due to the colder weather. Her hair was still loose around her shoulders, a red shawl letting the world know she was one hell of a warrior. He was glad to have met Jaleel's family because he understood so much more about Khat.

He smiled a little, happier than he'd ever been. In time, Khat was going to marry him, and he still couldn't believe it. Mike wanted to make sure that Mac knew about it. There were papers to be prepared for her and him to sign. He would write her down as the person who would receive everything he owned in life if he was killed, including the insurance policy. It wasn't a very happy thing to think about but in their business, it was a reality.

"Don't you want real eggs and bacon back at Bravo?" he teased.

Khat took a mane comb and pulled it down through Mina's long, thick black mane. "Yes." She saw him grinning at her. He was more than ready to get back to civilization and give that wooden saddle away. He might be a SEAL, but he hated riding in that creaky, uncomfortable saddle. Splinters in the butt and thighs were common. He was going to be happy to be patrolling on foot or being dropped by helo at night from now on. "I wonder if they'll have pumpkin pie at the chow hall?"

"It's that time of year," he said. "Why? You a squash person, too?"

Laughing softly, Khat patted the horses and put her tack tools away in a small box. Rubbing her hands down the thighs of her trousers, she walked back to him. "I love the holidays. I'm into overkill." She knelt down and took the heated MRE from him and let it cool a bit. "When I was little, my mother, Glenna, would make all kinds of Thanksgiving cookies. I used to help her." Khat laughed fondly. "I'm afraid I wasn't very good at putting frosting on them, though. I'd dip my finger into the bowl and eat a lot of it when I could get away with it."

Mike joined her with his MRE, their knees almost touching one another. "Your father didn't insist on a Muslim way of life for you?"

"No. My mother is spiritual. My father is Muslim, and he's devout, but I guess they agreed long before I was born, to not force me into one religion or another. I got to make my own choice."

"So you took after your mother?"

"I'm spiritual, not religious," she said between bites. "You?"

"Same way. My parents didn't push me one way or another."

"I guess I feel most at peace out in the open air," Khat murmured. "I love to sit with my back up against a tree, see fog move silently through a meadow…"

"Where do your parents live?"

"San Francisco. My father is part of a very successful engineering firm there. My mom loves the Muir Woods giant redwood trees. She would take me up to a park nearby, and we'd walk through them. I always thought it was a perfect place for a church of sorts. It was so calm and healing in that grove of redwoods."

"And you carry that memory with you to this day," Mike said, watching her face become pensive. "Maybe you'll take me up to Muir Woods? I'd like to experience it with you."

Khat smiled fondly. "That's a wonderful idea."

"I'll teach you scuba diving and introduce you to Mom Ocean, and you show me your favorite forest haunts growing up in the San Francisco area," Mike said. He wanted a chance to share happier moments in Khat's life. They had been overshadowed, perhaps buried beneath the past five years of her life. He saw her green eyes sparkle, a soft smile come to her mouth.

"I'll take you to the giant sequoias, too. There's a national park just east of Bakersfield, California. I'm so in love with those giant trees. That was another place of powerful healing for me. Another church of the woods." She gave him a warm look, her eyes filled with good memories.

"I like planning the future with you," Mike said,

meeting her smiling eyes. He saw such hope burning in them. Feeling as if a huge, invisible weight had lifted off his shoulders, or maybe feeling like he'd run the marathon and won her hand, hope threaded powerfully through his chest. Mike knew there was a long way to go with Khat. Nothing was going to be easy with her parents or dealing with her tortured past. He loved her, and that gave him infinite patience to help bring her back to the world he knew. A world of a solid, positive family, of being loved, of being able to laugh and start becoming a part of his world.

Khat nodded. "My whole world is changing," she offered quietly, finishing her MRE. "I feel unsettled about it, Mike. Scared in some ways, hopeful in others."

"It's always that way when we make a big change in our lives," he agreed. "The good news is we have each other. I'll help you walk through this change." He saw the love shining in her eyes for him.

"You've been there for me since we met."

"I'll always be at your side," he promised, his voice gritty with emotion.

"You have no idea how it feels to have you there, Mike."

"No one likes working or walking alone in life, Angel."

Khat stood. "We need to get packed," she offered. She knew Mike was looking forward to getting back to Bravo. She wanted to remain here. This was a familiar friend to her. A place of safety of sorts, as crazy as that sounded.

By the time they moved out of the cave, light rain was falling once more. Mike took the lead on his gelding, the rope to Mina tied to the back of his saddle as she carried the pack contents.

Khat had discussed the change with him because she usually tied Zorah to the cantle of her saddle. Mina's leg splint was starting to swell once again, and Khat didn't want to take a chance and make her lame. Instead, Zorah would be her mount and trade places with Mina. She never went against her feelings because it had saved her life so many times in the past. And Khat felt uneasy.

This time, she asked Mike to take Mina with him, leaving her able to move quickly, if necessary. Usually, she had the packhorse, but this time she wanted Mike to do it. With their NVGs on, she kept a quarter of a mile between them. Already having discussed the route to the next cave, she felt confident Mike would remember the way.

The air was near freezing, her breath white vapor. She was glad to be wearing the Kevlar helmet tonight because it kept her head protected. The warmth of the gloves felt good and so did the heavy wool of her Afghan clothes over her cammies. Khat noticed Zorah's small fine ears were moving around a lot. Was she hearing something through the rain? Picking up sounds human ears could not? Often she did, and Khat paid close attention to her mare's alertness. In the distance, thunder growled and lightning flashed, coming their way.

She wore her M-4 rifle on her back, the barrel pointed down to prevent water from getting into it. The goat path was fairly wide, maybe three feet in width, winding like a snake around the slopes of the nine-thousand-foot mountain. They'd be heading down to near seven thousand feet, and it would get warmer as the night progressed. Adjusting the mic near her lips, she knew their communications worked for a mile. The radio was hooked beneath her lapel of her cammies, protected from the rain.

Lightning flashed, ruining her night vision through the goggles. Cursing under her breath, Khat pushed them up on the helmet rail. Everything was black. She relied on Zorah to see well enough to stay on the goat path. Mike had just disappeared around a large turn with Mina in tow. She was alone.

Thunder rolled loudly around her, the air vibrating. She hunched her shoulders forward, hoping that the storm would pass them quickly, but instead, the rain increased substantially. Zorah suddenly stopped and froze.

Her heart rate went up, and Khat pulled the M-4 rifle off her back, taking off the safety, a bullet already in the chamber.

"Something's up," she warned Mike quietly into the mic. "Keep going, I'm going to check it out."

Anytime Zorah halted and froze, Khat knew Taliban was nearby. Her pulse ratcheted up as she pulled down the NVGs over her eyes, remaining where she was. Slowly panning up above her, she knew there was another goat path about a thousand feet above. It was devoid of riders.

She slowly panned the slope from where the horse had halted. Khat knew there was a small rocky depression where Taliban would sometimes sleep overnight. They'd come in at dusk, make their tea, eat and then sleep, getting up at dawn to begin their patrol of the area.

Standing up in her stirrups, Khat strained to look down the rocky slope littered with brush. Water ran down her cheeks, the rain slashing almost sideways in a sudden gust from the thunderstorm surrounding them. Damn. Where were they? She knew Taliban were nearby. Her skin was crawling with warning.

Zorah snapped her head around, ears pricked up, looking behind her.

Khat let out a gasp, twisting around in the saddle. Shit! There were fifteen riders coming around another curve, not more than half a mile from where she was at! Her mind spun with options. There was a thin goat path just ahead, moving up toward the ridgeline a thousand feet above them.

"Tangos half mile behind me," she whispered into the mic. "Get moving as fast as you can. I'm staying behind to stop them."

"I'm coming back," Mike said.

"No! I can handle this! Get the hell out of here! I'll meet you at the cave at dawn. I've done this before!" Her heart was pounding now. Every second wasted on talk was seconds that Zorah would need to climb the rocky, steep path without them being discovered.

"Roger," Mike growled, his unhappiness clear in his tone.

She heard the protectiveness in his voice. First, he couldn't turn around on this narrow goat path. Second, he had a packhorse in tow, which would slow him down. She pressed her heels into Zorah's flanks, heading forward at a gallop toward that small path. She would have minutes to set up a sniper op to stop the tangos.

Jets of white vapor shot out of Zorah's flared nostrils, her hind quarters digging into the rocky, muddy trail like powerful pistons. In minutes, the game Arabian had crested the top of the ridge, following the narrow goat path that moved down to the other side of the rocky slope. Dismounting, Khat dropped the horse's reins and led her to the opposite side of the ridge so she remained protected and out of the line of fire. She tied Zorah's reins to a low bush.

Khat hauled her Win Mag sniper rifle out of the nylon boot and quickly pulled out the bipods, settling the rifle just below the ridgeline, aiming on the other side the Taliban would be riding by. Finding a shallow depression, she set the sniper rifle up, turning on the Nightforce scope, the thermal imaging flickering on. Khat flipped up the protective lens covers at both ends.

Settling down in the rocks, the path clearly marked three hundred yards below, Khat pulled five mags from her H-gear. She slowed down her breathing, the rain coming in torrential sheets around her.

Khat knew once the riders came within view, they had no place to turn around. And it was nearly impossible to back a horse for a quarter of a mile on a dark, slippery, rocky path. The animals would be frantic, the sounds of the rifle scaring them, making them hard to handle. The enemy had no recourse but to try and ride past her and make the other curve half a mile away in order to seek protection.

If they tried to come up her narrow goat path, she'd stop them before they ever got close to her. There was a five-hundred-foot drop-off on the other side of the path; a rocky scree slope. If they tried to escape down it, their horses would break legs or their necks and fall, and most likely, the riders would be killed, as well. They didn't have options, and Khat knew it.

She felt the cold water dripping down her neck, soaking through the heavy wool *shemagh* around her shoulders. Putting her eye to the scope, she watched the slow progress of the Taliban. They were all hunched over, heads down, their AK-47s on their backs. The horses were weary. Her mind clicked off other possibilities. Normally, Taliban stopped at dusk to rest. This group had to have something they were carrying or was needed elsewhere to be out on a night like this.

Scanning the line of riders, the horses were nose to tail with one another. She saw a number of packhorses in between each rider. Probably fertilizer being carried in the panniers. If she didn't stop them, eventually, this group could run into Mike on the same trail. It would become a shoot-out, but he would be at a distinct disadvantage, firing behind at the tangos. This group had to be stopped now.

Mouth tightening, the rain continuing in sheets, wind gusting, Khat dialed in the windage and elevation. Her first shot would be from a cold barrel and often, the bullet was off target. The blustery wind could easily cause a bullet to miss its mark. Her breathing slowed down, her wet finger caressing the two-pound trigger. Khat would wait until they were almost in front of her. That way, she could start with the first rider and pick them off quickly down the line.

Her mind grew detached, making a thousand calculations on speed, trajectory, weather and her target.

The leader was in her sights. She could see his bearded face, his scowl, his face, wet and cold. She panned three riders down from him. Her heart thudded with fear. All three of them carried RPGs. That wasn't good. If one of them was able to get off a shot, she was well within easy distance and could be killed. The Win Mag did not have a muzzle suppressor to hide the flash from the shot. Taliban were skilled at seeing that flash and then would swiftly attack her position. Khat bit her lower lip, shifting her scope to the leader. *Damn.* Even if Mike were here, it wouldn't make a difference. She was relieved he was ahead of her with Mina, moving out undetected and unknown by this group. It was up to her to stop them. *Now.*

The first round struck the leader, throwing him off his horse, his hands and arms flailing like windmill blades as he flew over the edge of the slope. The horse skidded, turned sharply and crashed into the second rider and horse.

She got off a second shot. The booming sound was muted by the heavily falling rain. Khat took a third shot and missed. Dropping the mag out of the rifle, it took her precious seconds to slap the next mag into it. Quickly sighting through the scope, she saw the fourth man raising the RPG to his shoulder to fire at her. She squeezed the trigger, taking him out. The third man was next. Khat saw him fire the RPG at the same time she squeezed the trigger.

The RPG landed on the other side of the ridge, just above her. Khat opened her mouth as the concussions from the explosion tore by her. The red and yellow explosion lifted her off the rocks, throwing her into the air. She rolled, gripping her rifle. Rocks and dirt pelted down around her. For a split second, Khat remembered Zorah had been hidden on the side where the RPG landed. Her head rang. She couldn't hear anything, shaking herself, rolling back onto her stomach, knowing she had to kill the men below.

Sighting, Khat shot the next three tangos. Their horses were wild, nearly uncontrollable. She saw two horses leap off the trail, taking their hapless riders with them. They would all die on that five-hundred-foot fall.

Breathing slowly, controlled, Khat took out the next Taliban, trying to race past her position. She turned the rifle, looking for the last two of the group. They were whipping their horses, screaming at the packhorses who were wild-eyed, unsure of where to go, slowing them down, leaving them easy targets to shoot. She shot the last man in the group first. And then, as she swung the scope on her last target, she saw he had an RPG. And he had just fired it up at her. She fired back, taking him out.

Throwing her arms over her helmeted head, Khat opened her mouth, hoping like hell the enemy's RPG was not on target. The last thing she remembered was a huge *whump*, the earth heaving violently upward beneath her, and she was lifted into the air.

CHAPTER NINETEEN

MIKE CURSED SOFTLY, hearing the firefight miles away, the sounds echoing through the mountains. Twice, he'd tried calling Khat on his radio. There was no response. Frustrated, he knew that in this kind of weather, they'd get no air assets. A drone couldn't fly in this violent weather. They were essentially blind on the ground.

Fear snaked through him as he kept the soaked bay gelding at a steady, fast trot through the rain, Mina close behind. They were at least five miles away, at a lower elevation, the trail sometimes steep and slippery. Where was Khat? Why wouldn't she answer her radio?

There was no lightning now, the rain beginning to let up as the storm moved past him. It was 0300. Mike tried calling Khat every ten minutes. There was never an answer. His mind seethed with possibilities. The radio Khat carried could be low on batteries and therefore its range was limited. Or it could have been broken if she landed on it. Or rain had gotten into it. This wasn't the first time communications got fucked up in this mountain range. It happened all too often. His intuition screamed at him to go back.

He slowed his horse to a walk. His mind was working on other paths back to that area. He'd more or less committed all the larger paths to memory, but in the dark of night, things changed markedly. Mike wasn't as familiar with them as Khat was. She seemed to know where every last damned one of those trails were located. She'd had years to learn them all. He had only ten days to learn the intricate and complex trail systems.

Son of a bitch! He felt helpless. The trail had narrowed with absolutely no possibility of turning around. And even if he could, how could he get Mina turned around, too? It was impossible. There was a two-thousand-foot cliff above the trail and a thousand-foot drop off below him on the other side. He was trapped, with no way to ride back to help Khat.

Mike thought about calling Camp Bravo, to try and get them to send an Apache helicopter. He decided to make the call, hoping against hope. The entire region, as far as he could see, had early autumn thunderstorms raking the area.

He called directly to Ops. They informed him all Apaches were needed elsewhere and were grounded in his sector due to extreme weather conditions. Next, he called the CIA about a drone. They refused to put one up in the area due to weather issues. Calling J-bad, all air assets were out tending presently to other trouble spots; none were available for his area.

Cursing softly, Mike urged his horse into a trot, hoping like hell Khat was all right. He had heard two explosions, the sounds of gunfire in the distance, but then it all stopped. Praying she was on her way down the trail and that he'd meet her at their agreed upon cave, Mike felt terror in his gut. He didn't know why. But it was eating him alive.

KHAT FELT THE RAIN striking her face. Her head ached; her ears were ringing. She felt warmth trickling down

across her right cheek, mixing with the colder rain
slashing at her. Trying to move, her legs were trapped,
pain floating up through her. It took her minutes to remember what had happened.

The night surrounded her. She lay on her back, her
spine curved because of the sixty-five-pound ruck she
wore on her back. Slowly lifting her hand, Khat tried
to wipe away the mud and dirt across her face.

Shaking her head, she realized her lower legs were
buried in rocks and mud. Then she remembered everything. Blinking, Khat forced herself to lie still. Had she
killed all the Taliban? Or were they searching for her
up on this slope? Her heart pulsed powerfully through
her as she tried to take stock of her situation. Her ears
rang so loudly she could hear absolutely nothing, and
that scared her. She would never hear the enemy approaching her. Moving her hand over her head, she
realized her NVGs had been blasted off her helmet. It
was dark, and she couldn't see anything.

Moving her one leg, Khat slowly pulled it from beneath the rubble. Her boot moved, and she worked on
the other trapped leg. In moments, she was free. Rolling over on her belly, she felt dizziness wash through
her. The softly falling rain was washing away the mud
and blood on her face. Where was her rifle? Panic ate
at her. Khat automatically felt for her .45 in her holster.
It was still there, and some relief skittered through her.

She rolled over and got to her hands and knees, her
lower legs aching and bruised. Nothing felt broken.
Remaining crouched, Khat tried to hear through the
ringing of her ears. She felt blood trickling from her
right ear, the pain excruciating, realizing she'd blown
an eardrum in the blast.

Trying to take stock of her physical condition, to see if she had a wound or had a broken bone, Khat found none. She was a victim of being too close to a blast from an RPG. And maybe a concussion because she'd been slammed by the resulting pressure wave that had knocked her unconscious.

Reaching out with her shaking hands, Khat realized her helmet had been torn off her head. Where was it? Her NVGs were on it. She needed to locate her goggles and rifle. The cold was seeping into her bones, and she was soaking wet in near-freezing temperatures. The wind was less now, and she could see the thunderstorm had moved toward the south.

Her mind not working well, Khat concentrated on finding her helmet and goggles. Without them, she was toast. If she hadn't killed all the Taliban, they would be actively searching for her right now.

Moving slowly over the rocks, her knees taking the bruising punishment of crawling across the slope, her outstretched hand finally found her helmet. Joy tunneled through Khat as she settled it on her head. She pulled the NVGs down on the rail. She flipped them on. They still worked! Pushing off her hands and knees, Khat slowly rose. She was able to see clearly.

Turning, she scanned the slope below her. No one was coming up to get her. Then she looked down toward the goat path. There were five men lying dead on it. There were no horses around. They had run off or been killed by leaping and falling over the deadly slope below the goat path.

Wiping her mouth, Khat tasted blood. Her nose was bleeding, as well. Lucky to be alive, she knew she could

have died tonight. Her mind was mushy, and she wasn't
thinking coherently.

Sitting down, she fumbled for and found her radio. It
had been crushed. She was out of range to talk to Mike
on their personal headset channel. Sitting, eyes closed,
Khat tried to wipe her filthy hands off on her wet trousers. Most of it came off. She had to find her rifle.

Trying to stand, dizziness struck her, and she fell
down with a jolt. Pushing her palms against her closed
eyes, she knew she was in deep shock. Pieces of the
firefight came back to her. Her mind would shut down.
And then minutes later, it would come back and func-
tion. Pulling the NVGs back over her eyes, she rolled
onto her hands and knees. Khat felt nausea rising. Oh,
hell, she was going to vomit! It was nothing but dry
heaves as she crouched on her knees, her arms against
her belly, violently retching. The paramedic in her recognized the symptoms of a concussion. Finally, the
heaving stopped, and Khat forced herself to continue
to search for her rifle.

She finally found the rifle on top of the ridge, partially covered with rocks and dirt. With shaking hands,
she drew it to her, wanting badly for it not to have been
destroyed. The rain washed most of the mud away from
it. Looking through the scope, she saw it worked.

Turning it off, Khat pulled another mag from her
H-gear harness, released the emptied one from the rifle
and slapped in the new one. Now she wasn't completely
helpless, and hope filtered through her. She put the
sniper rifle across her back, barrel down.

Her horse. *Zorah.* Gasping softly, Khat felt fear. She
remembered only now that the first RPG fired at her
had landed on the other side of the ridge where her be-

loved mare was standing. A cry tore from her bleeding lips, and Khat lunged to her feet, turning and trying to stay upright as she slid and slipped time and again. Her legs collapsed beneath her. With a frustrated sound, Khat clawed upward. She struggled, crawling to the other side of the ridge.

A sob jammed in her throat. Below, Zorah lay dead. Tears stung Khat's eyes as she saw Zorah's beautiful head, her eyes glazed open, lying on her side, legs curved in toward her body, unmoving on the slope. Pressing her hands to her mouth, Khat sobbed. *No! Not Zorah! No!* Tears created warm paths down her cold, dirty cheeks. She tried to stand, the dizziness felling her. Crawling toward her, Khat sobbed brokenly, not caring who heard her.

She reached Zorah, lifting the horse's heavy head, placing it on her thighs, stroking her elegant dished face. Anguish spiraled into Khat's wildly beating heart. She bent over, pressing her brow against Zorah's head, sobbing. Her brave Arabian mare who had kept her safe, been her devoted companion for so many years, was dead. She had been courageous, stalwart and never shied away from a firefight or carrying medical supplies.

Moving her shaking, wet fingers across her horse's long neck, Khat felt her world coming apart. She cried raggedly, calling Zorah's name. It felt like an earthquake had suddenly ripped her life apart. Khat could still feel the warmth of Zorah through her thick winter coat, her fingers moving slowly, lovingly up and down her neck. The tears wouldn't stop, the sobs deep and shredding her heart apart.

Khat didn't know how long she knelt with her horse.

She had shut off her NVGs and pushed them up on the rail of her helmet, hugging her horse. She slowly became aware that dawn was coming. A hint of gray light silhouetted the unforgiving peaks of the Hindu Kush. She was shaking and trembling, cold and numb.

Gently easing Zorah's head on the slope, Khat tried to stand. Dizziness assailed her, but this time she remained on her unsteady feet. Sniffing, the tears still falling, Khat knew she had to leave her horse and find some kind of shelter. She didn't dare be seen out in daylight hours, too easily spotted by sharp-eyed Taliban. Her mind was still functioning sporadically. The weight of her ruck cut into her slumped, weary shoulders. Remembering there was a cave on this side of the ridge, a goat path roughly a quarter mile down from where she stood, Khat knew she had to find shelter. Her mind revolved back to Mike. Swallowing hard, a lump in her throat, she knew that sometime soon, he would reach the safety of their cave.

Wiping her numb cheek with cold, trembling fingers, Khat leaned down and touched her beloved mare one more time. "I love you," she whispered unsteadily. "I'll never forget you, Zorah…never…"

Khat pulled down her NVGs, picking a path down the disturbed soil and rock caused by the RPGs. Soon she located the thin goat path, one that was not used often, and walked unsteadily to the south. There was a cave about fifty feet down the slope about a mile away. She would find it and hide for the day, taking stock of herself and what she had to do next in order to survive.

Emotionally numb, Khat found the cave. Wanting to stop and dig out the satellite phone in her ruck, she staggered into it, glad to slide the heavy ruck off her aching shoulders. Finding a tunnel in the rear of the small cave, she hid behind the wall and sat down. There was enough light with the coming dawn. She shook with fatigue and shock.

Opening her ruck, Khat found a mess. Of the eight quarts of water she had in it, four were destroyed. Her heart dropped as she pulled the sat phone out. It was in pieces. A number of glass bottles filled with drugs were also destroyed. The entire ruck was soaked with the water from the exploded plastic jugs that had once held the liquid. Frowning, she remembered that she'd been on her belly, the ruck on her back, protecting her from the worst of the RPG pressure wave concussions. Her ruck had taken the massive pounding, not her body.

Without a working sat phone, she couldn't call for help. Mike wouldn't know if she was dead or alive. Her heart contracted with agony. There was no way to let him know, either.

Drinking deeply, she put the bottle aside, hungry. The two MREs were destroyed, as well, the food packets blown open, the bottom of the ruck a gooey mess. Digging into a side pocket, she pulled out two protein bars. She had food, and she had water. Bravo was probably twenty miles away. Not hungry, Khat forced herself to eat. The blood was drying against her temple and cheek, pulling at her flesh. The metallic copper odor made her nauseous.

Closing her eyes, she waited. She couldn't vomit. Not now. Forcing the sensation away, she opened her eyes and tucked the rest of the protein bar away into her pocket. Utterly exhausted, Khat stretched out beside the tunnel wall using the ruck as a pillow. Beside

it was her .45 pistol with a bullet in the chamber in case
Taliban appeared. The moment Khat closed her eyes,
she spiraled into sleep.

KHAT AWOKE DISORIENTED. She was sweaty and feeling
feverish. It was dark outside the cave. Freezing, she
waited, trying to hear any sounds through the still-
ringing in her ears. It was reduced by at least 70 percent, but it was tough to hear subtle noises or sounds
that might be nearby. Sweat trickled off her temples.

Khat pushed herself up into a sitting position,
thirsty. Finding the half-filled bottle of water, she
slugged down the rest of it. There was a dull ache in
her abdomen, and she frowned. Had she been shot?
Pulled a muscle in that area? Her mind was cleared,
but her memory kept shorting out. Touching the side
of her head, the blood had dried and flaked off beneath
her fingers. Grimacing, Khat wished for some water to
clean herself up, but she knew this cave was a dry one.

Doing a serious physical examination of her body,
Khat started at her head and worked down. She had a
gash in her scalp, and that's why she'd bled so heavily.
It was now clotted and had hardened, which was good
news. When she reached her abdomen, pressing the
quadrants, she felt a sharp pain lance deeply into her
gut. Grunting, she lay back, closing her eyes, feeling
around the tender area with her fingers. And then she
felt the opposite side on her back, thinking she'd been
shot. There was no bullet hole. No nothing.

The rest of her examination revealed a lot of swelling and bruises around her ankles and feet, but otherwise, she was in decent shape. Again, her stomach
rolled, and she felt like she was going to vomit. What

the hell was this all about? Flu? Drinking more water quelled the nausea.

Glancing at her watch, it was 2300. She'd slept a long time and felt more alert. Stronger. Forcing herself to eat, Khat shrugged into the ruck, slid the pistol into her holster and put on her helmet, pulling down the NVGs and slowly easing out into the cavern. It was empty.

As she walked silently to the opening, Khat could hear the wind. Her ears were returning to normal, able to pick up the subtle sounds around her. Looking up, Khat saw the stars above. No clouds. No rain. That was good.

Standing, she felt a twinge of pain in her abdomen. Rubbing it absently, she looked out into the night, her mind turning on the best plan in order to get back to Bravo. Had Mike made it to the cave? The FOB? God, she hoped so. He should be back at Bravo by now, if all went well.

And she knew he'd be raising hell to find her.

Wiping her mouth, Khat used her wealth of knowledge. About a mile down from the cave, the trail forked down a steep grade, heading directly to a Shinwari village ten miles below and situated in the valley. It was her best choice under the circumstances. If she tried to avoid Taliban patrols around Bravo, she stood a greater chance of being captured. The well-used goat path to the village in the valley was safer in many ways.

Khat felt fevered. Despite the cold air and gusts of wind, she was hot and sweaty. She had some kind of infection, but didn't know what had caused it. Maybe she was right; she'd caught the flu. It was that time of year for it to raise its ugly head.

Stepping back into the cave, she decided to give herself a shot of antibiotics, just in case. The only two bottles of drugs that weren't destroyed by the RPG concussion were the morphine and antibiotics. She'd gotten lucky. Her heart and mind turned to Mike. Love flowed through her, giving her a momentary reprieve. Never had Khat wanted to survive more than this coming day.

MIKE WAS IN with Mac in his office when Travis Cooper showed up.

"I took care of the horses," he told them. Hesitating at the door, he asked, "Anything else I can do, Mike?"

Exhausted, Mike said, "No. Thanks, Travis." He stunk of sweat, wet wool and filth. The moment he'd trotted up to the security gate at Bravo on his gelding with his packhorse, Mina, his only focus was in finding Khat. Mac had called in an Apache that had finally been cut loose from another engagement, had just refueled and was now flying over the area GPS coordinates Mike had given them. He was leaning down, hands on Mac's desk as the Apache was feeding them live video pictures of the area.

His eyes burned with fatigue. Mike had arrived at dawn, the weather clear in the FOB region. Mac had already been awake and at his office because Mike had called in about Khat and the earlier firefight. Travis had met him at the gate and taken the two horses to the barn while he ran to the SEAL HQ.

Wiping his face, feeling the grit beneath his fingertips, Mike intently watched the scan as the Apache approached the area. Where was Khat? God, where was she? He choked back the lump forming in his throat.

"There," Mac said, putting a finger on the screen. "Three or four Taliban horses dead on that goat trail."

Looking closer, Mike scowled. "Khat said over the radio to me that there were fifteen Taliban on horses approaching her from the rear on the same trail we were on."

Mac watched the Apache slowly move around the steep slope. "I'm counting seven horses dead, and I think there's at least ten dead bodies, all Taliban."

Nostrils flaring, Mike gritted his teeth. "I heard a lot of shooting and two RPGs being fired." The Apache flew along the trail. There were five more Taliban bodies on it. There were no other horses in the area, probably fleeing down the trail and disappearing into the night. "That's fifteen bodies. Now, where is Khat?" he growled.

Mac called the pilot and asked her to fly up above the goat path where all the dead bodies were at, to look at the ridge above the area. The pilot confirmed his request.

Mike's heart began a slow beat of dread. He saw two huge RPG-made craters up near the top of the ridge. "Damn," he whispered. But no body. Khat wasn't there. It would have been a perfect sniper firing position to take down that group of Taliban. His heart plunged. As the Apache flew over the ridge, he spotted Zorah's dead body.

"Stop!" he rasped. "Ask her to hover."

Mac gave the radio order to the Apache pilot.

Breathing hard, Mike looked closer. "That's Khat's horse. Jesus! She's dead," he muttered. Killed by an RPG. Where was Khat? Was she riding Zorah at the time? Mike rapidly scanned around the area. It was all wide-open scree, nothing but rocks of all shapes and sizes. Far below it, he saw a narrow trail.

"I don't see her," Mac said. "That's good news."

"Ask the pilot to turn on thermal imaging. Khat might be wounded nearby. We need to check it out," Mike said hoarsely.

The pilot acknowledged, moving up in elevation so that the ridge was completely viewable on both sides. Mike wiped his mouth, breathing irregularly, fear snaking through him. The screen now showed thermal imaging. Anyone who was alive and breathing would give off a heat signature. The Apache trolled slowly along both sides of the ridgeline. It then moved down to the goat path on the side Zorah had been killed on. Nothing. It then moved to the other side of the ridge, imaging the enemy and their dead horses. There were no heat signatures.

"She must have escaped," Mac said, his voice hopeful. He looked over at Tarik. "Look, I'll keep on this. Why don't you get a shower and a change of clothes?"

Mike didn't want to, his heart beating with dread. "She's got to be somewhere nearby," he muttered, refusing to leave. He didn't say the obvious: that another group of Taliban had taken Khat prisoner. A wash of violent fear savaged his strewn emotions.

"Tarik, get your ass out of here. I've got every possible asset out there looking for Khat. We'll find her. Get cleaned up, get some food and then come back here."

KHAT STUMBLED. THE PAIN in her abdomen had intensified with every mile she'd walked. Sitting down, thirsty, she gulped water. It was 0300. Fever was ravaging her mind now, and she grunted softly, feeling throbbing pain in her gut. Finishing the water, she tried to think.

Her progress had been slow because she had to always be aware in the dead of night, since Taliban camped then. She didn't want to accidentally run into a group.

Breathing irregularly, feeling like she was burning up, she knew the antibiotics would take forty-eight hours to really take hold and fight her infection. If the infection was bacterial. All flu was a virus, and antibiotics wouldn't touch it. She waffled on what to do.

Last night she was freezing. Tonight, she was burning up. The wool cloak she wore had dried out. Khat wanted to rip it off, rip all her clothes off to cool down, but she knew it wasn't a smart move. The brown wool colors blended perfectly into the night.

It was warmer now, and she figured she was at seven thousand feet. The valley below was at six thousand feet.

She sat down next to a tree to rest a moment, pulling out her compass. She made sure she continued toward the village that she couldn't see below. The goat path was heading in that general direction, as well.

Pushing the compass back into her cammie pocket, Khat groaned and gritted her teeth. Opening up her waistband because it was tight against her swollen abdomen, she gently moved her hand across the area. Ruthlessly, she searched her memory, her medical symptoms once her mind decided to work again. Shit. It was appendicitis! Not flu.

Khat tipped her head back against the tree trunk. Her mind wasn't working well. That would account for the nausea, the vomiting and the fever symptoms she had currently. This was the wrong place and time to get this. A cold dread moved through her.

Nostrils flaring, her breathing uneven, Khat sat up and pulled open her ruck. She had already taken a max load of antibiotics hours earlier and couldn't give herself any more for twelve hours after the initial dose. Hands shaking badly, she located the bottle of morphine and a new syringe and a clean needle. The pain was increasing with each breath. She felt faint from it. Fighting the agony, wanting to lie on her side and curl up into a fetal position, Khat pulled just enough morphine into the syringe to dull the pain, but not knock her out or mess with her mind.

She pulled up her sleeve, giving herself the shot of morphine directly into her brachial artery at the bend of her elbow. A zigzag of sudden, fiery pain made her moan. The emptied syringe dropped out of her nerveless fingers as the pain made her faint.

Khat awoke slowly, blinking, fever surging through her. She felt less pain. It took more minutes to connect the dots of what had happened, where she was presently located. Rolling onto her side, she sat up, dizzy. Hand moving to her abdomen, she breathed shallowly, fingers moving against the tender area. The morphine was taking hold, thank God. How long was she out? She had no idea.

Shutting her ruck, Khat struggled to her knees and slowly shrugged it over her stiff, tired shoulders. Looking up at the night sky, the stars twinkling, Khat wondered if there was a drone up there watching her. She saw no helicopters. No nothing. Understanding that drones were in high demand, Mike and the SEALs might not be able to get one over the area. Further, he had no idea where she was.

Sweat leaked into her eyes, and they burned and blurred her vision momentarily. She staggered to her feet, gripping the trunk of the tree for support. She had to get to the village or die trying. As she stepped out on the trail, weaving drunkenly from the high fever ravaging her, Khat sucked it up and put one boot ahead of the other. Every cell of her stubborn body was focused on reaching safety. Reaching Mike. She wanted to live! She wanted a chance to have a life with a man who loved her without question.

As a paramedic, Khat knew the ultimate outcome of appendicitis if it wasn't immediately addressed with emergency surgery: death. The appendix was swollen and would, at some point, burst. The toxic crap held in the sac would spew out all over into her abdominal cavity, infecting her, and she'd turn septic. The poisonous material would then flood into her bloodstream, and she would die from the blood poisoning. And at a certain point, no antibiotic in the world could stop it once it had burst.

In her fevered state, Khat knew her temperature could spiral up and reach a killing one-hundred and six degrees Fahrenheit. A temperature that high would kill her brain. She could die from infection or go braindead from high fever because the body's own defenses were trying to kill the infection before it killed her.

Either way, she was dead. How badly she wanted to live! Tears jammed into her eyes as she remembered Mike's hands loving her, his mouth worshipping hers. He'd infused her with the dream of a new, better life than this one. Was the irony that this life she finally wanted to leave would kill her before she ever got a chance? *Oh, God...let me live...let me live...please...*

As dawn crawled on the horizon, Khat was fighting to stay coherent. She was weaving, stumbling and falling. Her knees were bloodied and bruised. She saw the village below, perhaps a half a mile away. Was it a hallucination? Because half the time with the fever, she was imagining things. She heard voices. Mike's voice. She heard Mina's soft whinny. And then she'd heard the Taliban nearby. In her present state, she couldn't sort it all out. What was real? What was not? Khat didn't know.

Just as she got to the flat of the valley floor, Khat saw the gate to the Shinwari village being opened by a man. He didn't see her, too busy opening the huge iron gate. Stumbling, she tried to push herself into a trot. Wobbling badly, she saw the man lift his head, hearing her approach. His eyes widened and he froze as he saw her approach.

"I'm American," she cried out in Pashto. "I need help! I'm hurt! Please, help me!" Khat fell unconscious in the dirt, two hundred feet away from the stricken-looking Afghan farmer.

KHAT GROANED, FEELING a cool cloth against her brow. Opening her eyes, sweat pouring off her, she saw a young woman dressed in a dark brown robe with a pink scarf over her head, a worried look on her face, sitting beside her. She was gently sponging Khat's face and neck. Feeling a bed beneath her, Khat swallowed and tried to speak. Only a groan came out. Thirsty, she tried to sit up. Pain in her abdomen made her gasp and lie down, breathing hard.

"I need help," she said hoarsely to the woman in Pashto. "I need someone to ride to Bravo, to tell the SEALs I'm here. My name is Sergeant Khatereh Shinwari, US Marine Corps. Please? Can you do this for me?"

The woman nodded. "I am Nasreen. My husband, Mohsin, has already left. He is riding to Bravo, the closest base to our village, asking them for their help," she whispered shyly. "Are you thirsty?"

Khat nodded. "My ruck," she said, lifting her hand weakly, seeing it sitting in the corner of the room, "there's water in it. Give me that water?" Because the water Afghans drank was full of germs and parasites. She was in enough trouble without drinking polluted, dirty water.

The woman nodded and quickly stood. Khat saw she was in a small mudroom. There was a window, allowing sunlight into the area. She didn't know what time it was. The woman brought over the bottle, and she handed it to Khat.

Shakily, she unscrewed the bottle top. Trying to sit up on her elbow, she found she couldn't.

"Here, let me help," the woman whispered, sliding her arm beneath Khat's shoulders. She placed her small, delicate hand around the bottle, guiding it to her mouth.

Khat drank deeply, the water dripping out of the corners of her mouth. Finished, she pulled the empty bottle away, thanking her. "My name is Khatereh. I am from the Shinwari tribe. My family lives in Dur Babba. What is your name?"

"Nasreen," she said. "My husband, Mohsin, saw you as he opened the gate to our village this morning.

He ran back and called for help. Three men carried you in here. You are now in our home. You are hurt?"

"Yes, I have appendicitis. When did your husband leave?" Khat asked, feeling the fever eating away at her mind. She was dehydrated. She needed an IV to rehydrate her.

"Three hours ago," she said. "But he must be careful. The Taliban are nearby."

Nodding, Khat whispered, "Yes, they are."

"Are you hungry?"

"No," she managed, closing her eyes. "I need water, and I need to cool down. I've got a high fever..." Khat could tell that the woman, who was probably around twenty, didn't understand most of what she said. The pain was still minimal unless she tried to move. The morphine continued to do its job.

She sank into a feverish semiconscious state. Her mind was playing tricks on her, thinking Taliban were bursting into the room where she was. She could hear herself babbling nonsense, but the fever was amping up and soon Khat swam in the fevered heat of hell and nonstop hallucinations.

Mike...she needed Mike! If only the Afghan could get through to get her the help she desperately needed!

"HEY, TARIK," MAC BOOMED, "get in here!"

Mike ran down the hall, stopping at the chief's door.

Mac was on the phone. "Get down to the security gate. An Afghan named Mohsin is there, speaking in Pashto, and the Marines need an interpreter."

Nodding, Mike grabbed his hat out of his cammie pocket, threw it on and trotted out into the evening. The sun had set, the sky a deep blue. As he came up to security, he saw a small Afghan man waving his arms excitedly on the other side of the gate, his tired horse next to him. When the marines saw him arrive, they gestured him around the gate to talk to the Afghan.

"Hurry! Hurry!" the Afghan said, out of breath. "You must come. One of your SEALs is badly hurt!"

Mike scowled. The man was frantic, his brown eyes huge, sweating freely like his horse. Holding up his hands, Mike said, "Slow down, slow down. We don't have any SEALs outside the wire right now. What's your name and what tribe are you?"

"I'm Mohsin of the Shinwari tribe," he gasped. He pointed toward the north. "You must come now! Your SEAL is very badly hurt! In need of medical attention."

He wasn't making sense. Mike wondered if it was a Taliban ruse, a lie to drag them into an ambush. It had been done before. Looking over the bay horse, whose flanks were heaving from being galloped for a long way, he turned back to Mohsin. "How did you get through the Taliban lines?" he demanded, his eyes hardening.

Mohsin took off his rolled cap, "Very, very hard. They are everywhere! I wanted to get here sooner, but I had to hide many times to avoid them. They are angry. They're looking for someone." He wiped his darkly tanned brow. "I think they are looking for your SEAL. She is safe with us, but I worry. I think they are tracking her." His voice turned anxious. "Please, you need to protect us. We took her in. We have kept her safe, but I'm afraid. Afraid they will come to our village, looking for her."

Mike's breath jammed in his chest. "You said *her*?" he demanded hoarsely.

"Yes, yes! She wears SEAL clothes like yours." He pressed his palm to his eyes for a moment. He was shaken, his voice trembling from exhaustion and stress. "S-she was babbling. Once, she said her name is Khatereh Shinwari. She said to tell someone at Bravo that she is very sick. She needs help very quickly. Please," the Afghan begged, "you must believe me!" He gestured wildly toward the north. "My village is going to be attacked because she is there! She asked for *pashtunwali*, and we have given her help and protection. But the Taliban is angry. I'm afraid for my wife, my village—"

Mike nodded to the security guard to open the gate. Grabbing Mohsin by the shoulder, he yanked him forward. "You're coming with me."

Inside, Mac listened to what the Afghan had said. The man was shaking, literally. Mike asked Travis to sit him down in the big room and give him some water, food and watch him.

"There's his village," Mac said, pointing to the map on his laptop. "Twenty miles from here. A friendly, pro-American village."

Rubbing his jaw, Mike felt his heart thundering in his chest. "Mohsin said the place is crawling with Taliban. He thinks they tracked Khat to them."

Mac grimaced, getting on the phone. He called in the two officers and pretty soon, the small office was crowded with bodies. Mike stood back as the chief got the three officers up to speed. The LT, Jim Sanders, a man with a lot of years of experience, said, "Get a drone over there. I can't send in a Medevac if the Taliban is surrounding that village."

Mike remained silent. A sudden op like this took

time. Maybe more time than Khat had. Had she been wounded in the firefight? Making mental calculations, she had walked from that ridge down to the village in two days. It wasn't that far mile-wise, but if she was wounded, it would take her more time.

"Call in the Apaches," the LT ordered Mac. "I want them out there in front of us coming in like yesterday."

Mac got on the phone with the emergency request to the Black Jaguar Squadron.

The LT looked over at Tarik. "Get seven SEALs together, let them know we're going in hot. Kit up in—" he looked at his watch "—twenty minutes. I want everyone on the tarmac ready to load into a Chinook. You'll head up the team, Tarik."

"Yes, sir," Mike said, relieved. He didn't have to go far to find seven other SEALs. They were all lounging around in the big room, bored to death.

As soon as he gave the orders, the room flew into action. Mike turned and ran out the door, heading for his tent where his gear and kit were stowed. They were going in hot. The Taliban had somehow trailed Khat to the village.

As he ran, he knew the Taliban would enter the village even if the elder forbade it. They were not Pashtun, and therefore, weren't bound by that tribe's ethics. They took what they wanted. And they'd find Khat by process of elimination.

His mouth tightened as he ran down the dusty avenue, skidding to a halt in front of his tent. Khat could be dead before they even got on scene.

CHAPTER TWENTY

MIKE WAS NEVER so relieved as when the SEALs landed at the Shinwari village and Mohsin led them directly to where Khat was being cared for by his wife, Nasreen.

The Apaches were keeping the Taliban at bay, and they were hiding in the woods, so they couldn't attack them or the village. Khat was barely conscious, lying in the only bed in the house. As he entered the home, Mike felt a mountain of fear dissolve from around his shoulders.

The combat medic with him, Tate Johnson, introduced himself to Khat, giving her a quick examination. Mike wanted to rush to her side, kiss her, hold her, but knew he couldn't. Instead, he stood back, speaking to shy Nasreen, who had cared for the woman he loved. He thanked the woman for her courage to bring Khat into their household. Mike slipped Mohsin, who stood by his wife, four US hundred dollar bills into his hand as compensation. Nasreen's eyes grew large as her husband disbelievingly clutched the bills. And then she wept, her hand against her face, grateful to Mike. Mohsin bowed, thanking him profusely. Mike gripped his shoulder, thanking him.

If not for this Afghan's bravery to dodge the killing Taliban, they would never have known Khat was here. And four hundred dollars would feed them and their relatives for the year to come. It was the least Mike could do for them saving Khat's life.

The combat medic, Tate Johnson, looked up. "Probably appendicitis. She's stable, and I've just given her a mild dose of morphine to sedate her for the trip to Bagram. Let's rock it out." He stood, going to his huge medical pack. On the side of it was a stretcher that he quickly unfolded so that Khat could be placed on it and brought to the awaiting Medevac Black Hawk.

Mike moved forward, kneeling down beside Khat. Her eyes were cloudy, and her skin stretched taut, glistening with perspiration. "We've got you," he told her quietly, squeezing her hand. "You're safe, Khat. You're coming home with me." He leaned over, pressing a kiss to her brow. As he pulled away, he saw her mouth soften.

"Home," she rasped, her voice hoarse. "That sounds so good...with you...only you..." And she lost consciousness from the morphine.

Two DAYS LATER, Mike was sitting on the edge of Khat's bed in the private room at the Bagram hospital. She'd had surgery immediately upon being flown into Bagram. Her recovery was nothing short of a miracle. Her concussion, a level three, was improving.

He sat facing her, holding her hand, listening to the entire story of what happened to her and Zorah leading up to and through the firefight. Her fever was almost gone, and there was clarity in her eyes. He leaned forward and moved the tears of loss from her pale cheeks as she choked up about Zorah being killed by the RPG.

"I feel so horrible about her death," Khat sobbed, covering her tender abdomen with her hand because each one pulled at the surgical stitches. "She was so brave. I asked so much from her..."

"War takes so much from all of us," Mike agreed

with a rasp, sliding his hand over her clean red hair. "At least you still have Mina. She's at Bravo, and Travis is taking care of her leg for you. She's going to be fine." His voice thickened. "I'm sorry you lost Zorah…"

When she was finished weeping, Mike pulled out a set of orders from his pocket and handed them to her. He had already read them, and they were from General Maya Stevenson, ordering her back to the USA.

He watched Khat's expression as she read them. Hoping she would go along with them, not fight them, Mike was surprised by the relief he saw shining in her green eyes as she lifted her head.

"I'm ready to go home," Khat uttered tiredly, placing the papers to sit on the tray next to her bed. "I can take no more. Aunt Leeda wants me out of here." Her voice waned, and she gave him a weary look. "I have done what I can… I am only one woman."

"Home with me?" Mike asked, unconsciously holding his breath. He saw her lips compress and turbulence in her eyes for a moment.

"Yes, only with you." Khat placed her hand in his. "So much went through my mind and heart after the firefight, Mike. What was I doing? You love me. I love you. I have a mother who wants me home and living near her." She earnestly searched his somber face, held by the gold in his eyes. There was no question Mike loved her. Khat felt it, saw it, heard it, every day from him. "I guess—" and she frowned, looking away for a moment "—I guess I had blinders on. I saw no other life other than this one. Aunt Leeda giving her permission… That was so important to me." She clung to his gaze. "And you wanting to marry me? Do you know how wonderful that made me feel? To be wanted? Loved?

And I never had any dreams of ever being married." Her mouth curved faintly as she absorbed his intense look. "Until I fell in love with you. I never thought anyone could love me with my scars…my shameful past."

Mike moved a little closer, sliding his hands through her thick red hair that was a loose mantle around her shoulders. "Those scars are medals showing your bravery, Khat. To me, you are beautiful just the way you are. There isn't an inch of you I don't love." He kneaded her scalp, watching her eyes slowly shut, a soft hum in her throat telling him how much she enjoyed his ministrations. "You survived, Khat. Most wouldn't have, but you did." He smoothed the strands away from her delicate ears, smiling down at her. "We have a chance at a new life. Together. I'm more than ready to take that step. Are you?" Because Mike had never wanted anything more than Khat since he'd regained consciousness in that cave after she'd saved him.

Khat opened her eyes, drowning in his gold ones. "You are the bravest warrior I have ever known." She slid her hands up across his forearms, her voice shaking with emotion. "I want a life with you, Mike. I know it won't be easy, sometimes, but you have shown your willingness to work with me, love me despite my ups and downs. I still have to finish out my enlistment…"

"Those things will work out over time," he reassured her. Slipping his arms from her hands, he folded her long, graceful fingers into his. "The important thing is General Stevenson is ordering you to San Diego Naval Medical Center to recuperate. She's already got a job waiting for you at ST3 in their Intelligence section until your enlistment runs out. You'll be there with me. I have sixty days when our platoon returns to Coronado and I intend to spend every one of them with you, Khat. I have a condo that is owned by Gabe Griffin, a former SEAL, on the island. We'll live there with one another, love one another, have the time we deserve with each other. Sound good?" He caressed her cheek that had a little pink color returning to it. A tender smile pulled at his mouth, his voice husky with emotion. "And you can feed Sam, the harbor seal, every Friday when he drops by for his fish dinner."

"That sounds so good," Khat wobbled. "My mom lives in San Francisco. She'll be close, and that's good. I need her right now, too." She hitched a shoulder. "My father? I don't want to see him. I'm not ready for it."

"You don't have to see him," Mike promised her quietly, holding her hurt stare. "My parents live in Alpine, California, just north of San Diego. They're longing to meet you, Khat. They know I love you, and that you love me." He lifted her hand, placing a kiss on the back of it. She smelled of fresh Ivory Soap. "I have a surprise for you."

"Not a bad one."

"No, a good one."

"I've lost so much, Mike. I can't stand to lose anything more."

Mike understood the gravity of her words. He leaned forward, pressing a soft kiss across her lips, meant to heal Khat. She eagerly returned his kiss, her hands coming to rest on his shoulders, trying to draw him closer to her. The past two days had been rough on Khat in every way. Wanting to love this fierce woman warrior, but knowing with her surgery, that was out of the question for a couple of weeks, Mike whispered, "I love you, desert woman of my heart…"

Khat crumpled wearily against him as he gently eased his hand around her gowned shoulders. She had five years of tired that she carried within her. Clinging to him, her head against his shoulder, Khat felt hot tears of grief, letting go of the past, and running toward a joy she never knew could exist until Mike had stepped into her life.

He kissed the curve of her ear, strands tickling his nose. "Want to hear about that good surprise?"

Khat eased away, holding his gaze, feeling the warmth of his love sheeting through her. "Yes. What is it?"

"Mina," he told her quietly, holding her widening eyes. "My father asked his relative in Saudi Arabia to fly in a C-130 to pick her up here at Bagram. They are going to fly her to my father's black Arabian stud farm in Alpine for you." He grazed her cheek with his thumb, seeing the shock and then joy come to her eyes. "I wasn't going to leave Mina behind, Khat. She's been a major part of your life and has saved you so many times. She's just as much the warrior you are and risked her life time and again for you. Like you, she deserves some peace, happiness and a new, loving family who will surround her and make her one of them."

Choking on a sob, Khat managed a strangled, "Thank you... Thank you for doing that... I was so worried for Mina... I didn't know what would happen to her..."

Mike released her and sat up, his arm bracketing her hips, palms flat on the mattress, studying her. "Mina deserves a reward for all that she's done for you, Angel. Now, my father, Bedir, wants to know if you would like her bred to his black stallion. I told him that you needed some time to think about that."

"Does that mean that I can see Mina sometimes?"

Mike shrugged. "Sure, the horse farm is about twenty-five miles northwest of where we'll be living and working. My parents have invited us up to stay any weekend we want at their ranch. You'll have many, many miles of trails to ride your brave horse anytime you want."

"And her leg? Has it improved since you came back to Bravo?"

Nodding, Mike slipped his hand down her arm, feeling her strength beneath the warm skin. "Yes, Travis is looking out for her now. He's wrapping her legs for transit that will take place tomorrow." His voice fell. "You won't be able to say goodbye to her, Khat. The Saudi transport is coming in the morning to pick her up. They have a large padded stall prepared for her. She'll be fine. There's also a Saudi veterinarian on board who will accompany her all the way to my father's horse farm. She's in good hands."

"She'll be safe," Khat whispered, touched. "That's all I care about. Your father, Bedir, is so special." She managed a broken smile up at him, placing her hand against his bearded face. "Like you, Michael Tarik. You are an ancient warrior who has stepped into today's world, in my eyes. You have the heart, the morals and values of the finest of the old guard Middle Eastern caliphs and chieftains of so long ago."

"And I'm the luckiest man in the world to have you, Khat." Mike took her hand, kissing her opened palm, feeling her respond. Khat was exquisitely sensitive to the lightest of touches, and he silently promised her that when they started their new life Stateside, he was going to make her as happy as he could.

Mike knew there were a lot of hurdles ahead for Khat, knew her father was still a dark shadow in her life, still eviscerating her emotionally. From now on, he would shield her from him. Mike knew what a good father was because he had one, and he hoped that Bedir would gently show Khat the warmth and love that a parent should give to their child. He knew his parents would fall in love with Khat, and they would embrace her with their hearts, just as he had.

Life was never easy, and Mike knew that firsthand, but what Khat had endured and managed to survive? It was phenomenal in his eyes. To finally have this beautiful woman with the red hair and green eyes in his bed, at his side, being able to love her fully, was something he was going to look forward to. And later, when the time was right, they would marry.

Right now Khat was in the middle of a tremendous life change, and Mike had no wish to pressure her any more than she already was. She was giving up a way of life. That took guts.

A knot formed in his throat as he watched her smile softly up at him. How did he get so damned lucky? This woman was one in six billion, no other like her on this planet. And she was his. All his. Forever.

* * * * *

If you loved this book and these characters, there is more to their story in ON FIRE, an e-novella by Lindsay McKenna. ON FIRE is available now on www.Harlequin.com or at your favorite online retailer!

Don't miss Lindsay McKenna's next SHADOW WARRIORS novel, RUNNING FIRE, coming to you in May 2015! Only from HQN Books and available wherever you buy books and ebooks!

Turn the page for a peek at this exciting new story.

CHAPTER ONE

"READY, LEAH?" CAPTAIN Brian Larsen asked.

Chief Warrant Officer Leah Mackenzie picked up the mission information from the US Army 80th Shadow Squadron office. She looked outside, getting a bad feeling. It was raining at Camp Bravo, a FOB, forward operating base, thirty miles from the Pakistan border. "This is a lousy night," she told the MH-47 pilot. She saw Brian nod.

"It sucks," he agreed. "But we gotta make this exfil."

Leah followed him across Operations, helmet bag in one hand, knee board in the other. It was 2400, midnight, and they were to pick up a SEAL team one mile from the Af-Pak border. They had thirty minutes to meet the black ops team who had been out for a week hunting high-value target Taliban leaders.

Her heart picked up a beat as they walked quickly from Operations onto the wet tarmac. Their MH-47, a specially equipped Chinook helicopter that could fly in any kind of weather conditions, had been prepped by the ground crew and was ready for them to board.

The rain was slashing down, cold and quickly soaking Leah's desert-tan one-piece flight suit. It was June 1, and Brian told her rain was unusual at this time of year in eastern Afghanistan.

Bravo sat at eight thousand feet in the Hindu Kush

mountains. Leah had arrived three weeks ago, acclimating and learning the Shadow Squadron area that they operated within. She had replaced a pilot who had gotten appendicitis. And being the only woman in the 80th, she stood out whether she wanted to or not. It was time to take to the sky.

"This is a shitty area to pick anyone up in," Brian muttered. "You remember? It's a very narrow valley? With the mountains on the east side at fourteen thousand? And on the west side at ten thousand?"

"Yes," Leah answered. She'd worked hard to commit the terrain to memory. Black ops never picked up a team at the same spot—ever. It could be a trap or ambush the second time around. "What I don't like is we're landing too close to a series of caves. The Taliban routinely hide in them."

"Roger that one," Brian agreed grimly, studying the all-terrain radar on his HUD, head's up display. "The SEALs said they couldn't locate any tangos nearby, but that means squat. The Taliban hide in the caves and pop up with RPGs after we land."

Leah nodded. Her adrenaline was already flooding into her bloodstream. Should she tell Brian she had a bad feeling? That when she did, things went to hell in a handbag? "Is there any way this team can meet us out in that narrow valley?"

"No. Then they become targets for any Taliban sitting up high in those caves."

Mouth quirking, Leah felt her stomach tighten. She flew the Chinook in the long, flat stratus clouds, the rain slashing downward at four thousand feet. In ten minutes they'd hit the last waypoint and start descend-

ing, going in to the exfil area to pick up the awaiting
SEAL team.

She heard Brian talking with Ted over the intercom.
The crew chief would have to lower the ramp once
they began to descend into the pickup zone. Brian had
made his authorization request with Bagram Air Base,
where the major part of the 80th Shadow battalion was
stationed. No mission went down unless authorization
was approved by everyone. And it had just been approved. It was a go.

Leah listened to all transmissions while her gaze
constantly roved across the cockpit instrument panel.
Everything felt good and solid to her. She'd flown by
the seat of her pants since age sixteen, when her father, bird Colonel David Mackenzie, taught her how
to fly. The reason she got into the Shadow Squadron
was because he was the commander of this particular battalion. She was the only woman in it, and Leah
hoped other deserving women pilots would be allowed
to follow in her footsteps sooner, not later.

"I'll take the controls," Brian said.

"You have the controls," Leah said, releasing them.
Brian was worried about this pickup area and she was
happy to allow the pilot more experienced in this region to fly them in and out. She busied herself with
talking to the SEAL team on the ground and prepar-
ing the helo for the pickup.

At one thousand feet, she gave Ted the order to open
the ramp. Instantly, a grinding sound began throughout the hollow fuselage. The closer they descended to
the ground, the harder it rained.

The hair on the back of Leah's neck stood up. A
feeling of real danger washed through her. Compress-

ing her full lips, she watched as the Chinook came out of the low-hanging cloud cover at three hundred feet. Looking to the east, she saw the caves, all black maws. Their exfil was down below them, on a gentle slope that would be easy to land upon. Her heart rate picked up and she felt a strong thrust of adrenaline burning through her.

NAVY SEAL CHIEF Kell Ballard lay in his hide, fourteen hundred yards west of where he saw the Shadow helicopter dropping below the low cloud cover. He was hidden and dry, his .300 Win Mag sniper rifle covered with fabric to camouflage it from enemy eyes. He'd been watching through his Nightforce scope for any thermal activity other than that of his two SEAL brothers on the opposite side of the narrow valley who were about to be picked up. The problem was the rain was so heavy that Kell knew Taliban could be in those caves and even *he* wouldn't be able to spot them.

The whumping sounds of the twin engine MH-47 Chinook vibrated the air throughout the narrow-necked valley. He panned his rifle slowly, looking through his infrared scope at the helicopter descending.

Then he moved his scope farther down and to his left. He saw two thermal images of the SEALs, hiding behind brush, waiting for exfil. They'd been in contact with one another all week, although Kell's single sniper mission was different from their mission. He'd already been out here three weeks, waiting for an HVT to slip into Afghanistan. He was sitting on the mountain to intercept the bastard when it happened. So far, he'd just waited and watched.

He'd been in touch with one of the pilots on board

the Chinook, a Captain Larson. Kell had warned him that Taliban could be hidden in those caves. He had no way to find them unless one of them rose up and fired an RPG at the helo. He turned his scope toward those caves once more, trying to protect the helo, just in case.

Kell watched the Chinook swing over the valley, staying as far away from those caves as possible. But the valley was exceedingly tapered in shape, and the huge rotor circumference on this transport helo forced it to make a long, wide turn.

The Chinook was at one hundred feet, descending rapidly. Shadow pilots got in and out as swiftly as possible, knowing they were always vulnerable when landing and taking off.

Kell inhaled deeply, the night air moist and the rain punctured by the heavy echo of thumping blades. His heart rate slowed and he focused on the caves, watching the helo cautiously approach.

His intense focus was on the caves, moving his rifle scope slowly, right to left and then back again. Any heat signatures? None so far. His finger was on the two-pound trigger. He had a bullet in the chamber and two more in the mag. The wind gusted and whipped around his hide. The rain thickened, making his visual blurry. Kell's heart suddenly plunged. He saw three heat signatures suddenly pop up from a cave.

Son of a bitch!

All three Taliban had RPGs on their shoulders, ready to fire! There was no time for a radio warning as the first enemy fired his RPG at the helo. Kell pulled the trigger, taking out the second Taliban. Moving swiftly, he scoped the third one, firing.

Too late!

LEAH SAW A flash off to the right, out of the corner of
her eye, as Brian brought the Chinook down onto the
slope.

"RPG!" she yelled. And then, the entire center of the
helicopter exploded, shrapnel, fire and pressure-wave
concussions slamming Leah forward. She felt the deep
bite of the harness into her shoulders. Brian screamed
as the fire roared forward. Leah ducked to the left, toward the fuselage at her elbow, feeling the burning heat
and precious oxygen stolen from their lungs.

A second RPG struck the rear of the helicopter. The
thunderous explosion ripped off the rear rotor assem-
bly, the blades, flying razors shrieking out into the
night.

Leah's head got yanked to the right from the second
RPG hit. The entire cockpit Plexiglas blew outward.
Thousands of shards shattered and rained around her
like glittering sparkles, catching the fire within the
bird. She heard Brian screaming, fire enveloping the
entire cockpit. She smelled her hair burning.

The fire was so intense, Leah couldn't reach out and
get to Brian's harness. With shaking hands, she found
the release on her own harness. The whole helo was
tearing in two. Metal screeched and tore. She heard the
rotor just behind and above her head rip off. A loose
blade sailed through the cockpit. Because she was out
of her harness, she avoided most of the slicing blade's
action. It cut the other pilot's seat in half. Sobbing,
Leah knew it had killed Brian instantly.

Escape! Egress!

Choking on the smoke, Leah thought her fire-retardant
uniform was going to burst into flames any second now.
Fire roared through the inside of the broken bird. Gasping,

she crawled to the blown-out window to her left. Shoving her boots up onto the seat, she launched herself out the window. Leah felt immediate pain in her right arm, slashed by a jagged piece of Plexiglas left in the aluminum window frame.

She fell ten feet, hitting the rocks and mud below, tumbling end over end. Dazed, blood running down the right side of her head, she tried to get up. Her hands and legs wouldn't work. The black clouds of smoke enveloped her. The rain slashed at Leah's eyes, part of her helmet visor broken, exposing her face to the violent weather. Coughing, gagging, the smoke smothered her. She got on all fours and moved away as fast as she could. Air! She had to get air or she'd die of smoke inhalation!

The rocks bit into her hands and bruised her knees. Disoriented, Leah heard gunfire from her right and left. Collapsing to the ground, she crawled on her belly, so damned dizzy she wasn't sure where she was at or where she was headed. There was another explosion behind her. Part of the Chinook had ripped in half, the aviation fuel set on fire. The pressure wave struck her, smashing her helmet into the rocks. It was the last thing Leah remembered.

KELL CURSED RICHLY, leaping out of his hide and leaving his sniper rifle behind. He pulled the Sig pistol from his drop holster, crouching and sprinting down the slope. He had fourteen hundred yards to run before he would reach that pilot he saw fall out of the Chinook's starboard side window near the cockpit.

Slipping and sliding, the rain so heavy he could barely see even with his NVGs on, Ballard watched for more trouble. The two SEALs waiting for extract had immediately broken contact and were already on the run toward the cave where the RPGs had been shot from. They'd have to contact the platoon at Bravo for another pickup at a later date.

Kell breathed hard. The slippery soil slowed him down. He had dispatched all three Taliban. But were there more of them around that he hadn't seen through his scope? And that was the greater problem. He flipped up his NVGs because the roaring flames around the destroyed helo blinded his night vision capability.

The last he'd seen through his scope, the pilot was about a hundred feet west of the wreckage. He'd disappeared beneath the roiling, thick smoke. Where the hell could he be?

Circling the helo, staying well away from it, Kell entered the heavy smoke. Immediately, he started choking and gagging. Crouching low, moving swiftly, Kell began a hunt for the pilot. He had no idea if the man was dead or not. He was amazed even one of them had managed to get out of that flaming helo alive.

Kell almost stumbled over the body. He fell to his knees. The pilot was on his belly, arms stretched out in front of him, thrown forward by the second, bigger blast. Gasping, unable to see except by feel as more smoke poured into the area, Kell grabbed the man and threw him into a fireman's carry across his shoulders. Only, to his shock, he felt breasts resting against his shoulders.

What the hell? A woman?

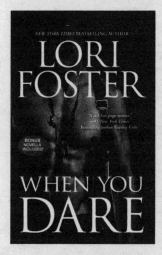

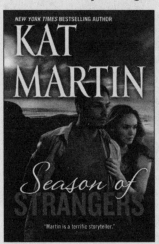

From the creator of *The Originals*, the hit spin-off television show of *The Vampire Diaries*, come three never-before-released prequel stories featuring the Original vampire family, set in 18th century New Orleans.

Available now!   Coming March 31!   Coming May 26!

Family is power. The Original vampire family swore it to each other a thousand years ago. They pledged to remain together always and forever. But even when you're immortal, promises are hard to keep.

**Pick up your copies and visit
www.TheOriginalsBooks.com**
to discover more!

HQN™
www.HQNBooks.com

REQUEST YOUR
FREE BOOKS!

2 FREE NOVELS
FROM THE SUSPENSE COLLECTION
PLUS 2 FREE GIFTS!

YES! Please send me 2 FREE novels from the Suspense Collection and my 2 FREE gifts (gifts are worth about $10). After receiving them, if I don't wish to receive any more books, I can return the shipping statement marked "cancel." If I don't cancel, I will receive 4 brand-new novels every month and be billed just $6.24 per book in the U.S. or $6.74 per book in Canada. That's a savings of at least 22% off the cover price. It's quite a bargain! Shipping and handling is just 50¢ per book in the U.S. and 75¢ per book in Canada.* I understand that accepting the 2 free books and gifts places me under no obligation to buy anything. I can always return a shipment and cancel at any time. Even if I never buy another book, the two free books and gifts are mine to keep forever.

191/391 MDN F4XN

Name	(PLEASE PRINT)
Address	Apt. #
City	State/Prov.	Zip/Postal Code

Signature (if under 18, a parent or guardian must sign)

Mail to the **Harlequin® Reader Service:**
IN U.S.A.: P.O. Box 1867, Buffalo, NY 14240-1867
IN CANADA: P.O. Box 609, Fort Erie, Ontario L2A 5X3

Want to try two free books from another line?
Call 1-800-873-8635 or visit www.ReaderService.com.

* Terms and prices subject to change without notice. Prices do not include applicable taxes. Sales tax applicable in N.Y. Canadian residents will be charged applicable taxes. Offer not valid in Quebec. This offer is limited to one order per household. Not valid for current subscribers to the Suspense Collection or the Romance/Suspense Collection. All orders subject to credit approval. Credit or debit balances in a customer's account(s) may be offset by any other outstanding balance owed by or to the customer. Please allow 4 to 6 weeks for delivery. Offer available while quantities last.

Your Privacy—The Harlequin® Reader Service is committed to protecting your privacy. Our Privacy Policy is available online at www.ReaderService.com or upon request from the Harlequin Reader Service.

We make a portion of our mailing list available to reputable third parties that offer products we believe may interest you. If you prefer that we not exchange your name with third parties, or if you wish to clarify or modify your communication preferences, please visit us at www.ReaderService.com/consumerchoice or write to us at Harlequin Reader Service Preference Service, P.O. Box 9062, Buffalo, NY 14269. Include your complete name and address.

SUS13R

LINDSAY McKENNA

77903	WOLF HAVEN	___ $7.99 U.S.	___ $8.99 CAN.
77882	NEVER SURRENDER	___ $7.99 U.S.	___ $8.99 CAN.
77851	HIGH COUNTRY REBEL	___ $7.99 U.S.	___ $8.99 CAN.
77772	THE LONER	___ $7.99 U.S.	___ $9.99 CAN.
77616	THE LAST COWBOY	___ $7.99 U.S.	___ $9.99 CAN.

(limited quantities available)

TOTAL AMOUNT	$ _____
POSTAGE & HANDLING	$ _____
($1.00 FOR 1 BOOK, 50¢ for each additional)	
APPLICABLE TAXES*	$ _____
TOTAL PAYABLE	$ _____

(check or money order—please do not send cash)

To order, complete this form and send it, along with a check or money order for the total above, payable to HQN Books, to: **In the U.S.:** 3010 Walden Avenue, P.O. Box 9077, Buffalo, NY 14269-9077; **In Canada:** P.O. Box 636, Fort Erie, Ontario, L2A 5X3.

Name: _____
Address: _____ City: _____
State/Prov.: _____ Zip/Postal Code: _____
Account Number (if applicable): _____

075 CSAS

*New York residents remit applicable sales taxes.
*Canadian residents remit applicable GST and provincial taxes.

HQN™

www.HQNBooks.com

PHLM0315BL

Praise for Lindsay McKenna

"A treasure of a book…highly recommended reading that everyone will enjoy and learn from."
—Chief Michael Jaco, US Navy SEAL, retired, on *Breaking Point*

"McKenna's latest is an intriguing tale…a unique twist on the romance novel, and one that's sure to please."
—*RT Book Reviews* on *Dangerous Prey*

"McKenna's military experience shines through in this moving tale…. McKenna (*High Country Rebel*) skillfully takes readers on an emotional journey into modern warfare and two people's hearts."
—*Publishers Weekly* on *Down Range*

"Gunfire, emotions, suspense, tension and sexuality abound in this fast-paced, absorbing novel."
—*Affaire de Coeur* on *Wild Woman*

"Another masterpiece."
—*Affaire de Coeur* on *Enemy Mine*

"Emotionally charged…riveting and deeply touching."
—*RT Book Reviews* on *Firstborn*

"Ms. McKenna brings readers along for a fabulous odyssey in which complex characters experience the danger, passion and beauty of the mystical jungle."
—*RT Book Reviews* on *Man of Passion*

"Readers will find this addition to the Shadow Warriors series full of intensity and action-packed romance. There is great chemistry between the characters and tremendous realism, making *Breaking Point* a great read."
—*RT Book Reviews*

"Lindsay McKenna will have you flying with the daring and deadly women pilots who risk their lives…. Buckle in for the ride of your life."
—*Writers Unlimited* on *Heart of Stone*

**Also available from
Lindsay McKenna
and HQN Books**